SE

INAMORATA

INAMORATA

·

JOSEPH
GANGEMI

·

VIKING

VIKING
Published by the Penguin Group
Penguin Group (USA) Inc., 375 Hudson Street, New York, New York 10014, U.S.A.
Penguin Books Ltd, 80 Strand, London WC2R 0RL, England
Penguin Books Australia Ltd, 250 Camberwell Road, Camberwell,
    Victoria 3124, Australia
Penguin Books Canada Ltd, 10 Alcorn Avenue,
    Toronto, Ontario, Canada M4V 3B2
Penguin Books India (P) Ltd, 11 Community Centre, Panchsheel Park,
    New Delhi – 110 017, India
Penguin Books (N.Z.) Ltd, Cnr Rosedale and Airborne Roads, Albany,
    Auckland, New Zealand
Penguin Books (South Africa) (Pty) Ltd, 24 Sturdee Avenue,
    Rosebank, Johannesburg 2196, South Africa

Penguin Books Ltd, Registered Offices:
80 Strand, London WC2R 0RL, England

First published in 2004 by Viking Penguin,
a member of Penguin Group (USA) Inc.

10 9 8 7 6 5 4 3 2 1

Grateful acknowledgment is made for permission to reprint an excerpt from "The tint I cannot take—is best" from *The Poems of Emily Dickinson*, Thomas H. Johnson, ed., Cambridge, Mass.: The Belknap Press of Harvard University Press. Copyright © 1951, 1955, 1979 by the President and Fellows of Harvard College. Reprinted by permission of the publishers and the Trustees of Amherst College.

PUBLISHER'S NOTE
This is a work of fiction. Names, characters, places, and incidents either are the product of the author's imagination or are used fictitiously, and any resemblance to actual persons, living or dead, business establishments, events, or locales is entirely coincidental.

LIBRARY OF CONGRESS CATALOGING IN PUBLICATION DATA
Gangemi, Joseph.
    Inamorata : a novel / Joseph Gangemi.
        p.   cm.
    ISBN 0-670-03279-4
    1. Philadelphia (Pa.)—Fiction.   I. Title.
PS3607.A46I53 2004
813'.6—dc21   2003053773

This book is printed on acid-free paper. ∞

Printed in the United States of America
Set in Adobe Garamond
Designed by Carla Bolte

FOR STACEY

and two others in my circle of skeptical inquirers,

Jon Cohen and Howard Sanders

Don't worry, my dear—I am quite used to skeptics—they generally turn out to be the most vulnerable and receptive in the long run.

—Noël Coward, *Blithe Spirit*

INAMORATA

PART ONE

GOING TO THE SPOOKS

· 1 ·

"Hypnotize her."

I looked at the girl Halliday had just shoved at me like a virgin sacrifice. She was a leggy little sophomore from Radcliffe, slim as a cigarette, with a black bob and painted brows that gave her a look of pretty astonishment. She gazed up at me in myopic perplexity, as if my face were a puzzle she'd completed only to find herself holding an unaccounted piece.

I looked at Halliday. "I beg your pardon?"

"Hypnotize her, Finch," he repeated. "Everyone knows you can do it."

"You're mistaken."

"Am I? Why don't we ask Dickie Hodgson's sister?"

Halliday gave me a challenging look. The smug son of a bitch knew he had me. I glanced past him to the nearest exit, clear across Emerson's student lounge, calculating the odds of making my escape before Halliday succeeded in drawing a crowd. A few years earlier I might've stood a chance, but ever since Prohibition attendance at the psychology department's illicit Christmas soirées had soared. The path to freedom tonight was blocked by a fox-trotting mob of besotted doctoral candidates. No, Halliday had me cornered. Though that didn't mean I was defeated.

"I can't hypnotize her, Wick."

"Why?"

"For starters"—I stalled—"she's tight."

"I am not!" The girl stamped the floor with one satin-shod foot. I threw her a look to keep quiet, but it was too late; she'd already managed to create a scene. Several of our classmates within earshot were drifting our way to investigate. And Halliday wasted no time encouraging them.

"Gather 'round, ladies and gentlemen," he called over their heads, playing carnival barker. "Our own Dr. Caligari is going to grace us with a demonstration of his formidable mental powers!"

Someone switched off the gramophone, and the music—a dance number called "Bit by Bit You're Breaking My Heart" by Charles Dornberger and His Orchestra—went silent, leaving only the susurrus of the inebriated crowd. As all eyes in the lounge turned our way my throat constricted and the roof of my mouth began to sweat. It was a recurrent nightmare come to life—the one consolation being that in the present version, at least, I was still wearing my trousers. God only knew what was going through the head of Halliday's girl at that moment. I felt a sudden and overwhelming wave of tenderness toward her, this girl whose name I didn't even know.

But when I turned to show her what I hoped was a reassuring look, I found Halliday's girl glaring at me. Arms crossed. One toe tapping the carpet in agitation. She gave me the withering look of an impatient prostitute, asked,

"Well, what are you waiting for?"

"I suppose . . . a pocketwatch."

Another bluff. All I'd needed was a birthday candle to get Dickie Hodgson's sister howling like a beagle that had heard a fire siren. As last-ditch efforts went, I gave this one even odds at succeeding. Thanks to the war, wristwatches were no longer considered effeminate, at least among the college set, while their stuffier, vest-dwelling forebears were quickly going the way of the pince-nez. Or so I sincerely hoped.

"Here!"

I cringed as the pocketwatch came through the crowd, passing from hand to hand until it arrived in my own—an absurd thing, heavy as a gold-plated turnip, its weight in my palm conjuring images of a firelit study, an alcoholic judge, a solemn retelling of some ancestor's decisive role in the Louisiana Purchase. I opened its gold cover and read the inscription: TRUTH LIES AT THE CENTER OF A CIRCLE. Maybe so for the watch's owner. But all I stood to discover at the center of the circle of onlookers now surrounding me was a very public embarrassment.

"The floor's all yours, sport," Halliday said.

I sighed, shifted my eyes to my reluctant assistant. "I suppose we should start by you telling me your name."

"Veda." Defiant.

"All right, Veda," I began, "I'd like you to take a few deep breaths to relax. . . . Go ahead . . . yes, that's right. . . . And when you feel you are ready, begin to focus your attention on this watch. . . ." And I set the watch swinging like a pendulum, back and forth, back and forth, before Veda's highly skeptical expression.

She resisted at first, then began to follow its motion with her blue eyes. I worried she was too intoxicated to muster the requisite concentration—for it takes significant mental displine to narrow the aperture of awareness, to still the incessant babbling of mind—but her animosity toward me seemed to have had a sobering effect, and after a moment her eyelids became heavy. Her descent into a trance state required little of me beyond the occasional encouraging word, though for our audience's sake, I made a great show of glowering menacingly and looking Mephistophelian—at least insofar as this is possible when one is twenty-three and shaves only every other day. At last Halliday's girl arrived at that place of equipoise between alertness and relaxation, and I knew that her inhibitions had reached their point of lowest ebb.

Unfortunately, I wasn't the only one who knew it.

"Witness, ladies and gentlemen," Halliday said, "the power men wield over the impressionable female mind!"

There were jeers from the crowd. Someone let out a piercing wolf whistle. I shot the whistler a sharp look and motioned for silence. Halliday's girl stood swaying like tapering smoke from an extinguished candle. She smiled, as if she were having a pleasant dream. Time to test her openness to suggestion.

"Can you still hear me, Veda?"

"Mmmmmm."

She drew out the syllable as if I'd fed her something sweet. The hairs along my arms stood up. I was frightened; also, I confess, not a little aroused. I fought the impulse to bring her out of it immediately, forced my brain to become a motion-picture camera recording the details of her own arousal: how her lips had swollen imperceptibly beyond their lipsticked borders, the gooseflesh giving pattern to her slender arms, the way her nostrils flared with each delicious breath. A shiver ran through her as if she'd felt a draft, and from my privileged vantage it became obvious she wasn't wearing a bust flattener beneath her silk dress.

Halliday appeared at my elbow. "Remarkable," he whispered, eyes traveling up and down the length of her. "You know, it strikes me that our Veda here would make an absolutely *smashing* Salomé—"

"Forget it."

"You're right, we can do better," he said ruminatively. "Something truly memorable . . . something she wouldn't dream of doing awake—"

"It doesn't work that way."

"What doesn't?"

"Hypnotic suggestion," I said. "I can't force her to do anything she doesn't want to."

"Because it's forbidden by the mesmerists' Code of Honor?"

"More like the mechanics of the human unconscious."

I watched Halliday stew on this with a sour expression. Like so many in those days, he had fallen in thrall to the behaviorists, pigeon trainers like J. B. Watson who dismissed human consciousness as a side effect of overstimulated nerves, and therefore unworthy of study. Halliday knew that when it came to the subject of the unconscious, he was woefully ill informed. I could see him weighing whether or not I was telling the truth. In fact I *was*. Contrary to popular belief, it's all but impossible to force a hypnotized subject to do something against her will—though I hadn't arrived at this understanding via any deep reading of Freud. Rather, I'd come by it as did most self-taught Svengalis: through trial and error, and a mail-order pamphlet titled *Hypnosis Explained!*

Halliday narrowed his eyes at me. He wasn't buying it.

"In that case why don't we put your hypothesis to the test, Doctor?"

Before I could protest he turned and began appealing to the crowd for ideas, working the house like an old vaudevillian. The suggestions that came back ranged from the silly ("Make her swallow a goldfish!") to the sadistic ("Convince her that her hair's falling out!"). Someone shouted we should give her a glass of water and convince her it was champagne, a suggestion I found privately amusing in light of the fact that the fellow who'd made it was at that moment drinking a dilute solution of ethyl alcohol that some bootlegger had sold him as "gin."

After a minute of this Halliday shook his head, dismissing the

uninspired suggestions wholesale. Fearing he was losing his audience, he seized me by the elbow, hissed a few inches from my ear,
"For God's sake, Finch, I thought Jews were supposed to be
clever! Now come up with something quick, before you make us
both look like fools."

There it was. *Jew.* I'd always suspected the question of my race
shadowed me about campus, but until that moment I had never
encountered the rumor firsthand. That it was incorrect—Finch
was short for Finnochiaro; I had been raised a Roman Catholic—
was beside the point. My face grew hot. My hands clenched into
fists. I felt the cocktail of adrenaline and alcohol in my bloodstream threatening immolation. . . .

And then a sudden, anesthetizing *calm.* It settled over me like a
narcotic shroud, cooling my blood, suffusing me with an un-
earned confidence. I looked at the hypnotized girl awaiting my
instructions. Looked at Halliday.

"Something clever, you say?"

"Preferably before the New Year, old sport."

"Something she wouldn't dream of doing awake . . ."

"Otherwise where's the fun?" asked Halliday with a wink to
his audience.

"All right," I said, and, turning to Halliday's girl, instructed
her, "Kiss me."

A stunned silence—the sound of the crowd's drawing a collective breath and then holding it as they awaited Veda's response. At
first she showed no sign whatsoever of having heard, but then, after a delay of several seconds, a faint smile appeared on her
painted lips. My heart thrilled as her cool arms encircled my
neck, everything happening in an uncontrollable rush now, like
the moment gravity seizes your sled and you begin hurtling
downhill. Suddenly we were kissing, or rather she was kissing me:
hungrily, with open mouth and tiny noises from her throat I can

only describe as feral. I would like to say I glimpsed Halliday out of the corner of my eye going white as a ghost, but that would be a lie. The truth was, I was too busy being devoured to be aware of anything beyond the catcalls of the crowd—

Until the scream.

"Rats!"

They came scurrying across the Oriental carpet, two dozen healthy adolescents scrambling among leather brogues and ladies' boots. They were bald as Trappist monks, their tiny pink scalps shaved smooth for stereotaxic surgery. I knew because I'd been their barber, as well as caretaker. I heard a squeal as one of my rodent charges met its demise beneath a Louis heel, and, shoving Veda aside, I threw myself headlong into the throng. More screams and, floating above it all, some prankster's cruel laughter. I crawled on all fours through the forest of trouser legs and shapely ankles in silk hose, trying to round up as many rats as possible. But no sooner had I corralled a wriggling armful than I took a wingtip to the temple that dropped me to the carpet— stunned, spectacles knocked askew. The rats scattered to the four corners of the room and one by one met their fate beneath the feet of the stampeding herd of flappers and philosophers.

· · ·

An hour later I waited in an uncomfortable chair outside the office of the chairman of the psychology department, Dr. William McLaughlin, a man I had never met. That our introduction would take place under such inauspicious circumstances—the middle of the night, in the aftermath of an incident that had left thirty laboratory rats dead or missing and a faculty member's experiment ruined—only deepened my depression. To be perfectly honest, it wasn't the dressing-down I most feared. It was being fired.

I stared at the windows, miserable. Outside Emerson Hall a light snow was busily erasing the brick walks of Harvard Yard, prelude to another nor'easter. Already the winter was off to a punishing start, with a foot of fresh snow delivered to our doorstep each weekend like the Sunday paper. With the snow came a blistering cold off the Charles that in its more inspired gusts brought tears to the eyes of poor bastards like myself who were unlucky enough to live on the outskirts of Cambridge. (The only thing that had spared my lesser extremities from frostbite was the fact that I kept a mental list of every radiator in a three-mile vicinity, and had mapped the shortest routes between them.) Tonight I would be making the trek home sans overcoat, since in the hullabaloo following the party someone had walked off with it, leaving me only my muffler and gloves. I consoled myself that I'd been meaning to get a new coat anyway, though it remained in question exactly how I was going to afford it. My father's checks had stopped; I had spent all but $1.30 of my last paycheck and for the last three nights had been subsisting on ketchup sandwiches. It occured to me now that if I were to lose my job feeding and watering the department's various colonies of lab rats, I might simply lie down in the most comfortable-looking snowbank I encountered on my walk home and go to sleep. I dimly recalled something from my brief tenure in medical school (courtesy of one of our more ghoulish professors) about hypothermia's being among the more painless means of suicide. . . .

"He's ready for you, Finch."

A chastened Halliday had emerged from McLaughlin's office looking several inches shorter and considerably less conceited. I rose. As we passed one another in the doorway, Halliday gave me a shove with his shoulder that sent me into the frame. I struck my funny bone on the doorknob and winced.

"Dreadfully sorry," Halliday said with a look that implied he was anything but.

Inside the office McLaughlin stood at the windows contemplating the snow. Given the ungodly hour, I had half expected to find him in dressing gown and pajamas and was surprised to discover him dressed for the lectern in an exquisite Savile Row suit of worsted wool, complete with French collar and cuff links. On the whole I would have preferred the pajamas, since the notion of his rising stiffly from his bed and walking to the bureau to solemnly select cuff links deeply unsettled me.

"Take a seat, Mr. Finch," he said without turning.

I hurried to the nearest leather chair across from his great mahogany desk. He proceeded to ignore me, employing that tried-and-true technique of displeased parents of Leaving Me to Think About What I'd Done. The silence grew heavy, the only sounds an occasional gurgling from the radiator and my own stomach. I glanced around the office and was surprised to see on the bookshelves among the standard texts on social psychology (including McLaughlin's own, currently in its third edition) several occult works with titles like *On the Threshold of the Unseen* and *Modern Spiritualism*. And there on the wall, beside the framed diplomas from Harvard and Oxford (a D.Sc., awarded in 1889), what appeared to be a certificate of recognition from the American Society for Psychical Research. But before I could examine the calligraphy any more closely, McLaughlin spoke, and my interrogation commenced.

"I wonder, Mr. Finch," he began, his voice bearing the hint of a British accent, "if you wouldn't mind sharing your thoughts on how Professor Schneider's rats might have escaped from the basement?"

"I assume it was someone's idea of a practical joke."

"Yours?"

"Certainly not," I said, appending a hasty "—sir."

"I see."

This exchange took place without his ever once turning to look at me. Another uncomfortable silence fell, after which he announced, apropos of nothing, "I don't much care for Prohibition. To be perfectly honest, I see no reason a man shouldn't enjoy a drink at the end of the day . . . or the academic term, as the case may be. Preferably sherry of course"—finally turning from the windows—"though I'm told the cocktail of choice among graduate fellows is wood alcohol or similar industrial solvents, isn't that right, Mr. Finch?"

I sat forward in my chair, readying my defense. "I wasn't responsible for the bootleg gin. And as for Professor Schneider's rats, I'm *positive* I locked his laboratory after the six-o'clock feeding. Someone must have stolen the key from the office—or from one of the janitors. It really wouldn't be all that difficult to—"

McLaughlin raised a hand to silence me. He opened his jacket and hooked his thumbs in his vest pockets, a signature pose I'd seen caricatured once in an underground student newspaper. The caricaturist had done an admirable job capturing the face I saw now scrutinizing me, the fair Irish skin and wisp of white hair, the distinguished features beginning to turn brittle with the years, like paper; but he hadn't done justice to McLaughlin's eyes, blue as a newborn's and just as inquisitive. They studied me behind rimless spectacles for a good half minute, rarely blinking as they decided my fate. At last McLaughlin spoke.

"It occurs to me that perhaps the department is wasting your talents having you care for Professor Schneider's rats."

Here it came. A note of desperation crept into my voice.

"Please, Professor, if you'll only let me explain—"

"That won't be necessary, Finch."

"But I *need* this job," I pleaded. "If you let me go, I'll have to leave Harvard—I'm barely holding on as it is. I'm not like Halliday; my father isn't a senator."

McLaughlin's ears pricked up. "And what does he do?"

I frowned in confusion. "Who?"

"Your father."

No doubt my hesitation was as telling as my reply: "He's a greengrocer in the North End."

"Ah! I suspected a barber."

"What gave you that idea?"

McLaughlin took a seat behind his desk, explained, "You came to us as a transfer student from the medical college . . ." Opening a file folder before him, he consulted my transcript, continuing, "Given your excellent grades there, I can only assume you chose to leave for personal reasons—that medicine was never your dream in the first place. Nothing unusual in this, of course. You aren't the first student who allowed the prevailing winds of parental opinion to steer him toward an unsuitable profession. As a parent myself, I can understand the temptation to live vicariously through one's children. I asked myself what merchant or tradesman would hold medicine in symbolic esteem and recalled that in many Italian immigrant communities medical advice and folk remedies are often dispensed by the neighborhood barber." Closing my file, McLaughlin concluded, "In other words, Finch, I made an educated guess—an incorrect one, as it turns out."

As incorrect guesses went, his wasn't far off the mark. My father had studied medicine for a year at the University of Bologna before emigrating to America, and he still kept an anatomy text close at hand in the fruit stall for the occasional sidewalk consultation. Yet impressive as McLaughlin's performance was, it still contained a few leaps in logic I couldn't follow.

"But how did you know I'm Italian?"

Now it was McLaughlin's turn to look confused.

"I should think that was obvious. You have Mediterranean features."

A surprised laugh escaped me, but when McLaughlin gave me a questioning look, I only shook my head to indicate that it would take too long to explain. I asked my one remaining question:

"Why didn't you assume that my father was a doctor?"

McLaughlin handled this with kid gloves. "In my experience, Finch, physicians' sons don't need to work so many jobs to afford their tuition."

Despite the sympathetic look he showed me, I felt myself redden. "He's actually quite successful," I found myself saying in my father's defense. "I was selling him a bit short calling him a green-grocer. He's really more of an importer."

"Of course."

"He's just disappointed, you understand. He had his heart set on me being a physician. I tried explaining to him psychology was potentially just as lucrative, that people like Brill and Watson are making a killing on Madison Avenue with what they've learned in the lab. . . ."

"Very true."

"In any case, I'm certain once he cools down he'll come around and I won't have to work as many jobs."

"No doubt he will. But in the meantime . . ." McLaughlin turned in his chair, began searching through a pile of journals stacked on the radiator. "I believe I can offer you an opportunity that will help consolidate your extracurricular jobs into one better suited to your abilities."

Turning back, McLaughlin slid a magazine across the desk

toward me. "Are you familiar with the *Scientific American*?" he asked.

"Somewhat."

This was an understatement. *Scientific American* had been a staple of my childhood, the reading I'd graduated to after exhausting the oeuvre of Verne and Wells. Full of articles on advances in radiography and illustrations of airships and super-locomotives, its glossy pages had fueled my romantic imagination and for a brief time filled my twelve-year-old head with thoughts of being an engineer. (Or some days—an airship captain.) Until, that is, my father quashed the idea. To his way of thinking, engineering was little better than a glorified trade. I don't believe he'd ever met an actual engineer, unless it was to sell him an apple on his way to work, but this didn't prevent him from dismissing the profession. Tinkerers, that's what *l'ingegneri* were to my father. Crackpot inventors whose children went hungry. And so he banned the *Scientific American* from our household, before it could have a further corrupting influence on his only son—who was already exhibiting signs of being a bit of a dabbler.

"Turn to page 389," McLaughlin said now.

It had been more than a decade since I'd last held a copy of *Scientific American* in my hands, and as I thumbed through the pages of last month's issue—November 1922—it pleased me to see that the magazine hadn't changed significantly. Here were feature articles on "The Largest Cruising Airdrome" and "Finger Prints Via Radio," alongside brief updates on advances in civil engineering and recently patented inventions. It lifted my spirits to find that it even smelled as I remembered, like glue and linotype.

I found the page McLaughlin indicated and beneath the headline A SQUARE DEAL FOR THE PSYCHICS read the following announcement from the *Scientific American* editors:

$5,000 For Psychic Phenomena

As a contribution toward psychic research, the SCIENTIFIC AMERICAN pledges the sum of $5,000 to be awarded for conclusive psychic manifestations. . . . The SCIENTIFIC AMERICAN will pay $2,500 to the first person who produces a psychic photograph under its test conditions and to the full satisfaction of the eminent men who will act as judges . . . and $2,500 to the first person who produces a visible psychic manifestion of other character. Purely mental phenomena like telepathy, or purely auditory ones like rappings, will not be eligible for this award. The contest does not revolve about the psychological or religious aspects of the phenomena, but has to do only with genuineness and objective reality.

I couldn't help stating the obvious: "That's a lot of money."

"Indeed," McLaughlin said, "which is why the editors of the *Scientific American* have asked me to head the panel of judges who will evaluate the candidates. As you might imagine, a cash award that size is drawing all sorts of questionable characters out of the woodwork."

Who could blame them? With twenty-five hundred dollars, I could have lived in high style, with enough left over to purchase a car—and not just any secondhand flivver, but a sporty new Pierce-Arrow with velour upholstery and an electric starter. The type of automobile that got one invited to the petting parties our campus chaplain was always sermonizing against. Pity, then, that my attitude regarding supernatural phenomena was highly skeptical; otherwise I might have immediately borrowed a Ouija board and had a crack at the prize money myself. But at least I might still profit from the contest.

"You mentioned something about a job?"

McLaughlin nodded. "I need a graduate assistant. An assistant, it just so happens, with precisely your combination of skills."

"I'm not sure I know what skills you're referring to."

"Professor Blackton tells me you're a fellow who knows his way around a soldering iron, isn't that right, Finch?"

"I suppose so," I admitted. "He hired me to build him a rheostat for an experiment he's planning. Something about visual acuity in varying light."

"Excellent."

"But you could probably find a hundred undergraduates in the school of engineering who could do the same."

McLaughlin raised an eyebrow. "Are you trying to talk me out of hiring you, Finch?"

"No."

"Good, because I've made my decision."

McLaughlin sat forward in his chair, glancing down through the spectacles clipped to his nose at some figures on a piece of departmental stationery. "Now. Most weeks the position will require only a few hours of your time, though there will be occasions when I require most of it. The salary is the same regardless—fifteen dollars a week, as well as a deferral for a portion of your tuition. I trust this will be sufficient to keep you with us at Harvard—yes, Finch?"

I was speechless. At last I managed a nod.

"Good."

We discussed a few administrative details, and then before I knew it the job interview was over and we were shaking hands. As McLaughlin ushered me to the door of his office he suddenly said, "I wonder if you wouldn't mind my asking a personal question, Finch?"

For fifteen dollars a week he could have asked me how frequently I masturbated and I would have answered him.

"Were you raised in a religious household?"

"My family is Roman Catholic."

"Devout?"

"I was an altar boy."

"Ah."

McLaughlin seemed to glean a significance in my answer I knew it didn't merit, so I added quickly, "It wasn't my idea."

"No, I don't suppose it ever is!" He seemed amused by this, then continued his strange line of questioning. "Tell me, are you still practicing?"

"I haven't set foot in a church since my mother's funeral."

"I see."

We had arrived at the office door and stood on opposite sides of the threshold. McLaughlin thanked me for indulging his personal questions, shook my hand a second time, and wished me good night. He was about to shut the door when he hesitated, telling me in parting, "You know, you really should reconsider your policy on churches, Finch. Next week in Manhattan if we have time, we'll pay a visit to St. Patrick's. I think you'll find it has the most remarkable light."

And with that he closed his office door, leaving me dumbstruck, since never once during the entire time I was in his office had he mentioned anything about a trip to New York.

· 2 ·

The trip by rail from Boston to Manhattan took seven hours, during which time McLaughlin napped, graded seminar papers, caught up on his correspondence, and generally ignored me. All of which suited me fine, silence being to my mind infinitely preferable to seven hours of strained conversation. Some might have been hurt or insulted by McLaughlin's seeming lack of interest, but I considered it an encouraging sign that he expected our association to be a long one, offering plenty of future opportunities to become better aquainted. And God knows I had more than enough to keep me busy for the duration of the journey, thanks to the stack of journal articles and book excerpts McLaughlin had given me to read. A short course in the history of spiritualism.

Some of it I had encountered before, thanks to a magpielike interest in anything that sparkled with the Strange—hypnotism being a prime example. (No doubt a psycho-analyst would have said I was compensating for childhood feelings of powerlessness and inefficacy by hoarding secret knowlege, but I chose not to pathologize what seemed a harmless, if somewhat morbid, curiosity.) Therefore I was already familiar with the infamous Fox sisters of Hydesville, New York, whose spirit rappings had inaugurated the Spiritualist movement in 1848. By 1888 interest in

Spiritualism had gathered sufficient momentum to survive the Fox sisters' confession that it had all been a childhood prank, that they had manufactured the ghostly rapping noises by cracking their toes. Now in the thick dossier McLaughlin had provided me I picked up the story where my prior knowledge left off: how Spiritualism, transplanted overseas, had quickly taken root in superstition-rich foreign soil, bearing fruit in the form of England's Goligher Circle and Italy's Eusapia Palladino; and how the movement inspired a dozen hybrid religions, from the occultist Theosophy to the faith-healing Christian Science. I read about the movement's wane at the turn of the century, and although I didn't need any articles to know that it had recently recaptured the public's fascination, McLaughlin had provided one: the Royal Edinburgh Mental Hospital annual report for 1920, in which Physician-Superintendent George M. Robertson had written, *"Those who had sustained bereavements during the war and bore them with equanimity in the days of crowded incidents . . . find it much harder to bear up now, although some time has lapsed. Many, as a solace to their feelings, have taken an interest in Spiritualism. . . ."*

I had dismissed this renewed interest in séance parties—"going to the spooks," we called it—as just another fad, something to do with your card table after you'd tired of mah-jongg. Each year seemed to bring a clutch of silly new national obsessions, from the newest dance craze (the fox-trot) to the latest campus stunt (swallowing goldfish). I had long ago given up trying to keep current with the Latest and Greatest, for no sooner would I master the steps to one than the fickle public would turn suddenly like a school of minnows and swim off in another direction. But the more I read about the Spiritualist revival, the more I began to appreciate that it wasn't a craze so much as a persistent rumble of a deeper hunger, one that waxed and waned, certainly, but never faded altogether; and the more I understood this, the more I came to appreciate the fascination the phenomenon held for the social scientist.

To say nothing of the magazine editor. The *Scientific American* had been among the first publications to capitalize on this public craving for all things metaphysical. As our train rattled south through Rhode Island, I began reading the articles the *Scientific American* had fed its hungry readers throughout 1922. One month the magazine ran a profile of a spirit medium, or "sensitive," as the psychics were sometimes known; the next it offered a descriptive tour of Berlin's famous Grunewald psychic laboratory. There were photos of spirit hands the Polish medium Franek Kluski claimed to have captured in paraffin wax. There was even a lengthy debate among a panel of experts on the chemistry of ectoplasm, the albuminous exudate that on very rare occasions poured from the orifices of physical mediums in trance and was often exposed as nothing more otherworldly than cheesecloth. The *Scientific American* had brought 1922 to a rousing close with the announcement of the five-thousand-dollar "inducement" for conclusive evidence of psychic phenomena. To hedge against criticism that it was all just a publicity stunt, the editors had assembled an independent panel of judges comprising prominent members of academia and the press and chaired by the president of the American Society for Psychical Research, William McLaughlin—a man whose moral probity was beyond reproach. In addition to lending the contest legitimacy, McLaughlin could be counted on to keep it from turning into a sideshow, a very real danger given the sizable cash prize on offer.

"New Haven! New Haven!"

I glanced up from my reading as the conductor moved through our compartment announcing the next station stop. Across from me McLaughlin was resting his eyes, arms folded across his vest and head inclined slightly forward, so that it was impossible to tell whether he was sleeping or merely deep in thought. I studied him, trying to reconcile what struck me as contradictory titles: Distinguished Man of Science and Preeminent Psychic Researcher. All along I had assumed that McLaughlin's opinion of the supernatural was similar to my own, that is to say, highly skeptical. Why, then, had he allied himself with so credulous an organization as the American Society for Psychical Research? Became its president, no less!

But eclipsing this question in my mind was a more immediate practical concern: Exactly what duties did the position of "assistant psychic researcher" entail? On this subject my new employer had remained frustratingly vague; all he would say was that he needed me to accompany him down to the New York offices of the *Scientific American* the day before the first scheduled séance and that in addition to a shaving kit I should be sure to pack my soldering iron. Of course I was in no position to refuse and had arrived at Boston's South Station bright and early that morning with overnight bag in hand. But now, as we entered the final leg of our journey, I began to wonder if I might not have once more committed myself to an undertaking at which I would ultimately fail.

. . .

We arrived at New York's Grand Central Terminal in the early afternoon and, after a quick lunch at the cavernous white-tiled Oyster Bar beneath the concourse, caught a taxi downtown to the *Scientific American* offices at 233 Broadway—the Woolworth Building. Built in 1913 at a cost of $13 million, the Woolworth was then entering its second decade as the tallest building in the world. Climbing out of the taxicab, I craned my neck to peer up its fifty-eight stories of terra-cotta arches and spires and flying buttresses, appreciating for the first time why the regal skyscraper was nicknamed the "Cathedral of Commerce." Its lobby could easily have hosted a coronation, with its terrazzo ceilings of turquoise and gold and its great mezzanine frescoes depicting Labor and Commerce.

We were met at the bronze elevators by Malcolm Fox, an editor of the *Scientific American*, who was acting as secretary to the investigating committee. A jowly, good-natured fellow in his fifties who looked as if he had just awoken from a nap, Fox inquired if McLaughlin and I had had lunch and then looked comically disappointed after learning we had. I suspect he'd been hoping to enjoy a second lunch on the magazine's expense account. But we accepted his offer of coffee, and Fox sent an office boy out to a nearby diner with instructions to pick it up along with a dozen or so of a certain Greek pastry he enjoyed.

Ten minutes later the office boy returned with the coffee and baklava just as the three of us had settled into chairs in Fox's sunny corner office.

"Tell me, young fellow," Fox asked as he offered me a pastry, "what first interested you in the field of psychic research?"

"I—"

"Finch here is quite clever with his hands," McLaughlin said. "I hired him to build us a device to control the medium we're testing tomorrow."

Fox frowned. "Don't you think it's a bit premature to talk about controls before we've even conducted an initial sitting?"

"You've read his testimonials, Malcolm. You can't tell me it isn't obvious to you how this Valentine fellow achieves his effects. Why else would he insist on conducting séances in total darkness?"

"I prefer to go into it with an open mind."

"I'm sorry," I cut in, "but I'm not sure I understand what sort of 'device' I'm supposed to be building."

"He wants you to build him a mousetrap," Fox said.

McLaughlin made a face at this gross oversimplification. " 'Mousetrap' implies I'm interested in *catching* Valentine, which isn't the case. I'm only interested in *controlling* him." He lit his pipe and sucked on its stem; then, thinking that the subject warranted further comment, he said through the smoke, "I'm not interested in unmasking false mediums, Malcolm. I'm interested only in their phenomena. Whether it is genuine. Whether it can be explained by the laws governing our physical world. Whether it warrants further study under more rigorous controls. When you say I mean to 'trap' Valentine, you suggest I carry some personal grudge against the man, when the truth of the matter is, I have no opinion one way or the other regarding him or why he might want to deceive us. I'm concerned only that we make it as difficult as possible for him to do so—which, as I mentioned before, is my reason for bringing Finch."

"What do you have in mind?" Fox asked.

McLaughlin turned in my direction. "Correct me if I'm wrong, Finch, but doesn't the human body possess a certain low level of electrical conductivity?"

"Very low," I said. "Skin is a pretty far cry from copper. You're talking something on the order of a million ohms of resistance."

"That much?"

"You might be able to cut the resistence in half," I said, "if you drank a lot of fluids and salt. Why?"

"I was hoping that if we introduced a small amount of electricity into the circle of joined hands, we could create a kind of rudimentary circuit—"

"And electrocute the whole committee!" Fox exclaimed.

"Not necessarily," I said, seeing now what McLaughlin had in mind. "Even with five million ohms of resistance in the circuit, a six-volt battery would generate a measurable current of"—reaching for a pencil among the photos of Fox's grandchildren, I scribbled a quick calculation—"one point two uAmps. That's such a small amount you wouldn't even notice it."

"But would a galvanometer?" McLaughlin asked.

"Yes," I said, "if your medium broke the circuit, a galvanometer would read zero."

McLaughlin looked pleased. He turned to Fox, who was following all of this with the confused expression of the Victor dog listening to His Master's Voice. "I assume you can help Finch here with any electrical supplies he might need, Malcolm?"

"Hm? Oh. Certainly."

"Splendid," McLaughlin said, and with this piece of business concluded, he continued to the next items on his agenda.

· · ·

It took me no time at all to engineer and field-test what I'd come to think of as McLaughlin's "spook circuit," employing a half dozen batteries and a d'Arsonval galvanometer. With these duties complete, I was granted an afternoon's furlough and went on a walking tour of the city, with a brief detour through the Bowery, where a nickelodeon was screening an educational film on "The Secrets of a Happy Marriage." Afterward, as an act of contrition— and because I'd promised McLaughlin I would do it—I paid a visit to St. Patrick's Cathedral, that twin-spired Gothic fortress at Fifth Avenue and Fifty-first Street. (I'd been memorizing Manhattan street addresses all day; I thought it would make me sound worldly back home in Cambridge.) I entered the vestibule and automatically dipped my finger in holy water to cross myself. Force of habit. I ducked into the nearest pew to avoid an awkward genuflection and spent the next few reflective moments trying to appreciate exactly what it was about the light that had so impressed McLaughlin. It filtered in through the stained glass, a diffuse radiance that accumulated near the cathedral's vaulted ceiling like weather. Looking at it, I was reminded of those interminable Tridentine masses of my youth, when I'd pass the time counting how many seconds it took for the little clouds of incense to drift from the priest's censer all the way up to the sunlit ceiling. These were my recollections of a Catholic childhood: boredom and bruised knees and odd-smelling priests. After ten minutes in St. Patrick's, I regressed to my fidgety twelve-year-old self, and when I couldn't stand it any longer I rose to my feet and quietly slipped out.

Back on the streets of midtown, I treated myself to a sandwich at a Horn & Hardart, then spent the final hour of daylight experimenting with the subway back to the Woolworth. When I finally arrived, I found the *Scientific American* offices in an uproar: During my absence it had been learned that the medium, Valentine, intended to break with orthodoxy and conduct tonight's séance without the usual joining of hands. Which meant all my work on McLaughlin's spook circuit had been for nothing.

I hurried to the library, where I'd been told I would find McLaughlin supervising final preparations for that evening's events. Two janitors were perched on wooden ladders, draping the windows in black muslin. McLaughlin looked up as I entered.

"Ah, Finch, how was St. Patrick's?"

I ignored the question and asked him breathlessly, "What are we going to do about Valentine?"

"Nothing, tonight," he said matter-of-factly; he seemed to be taking the setback in stride. I wish I could have said the same, but to me the news had come as a devastating blow. McLaughlin saw my look of dismay and said, "Cheer up, Finch. This sort of thing happens all the time. We'll just have to be more clever tomorrow."

And with that he dispatched me on a dozen small errands, to distract me from my disappointment. I spent the next hour on these details: helping the man from the Dictograph Products Company set up a transmitter on one of the library's shelves; running its wires out the library window, around the corner of the building, and back inside a small adjoining room; installing a stenographer in these cramped quarters, where she and I would eavesdrop via the Dictograph's receiver on the séance. And all the while racking my brain for some new device to replace McLaughlin's spook circuit.

At six-thirty the other members of the investigating committee began arriving at the *Scientific American* offices. First to appear was H. H. Richardson, the Princeton mathematician, a perilously slender man of about forty who tried to overcompensate with fine clothing—tonight a double-breasted suit of navy pinstripe and a pair of oxfords polished to a high sheen. He scowled at me when I told him my name as if I'd just proposed an impossible integer, then handed me his hat and camel-hair coat and continued past without ever once opening his mouth to speak. Fox returned from supper a few minutes later, smelling of cigars and brandy; when I told him the others were waiting in the library he blinked at me and said, "Very good, French." Last to arrive was Flynn, the reporter from the *Times*, a nicotine fiend with red hair and sharp English features; when I offered to show him to the library, he winked at me and asked for directions to the lavatory so he could catch one last smoke—though I suspected what he really intended was to chat up the few secretaries who hadn't yet left for the night. The committee was a motley bunch, and yet I knew that each in his own way was quite accomplished in his field. Despite his rather staid demeanor, Richardson possessed a restless intelligence and was something of a polymath, having published essays on everything from numerology to numismatics; Flynn had distinguished himself at the *Times* with a series of hardboiled articles on Houdini's own tireless—

and characteristically self-aggrandizing—campaign against bogus Spiritualists; and even poor witless Fox had succeeded over the course of his careeer to produce several well-regarded works of popular science.

At seven-thirty the guest of honor made his entrance. George Valentine was a man of medium build and average height, but that was where any affiliation with normalcy ceased. When I told him my name, he turned his somnolent gaze toward me, and I found myself staring into two eyes so black they looked like holes punched in tin. And yet these were not the most disconcerting of his features; that distinction belonged to his utter lack of hair. Beneath his camel overcoat he was clothed in a silk dressing gown embroidered all over with Oriental symbols in metallic thread, the sort of outfit I imagined addicts wear in an opium den; and where this revealed his chest and arms and ankles I glimpsed pallid skin entirely devoid of hair. He was bald as an egg, and seemed to be missing not only his eyebrows but also the lashes. Whether by choice or affliction, Valentine was smooth as a newborn, and the effect in a grown man of forty-some years was highly unnerving: like a creature who had escaped his jar of formaldehyde and matured somewhere out of reach of daylight.

Valentine followed me to the library, where I was more than happy to part company with him. I hurried to the adjacent room, where the stenographer was waiting. Together we huddled by the Dictograph machine and waited for the proceedings to begin.

The library lights were extinguished, and the séance got under way at eight o'clock with an inaugural recitation of the Lord's Prayer. Valentine led the circle in an off-key rendition of "Rise Up, Christians, and Rejoice," and after the hymn was concluded, the medium could be heard on the Dictograph invoking the ether:

"Welcome, spirits."

The whole thing was unsettling, and when McLaughlin announced a few moments later that he was observing "a faint luminescence, bluish in hue," I will admit I felt my hackles rise, though I had read how easily such spirit lights could be faked with an electric torch and a swatch of colored paper. For the next quarter of an hour I sat riveted by the Dictograph, hanging on its every amplified cough and inaudible word. The supernormal phenomena during those fifteen minutes were all easily discountable, the sort of things Valentine could produce without ever leaving his chair: spirit lights, animal chirps and whistles, a mewling the medium attributed to an unbaptized child crying for its mother in purgatory. This last functioned as a kind of macabre act-topper before an interlude of silence, as if the spirits needed rest between sets—like jazz musicians. Valentine said another prayer and led the circle in another hymn, and a moment later the séance moved into its second act:

"Something just brushed my face!"

It was Fox, his voice an octave higher than usual. I felt my heart quicken. Valentine was out of his chair! I looked at my watch—8:23. I followed the second hand's sweep around the dial as the stenographer scribbled frantically beside me to keep pace with the flurry of excited voices.

"Now it's exploring my pockets." (McLaughlin)
"It's blowing in my ear!" (Flynn)
"I beg your pardon!" (Richardson)
"Ouch!" (Fox)

These continued for the next thirty-eight seconds, before tapering off into a silence that could signify one thing only: Valentine had returned to his chair.

In the adjoining room I shared with the stenographer the air had grown stale thanks to the heat I was putting off—not to mention the smell from my underarms that I hoped my cubby companion didn't detect. A bead of perspiration itched beneath my collar; I swatted it angrily and, with my hand still cupping the back of my stinging neck, listened as Valentine thanked the spirits and brought the séance to an end.

. . .

That night I lay tossing and turning in bed, staring at imaginary electrical diagrams on the bedroom ceiling. I was staying in the handsome old home of a Harvard alumnus on West Fourth Street. I was still awake when the ceiling began to lighten in the early hours of morning. I had a throbbing headache and no solutions to show for it, and my concentration was broken by gruff voices speaking Italian outside the window. My host had warned me that stonemasons were currently renovating the brickwork across the alley; many of the older homes in that part of Greenwich Village had been built before the Civil War, and their oystershell mortar had begun to crumble after seven decades of weather. I sat up in bed and looked out the third-story window to watch the masons next door on their precarious scaffolding. The iron framework trembled as they scrambled over it like sailors in a ship's rigging. After several minutes the men finished their breakfast and set to work, the wooden platforms bowing slightly beneath their weight, lending a springiness to each stride. I watched for several minutes more, fascinated, without quite realizing for the longest time what it was that had seized my interest. And then all of a sudden I saw it: The wooden planks. The way they bowed underfoot . . .

I leaped out of bed and began searching for my trousers. Twenty minutes later I had commandeered my host's dining-room table and was covering it with the electrical schematics pouring out of my brain as quickly as I could sketch them. My host's bemused wife brought me two aspirin tablets, and I scalded my throat gulping them down with coffee. And yet I couldn't have cared less about my headache or the fact that I'd barely slept the night before, now that I had stumbled on the solution to the Valentine dilemma.

I worked like a demon the rest of the day, scouring lower Manhattan for the parts I needed, and by nightfall I had managed to see my contraption completed. As the business day came to a close and the office building was invaded by cleaning ladies, I demonstrated my device to McLaughlin, who gave it his provisional blessing. He reserved any praise for my ingenuity until the device had proven itself, for the real test was at that moment en route to 233 Broadway in a taxicab. I scrambled to get the device in place and managed to do so in the nick of time—just as Valentine came strolling through the doorway of the *Scientific American* offices and announced himself ready for the second night's séance.

By seven the committee had once more assembled in a circle, with Valentine—dressed tonight in a satin cape embroidered with strange symbols—occupying the center chair. Once more the lights in the library were dimmed, once more an opening hymn commenced by the untrained tenors. Once more the stenographer and I listened from the next room . . .

But this time I was ready for Valentine to leave his chair.

It happened the first time precisely eighteen minutes later. In the dark library, Valentine slipped from his chair . . . unaware that directly beneath it, hidden by the Oriental carpet, were two thin pieces of fiberboard sandwiching a dozen spring contacts. In essence a giant switch that remained "on" so long as the medium's weight in the chair held the boards closed. The moment Valentine left the chair, the spring contacts opened; and a dozen yards away, in the tiny room where the stenographer and I huddled, the lamp I'd wired to the fiberboard switch went dark. I signaled the stenographer to make careful note of the time in her transcript. Only after I'd seen her do it could I release the breath I'd been holding for the last sixty seconds. My heart was racing, my mouth was dry; it was all I could do to keep from bursting into the library and pointing an accusing finger at Valentine. But I tempered my impatience with the satisfaction of knowing that each time Valentine left his chair—and he would do it eight more times over the next ninety minutes—he was adding another damning data point to our evidence against him.

The séance concluded a few minutes before nine o'clock. As Valentine lingered in conversation with the other committeemen, McLaughlin took me aside to confer quietly over the transcript. He listened to the evidence without expression and only grunted when I'd finished. I was exultant, but McLaughlin seemed to take no pleasure in the news. He called the other committeemen into private counsel, and when they emerged from deliberations ten minutes later, it was McLaughlin who delivered their verdict.

"I'm afraid we cannot award you the *Scientific American* prize, Mr. Valentine."

"What?"

"We believe that the psychic manifestations witnessed here tonight were all produced by normal means."

Valentine looked stunned. He pressed for an explanation. McLaughlin calmly lifted back the Oriental carpet to reveal my fiberboard switch, then took him to the adjoining room to see the lamp, and concluded his tour finally by showing Valentine the séance transcript, where every instance of his legerdemain had been meticulously recorded. Valentine listened, growing quiet, and after what seemed a long while looked up. But the medium wasn't interested in confronting his accusers—he was looking for me, architect of his unmasking; and when his eyes found mine, I saw color come to his face for the first time. In those black eyes I saw a fury so cold it seemed to drop the temperature in the room ten degrees. Fortunately, Valentine seemed to understand he was outnumbered, and so I was spared an assault. The medium gave his cape a theatrical twirl before storming off into obscurity. Several months later, when the *Scientific American* published its account of the evening, he would be referred to only as "Mr. X" and, except for that pseudonymous mention, would never be heard from again.

But before I leave that night, I want to mention one more moment of importance it held for me—maybe the most significant of all. It occurred after Valentine had gone and the stenographer was sent home and the other committeemen had left in search of a speakeasy. The building was quiet, and my thirty-six hours without sleep were finally catching up to me. As I was gathering the pieces of my spirit chair, I looked up and saw McLaughlin watching me from the doorway. He was standing in silhouette, so I couldn't read his expression. But it was what I heard him say that mattered.

"That was fine work you did tonight, Finch."

"Thank you, sir."

"Have you given much thought to your dissertation topic yet?"

I admitted, "Not as much as I should, I'm afraid."

"You might consider something in the field of parapsychology," McLaughlin advised. "You have a talent for it—something few so-called experts in the field do, in my experience. If you should decide it might interest you, I would be happy to act as your faculty adviser, oversee your research and so forth. In any event, give it some thought, Finch."

"I will," I said, unexpectedly moved by his offer. "Thank you, Professor."

"You're welcome," said McLaughlin, and, putting on his hat, departed.

· 3 ·

In its July issue, the *Scientific American* published the findings of its first psychic investigation, in a lengthy account written by committee secretary Malcolm Fox. I bought the magazine the day it appeared on newsstands in Harvard Square and scoured its pages for any mention of my spirit chair. To my delight I found the chair described in considerable detail—several column inches—though my part in its design received no mention. A chart compared the psychic phenomena and the medium's location at the time each one occurred (in or out of his chair); the evidence was presented under the heading "The Deadly Parallel." The article concluded, *"It is the opinion of this committee that Mr. X has failed to provide convincing evidence that his mediumship is genuine."*

On the whole I felt it was a fairly evenhanded account of the Valentine séances. And yet as the summer went on, the *Scientific American* received sharp criticism from Spiritualist publications like *Light* and the *International Psychic Gazette* for sponsoring what they considered to be a witch-hunt. Rumor spread through the Spiritualist community that the *Scientific American* investigators were nothing but a bunch of godless debunkers, no different from (as a typical correspondent wrote) "that low-minded Jew, Houdini." With the exception of the few anti-Semitic remarks directed at his friend Houdini, the professor wasn't particularly upset by these letters, though he did share with me his concern that such sentiments might hurt the investigation by discouraging other mediums from coming forward.

Fortunately, his fears proved premature, and in August a second medium surfaced with the necessary affidavits to qualify for consideration. But before I could pack my bags for New York, I received notice of an unexpected change in plans. The professor's rheumatism had flared up in the last few weeks, and in spite of regular hydrotherapy and a protein-restricted diet, he was finding it increasingly difficult to walk—and all but impossible to travel. In light of this, the other members of the investigating committee had offered to come to Boston. Schedules were consulted, and the week of August 5 chosen for the first séances.

I was given the assignment of securing a suitable space for the occasion and making any other necessary preparations. With the help of McLaughlin's secretary, I reserved a suite of rooms at the Copley-Plaza Hotel; with the help of his wife, I planned the menu for a formal dinner on Arrival Day; and with the help of Western Union, I corresponded with the medium in St. Louis to see if she needed anything beyond the usual darkened room and circle of chairs. This last item on my crowded to-do list turned out to be the least complicated, when the medium wired back:

CHAIRS UNNECESSARY STOP REQUIRE ONLY STATIONERY CARDS (75) HEAVY STOCK

On August 2 tragedy befell the nation: While on tour of the western states, President Harding died of cerebral apoplexy brought on by a bout of ptomaine poisoning (contracted from a batch of bad crabs that had been given him as a gift from the people of Alaska). As the sphinxlike Calvin Coolidge was sworn into office, McLaughlin and the rest of his committee debated whether to postpone the Boston meeting. Finally they decided to proceed with the séances scheduled to begin August 9, a week being deemed an appropriate period of mourning for a president who was liked but not beloved.

And so it was that the *Scientific American*'s investigating committee—Princeton's Richardson, Flynn from the *Times*, secretary Fox, and chairman McLaughlin—convened once more, on an unpleasantly humid Friday evening. To my horror I discovered when I arrived that night at the front desk of the Copley-Plaza Hotel that I'd accidentally booked the honeymoon suite; luckily, when I arrived upstairs, I found the other men entirely unfazed by the feminine décor, the gilt wallpaper and Louis XIV chiffonier and canopy bed with its gold brocade pillows. They were too busy speculating about what the evening would hold, and in particular whether the message medium from St. Louis would finally prove to be the genuine article.

She had arrived earlier that afternoon at South Station. She called herself the Reverend Betty Bell Harker, though she wasn't affiliated with any church. She claimed to be able to produce spirit writing on blank stationery cards through the intercession of a kind of astral stenographer she'd christened "Ivy." She arrived at the hotel at the appointed hour, seven o'clock, smelling of camphor balls and swaddled in so many threadbare sweaters it was difficult to estimate the exact dimensions of the grandmother underneath. I presented her with the stack of heavy-stock index cards she'd requested, and she immediately got down to work.

First she examined each card individually: running her fingers along its edges, scrutinizing its grain, even holding it to her nose and giving it a good sniff. A dozen cards were rejected at the outset, some set to the side for the time being, while others were immediately ripped into confetti, so that by the time she was finally satisfied with the remaining deck, it was difficult for any of us watching to remember how many cards had been eliminated. This would prove to be no accident.

At last the Reverend Betty Bell Harker was ready to invoke her spirit stenographer, Ivy. She began plucking the petals from a bouquet on the windowsill, which she proceeded to distribute carefully between each card in the deck. These, she explained, provided the organic "ink" her spirit stenographer needed to write her messages. Then the reverend held the deck of cards over the heads of members of the committee she identified as psychic "magnets"—it just so happened I was one—and made us join her in a few quiet prayers.

Unfortunately, this elaborate performance yielded nothing in the way of spirit messages, and after an hour and a half, the session was reluctantly declared a blank. The Reverend Betty Bell proposed that she return tomorrow, at which time she was certain Ivy would be "finished pouting." As a gesture of good faith, she left the deck of blank stationery cards in McLaughlin's care. Then she bade everyone good night and breezed off in a cloud of camphor.

"All right, gentlemen," McLaughlin said as soon as the Reverend Betty Bell had left the hotel suite, "how many cards do you estimate just walked out of this room?"

"I lost count," Richardson said. "Two?"

"In her brassiere alone," Flynn said, removing a hip flask and taking a belt. He smacked his lips and passed the flask, continuing, "Then figure a second pair in the old gal's unmentionables."

"So your estimate is four?" McLaughlin said.

"At least."

Fox had been listening to all this with a puzzled look and couldn't stand being left out of the joke any longer. "I'm afraid I don't follow," he said. "What are you estimating?"

"Oh, for crying out loud," Flynn said, rolling his eyes. "Didn't any of that complicated hocus-pocus in the beginning tip you off, Fox?"

"All that shuffling and sorting," Richardson prompted.

"And the sniffing!" Flynn added. "Don't forget about the sniffing!"

But Fox only looked more confused. Finally McLaughlin was forced to spell it out for him: "She's a cardsharp, Malcolm. She uses sleight of hand to slip an unspecified number of cards from the deck and leaves with them concealed somewhere on her person."

There was a long pause, and then a light of low wattage suddenly dawned in Fox's brain. "I thought it seemed awfully hot for all those sweaters!"

"Precisely," McLaughlin said. "No doubt she's holed up somewhere right now sipping a gin and tonic and composing the spirit messages that will miraculously appear tomorrow—"

"After she slips them back into the deck," Flynn finished.

"That may very well be the case," Fox said, drinking from Flynn's hip flask and handing it past me to the newspaperman, "but we'll need more than circumstantial evidence to disqualify her."

Despite its source, this would prove to be the evening's most important observation. After considering Fox's warning for a moment, McLaughlin asked, "How many cards are left in the deck?"

Richardson performed a quick count. "Sixty-eight."

"And we started with seventy-five," McLaughlin said, as much to himself as to the rest of us. Finally he looked back at me and said, "Fetch the wastebasket, Finch." I found it beneath the dressing table and overturned it carefully. Out came a shower of white confetti. McLaughlin instructed me to try reassembling the bits of stationery, like a jigsaw puzzle, but it didn't take long to see this was only an exercise in futility.

"What about a scale?" I suggested.

A half hour later, I regretted ever having opened my mouth, as

I was sent out to search the whole of Back Bay for an all-night pharmacy. At last, I managed to find a druggist who would lend me one of his chemical scales. I returned with this to the Copley-Plaza honeymoon suite, where we weighed the confetti and found it to total 11.84 grams—approximately four cards' worth.

So now we could say with some confidence how many cards the Reverend Betty Bell Harker had sneaked out of the hotel suite concealed somewhere on her person:

$$
\begin{array}{r}
75 \text{ (the original total)} \\
-\,68 \text{ (the current total)} \\
-\;\;4 \text{ (the confetti)} \\
\hline
3 \text{ cards unaccounted for}
\end{array}
$$

But that still left the question of how we were going to catch the woman in the act of surreptitiously returning them to the deck. And it remained unanswered when the clock on the hotel suite's dressing table struck midnight and the five of us reluctantly adjourned for the evening.

· · ·

Given the nonmechanical nature of the problem, McLaughlin did not expect me to come up with any answers. Which is why I was excited the next morning to be able to tell him I'd found one.

I turned up on his doorstep early. His wife, a graying Quaker beauty given to plain speech and peasant dresses, insisted I join her husband and his ancient dachshunds on the patio for coffee and scones. These days anyone who set foot inside Mrs. McLaughlin's household did so with the understanding that his diet would be subject to the same scrutiny as her convalescing husband's; and the few times I'd met her, she hadn't been shy about telling me I was underweight. Therefore, a few minutes later, when I began outlining my plan for the professor across the patio breakfast table, I had no choice but to do so with a mouth full of warm scone and lemon curd, under Mrs. McLaughlin's critical eye, a pair of old dachshunds yapping around my ankles and fighting for crumbs. As if these weren't distractions enough, the youngest of the four McLaughlin girls—Carolyn, the only daughter still at home—had reached sufficient age (fifteen) and attractiveness (a butterscotch blonde) to act as a kind of pretty irritant flitting about in the corner of my eye.

These distractions notwithstanding, I managed to make it through my proposed solution to the dilemma of last night. And this time McLaughlin's approval was immediate.

"You're beginning to show a real knack for this, Finch."

At that moment his wife appeared at my shoulder with fresh coffee and, with a disapproving look at my half-eaten scone, said, "Although thy appetite leaves something to be desired."

McLaughlin leaned forward, a twinkle in his eye. "You'd better pick up the pace, Finch," he warned, apropos of his wife's Quakerisms. "When she starts in with the 'thees' and 'thys,' she means business." He gave a sly wink, as much for his wife's benefit as my own, and her frown of disapproval might have been convincing if she hadn't betrayed it with a girlish gesture—tucking up a strand of hair that had escaped its bun. I blushed and stared down into my coffee, experiencing the cozy embarrassment of a child who's just stumbled on his parents kissing in the larder. I took a second scone and slathered it with enough clotted cream to appease Mrs. McLaughlin; satisfied, she whistled for the dogs to follow her inside and left the professor and me alone on the patio to get down to our own pressing business.

Foremost was a discussion of how to implement my solution. McLaughlin pointed out that my proposal was almost *too* simple; he feared that the medium might become suspicious if we didn't take precautions to throw her off our scent. We spent the next hour discussing ways of doing this, and once we'd settled on several ideas, he sent me off to investigate the options available to us.

McLaughlin was right: My solution was ridiculously simple, and it took me all of an hour to set the trap itself. But the task of *disguising* the trap was another matter entirely, and it occupied most of my afternoon. By the time we reconvened at the hotel, however, everything was in place—the jaws of the bear trap set and any signs of subterfuge carefully disguised by leaves and branches . . .

The Reverend Betty Bell Harker arrived at the Copley-Plaza promptly at seven, well rested after a day of sightseeing (which, it would turn out, entailed putting half of Quincy Street on layaway in anticipation of the *Scientific American* prize money). To the medium's surprise, I had arranged for her to be greeted by a nurse from Massachusetts General Hospital.

"Good evening, ma'am," the steely nurse said, opening the door of the honeymoon suite. "These gentlemen would like me to conduct a thorough search of your person—with your permission, of course."

To her credit, the medium disguised her surprise well and hesitated only a few seconds before granting her consent.

"Gladly, Sister."

The nurse escorted her into the adjoining bedroom. Ten minutes later the nurse emerged to report that her search had revealed nothing out of the ordinary. I wasn't surprised: I'd given the nurse explicit instructions to conduct her thorough search so unthoroughly that even an amateur could elude her. The whole thing was a ruse, part of McLaughlin's plan to put the medium on the defensive.

As were the tiny pinpricks I had made that afternoon in several random cards in the deck. These the reverend detected almost immediately, as the professor had hoped she would, and the effort to find and eliminate every card marked with a pinprick absorbed so much of her attention and energy that she overlooked entirely the real trap we'd laid for her. It took her a good twenty minutes, during which it was all I could do to keep a straight face.

Finally, satisfied that she'd eluded our attempts to trip her up, the Reverend Betty Bell was ready to continue. Once more she plucked flower petals from the bouquet of flowers and distributed them between the cards. Once more she held the deck above the heads of various "magnets" on the committee as she invoked Ivy. And just as we'd predicted the night before, this time the spirit stenographer made good on the reverend's promises: Among the blank cards, we now found three messages of metaphysical greeting—the sort of wish-you-were-here sentiments your Aunt Hattie might write on a postcard from Atlantic City. Two of these greetings were scribbled in a vivid red botanical "ink," while the third was scripted in a kind of gold filigree—and was signed by no less illustrious a ghost than Harvard's own departed dean of psychology:

> *How happy I should have been for an opportunity such as this!*
> *—William James*

A nice touch, I thought. You couldn't fault the old girl on creativity. Having concluded her demonstration, the Reverend Betty Bell collapsed and allowed herself to be carried by Richardson and Flynn to the settee.

While a cold compress was applied to her brow, she asked when she might expect to hear her victory announced in the press and, more important, whether her winnings would come in the form of cash or banker's check. With the compress over her eyes, she couldn't see the amused look that passed among the men in the hotel suite or the more solemn glance McLaughlin threw my way, indicating it was high time we put an end to this.

"Excuse me, Reverend," I began as gently as I could, "but there's something I need to show you."

She sat up on the settee, the washcloth sliding off her eyes and landing with a wet plop in her lap, and she saw me holding up the blank deck beside her three message cards. I could see her trying to comprehend what she was seeing: The three message cards were bigger than the deck.

"I don't understand . . . ?"

I explained it to her. I'd had the stationer trim the deck by one thirty-second of an inch that morning, gambling that she would never notice such a tiny discrepancy without a close inspection and an even closer side-by-side comparison. And in fact she hadn't noticed; she'd been too flustered by the nurse's examination, too distracted by the pinpricked cards, to see she was setting foot in a simpler trap—until it was too late, and she felt its iron jaws clamp shut on her ankle.

What happened next caught me completely off guard. All that afternoon, as I'd gone cheerfully about the business of baiting my trap, I'd given very little thought to how I would feel when it finally sprang. I suppose if I gave it any thought at all it was to fantasize about the aftermath—the praise from the other men, their claps on the shoulder and invitations for drinks, my ascension into their ranks as a colleague and equal. But now that the moment had arrived, now that I'd heard the sound of my trap's spring-loaded jaws clamping shut on their victim, I found that I didn't feel triumphant after all, or even particularly happy. Tasting victory, I found it bittersweet: soured by an unexpected sympathy for this little medium I'd just bagged.

She looked at me with the rheumy eyes of a heartbroken grandmother, and I felt a sharp tug in my chest. I tried biting

down on that inconvenient thread of conscience, like a man trying to free himself from a fishhook, but it was no use.

And then the Reverend Betty Bell Harker leaned forward and
hissed something under her breath that took care of it for me.

"Cocksucker."

. . .

In the weeks that followed, I would come to regard the Harker
Affair as a kind of personal best I wouldn't surpass anytime soon.
If this sounds strange, given the simple methods I had used to
"control" the reverend (in the experimental sense), I should point
out that simplicity is the essence of all good experiments, the
quality that keeps them seaworthy through the hostile waters of
peer review and sees them safely into port—or, in this case, print.
Admittedly, the *Scientific American*'s review process wasn't the
same rough crossing one encountered in the academic press, but
it still felt like a personal victory when Fox's article on the Harker
Affair withstood the scrutiny of the magazine's internal board of
review and was published, in the fall of 1923, under the title "Another Mediumistic Failure."

Once again my name went unmentioned. But this time the
oversight didn't sting so much. *I* knew how instrumental I'd been,
and it was gratifying to know that McLaughlin did, too.

My prediction that this would remain my high-water mark
proved correct, though not for the reasons I originally thought.
In the weeks following the Harker Affair, two more mediums
were tested in quick succession and just as quickly eliminated;
both came from the bottom of the barrel and required little input
from me to disqualify. One was a Rhode Island portrait photographer who attempted to pass off double exposures as spirit
photos. But when the committee asked him to use the plates
they provided, his ghostly images ceased to appear. The second

medium was little more than a glorified escape artist—literally, as
the committee learned when it received a phone call from the
man's keepers at Danvers Asylum. In both cases I was relegated to
the role of bystander, which is why I'll spend no more time com-
menting on them here.

By mid-October the editors of the *Scientific American* began
grumbling that perhaps the magazine's critics were right: Maybe
McLaughlin and his committee *were* engaged in a witch-hunt.
Four mediums had now fallen before the investigating committee; could it be that their criteria were too strict? With the end of
1923 looming, the editors began to worry that reader interest
couldn't be sustained into a second calendar year. After all, the average *Scientific American* reader didn't give a good goddamn
about investigative rigor (or so the argument went); he wanted to
be entertained as he was being informed—in short, he wanted a
little spectacle. Skepticism didn't sell subscriptions. Oh, it was
amusing enough for a few issues to follow our intrepid investigators as they outwitted bogus mediums, but in time these
cliffhangers had to reach a thrilling conclusion, didn't they?

No, they did not, McLaughlin responded in a strongly worded
letter to the editors of the *Scientific American* dated October 23.
He followed this one day later with a missive to his committee,
urging them to remain vigilant.

"Gentlemen," he wrote, *"We are not charged merely with adju-
dicating a contest. We are charged with investigating the Truth."* His
letter went on, *"We have been asked to defend the public's interest,
not assuage its impatience. When it becomes enamored, we must remain aloof. When it is credulous, we must remain skeptical. And
most of all, gentlemen, when it clamors for resolution—as it is clam-
oring now—we must be resolute."*

I remember looking up from a draft of this letter in McLaughlin's office and feeling strangely moved. Certainly his words had

strengthened my resolve—though mine was never in question. It was Fox, unsurprisingly, who'd shown the first signs of cracking. The *Scientific American* lackey had circulated his own letter the week before, in which he wondered if the committee might not be holding these spirit mediums to an impossible standard.

"Isn't it conceivable," Fox had argued, "that an otherwise genuine medium might from time to time be forced to resort to trickery, when the spirits prove fickle?"

It was just this sort of sophistry McLaughlin most abhorred, in research and in life. Which is why he spent the better part of November lobbying by phone and post and wire to ensure that Fox's slippery logic didn't gain a foothold with Richardson or Flynn.

It was in the midst of this campaign that a letter of a different kind appeared one autumn day in McLaughlin's cubby. It came in an envelope of cream vellum and was postmarked Crowborough, Sussex. The correspondent had been following the *Scientific American* investigations with great interest from his estate in the south of England and wished to bring to the committee's attention Mrs. Arthur Crawley, a young Philadelphia socialite who possessed (the writer enthused) *"quite the most remarkable mediumship I have yet encountered."* The letter was signed Sir Arthur Conan Doyle.

At the time Conan Doyle was among the world's foremost psychic authorities—some would say apologists—and certainly its most ardent believer. McLaughlin knew the novelist from his days as president of the British Society for Psychical Research, had on several occasions been the guest of Sir Arthur and Lady Doyle at Windlesham, their Sussex estate, and had seen firsthand how seriously the couple took the subject of psychic research, not to mention their newfound religion. Conan Doyle had first professed his faith in Spiritualism publicly in October 1917, at a meeting of the London Spiritualist Alliance. Many people attributed Doyle's interest in Spiritualism to the death of his son Kingsley in the war, but in fact, McLaughlin told me, the seeds of Conan Doyle's latter-day obsession had been sown in séances the young physician had attended during the last century. Over the decades these seeds had taken root and spread like a creeper, to the point where they now threatened to crowd out the cash crop that had first made Conan Doyle's fortune—fiction. These days the author was spending less and less of his time writing novels and more of it in séances and lecture halls. Which would have been a respectable pastime for a retired author if Conan Doyle had approached his psychic research with anything resembling scientific rigor; but he and Lady Doyle were so trusting, had become such easy marks, that even the couple's friends—like the McLaughlins—worried that the creepers had begun to loosen the stones of the foundation itself.

Therefore an endorsement from Sir Arthur Conan Doyle was neither very unusual nor so compelling as it might first seem. Yet his endorsement still held some currency, certainly enough for me, who had thrilled to his fiction as a boy and found in its pages my first lessons in a detective's inductive reasoning; and ultimately enough for the more circumspect McLaughlin, who, against his better judement, continued to extend his old friend a line of credibility long after other creditors had cut him off.

And so before the day was through, McLaughlin had dispatched me with a letter for the evening mail, extending his personal invitation to this Crawley woman in Philadelphia who had so impressed the creator of Sherlock Holmes.

· · ·

While we awaited her reply, McLaughlin made a few inquiries of his own into the background of Sir Arthur's society psychic. He phoned several colleagues from the Philadelphia chapter of the American Society for Psychical Research, who confirmed Doyle's opinion that she was a woman of good character, and contributed additional details: She was thirty years of age, married for the last decade to a surgeon some twenty years her senior; the couple was childless. On the question of her authenticity, none of these Philadelphia contacts could comment; it seemed she'd only recently become aware of these latent psychic talents herself—accidentally, in December of '22—and was reluctant to share them beyond her family and a few trusted friends. For Conan Doyle she had made a rare exception, because her husband was an admirer of such long standing; all other requests to join her circle were met with a polite but firm refusal. Which was a pity, since her powers were rumored to be formidable.

And yet despite these forewarnings, we were still surprised when we finally received Mrs. Crawley's reply one week later:

Philadelphia, 1 November, 1923

Alas, my dear professor, I must decline your kind invitation, as I consider what is happening to me to be a gift from God & not a fit subject for scientific inquiry.

(signed) Mrs. Arthur Crawley

Well, I thought, *that puts an end to that.* But McLaughlin seemed to take the news especially hard, and this confused me. Hadn't he written her only as a courtesy to Conan Doyle? Why, then, did he seem so upset when she turned our invitation down? Attempting to reconcile these inconsistencies, I though back over the last few weeks. I had noticed that McLaughlin seemed uncharacteristically short-tempered, and easily fatigued in the afternoons. I'd assumed this was due to his rheumatism and its attendant frustrations, but now I recognized these as symptoms of the tremendous pressure he must have been suffering, caught between the rock of the *Scientific American*'s demands and the hard place of his uncompromising ethics. McLaughlin's reaction to the Crawley letter forced me to face the truth: No matter how stirringly he wrote to the other committeemen about duty and vigilance, privately he worried he was failing them. Seeing the professor in this new light was troubling, because by this time he was an idol to me; and, like most young men, I wanted my idols cast in twenty-four karats—not cheapened by the baser metals of hesitancy or self-doubt.

And so it pained me all the more to see him commit what I considered a further compromise, dashing off a second letter to Doyle's society psychic—a religious fanatic so far as I could see—and virtually begging her to reconsider.

Though she once more declined (this time citing her husband's mistrust of publicity) Mrs. Crawley seemed to enjoy this exchange with McLaughlin and left the door open for future correspondence. This continued for much of the month and became a kind of courtship dance conducted by post and wire:

WHAT IF COMMITTEE GUARANTEED ANONYMITY MIGHT YOU RECONSIDER

A KIND OFFER BUT UNFORTUNATELY LEAVES UNRESOLVED THE ISSUE OF $ HAVE NEVER BEFORE ACCEPTED PAYMENT FOR MY GIFTS AND ADMIT I FIND THE IDEA DISTASTEFUL PLEASE ACCEPT SINCEREST APOLOGIES MINA

PERHAPS A DIFFERENT SORT OF HONORARIUM THIS WOULD NOT BE UNPRECEDENTED AS EUSAPIA PALLADINO FELT AS YOU DO BUT WOULD ACCEPT SMALL GIFTS JEWELRY ETCETERA OF SENTIMENTAL VALUE IN EXCHANGE FOR READINGS

MISS PALLADINO SOUNDS LIKE A FASCINATING WOMAN THOUGH
NOT BLESSED AS I AM BY A GENEROUS HUSBAND WHO PROVIDES ALL
THE ORNAMENT A WOMAN COULD DESIRE

EUSAPIA PALLADINO NOT HALF SO FASCINATING AS MRS CRAWLEY
PERHAPS A CONTRIBUTION TO A FAVORITE SOCIAL CHARITY PLEASE
RECONSIDER

This met with a silence of several days, until McLaughlin began
to worry that his persistence had lost its charm. And then, finally:

MY HUSBAND PROPOSES A FELLOWSHIP ESTABLISHED IN CRAWLEY
FAMILY NAME TO SUPPORT WORK OF FUTURE RESEARCHERS THIS
WOULD BE ACCEPTABLE PLEASE ADVISE

McLaughlin was so delighted to win her over that he didn't
give a second thought to the difficulty the trip would cause him,
for Mrs. Crawley disliked winter travel and had made it a further
condition that the *Scientific American* committee should come to
her. Over his wife's protests, McLaughlin agreed.

With these terms in place, all that remained was to pick dates
for the sittings. The Crawleys consented to the first week of December and graciously made available their home in the Quaker
City's Rittenhouse Square to any guests for whom the Bellevue-
Stratford would not suffice. By Thanksgiving everything had
been arranged, all schedules cleared, and the necessary reservations confirmed.

And then, two nights before we were to leave—disaster.

· · ·

"He's in his study sulking," Mrs. McLaughlin said, handing me a
tray of soup and crackers. "Why don't you take him his supper."

I carried the tray into the study, where I found McLaughlin
in a rattan chair staring moodily into the fire. His right leg was

encased from ankle to hip in a white plaster cast, thanks to the spill he'd taken on his icy front walk that morning.

"Professor?"

He scowled in my direction. "What the devil are you doing with that tray, Finch?"

"Attempting not to spill it."

He made a disgusted sound. "More soup. Is she trying to drown me?" He bellowed toward the kitchen, "It's a broken hip—not the grippe!"

"Where would you like me to put this, Professor?"

"Pour it in the ficus."

Ignoring these instructions, I set the tray on an ottoman and chased the dachshunds off the couch so I could sit across from him. After what seemed an appropriate period of silent commiseration, I asked quietly, "Is it very bad?"

"That depends on your opinion of *walking*," he muttered, and then he rattled off the laundry list of injuries he had sustained in his fall: two cracked ribs, a bruised kidney, a sprained wrist, a fractured pelvis. . . . (How so much damage could result from an accident that hadn't involved a motorcar or farm equipment escaped me, until I remembered that McLaughlin hadn't been in the best of health to begin with; his arthritis had no doubt contributed to his fall.) He was looking at a twelve-week convalescence confined to a wheelchair, after which he would graduate to a pair of crutches and eventually—if he was lucky and if he followed a rigorous exercise regimen to strengthen his atrophied muscles—a cane. But he would always have a limp, and his days of running for trains were over.

"So there you have it," McLaughlin concluded. "I am officially an invalid."

I didn't know what to say, and so for a long time I didn't say anything. It was the worst possible news, worse even than any of the scenarios I'd envisioned as I'd hurried over here—and I was an imaginative catastrophist. I felt an overwhelming urge to make myself useful and was grateful therefore when he surfaced from his brooding and ask me to fix him a drink. I went to the bookcase where he kept a decanter of whiskey and returned with a double. He sipped it, made a face, and settled back into his black mood. I coughed into my fist by way of announcing I was about to leave.

"I suppose I'd better phone the rest of the committee and tell them Philadelphia is off."

"Are you out of your mind, Finch?" McLaughlin snapped. "After all I've had to go through to get this Crawley woman to sit for us? We can't cancel now!"

"I meant 'postpone,' " I said. "She sounds like a reasonable enough woman. I'm sure once she hears the circumstances, she won't mind waiting until you're well enough to travel again."

McLaughlin looked glum. "Even if she *is* willing to wait, the *Scientific American* won't be."

"No?"

"They're uncomfortable as it is with how long this contest has dragged on—even though I've been warning them from day one it could very well take years. But then, they're tired of listening to me. They'd much rather hear what Fox has to say."

"Why, what is he telling them?"

"That he's found their winner," McLaughlin said, seizing a fireplace poker and stirring the fire with stabbing, agitated motions. Sparks swarmed like hornets and escaped up the flue. "The contest has succeeded in what it was intended to do—increase subscriptions and garner publicity. Now it has outlived its usefulness. Fox's employers are under tremendous pressure to award their little 'inducement'—from readers, the press, the Spiritualist community. If it were up to the editors, they would have awarded the five thousand to that straitjacket contortionist we tested last autumn—what was his name again?"

"Eugene Polini."

"That's right." McLaughlin swirled his drink around in his glass, said to the diminishing ice, "So you can imagine how ecstatic they must be to have found this 'society psychic.' She's young, educated, comes from a good family. And it gets better: She doesn't even want the money! Stop the presses and phone the governor! We'll devote an entire issue to her!" He tossed back the remainder of his drink as if to kill the sarcasm.

I cautiously ventured, "They'll still have to test her."

"Yes, I expect they will go through the motions."

"You won't let them."

"I won't have any say in the matter."

Frustrated, I began pacing before the fire. The dachshunds raised their heads to watch me.

"Isn't there anyone you trust who can go in your place?"

"On such short notice—no."

"What about Houdini?" I knew they were friends and had collaborated on articles about various techniques used by bogus mediums.

"He's touring the Continent."

I stopped pacing, struck by a sudden thought. "What about me?"

Up went McLaughlin's eyebrows. "You, Finch?"

"I can hire a stenographer to keep transcripts of the séances and telephone you first thing every morning with a status report." I was talking quickly, knowing if I slowed long enough to think about what I was proposing, I'd suffer the same fate as a tightrope walker who risks a peek at the ground. Incredibly, McLaughlin seemed to be giving my eleventh-hour suggestion serious consideration.

"*Scientific American* won't be very happy about it. . . ."

"No."

"And I expect Fox will try to filibuster. . . ."

"I wouldn't put it past him."

"But then, I don't see how he has a leg to stand on," he concluded. "The charter is quite clear on the matter: Each of us may designate an alternate to serve in his place, in case of emergencies."

"I think this qualifies."

McLaughlin looked up at me. Though the spark had returned to his blue eyes, his words were cautionary. "You realize Fox will do everything in his power to undermine you, yes?" Without waiting for my answer, he continued, "I can give you my seat in the séance circle, but I cannot force the others to respect you. If this Crawley woman is half as impressive as Conan Doyle says she is, Fox will move quickly to have her declared winner. If she is pretty to boot, Flynn won't require much persuading—remember, he has his own editors to please, who would like nothing more than an exclusive interview with a photogenic spirit medium. Which means if you intend to keep this investigation from concluding before it's begun, you are going to have to win over Richardson."

I listened to all this without comment, my initial surge of confidence subsiding to sea level. Prickly little doubts began to appear among the tide pools, like starfish. But I put on a brave face and asked, "Do you think Richardson will listen?"

"To reason, yes," McLaughlin said. "He's the most sensible of the group. Also, he and his wife were once the victims of a bogus spirit medium—they lost their only child to the influenza; a daughter, if I remember correctly—so if you present him with a solid argument for withholding his vote, he will not hesitate to force the committee into deadlock. But be warned that even Richardson won't hold out forever; you will have to be very clever if you expect to keep him in your corner."

I nodded, trying not to let McLaughin see how overwhelmed I was by his confidence. What had started as elation was beginning to feel like a crushing responsibility, and I cursed myself for suggesting the lunatic scheme in the first place. What had I been thinking? I knew next to nothing about Philadelphia and even less about internecine politics. McLaughlin was right: Fox would never respect my opinion. I'd be lucky if he even let me speak. I might carry McLaughlin's vote, but I would never wield his authority. But then I didn't see what other choice I had than to represent him in Philadelphia. True, I could simply shrug my shoulders and accept this stroke of bad luck, but that would also mean accepting the end of the only job I'd ever shown any talent for, unless you counted shaving Professor Schneider's lab rats.

"Finch."

I roused from my woolgathering. "Sir?"

"If you don't mind, I'd like another drink," he said, holding out his glass, "and while you're at it, I suggest you make yourself one as well. We have a very long night ahead of us."

· 4 ·

I booked passage on an overnight train with the intention of getting a jump on the rest of the committee and arriving early in Philadelphia, but when my train was delayed by an overturned freight outside New Haven, I quickly saw my lead dwindle and disappear altogether. After an interminable delay, the tracks were cleared and we got under way again. We crawled into the Quaker City a little past five the next afternoon, seventeen hours after I'd departed Boston and a full six hours behind Fox and Flynn and Richardson.

All this I offer to explain my poor first impressions of Philadelphia. The bustling Broad Street Station, which at any other time would have thrilled me with the romance of arrival—with its train shed like an iron cathedral, its steam-belching locomotives and busy redcaps—impressed me now only as crowded and oppressive and loud. It was rush hour, and I had to fight my way through a crush of people decamping for the Main Line suburbs, the Haverfords and Bryn Mawrs and Villanovas I heard being intoned around me from a monotonous loudspeaker. At the time I was too unseasoned a traveler to appreciate it, but I've since come to understand that something secret and true about a city's nature resides in its place-names, and so one's best introduction to an unfamiliar town often lies simply in *listening*. Thus did my education in the secret Philadelphia begin that day, before I'd even left the train station, gleaned in snippets of local talk and overheard conversation: mysterious words like "Passyunk" and "Neshaminy" and "Wissahickon" and "Schuylkill" (which was pronounced "Skookle" and not, as it appeared, "Skoilkill"). Of course, I was unaware it was happening—I was too busy playing the role of World-Weary Traveler, which consisted of walking briskly and glancing at my watch a lot—but these ancient Indian names, thick with sibilants, whispered at something fundamental about Philadelphia, that small town that masquerades as a city, where news travels fast and gossip faster.

All of which is my roundabout way of saying that a harried young stranger to a city was still capable of picking up a thing or two about his new surroundings, through osmosis if nothing else. Yet by the time I fought my way out of the station and into the open air of center city, I was ready to set down my suitcases and take a more active role in my acclimation.

From the vantage of Broad Street, first impressions of Philadelphia are misleading: With its massive City Hall, set down amid what seems an endless avenue, and its claustrophobic canyon of granite office buildings, it could easily be New York—say, Lexington Avenue at the mid-Thirties. But Philadelphia isn't New York, as I would learn. For one thing, Broad is its only endless avenue, and you need only travel a few blocks in any direction to escape the shadow of its few skyscrapers. A couple of blocks off Broad Street, Philadelphia becomes what it most emphatically is—a city of neighborhoods. In this, and in its omnipresent Colonial touches, the brickwork and cobblestones and trinity row homes, it reminds me most of Boston, if Boston experienced a sudden surge in heavy industry. For in addition to its neighborhoods, Philly is a city known for manufacturing things: carpets, and streetcars, and Stetson hats, and lawyers.

I would come to know all this in time. But at the moment I was too overwhelmed by the giddy disorientation of emerging in the midst of a strange city at rush hour to take in anything more subtle than the broadest brushstrokes: the gridlock of trolleys and delivery vans and motorcars; the din of wheezing auto horns and trolley gongs and horse hooves and chain-drive transmissions; the odors of exhaust, manure, cold asphalt. I'm a head taller than most people, and so I looked out on a sea of hats as pedestrians parted around me and pushed past me and generally looked annoyed at me for standing motionless on the sidewalk like a stubborn lemming. When I grew tired of being jostled, I tried hailing a taxi to the Bellevue-Stratford and was enlightened by an angry cabdriver that I was standing within sight of it.

The Bellevue-Stratford, with its gilt ceilings and acres of Italian marble, was the kind of grand hotel I imagined royalty frequenting, and opera singers tenanting, and insolvent types like myself avoiding altogether if we did not want to draw hostile stares. I hadn't learned yet that the grandest lobbies are still public places and therefore possess a high tolerance for riffraff. And compared to riffraff, I was reasonably presentable: My coat was decent and concealed the worst of my shirt's wrinkles, and I'd worn my Harvard tie on the principle that one should always dress for travel. I suppose, then, if I was noticed at all, I was taken for a cub reporter—or a junior law clerk, delivering divorce papers to some disreputable guest. At least I hoped I was taken for a professional, rather than what I actually was: a member of that "new class of American social failure" (as William James called us), the professional student. I loitered awhile by a potted fern, half expecting at any moment to be swarmed by angry bellhops—a trespassing germ beset by liveried leukocytes—and only after I was ignored by a dozen of them did I feel confident enough to approach the check-in desk. Where I learned there are subtler ways of ejecting the unwanted.

"I'm sorry, sir," the obsequious clerk told me, pursing his lips as he searched his reservation book, "but I'm afraid I don't see your name."

"Are you sure?" I repeated my name for him, tacking on my usual clause "—like the bird." He humored me by pretending to make a second search of his book, and it was while he was running his thumbnail down its list of names that I heard a voice call to me across the lobby.

"Finch!"

I looked up and saw Flynn approaching with Richardson and Fox, all three men looking well rested and dressed for a night on the town. Flynn's red hair shone with Vaseline, and he smelled as if he'd dipped himself in tonic; when I shook his hand (he was a southpaw), I noticed he no longer wore a wedding band. Fox was looking more pear shaped than when I'd seen him last, nearly five months ago; the three-course lunches were taking their toll on his waistline, as well as his nose, which was beginning to resemble a scarlet geranium. The triumvirate was completed by Richardson; aloof as ever, the mathematician hung back from the others studying the grand lobby's gilt ceiling.

"So I see you made it in one piece, hey, kid?" Richardson said, lighting a cigarette.

"I almost didn't." And I started to tell them about my travel woes.

"Save the stories for dinner, kid—we've got reservations at Bookbinder's."

"Reservations for *three*," Fox said pointedly.

"They'll squeeze in a fourth," Flynn said, then threw an arm around my shoulder. "Stash your bags and shake a leg." He gave a shrill, ear-piercing whistle and shouted across the lobby— "Richardson! Quit your daydreaming and grab us a taxi!"

"There's been some sort of mixup," I told them. "The hotel can't find my reservation."

"What's this?" Fox said, feigning surprise. He stepped to the desk to intervene on my behalf and made a great show of insisting the desk clerk have another look at his reservation book. I felt like I was watching a skit for two actors—and bad actors at that.

"His name should be there under *Scientific American*."

"I'm sorry, sir."

"There must be some mistake," Fox said. "I'm quite certain I instructed my secretary to book *four* rooms."

"The reservation says only three guests."

"Is there nothing you can do to accommodate this young man?"

"I'm afraid at present we're fully occupied, sir. We're hosting a convention of chiropodists."

"I thought the elevator smelled a little ripe," Flynn quipped.

"That explains the conversation I just overheard," said Richardson, sauntering over. "Did you know New Yorkers have the nation's smallest feet?"

"For Christ's sake," Flynn said, glancing at his watch, "our crab cakes are getting cold!"

"Go," I told them. "I'll stay here and sort this out."

"Are you sure?" Fox asked.

"I'm too tired to eat anyway."

"Attaboy, kid," Flynn said, pumping my hand exaggeratedly. "We'll bring you back a coupla dozen oysters." And with the others in tow, he hurried off toward the taxi stands.

I turned back to the desk clerk. This time I took a new tack, appealing to his emotions and our similar ages: I told him how I'd

been traveling for the better part of a day, how I hadn't eaten anything since breakfast, how desperate I was to find a bed in which
to collapse. I hinted that the *Scientific American* work that had
brought me to his city was the sort of thing that won Nobels and
let him draw his own conclusions how my lack of a good night's
sleep might negatively affect the course of medical science and
national security and the course of Human History. It was a good
speech—I don't think a Barrymore could've done any better—
and it seemed to elicit the right sort of sympathetic noises from
the desk clerk; but when it was finally over, he remained dry-eyed.

I had reached the end of my arguments, and so when the clerk
offered to phone around to other hotels in the vicinity and try to
find me a room, I let him. While he dialed, I stood there doing a
slow burn, imagining my *colleagues* cozied up in a restaurant
somewhere laughing at my predicament. I could just see Fox in
his lobster bib, his little smirk glistening with clarified butter. It
was this image finally that made me reach on impulse across the
check-in desk and disconnect the startled clerk.

"Don't bother," I said. "I've decided to stay with friends."

I wanted to add, *Dr. and Mrs. Crawley,* just to see the reaction
on his face but decided the satisfaction wasn't worth the price of
their privacy. And so I said nothing, only picked up my bags and
left the grand lobby of the Bellevue-Stratford Hotel.

· · ·

The Crawleys had offered, after all—at least that was how I justified to myself what felt like a bold decision: to show up unannounced on the couple's doorstep, suitcases in hand. It was a
difficult decision for me, as I tended to worry excessively about
"putting folks out" (my father's phrase), when in fact they weren't
inconvenienced in the least, just as I've always been uncomfortable accepting favors, or gifts, or even compliments. More of my

father's influence, I suppose. He was a man fiercely committed to paying his own way, if for no other reason than the right it afforded him to complain about those who did not, or wouldn't, or couldn't. (He was no progressive, my father.)

And so I had this excessive worry, and the excessive heat it seemed to generate, to keep me warm as I walked through the frigid night away from the Bellevue-Stratford. Whether it was due to the cold, or my exhaustion, or the exhilaration of having done something out of character, before I'd gone two blocks I had become positively giddy at my decision, which seemed to return to me in one fell swoop the advantage I'd been losing by degrees all afternoon. A block later my stride had lengthened, and I was whistling a Christmas carol and greeting Philadelphians young and old as I passed them on the sidewalk; and when a pretty young mother admiring a Christmas window beside me saw my suitcases and asked what had brought me to the city, I heard myself replying, "I'm a chiropodist."

Bidding her good night, I cut across Rittenhouse Square—a lovely little park of stone walks and dry fountains and winter-bare trees, fronted on all sides by the elegant apartment buildings of the vertical rich—and slipped down the first numbered street I could find. Within minutes I was in a neighborhood that could just as easily have been Back Bay, or Beacon Hill, or for that matter Greenwich Village, with brick sidewalks and wrought-iron fences and town homes lined up like volumes in a library. And in fact the street I'd come looking for, Spruce, must have been a respectable address for the city's wealthier physicians, since every third residence I saw bore a nameplate of polished brass. This made my search all the easier, and in no time I found the address I was looking for: Number 2013 Spruce Street, private residence and medical office of A.W. CRAWLEY, M.D.

A light was burning in the drawing-room window, and I saw a

Siamese watching me from the sill, tail twitching the chintz curtains. I rang the bell and said a silent prayer I wasn't arriving in the middle of their dinner. A few houses away, a kid of about twelve dressed like an English schoolboy in woolen stockings and cap watched me. I rang the Crawleys' bell again. Inside, a small dog began barking. I heard it scrabble across hardwood floors and sniff on the other side of the mail slot. This was followed by the sound of heavier footsteps and a voice scolding the dog softly in a foreign language, and a moment later I found myself greeted by a dour Oriental cradling a Boston bull terrier in the crook of his arm like a baby.

"*Sino po kayo?*"

"My name is Martin Finch. I'm here with the *Scientific American* investigating committee. I wonder if I might be allowed to see Dr. and Mrs. Crawley?"

"Not home!"

I thought perhaps he hadn't understood and was mistaking me for a nosy reporter. I launched into an overenunciated explanation of how I had been turned away by the Bellevue-Stratford, and, after listening for a moment, the butler cut me off with an impatient gesture.

"Yes, yes," he said, as if he'd heard this all before, and then to my surprise motioned me inside. "*Tuloy.* Come."

I gave a final look at the little English schoolboy watching me up the street, and then I stepped inside. The front hall was fragrant with the frying-oil smell of Filipino cooking, for while I hadn't interrupted his employers' dinner (the Crawleys were out for the evening attending a concert at the Academy of Music) I *had* managed to interrupt the butler's.

He closed the door and set down the Boston terrier, which commenced a close inspection of my trouser cuffs. The butler took my coat and hung it in a hall closet while I stood there feeling awkward and ill proportioned beside him. He was small, no more than five-three or -four, but powerfully built in a compact way, not unlike the terrier. I guessed him to be about fifty years old, though he had little gray in his hair; and while his Christian name was Pacifico, most people, I would learn, called him "Pike." Which struck me as ironic at first, a pike being a tall, thin medieval weapon meant for impaling, until I remembered that a pike was also a particularly toothy and aggressive breed of sport fish. Fitting, since I wouldn't have put it past this Pike to deliver a wicked bite.

I don't mean to paint him as inhospitable. Quite the contrary: Once I was inside, he warmed to me, flashing a toothy grin when I turned beet red at a taste of the fiery dish he was cooking—a highly spiced mix of shrimp and rice noodles and vegetables he called pancit luglug. He insisted I join him, and I found I was hungrier than I thought. We ate in the kitchen, a place guests rarely saw; but with the Crawleys at the symphony, and the housekeeper off for the evening, 2013 Spruce was enjoying a welcome respite from its usual formality.

And this was the most formal of households. As the butler had been leading me to the kitchen, I'd glanced into the rooms we passed and tried to glean some insight into the character of my hosts. What I had initially taken for the drawing room turned out to be Crawley's medical office: a small reception area with an uncomfortable-looking low divan where patients could wait and a connecting door leading to what I assumed must be a consultation room. A little farther along the hall I saw the parlor, furnished with several brooding pieces, a few somber oils (mostly hunting scenes, stags on the hoof, and that sort of thing), a dark hearth made of what I would learn was Egyptian marble, and a Dresden clock on the mantel ticking off the seconds to doomsday. I tried to find something to admire in the other framed oils I passed in the hallway but couldn't imagine anyone liking them, unless he was a depressive; landscapes all, they seemed to capture the rolling Pennsylvania countryside at the precise moment the sun has gone behind a cloud.

In all these furnishings I had looked for some evidence of a feminine touch, but could find none. In every way it was the home of a Victorian gentleman, suspended in time like a medical specimen, in a preservative formula equal parts moral rectitude and unsmiling tradition, and it made me a little sad to imagine a woman of thirty living here. But then I reminded myself I hadn't seen the other floors yet, the sitting rooms and sewing rooms and studies and bedrooms where people did most of their living. And it *was* encouraging to know that Mrs. Crawley kept pets—and pets of such different character as a Siamese and a terrier; it hinted at a warmth, a playfulness missing from the décor, and perhaps a philosophy as well, a yearning to reconcile the yin and yang of conflicting animal natures. You can see how my own instincts to fill in the blanks on an incomplete canvas had already begun work on Mina Crawley.

Around greasy bites of lumpiang Shanghai, a sort of fried roll filled with cabbage and shredded pork, I attempted to learn more from Pike about his enigmatic employers.

"Have you been with the Crawleys a long time?"

"Twenty-five year with Dr. Crawley."

"That long! How did you come to work for him?"

"Spanish War," he said, meaning that tropical conflict of a quarter century ago, Roosevelt's war, fought on dual fronts in Cuba and the Philippines. With some effort I managed to extract the story from Pike: his wounding in skirmish fighting with the Spanish oppressors, his cruel imprisonment for weeks without medical treatment in a prison at Cavite, his liberation after

Dewey's fleet defeated the Spanish in the Battle of Manila Bay, his second rescue—this time from gangrene and certain death—by a young American surgeon aboard the *Olympia,* who managed to save Pike's life but not his leg.

Pike lifted his trouser cuff and showed me the prosthetic, two shades lighter than his caramel skin. The surgeon had been a young Arthur Crawley.

"After war Dr. Crawley wants to stay," Pike said, "and I want a job for only one leg!" Thus was the partnership sealed. After a decade of peripatetic wandering along the length and breadth of the South Pacific, Crawley had had his fill of tropical medicine and returned home to Philadelphia. And brought Pike with him.

I was curious how the arrival of a woman in this bachelor household had affected the longtime partnership, but of course this wasn't a question I could ask. Yet I wanted to bring the conversation around to Crawley's wife, so I asked, "Do Dr. and Mrs. Crawley go abroad much?"

He shook his head. "She is afraid."

"Of foreigners?"

Pike gave an inclusive shrug to suggest that this was only one of a long list of phobias: "Of the lightning, the big dogs, espiders . . ." His eyes glittered with boyish mischief as he added, "My leg."

"Your leg?"

"Once Dr. Crawley make me stand it in the corner by the bed."

"When?"

"The honeymoon!" Pike said gleefully. "Mrs. Crawley, oh she scream!"

His shoulders shook with laughter. I couldn't help joining him, though part of me thought the practical joke a bit morbid—not to mention a strange way to embark on a marriage.

"I'm surprised Mrs. Crawley is so skittish," I said. "I would think a woman who can speak to the dead wouldn't be afraid of anything."

A shadow passed over the Filipino's expression then, and I knew I had gone too far. His face set like cooling custard: guilty for laughing at his mistress's expense, wary of me for having encouraged him.

"Mrs. Crawley is *bukal sa loob*," he said guardedly. "She is a Christian lady."

"I'm sure," I said. "I didn't mean to suggest otherwise."

The silence between us became unbearable. I glanced at my watch, stifling a yawn, and asked, "When did you say you expect them home?"

"Late."

Pike rose stiffly; I didn't expect to be offered coffee. I watched him scrape the leftover pancit into a bowl for the dog and then begin washing the dishes.

"I hope I can stay awake long enough to meet them," I said, eager now to make my exit. "Perhaps I'll read awhile."

Pike directed me to Arthur Crawley's library on the second floor and offered to take me there as soon as he had finished with the dishes. I assured him I could find it myself, then thanked him for sharing his supper and beat a hasty retreat.

Upstairs, I found the library without difficulty. It was as somberly furnished as the rest of the house, though now I found the effect reversed: Where the parlor had been uninviting, here the walnut shelves and Oriental carpets and deep shadows drew me in. I walked the room's perimeter, my head canted to read the titles stamped in gold on the handsome leather-bound books. The collection was eclectic, medicine shelved alongside metaphysics, with a few volumes of Edwardian erotica by Anonymous (*"My weapon was rubbing against the upper part of the openings of her furrow . . . the index of my right hand slowly penetrating her hot fundament."*) courtesy of the Olympia Press. Two shelves were devoted to Mrs. Crawley's interests, for the most part popular novels and nonfiction works such as Lucy Abbot Throop's *Furnishing the Home of Good Taste* and Rémy de Gourmont's *A Natural Philosophy of Love*. Doubting I would find much to entertain me among these, I pulled down one of Crawley's medical texts, enticingly titled *The Illustrated Female Anatomy*, and took a peek inside—saw that the etchings had all been made from cadavers. The smell of the binding rose up to my face, became to my confused nostrils the reek of formalin. I slammed the book shut, replaced it on its high shelf, and selected instead something less inclined to give me nightmares: a copy of that infamous blue book *Ulysses*, privately published by a Parisian bookstore the year before to circumvent French obscenity laws. I stirred the embers in the fireplace and then settled down in a leather club chair. I had read Joyce's short stories but none of his longer, more adventurous fiction. Yet like so many scandalous books, this one defied easy skimming for its racier passages, and Arthur Crawley hadn't been considerate enough to underline any. Despite my best efforts to remain awake and meet my hosts, I kept nodding off. At one point I woke and saw that the dog had joined me in front of the fire; then my eyelids grew heavy again, and finally closed.

I am usually a light sleeper, particularly in unfamiliar surroundings, so it's possible I was in some state of half sleep when the Crawleys returned later that night, and I incorporated their homecoming into my dreams. Therefore I can't claim with any certainty which of the following was real and which imagined: the voices speaking quietly below, or the sounds of soft footsteps creeping up the stairs, or the strange gray faces peeking around the library door at me like those of concerned parents. . . .

Or those other sounds I dreamed much later, in the stillness that fell over the sleeping house after the grandfather clock finished chiming an uncertain hour: a woman's soft cries—or were they a man's?—lost in the walls, small and quick and quickening, a whimper that climbed each second to a plateau of greater urgency and then surpassed it, before subsiding, at long last and what seemed hours later, into silence.

· 5 ·

In the morning I met them.

"Mr. Finch!" Mina Crawley said, rising from the breakfast table to greet me; for, despite how late they had returned from the symphony, she and her husband had risen very early and were already finished with breakfast by the time I came downstairs, sheepish and stiff from my night sleeping upright in the library.

One look at Mina Crawley made me forget my sore neck. I don't know what I had expected—a church mouse, perhaps, dowdy and plain. But Mina Crawley wasn't plain; she was one of the loveliest women I had ever seen. I don't mean the most beautiful, for judging strictly by the standards of the day—the slim hips and boyish chest of the athletically inclined girlfriend or dance-happy flapper—Mina wasn't beautiful at all and would be considered by many as merely pleasant looking, in that chastely modest way of Sunday-school teachers and maiden aunts. Yet there was something remarkable in Mina's modesty that simultaneously compelled me to look closer and glance away. She was dressed simply, in a tea dress of pale blue serge, with a lace collar and a bit of embroidery on the sleeves. She wore her chestnut hair at unfashionable length, pulled back from her face and secured with a tortoise comb. Her features were open and friendly, a pastel sketched in a sunny park by a Parisian art student who had paid special attention to her eyes: adding fine lines at their corners to accommodate their curiosity and humor, softening the irises with the tip of his little finger to suggest their kindness.

"Mr. Finch!" she said warmly, taking both my hands in her own. "Arthur and I are so pleased you have decided to be our guest."

Crawley, shaking my hand when his wife had finished with it, added, "Though tonight I hope you'll let us offer you a bed!"

If Mina Crawley was a pastel, her husband, Arthur, was a study in charcoal, all sharp angles with heavy shading. His eyes were deep smudges, and though presumably he had shaved less than an hour ago his beard was already a visible shadow along his jaw. He was handsome, in an ascetic sort of way, tall and straight as a furled umbrella. Like many very slender men, he wore a double-breasted suit to give him more substance. The years hadn't thinned his hair, which he wore close and parted on the side and which was so black as to almost look laquered. Yet despite Arthur Crawley's wealth, despite his good looks and charming wife, I found myself liking rather than resenting him—as I often resented privileged men. I suppose it was the genuine good humor with which he greeted me, a smile as welcoming as his wife's, that made me reassess my earlier impressions of the surgeon's dour household: Maybe it knew more laughter than I'd originally assumed.

"I didn't want to be rude and go straight to bed," I said, explaining why I had spent the night in their library. "I was trying to wait up for you, but I'm afraid fatigue got the better of me."

"Of course it did," Mina Crawley said, giving my arm an understanding pat. "After traveling all that way. You were sleeping so soundly in the chair we were afraid to disturb you."

"Though I did consider having Pike throw you over his shoulder in a fireman's carry," Arthur Crawley said.

"Oh, Arthur, hush—you did not," his wife scolded.

"She's right," Crawley conceded. "I know the old pack mule's capacity. He can't manage more than seven stone anymore, and you're . . . what?" He eyed me up and down, estimating my weight. "Ten, I should think, yes?"

"However many make up a hundred and fifty pounds."

"Nearly eleven," Crawley said.

"And that's too little," Mina added, leading me to the breakfast table. "Come. You must be famished. Tell Mrs. Grice what she can make you." And she gestured to a shapeless older woman in an apron and gingham dress waiting in the kitchen doorway.

"Just coffee, thank you."

"A man after my own appetite!" Crawley said, and I saw his egg sitting untouched among the breakfast dishes.

Mina frowned at her husband. "Darling, I do wish you would eat *something*. If you won't do it for me, you must try for your patients' sake. You don't want your hands to shake."

"No, we certainly wouldn't want that," Crawley said with a rakish wink in my direction. "Someone might lose an extra ovary!"

"Oh, Arthur!"

Crawley looked pleased to have gotten a rise out of his wife. He crossed behind her chair and bent to kiss her cheek. She pushed a piece of toast between his lips; he took a bite and said to her, "I'll be home early, my dear. I made certain to schedule no surgeries after four." To me Crawley added, "I hope *you* aren't prone to the shakes, Mr. Finch. Your committee is in for more than a few shivers this evening."

"Please, call me Martin," I said. "And we're very much looking forward to it."

At this Crawley nodded, wished us good day, and left. Mina Crawley smiled at me, and I felt color come to my cheeks. She seemed more present to me now that he had departed. Mrs. Grice returned from the kitchen with a fresh pot of coffee, a boiled egg, and a few fried slices of something called scrapple ("In case you change your mind, lad"). The terrier and the Siamese followed Mrs. Grice in from the kitchen.

Mina Crawley lifted the dog into her lap, fed it a crust, and told me apologetically, "Arthur says I spoil them."

"I don't know where he gets that idea," I said, surprised to hear myself teasing her. When had she become a friend?

"I know it's a cliché to call them my children," Mina said, rubbing her cheek against the dog's, "but that's exactly what they are—my children."

The Siamese was twining around my ankles, pushing itself against my shins in that frankly sexual way that has always made me uneasy around cats. "How did you manage to train them to live together without fighting?" I asked, hoping she didn't notice me shove one of her babies away with my shoe.

"Oh, it's easy," she said, "if you raise them together from infancy. They don't know they're supposed to disapprove of one another."

"When I was a child," I said, "I thought dogs were male and cats were female, and they were all married, and that's why they fought all the time." Her look of amusement encouraged me, so I added, "Which probably says more about my parents' marriage than my own limited understanding of zoology."

As soon as I said it, I worried this might be revealing too much, but Mina's smile reassured me; and anyway, she seemed more interested in an earlier part of my story. "Married!" she said, laughing at the ridiculous idea. "But what sort of offspring would they make?"

I blushed, finally admitting with some embarrassment, "Squirrels."

"Of course!" she said. "Because they climb trees . . ."

". . . and chase birds . . ."

". . . and will root through the trash if you let them!" she said, delighted. The terrier licked her, and she set it back down on the floor. The cat approached it, purring, and pushed its diamond-shaped head against the dog's moist pug nose.

"Do you think they sense them?" I said, indicating her pets. "The spirits?"

Mina Crawley looked at me. "What a funny question."

"I only ask because of my father. He thinks his spaniel can see my mother's ghost—since it whines every night at the closet where her wedding dress is kept."

Mina reached out reflexively to cover my hand with her own. "I'm so sorry to hear your mother is no longer with you."

"Thank you," I said, then offered my standard disclaimer: "It was a long time ago. I'm ashamed to admit sometimes it's hard to even remember what she looked like."

"It must be a great comfort to your father to think of her nearby."

"I would think he'd find it more comforting," I argued, "to believe she's in a better place than our old cedar closet." Though that was probably better than the reality: a rotting pine box.

"And why do *you* think your father's spaniel whines?"

"Squirrels in the eaves."

She gave me a look of teasing disapproval.

"I'm beginning to think squirrels are your explanation for everything, Mr. Finch."

"Martin."

She showed me a smile. "If you would like, I can ask Pike to show you our attic before this evening's sitting."

"Actually," I said, relieved she had broached the subject without my asking, "if you don't mind, I *would* like to inspect the premises at some point this afternoon. Only because we've never conducted a psychic investigation outside of a controlled environment. And our readers expect us to be thorough."

"Of course, Martin," she said, and for no good reason I felt curiously pleased to hear her call me by my first name.

. . .

Mrs. Crawley made good on her offer, leaving the butler with instructions to show me any room in the house I might wish to inspect. Then she left in a taxicab for the day's errands, which included taking a box of old clothes to a relief mission and visiting St. Patrick's Catholic Church, just off the square, to light a penny candle—a ritual she performed every afternoon before a séance.

Pike was sullen and suspicious as he accompanied me throughout the house, limping along on his prosthetic leg, and I did my best to ignore him and focus on my task. Which was all the more difficult because I didn't know what I was looking for: evidence of trickery, of course—the trappings of theatrical illusion, false walls and secret panels, that sort of thing. But how do you catch a magician without seeing his (her) act first? Still, I needed to be thorough, so at the very least I could report back to McLaughlin I had accomplished more during my stay than enjoying the Crawleys' hospitality.

So Pike and I started in the attic and worked our way down to the basement, a painstaking journey that ate up the better part of the morning and left me with cobwebs in my hair but no more idea of what I was looking for than when I started. The attic had been crammed with souvenirs of Arthur Crawley's decade-long sojourn throughout the South Pacific and Orient: ornamental screens, rich carpets, teak furniture, along with a great deal of native art, stoneware and batik and baskets and weavings of every stripe. I wondered why more of these hadn't made it down to the lower floors, incorporated into the home's décor. The town house could certainly have used a fresh breath of island paganism to blow away all this stuffy Anglican civility.

After the attic Pike and I descended to the apartment below, an odd assortment of rooms he shared with the widowed Mrs. Grice: bath, bedrooms, kitchenette, sitting room—all neat as a pin, not a dust mote stirring in the strong sunlight. (And, as was so often the case in old houses, these rooms seemed the sunniest of all; not to mention those offering the most interesting views of the city—an endlessly fascinating tableau vivant of rooftops and chimneys and pigeons and blue skies.) But with Pike lurking, I felt uncomfortable giving his private quarters any more than a cursory looking over, and so after only a few moments, I indicated I was ready to move on.

The third and second floors were the Crawleys' main living quarters. I spent a good quarter hour inspecting the locked room at the back of the third floor where Mina Crawley held her séances. Except for a table and chairs, it was unfurnished, with bare wood floors and curtainless windows overlooking an alley and the brick wall of the neighboring house. If the light weren't so poor, it would be exactly the sort of cozy space new parents might choose for a nursery—which led me to wonder why the Crawleys were childless. I could see how Crawley might consider himself too old for fatherhood, but was that reason enough to deny his wife? Perhaps there was some medical condition to blame; they wouldn't be the first of fate's ironic pairings, this gynecologist and his barren wife.

The second floor suggested a third possibility, as it seemed the Crawleys slept in separate bedrooms. Of the explanations for the couple's childlessness, this seemed the least likely, and I didn't give it serious consideration. I wasn't so stupid as to think a short hallway was enough of an obstacle to discourage a man from visiting his wife. God knows if it had been I who was married to Mina Crawley, it would have taken a small continent. Maybe I would catch them at it, since the guest bedroom where I would be staying shared the same hall. Then I remembered the strange sounds I had dreamed the night before—and wondered if maybe I already had. My tour of the second floor concluded with Mina's powder room, an inner sanctum of Italian tile filled with two of every species of night cream, face powder, eyebrow brush, tweezer, lip salve, and mascara. There was a container of Persian Muscle Oil, and beside it something called Golden Peacock Bleach Creme, which promised to make skin four shades lighter in three days. More than anywhere else in the house, I felt here as if I were trespassing, and so I set the jar of bleach creme down where I had found it and quietly backed out of the powder room.

Downstairs, I had Pike show me the only place I hadn't yet explored on the first floor, Crawley's medical office. Beyond the small waiting area was an unremarkable treatment room: an adjustable table for pelvic examinations and simple office procedures; a glass cabinet containing various unpleasant-looking instruments, specula and such; and a great expanse of walnut desk, the altar from which Crawley, as high priest, might reveal what he'd divined from his patients' entrails. Except for a few nods to aseptic technique—a washstand and bottle of biniodide of mercury, a tray of used instruments waiting for pickup by a local steam-sterilization service—it could have been a medical office from the 1850s, and I wouldn't have been surprised to learn that Crawley still kept an electric vibrator in a locked cabinet somewhere for the therapeutic manual relief of his more "hysterical" patients.

I concluded my inspection tour in the cellar. There, among the coal bins and boilers and gardening tools and his-and-hers bicycles, I discovered . . . nothing. Not so much as a stash of bootleg gin. And so I returned upstairs, satisfied that as far as I could see, the house had nothing to hide in the way of trapdoors or secret passages, and that any skeletons Arthur and Mina Crawley might have had in their closets prior to my arrival had been carefully disinterred and taken elsewhere.

· · ·

I reported as much to McLaughlin after lunch, telephoning him from a corner "apothecary" (the genteel old neighborhood didn't have any chemists) so our conversation wouldn't be overheard. McLaughlin was on his way to another specialist and could spare only a few minutes to discuss the upcoming séance. He concurred that it was impossible to design controls for tonight without a clear idea of what Mina Crawley had in store for us. But he made two recommendations to hedge against accomplices: that I should request that the staff be given the night off and that I should seal all the doors into the town house with wax impressed with my thumbprint. I agreed to both of these prophylactic measures and promised to call again first thing in the morning.

Immediately after hanging up with McLaughlin I felt a tightness in my chest. The chemist, noticing my look of discomfort and assuming it was indigestion, offered soda water with cream and shaved ice. I asked for a Bromo-Seltzer instead. The old-timer looked disappointed but found some under his zinc counter for me anyway. I paid him for the phone call and the Bromo and then hurried back outside to the twentieth century.

Despite the Bromo, my indigestion lingered throughout the day, to the point where I declined Mrs. Grice's offer of afternoon tea and began worrying I would have no appetite for the elaborate dinner she was preparing to welcome the *Scientific American* committee. Or worse—that I might even be too indisposed to participate in the séance. In hindsight I see I was only suffering from a nervous stomach, compounded by a healthy dose of guilt. Guilt because, without intending to, I found I had grown to *like* Arthur and Mina Crawley, these kind people who had opened their home to me and granted me their trust, these kind people I must do everything in my power now to unmask as frauds. But as I lay on my bed that afternoon, fully clothed and groaning, I didn't understand that my suffering was entirely psychosomatic. To the contrary—I was convinced I had ptomaine.

Finally, around four o'clock, I decided a walk might clear my head and settle my stomach. I fetched my gloves and coat and went downstairs in search of Pike, who I thought might like an afternoon off from dog walking. The butler received my offer with great suspicion, but in the end he relented and handed over the leash.

For the next hour the terrier led me on a brisk tour of every tree, garbage can, bird dropping, and fire hydrant in a ten-block area, and if there was no stationary object to mark, he would simply squat like a female and squeeze a few drops in the middle of the brick sidewalk. By the time we made our way back to Spruce Street my own bladder was full to bursting, though my head was no clearer than when we'd departed, and my stomach felt even worse.

As we rounded the corner onto Spruce, I caught sight of someone in the alley beside 2013: a hobo, I thought at first, come to beg at the kitchen door. He was a thin and haggard fellow in the filthy clothes of a chimney sweep, with sallow features and eyes like smudges.

"Hello?"

The leash went taut in my hand: The Boston had spotted him, too. Hearing me, the man withdrew into the shadows, which was when the dog began barking and straining at his lead in earnest. The little brute was surprisingly strong, and I let him pull me along in pursuit of the man we'd both seen.

The sun was going down, so that the alley was plunged in deep shadow. Though the man had looked too sick to be dangerous, I wasn't in any hurry to encounter him in the dark, and so I resisted the terrier's pulling and called hello again into the gloom— the way you are supposed to make noise when entering bear country. At the opposite end of the alley, a trash can suddenly overturned, and moments later the terrier stopped barking. Whoever the man had been—whatever business he'd had in the alley— he was gone now.

While the terrier urinated a final time against the side of the house, I looked up and saw a window three stories above, and I realized it belonged to the séance room where we'd all soon be convening. Beneath the window was a small ledge I hadn't noticed earlier in the day, when I'd made my inspection tour of the house. I couldn't tell from the ground if the ledge was wide enough to stand on and made a mental note to open the window later and check. Not that I intended to climb out on it; that would require someone less paralyzed by heights. Nor did it especially matter, since I saw no conceivable way anyone other than a human fly might make it up to the ledge from below.

The terrier lowered his leg and scratched the ground a few times like a chicken. Before it could get any bright ideas about prolonging our walk, I gave its leash a tug, and together we went inside.

. . .

"My goodness, Finch," Richardson said immediately after arriving that night, "you look like a boiled owl. What have you been drinking?"

We were in the parlor, awaiting the arrival downstairs of our hosts, and I had just refused Pike's offer of sherry.

"I think Finch flew into a vat of the local panther sweat and got his wings wet!" Flynn said with a leer. "Fess up, kid—where'd you find the scatter? Was there a pretty girl there?"

"I haven't been drinking."

"I should hope not," Fox said, playing the disapproving headmaster. "I don't think I need to remind you that you are representing Professor McLaughlin and Harvard University at these proceedings."

"No, you don't need to remind me," I shot back irritably, and found myself in the uncomfortable position of putting down a rumor by admitting to an unflattering truth, in this case that I had the constitution of a Camp Fire girl. "I'm just a bit anxious about tonight," I said. Then, lowering my voice to a whisper, "And I may have eaten some bad scrapple at breakfast."

"Hell, I could have warned you about that stuff!" Flynn said, laughing. "You do know what parts of the pig the Pennsylvania Dutch use to make that stuff?"

"What?"

"Everything but the squeak!"

At that moment Pike happened to be serving canapés and, overhearing this, shot me a hostile look. Wonderful, I thought, now it would get back to Mrs. Grice I had been complaining about her cooking. I was well on my way toward offending the entire household.

"Good evening, gentlemen," a voice said, and all eyes turned in unison as Arthur and Mina Crawley made their grand entrance. Mina wore a chemise gown of embroidered silk decorated all over in complicated beadwork; the whole thing was the color of champagne, as were the combs securing her hair in a complicated chignon. Her husband was turned out in the full soup-and-fish of an Edwardian diplomat, complete with white gloves and tails and silver-topped cane. As introductions were made and we eventually moved into the dining room, I was pleased to see Mina having the same effect on the others as she had had on me that morning. Fox became courtly and bashful, Richardson tripped over himself in his rush to agree with her every comment, while Flynn stared at her with a look of such animal wantonness that I nearly kicked him under the table.

Arthur Crawley seemed accustomed to having his wife admired by other men, and even to enjoy it. And so, as Pike served the first courses—croutards of sweetbreads followed by a chilled soup called vichyssoise, which the menu informed us had been created by the chef of the Ritz-Carlton in New York—Crawley encouraged his wife to tell the story of how she had first discovered her psychic gifts, while we hung on her every word.

"It started as a lark," she said, "as so many serious things do."

"Indeed," Richardson agreed; Fox said, "So true."

Mina continued, "My husband was always the one with an interest in spiritism—"

"Much to the chagrin of some of my medical colleagues," Crawley interjected.

Mina looked at her husband with sympathy. "Poor Arthur, he has had to endure such ridicule."

"Most of it good-natured," Crawley said with a dismissive wave of the hand. "I mention it only to make a point about the limited imaginations of so-called learned men. But please—continue with your story, my dear."

"Anyway, my cousin and her husband were visiting for the Christmas holidays, and we thought it might be amusing to try a séance. So Arthur had Pike build a Crawford table—"

"A table specially made without screws or nails," Crawley explained.

"—And we held our first sitting upstairs, on the third floor. Where we'll be tonight," Mina said. "I don't think any of us really expected anything more than a few shivers, perhaps a mysterious noise or two. But once the lights were out and we joined hands in the circle, we experienced significantly more than just a few shivers. . . ."

The room had fallen silent, and I noticed that I wasn't the only one who had lost interest in his vichyssoise.

"Immediately the table started trembling, as if a train were passing close by, until this tremor became so violent that it began banging against our knees. I was frightened and insisted Arthur turn on the lights. But the table would not be pacified, and when my cousin's husband tried to escape, it followed after him like an angry dog—"

"Chased him out of the room," Crawley said, "and all the way down the hall. Poor bugger had to climb up on a bed in the guest room to escape it!" Crawley and his wife exchanged a smile at some private joke, which she explained for our benefit.

"Forgive us, but we don't much like my cousin's husband."

Pike cleared away our soup bowls and began serving the fish course, which the handwritten menu informed me was sole meunière with pommes Parisiennes. To distract myself from the fact that there were three more courses to get past my nervous stomach, I asked, "Was that the end of it?"

"That evening, yes," Mina said. "But of course it was only the beginning in a larger sense. Of something wonderful, that has blessed our marriage . . . and brought us so many new friends." And as her eyes filled with emotion, she raised her wineglass to toast us.

After we'd finished the toast and the fish and had our wine-glasses replenished and our empty plates replaced with ris de veau and vegetable marrow farcie, Crawley described the experiments he and Mina and the second couple had conducted over the week between Christmas and New Year's a different person sitting out of the circle each night, until via this process of elimination, they had identified Mina as the locus of the paranormal activity.

"Arthur calls me his little psychic lighthouse," Mina said, like a child trying to recall a verse she had been asked to perform for guests. "Shining into the next world like a, like a . . ."

She looked to her husband for assistance, and Crawley took up the description: "Like a beacon, shining into the great lightless ocean that is awaiting us all on the other side of this life."

It was a convincing performance, and I felt gooseflesh along my arms. Crawley's image of the dead adrift on a black sea haunted me through the remainder of the meal, and, judging by the silence of my colleagues, I wasn't the only one.

After lady cake and peaches in Chartreube jelly, the meal finally concluded, and we rose from the table and retired to the parlor for coffee and brandy. Mina excused herself quietly and disappeared upstairs to change into more comfortable clothes for the séance. I took Crawley aside and requested that Pike and Mrs. Grice be sent to the moving pictures after they'd finished clearing the table; he raised an eyebrow but consented without argument and went into the kitchen to tell them. A few minutes later they left in their hats and overcoats, and I locked the door behind them.

"Can someone lend me a hand?" I asked.

Flynn volunteered, and the other men gathered around to watch what I was up to. I gave Flynn the stub of candle I'd purchased earlier that afternoon on McLaughlin's instructions. We lit it and collected the drips of molten wax in my handkerchief. While the wax was still soft, I flattened it out to the size of a half-dollar, then pressed this across the crack between the edge of the front door and its jamb. I worked quickly so the wax seal was still soft enough to take an impression from my thumb.

"That's one down," I said, then gestured for Flynn to follow me so we could repeat this process on the kitchen and cellar doors, as well as the more accessible windows. In all it took thirty minutes to seal all the entrances to the house, and when we finally returned from the cellar, we heard Mina calling down that she was ready for us to join her upstairs.

"Shall we, gentlemen?" Crawley said, returning from his medical office with his black doctor's bag. He gestured for us to follow, and we fell into line behind him. We made an odd procession, five strangers marching in solemn single file. I brought up the rear, my heart sinking with each step on the creaking stairs.

A moment later we arrived on the third floor and crowded into the small room I'd come to think of as the nursery. Mina was waiting. She had changed for the occasion into a loose tunic of many layers, the outer ones diaphanous, and a pair of satin house slippers. It was the sort of getup you see in modern-dance recitals, and it added an unfortunate note of bohemianism to what were already questionable proceedings.

A kerosene lamp rested at the center of the Crawford table, throwing flickering light that made the cramped little room feel even smaller. The windows had been blacked out with heavy muslin, a precaution to prevent any ambient light from leaking in and startling the spooks away. Overkill, in my opinion, given that the alley screened out the streetlight and the winter overcast had taken care of the moon. Besides the kerosene lamp, there was a hatbox on the Crawford table filled with an assortment of trinkets: a ring of hard rubber, a ukulele, a short baton, a doll's head—each decorated with luminous paint so it would be visible in the dark. Mina invited us to inspect these trinkets, and while we did, Crawley went to the gramophone in the corner and began opening its cabinet doors. It was an expensive model of polished cherry, equipped with an electric repeater. With one eye I watched Crawley replace the old steel needle with a new one, then remove a phonograph record from its sleeve and, holding it by its edges, carefully inspect its grooves for dust. His movements were fastidious to the point of being fussy, and I had the sense I was watching a performance as ritualized as a Japanese tea ceremony.

At last Crawley turned and asked his wife, "Are you ready, my dear?"

"I am," Mina said dreamily, and welcomed us to take our places around the table. I was pleased (and secretly flattered) to learn that the Crawleys meant me to occupy the seat between them. As we all took our seats, Crawley opened his black bag and prepared an injection for his wife.

"What is that you're giving her?" I asked.

"It's called 'Twilight Sleep,'" Crawley said as he immobilized Mina's arm with one hand and with the other found her vein. Her eyes fluttered as she felt the needle's sting, though I couldn't tell if her expression was one of pain or relief. "It's a mixture of a henbane derivative called scopolamine along with—"

"Morphine!" Fox said in surprise, and when we all turned to him, he explained, "My wife received it at the birth of our youngest daughter. To this day she claims she doesn't remember a thing about the delivery."

"Precisely," Crawley said, sliding the needle out and putting it away in his bag. He massaged his wife's arm to speed the drug on its way through her bloodstream, a gesture at the same time both tender and clinical. "I'm sorry to say it's fallen out of fashion as a drug for painless childbirth. I give it to Mina before her séances to minimize her suffering."

"Does she often suffer?" I asked.

"Only sometimes," he said, but did not elaborate.

Satisfied that the drug was taking effect, Crawley rose to wind the gramophone, then hurried back to the circle in the few crackling seconds before the needle found the song.

We heard the opening measures of "Yes! We Have No Bananas," a rather silly tune, then popular in dance halls, that seemed to have been written especially to annoy me. My bemusement must have shown, because Crawley leaned over and whispered in my ear, "We've experimented with more sentimental songs, but Mina's spirit control seems to prefer this—"

"Shhhh." The sound issued from his wife's lips without her being aware of it, for her eyes were closed now, and she seemed to be entering a light trance.

All of a sudden, I experienced one of those moments when you step outside yourself and look back on the scene as clearly as a diorama in a natural-history museum—Mina swaying in her chair, five grown men holding hands, that insipid song playing on the gramophone—and I thought we could not have looked more absurd. I felt my face flush with embarrassment for myself, for my hosts, for the blindly yearning human race.

But when I looked around the table, it seemed I was the only one who felt foolish. The others were all watching Mina Crawley with the grave faces of men in a medical amphitheater, and when the song ended, the silence in the room was so absolute I could hear Mina breathing. She had stopped swaying, and appeared to have reached whatever place within herself she'd been seeking.

Crawley let go of my hand and reached across the table to extinguish the oil lamp. The room went black. I experienced a wave of vertigo, until those organs of proprioception in brain and inner ear reoriented me in the dark. I experimented with eyes open and shut to see if I could distinguish the subtleties between the two darknesses. It was interesting to note how the acuity of my other senses increased in the absence of sight. I heard the gurgle of someone's digestion, smelled the brilliantine in Crawley's hair, felt the air growing stale in the nursery.

And then—a gust of unexpected chill. To my left I heard Mina give a low groan, the sound of a sleeping woman having a nightmare. From downstairs we heard the musical crash of a cat landing on piano keys, until this cacophony was followed by an expert glissando. Then, from the middle distance of the stair landing, the old grandfather clock chiming an impossible hour: thirteen. The hour in between. The hairs stood up along my arms, and my mouth went dry as we heard heavy footsteps approaching the locked room. Whatever was approaching now stood just outside the door. My nervous system had become so sensitive that when Mina shuddered a moment later, I felt a valve in my heart register her tremor like a seismograph. Her hand tightened on mine to stop herself from pitching forward, and she convulsed, and for the first time I became frightened—

From somewhere inside the room with us we heard a man's deep guttural laugh and understood that our six had been joined by a seventh.

. . .

"Will she be all right?" a shaken Fox inquired a few minutes later as we helped Crawley carry Mina to a fainting couch in the downstairs parlor. Soon after the eerie laughter in the dark, the phenomenon had abruptly stopped and Mina started to awaken. But though the visitation had been brief—the luminous trinkets remaining motionless on the Crawford table before us—the séance had taken a great toll on Mina.

Now she could barely stand. Her hair had fallen from its

chignon, and somewhere on the trip from the third floor, she had lost one of her satin slippers. She was limp as a survivor of the *Lusitania,* fished from icy waters and as yet unaware of her surroundings.

"She'll be fine," Crawley answered as he prepared an injection. He beckoned Flynn over. "Squeeze her hand; it helps to raise the vein." Flynn didn't need to be asked twice. He knelt beside Mina and took her hand in his own.

"What are you giving her?" Flynn asked as Crawley lightly tapped the crook of his wife's arm to bring the cephalic vein to the surface.

"Five grains of caffeine with phenaecetin." He pushed the hypodermic in.

"To prevent migraine?" I asked.

Crawley shot me a surprised look. "That's right."

Richardson asked in a voice hushed with concern, "Does she suffer migraines after every séance?"

"Depends how near she is to her menses," Crawley said with a clinician's casual disregard for modesty.

While Crawley ministered to Mina, I examined the piano we had heard playing earlier: an old upright, one of those staples of the Sunday sing-along, the ivories beginning to yellow like the smile of a dowager who'd drunk too much tea. Drawing as little attention to myself as possible, I lifted the hinged top and had a peek inside. I smelled tung oil and old felt, saw dust on the harp's strings. I sneezed, and the lid slipped from my fingers, slamming shut with a loud bang. So much for drawing as little attention as possible.

"He likes to doodle," Crawley said, "but he can't play."

"Who?"

"Mina's spirit control," Crawley said. "Oh, from time to time, he will bang out 'Chopsticks' or the first few measures of 'God Rest Ye Merry, Gentlemen'—I suspect that's his idea of a little joke—but beyond these his repertoire is quite limited."

"Do you have any idea who it might be?" I asked, curious about the presence we had all felt—or perhaps only imagined—upstairs in the séance room. But before Crawley had a chance to either answer or evade my question, his wife let out a groan.

"She's coming 'round!" Flynn called.

Mina's eyes fluttered open and saw Flynn keeping vigil at her side. She gave him a smile of such drowsy intimacy that I wondered if she mistook Flynn for her husband, and I confess I found myself wishing it were I on the receiving end of her confusion.

"Darling . . . ," she whispered.

For all his reputation as a lothario, Flynn reddened.

"We should let her rest," Fox said, speaking for the group. "It's late, and I'm sure there's a great deal we need to discuss among ourselves before bed."

"As if I'm going to get any sleep tonight," Richardson said under his breath.

"To hell with sleep," Flynn said, "I need to get to a telephone, see if I can still make the early edition."

"Wait," I said. "What are you going to report?"

Flynn heard the caution in my voice and frowned. "You were there, kid. You trying to tell me you didn't hear what I did?"

"I'm not yet sure what I heard." Which wasn't true, since I could still recall very clearly the sound of the parlor piano, the clang of the grandfather clock . . . and of course that sinister laughter. But in an effort to remain open-minded, I said, "I propose we sleep on it, take a fresh look at things in the morning."

"Sweet dreams, son," Flynn said. "You can read my column over breakfast. Maybe that'll help you make up your mind."

"No, Finch is right," Richardson said, proving himself an unexpected ally. "This was only the first sitting. We mustn't rush to any judgment. Don't you agree, Malcolm?"

But Fox was with Flynn. "I'm satisfied by what I've seen and heard this evening."

"You may be," I said, resigning myself to the fact that I was about to make an enemy, "but as long as a majority vote is needed to declare a winner, you'll just have to wait until the rest of us are satisfied as well."

Fox darkened at this challenge to his authority. But there was little he could do about it, and so when Crawley returned with the coats, Fox snatched his and stormed off into the night with the others in tow.

"Oh, my," Crawley said, looking down at his sleeping wife, then up at the Dresden clock on the mantel. "I had hoped Pike would be home by now to help me get her to bed. I don't suppose you'd mind helping me carry her upstairs, would you, old sport?"

"Not at all," I said. "She can't weigh much."

"Ah," Crawley said, groaning under her dead weight, "pity she isn't awake to hear you say so!" Together we managed to get Mina to her feet and, each supporting one side, up the stairs. We poured her into the four-poster bed as gracefully as we could, which was about as gracefully as unloading a sandbag or a sweetly snoring sack of coffee.

"Let me just fetch her a nightgown," Crawley said, and he disappeared down the hall, leaving me wondering if he might actually ask me to assist in undressing her. Mina stirred and stretched on the cool sheets like a satisfied cat, and when I looked up, I found her smiling dreamily.

"Kiss me . . . ," she whispered, her eyes still closed.

Of course I didn't. She was only talking in her sleep. But she repeated her request, this time with greater insistence.

"Kiss me, darling. . . ."

She said it with such sweet innocence, like a child asking for a bedtime kiss, that it seemed unkind to refuse her. Or so I justified it to myself. I leaned across and touched my lips briefly to her own, and when I pulled away, I saw that she was smiling.

"That was a pretty kiss. . . ." She seemed to drift off again.

"Talking in her sleep?"

I turned sharply and saw Crawley standing in the bedroom doorway with a flannel nightgown and a second blanket for the bed. I had no idea how long he had been standing there or how much he'd seen.

I cast about for the most convenient lie. "She was saying something about being cold."

If Crawley knew I was lying, he betrayed no sign of it. He showed me the comforter, his eyes still on my face.

"I brought this to cover her," he said, then seemed to watch me for a reaction as he added, "after she's undressed."

I had no idea how to read his expression. The light was too poor, and I had too little experience with jealous husbands to know if that was who was standing before me now. And so I faked a yawn, stammered something about the lateness of the hour and my great exhaustion, and hurried from the bedroom.

· 6 ·

The next morning at breakfast, neither Crawley nor his wife treated me any differently, nor any less graciously, than the day before.

Mina was ravenous, as she always was after a séance. Her eyes lit up as Mrs. Grice set before her a breakfast fit for an Amish farmer: eggs and potatoes and ham and scrapple and rye toast with apple butter. Mina frowned when she saw my plate, a mirror of hers—with one glaring omission.

"One moment, Mrs. Grice," she said. "You seem to have forgotten to serve our guest any scrapple."

"I'm told it don't agree with him," Mrs. Grice said with a pointed look in my direction, then marched off haughtily to her kitchen.

"Now, whatever was that all about?" Mina said. "Arthur, I wish you would talk to her. She's been so temperamental lately."

"What's that?" Crawley asked, lowering his newspaper.

"Mrs. Grice—"

"I'm fine, really," I said, eager to let the matter lie. "I have more here than I can possibly eat."

After breakfast Crawley left strict instructions with his wife to spend the day resting. We departed the house together soon after.

Crawley offered me a lift to the Bellevue on his way to Jefferson Hospital, and though it was only a short walk to the hotel, it was such a cold morning—Crawley's driver, dressed in storm coat and cap, was busy vigorously scraping frost off the windshield while the idling car filled the street with clouds of pearly exhaust—that I accepted and climbed into the Peerless's backseat. A moment later Freddy, the driver, a Cockney import who resembled one of the Tower of London's more jovial executioners, took his place behind the wheel and said, "Morning, guvs."

We set off on the short trip. I regretted that it wasn't longer, so I could've had more time to enjoy the sedan's plush interior: its mahogany trim, the thick-pile English carpet, the silk taffeta window shades. The Peerless felt more like a yacht than an automobile and, under Freddy's confident command, rode like one as well—high in the water and with a regal purr.

As we motored through the tree-lined (and tree-named) streets around Rittenhouse Square, Crawley suddenly turned to me and asked with utmost casualness, "Did my wife happen to ask you to kiss her last night?"

I tensed. Freddy's eyes met mine in the rearview mirror.

"She was half asleep," I said. "I'm sure it was innocent."

A smile quirked Crawley's lips. "Well, there's no question about its being innocent!" he said—louder now, for Freddy's benefit. I heard the driver chuckle.

Crawley looked out the window as we overtook a delivery cart and dray horse, then said meditatively, "She's often very affectionate, my wife . . . afterward." He turned from the window to smile in my direction, and despite my difficulty reading him in the past, now his insinuation seemed clear. What remained unclear were his motives for this rather unappetizing bit of sexual boasting. Did he need the world to know that his wife still found him attractive, despite the difference in their ages? Or was this something more specific to me—a warning from an old bull moose to a young interloper?

Either way, I knew I should send him a clear signal I meant him no threat, so I responded as diplomatically as I could, "You're a very lucky man."

"Yes, I truly am."

Any trace of boasting or warning or whatever it had been vanished from his face and was replaced by tenderness.

"She is my treasure, Finch. I confess sometimes I am torn between hoarding her for myself and sharing her with the world."

"You mean her psychic gifts?"

But Crawley hadn't heard me, as he was too busy reminding Freddy to drop me at the Bellevue-Stratford. I tried to suss the subtext of this conversation and what Crawley meant me to understand. It didn't occur to me that I might simply be an excuse for an older man to have a conversation with himself.

And so I climbed out of the Peerless outside the hotel's Locust Street entrance understanding less about the Crawleys' marriage than I had when I entered the car only a short while earlier. Arthur Crawley rolled down his window with one of the car's silver-plated handles and made a request that only deepened my confusion.

"I say, Finch, would you mind doing me a great favor?"

"Not at all."

"If it's not too much trouble, would you pop in on Mina this afternoon and keep her company? Make sure she doesn't overtax herself?"

I agreed, and Crawley smiled in gratitude and told Freddy to drive on.

I stood there on the sidewalk and raised my hand in farewell as the car pulled away from the curb and disappeared into the morning traffic.

I was a half hour early for my meeting with Fox and Flynn and

Richardson, so I took the opportunity to duck into a phone booth in the Bellevue lobby and call McLaughlin.

"What number, please?" the switchboard operator asked.

"Klondike 5-6565."

While I waited for her to connect the line, I watched a delegation of well-dressed chiropodists pad by in their stockinged feet on their way to the reflexology seminar then assembling in the main ballroom. McLaughlin answered a moment later and told me he had already received a histrionic call from Fox at an ungodly early hour.

"I'm sure he had kind things to say about me," I said.

"I took it as proof you are doing a good job," McLaughlin said, and despite the three hundred miles separating us, I could sense his wry smile. "Now I would very much like to hear *your* impressions of last night."

I recounted the events as dispassionately as I could, with a minimum of editorializing: the piano, the grandfather clock, the approaching footsteps, the unsettling laughter—most of all the powerful sense that we had been joined by an intelligent *presence*. I told him about Mina's convulsion and the great toll the séance seemed to take on her. I *did* omit, however, any mention of the good-night kiss that had caused me such confused feelings.

"And your wax seals?" McLaughlin asked when I'd finished.

"All intact."

"Interesting." he said. "Though that does not rule out the possibility she employs an accomplice—someone already hidden in the house, for instance."

"I suppose."

"Or someone of diminutive stature, who might easily slip through a window you overlooked. A female accomplice, perhaps. Or, for that matter, a child."

I thought of the little boy who had watched me with such

suspicion when I first arrived on the Crawleys' doorstep. Had he been up to something more than playing?

"It's possible," I admitted.

Might the boy have been hired for a few pennies to size up the *Scientific American* investigators? Was a child even capable of faking the eerie phenomena we had experienced last night?

"Finch."

"Sir?"

"I had been hoping for a bit more of a dialogue."

"I'm sorry, Professor, I was just thinking."

"About?"

"Accomplices," I said. "To tell you the truth, I find the whole idea a little far-fetched."

"I am open to alternative explanations."

"I wish I had some."

A pause, in which I could almost hear McLaughlin's scowl.

"This isn't like you, Finch."

"This isn't like anything I've encountered before," I said as I worked a splinter loose from the phone booth's grain with my thumbnail.

"What bothers you about it?"

That she seems genuine, I wanted to blurt out, but I bit my tongue. It was an admission I wasn't capable of making yet to myself, let alone McLaughlin. At that moment the heavy silence inside the phone booth reminded me of the confessionals of my youth, though I had never before felt such fierce confusion or shame. McLaughlin waited, composed as any parish priest, and, like the reluctant penitent I had been at twelve, I conscripted a half-truth to stand in for my more egregious sins.

"It bothers me I can't figure out their motives," I began. "The Crawleys don't seem overly religious. They don't want any publicity. And they certainly don't need the five thousand dollars."

"Ah, I see," McLaughlin said. "So you have decided it isn't enough to be an investigator. Now you want to be a prosecuting attorney as well?"

"I only mean it might help me understand what happened last night."

"Quite the opposite!" he said, and launched into a lecture similar to the one I'd heard him give Fox months earlier, before the Valentine séance: "You are investigating phenomena, Finch—not Mina Crawley. Her motives are entirely irrelevant and can only confuse the issue. Does a chemist need to know nature's motives for making an atom in order to measure its valence? Does an oncologist need to understand a patient's politics in order to make his diagnosis? Of course not, or else we would call them alchemists and faith healers. That is why the behaviorists, for all their faults, have been such a good influence on our field—by stripping away all the sentimental variables like emotion from our research, by forcing us to adopt the discipline of the natural sciences, by shaming us into removing our philosophers' robes once and for all and donning lab coats."

And regarding human beings as little more than trained pigeons, I thought. (Or, as a behaviorist might say, "muttered silently to myself," since they also didn't put much stock in such unquantifiable nonsense as *thinking.*)

"Do you understand what I'm trying to tell you, Finch?"

"I believe so," I said, then paraphrased him: "Don't think too much."

"Nor too little," he corrected. "That's what Fox is for."

He meant this as an olive branch, and I gave a halfhearted laugh to show him I had accepted it. But I didn't feel any less conflicted.

"It still isn't going to be easy, Professor."

"Last night was that convincing?" McLaughlin asked, and I told him yes. He chewed on this a moment, before offering his counsel. "Forget for a moment my disparaging remarks about the philosophers. They do have a tool that may be of use in the present situation, something called 'Ockham's razor.' Are you familiar with the term?"

"It rings a bell. Remind me."

"With Ockham's razor," McLaughlin explained, "we cut away all explanations except for the simplest, on the principle that the simplest are often the most likely."

"I'm not sure I follow."

"Apply Ockham's razor to the phenomena you witness in Mina Crawley's company," McLaughlin said, "and ask yourself how you might reproduce them. If you can reproduce them with the simple tools of a magician's stagecraft, then you must assume this is how the medium and her confederates are producing them."

I frowned. I didn't like thinking of Mina in these terms. But I didn't comment, only checked my watch and told McLaughlin the others were expecting me upstairs. We agreed to speak again tomorrow, and I was about to hang up the line when he offered this Oriental proverb as his parting advice.

"Remember, Finch—you are there investigating the arrow, not the archer."

. . .

Upstairs, I did what I could to check my personal feelings for Mina Crawley at the door of Fox's hotel room. And thus did I find myself in no time at all playing devil's advocate, arguing a position I hadn't yet accepted myself: that what we had seen and heard last night in the Crawleys' home was bogus.

"Enough!" Fox said, "I'm not going to stand here and allow you to slander people of such culture and . . . and *refinement!*"

"I'm not slandering anyone," I said. "I'm asking us to look at the arrow and leave the archer out of it."

"Arrow?" Fox said. *"Archer?"* He turned to Richardson and Flynn, who, like any self-respecting jury, were feigning interest in the opposing arguments while they waited for their next meal. "Do either of you know what the deuce he is talking about?"

"He is removing our hostess from the equation," Richardson said without looking up from the morning paper, "so her charms cannot cloud his judgment. As opposed to you, Malcolm, who seem convinced solely on the evidence of a few spooky noises that she's the next Oracle of Delphi."

"He's just being McLaughlin's mouthpiece," Flynn countered, shaking out a cigarette from a crumpled pack of Ramses. "Pretty good impression, too. Sounds nearly as constipated as the old man."

I felt my blood rise. "You wouldn't say that if he were here."

"Probably not," Flynn said, striking a match. "The prof usually doesn't let any of us get a word in edgewise."

I narrowed my eyes at him. "Oh, I don't know—you seem to have a pretty slim vocabulary. I'm sure you could manage to slip one in."

I had meant to draw blood, but Flynn only laughed.

"Ha! Score one for Joe College!"

I might have leaped across the bed at him then and probably gotten myself a good beating, if at that moment there hadn't been a knock at the door. Fox answered. A bellhop wheeled in a breakfast cart, and for the next ten minutes they forgot about me altogether. I stood there fuming, imagining broken glass in their scrambled eggs.

After a moment Flynn remembered me standing there and said around a mouthful of kippers and eggs, "All right, Counselor.

For the sake of argument, let's say Mrs. Crawley *did* have an accomplice downstairs making all those noises. A neighborhood kid, the Tooth Fairy—whoever." Flynn pushed away his breakfast and reclined on the bed, crossing his stockinged feet at the ankles. He stuck a cigarette into the corner of his mouth and gestured at me with the unlit match as he continued, "But that doesn't explain what went on inside that room—a *locked* room, I might add."

I opened my mouth to reply, then shut it again. I looked to Richardson for help, but he gave a shrug that said I was on my own. Out of the corner of my eye, I could see Fox looking smug.

"I'm waiting," Flynn said, striking his match on the bedside table. Jittery from the black coffee, he jiggled one of his feet, clad in an old black sock that desperately needed darning. I found myself staring at a hole in the toe—and was struck by a sudden idea.

"I'll be right back."

"Finch, where the hell are you going?"

But I didn't linger to explain. I dashed out of the room and caught the first express elevator downstairs to the Bellevue's main ballroom—where I hoped that I might recruit an expert witness capable of making my case with greater dexterity than I.

When I returned fifteen minutes later, it was in the company of a fastidious little man in a brown tweed suit, with what impressed me on the elevator ride up as a matching brown tweed personality.

I ushered him into Fox's room, said to my colleagues, "Allow me to introduce Dr. Delmar Munson of Cincinnati, Ohio."

"Good morning, gentlemen," Dr. Munson said with a courteous nod. Then, without further ado, he proceeded to the nearest unoccupied chair, had a seat, and began unlacing his Oxfords.

"What's this about, Finch?" Fox asked.

"Dr. Munson is a chiropodist," I said, and beckoned Fox and Flynn and Richardson to join Munson and myself at the breakfast table. I made them join hands in a circle, as we had the night before, and then indicated to our guest that the floor was his.

"Whenever you are ready, Dr. Munson."

With a single deft move, Munson brought his bare feet up from under the table. Before the astonished eyes of Fox and Flynn and Richardson, he seized an uneaten piece of toast with the toes of his left foot while rooting among the breakfast utensils with his right. And though his hands were immobilized, he demonstrated that this did not hinder him in the least from buttering his toast, pouring cream in his coffee, or turning the pages of that morning's *Inquirer*.

"As you can see," Munson explained, "with a bit of practice, the pedal extremities are every bit as agile as the hands."

I thought I detected a hint of long-held grudge in this observation. Munson offered Fox the buttered toast with such nimble insistence of his left foot that Fox had no choice but to take a bite. Flynn shook his head in amazement and said, "I'll be damned," while Richardson nodded in my direction and conceded with a wry smile, "*Quod erat demonstrandum,* Finch."

Dr. Munson put his shoes back on, shook hands all around, and bade us good day. I closed the hotel door behind him and turned to face my colleagues.

"Now, gentlemen," I began, "shall we discuss how we're going to control tonight's séance?"

· · ·

As I walked home from the Bellevue later that morning I was surprised to look up and see the little English schoolboy playing in the street a few doors down from 2013 Spruce, dressed in white gaiters and a knit cap with earflaps. He was busy trying to remove a pane of ice off a puddle intact, and so he didn't notice me watching. On an impulse I called to him.

"Hey, kid."

He looked up and froze.

"Hey, kid, come here."

This time he shook his head vigorously. I didn't want to shout again, so I walked over to him. As I got closer, I saw his worried expression, though it was impossible to tell if this was guilt or just a little kid's general wariness around adults. Up close I saw he had pale freckles and rather girlish features, and I guessed he was the lonely sort of kid who had a great deal of experience playing by himself.

"What's your name?"

"Edwin."

"Do people call you Eddie or Ed?"

"People call me Edwin."

I rooted around in my pockets until I found a nickel, then factored in the quality of the kid's clothes and his expensive address and dug up two bits instead—enough for an entire Saturday at the moving pictures or sufficient candy to trigger diabetic shock.

I held out the quarter but demanded information before giving it to him.

"You ever been inside that house on the corner over there, 2013?"

Little Edwin looked past me and turned two shades lighter when he saw which place I meant.

"Creepy *Crawleys'*?" He shook his head even more violently.

"You sure? Mrs. Crawley never hired you to do any special 'chores' for her?"

He seemed so genuinely appalled at the notion of working for the neighborhood ghouls that I decided he must be telling the truth. So I dropped the quarter into his mitten and left him to return to his solitary play, then walked back to 2013 and climbed the front steps to the lair of the Creepy Crawleys.

"Martin!" Mina had on her Jaeckel mink and was in the process of selecting a cloche to match when I walked through the door. Now she clapped her hands like a little girl on Christmas morning. "I was so hoping you would return in time for lunch! No, no, don't take your coat off!"

"We're going out?"

"I want to take you to an adorable little table d'hôte I know around the corner."

"I don't know if we should. We'll get in hot water with Dr. Crawley."

She looked up at me. "How?"

"I'm supposed to keep you from overtaxing yourself."

"It's settled, then," Mina said, pulling a knit cloche down over her ears. "You just *have* to come with me to Madame B's and make sure I don't strain myself speaking French."

As we left the house, I was surprised to discover that it had begun snowing. Mina gave a small cry of delight, as if she'd never been outside before, her face upturned to the white sky. Snowflakes settled on her long eyelashes and stayed there until she blinked them away. She took my arm, and together we descended the front steps, setting off through the magical squall—the kind that comes early in the season and almost immediately vanishes, as if the season couldn't make up its mind. We hurried along the brick sidewalks, Mina holding my arm, I acutely aware of my arm being held. The pressure of her hand seemed to awake in me an entire second set of senses, so that I noticed for the first time how winter light transforms a cityscape from a watercolor into a daguerreotype, could appreciate how much more interesting trees were without their leaves and how much farther sound travels in December. I noticed also small details of the neighborhood that had escaped me until now: the narrow side street with its row of old stables, the wrought-iron boot scraper outside a corner mansion, the funny little meetinghouse welcoming guests to learn about the "Religion of Business." I noticed also the dark looks Mina drew from the governesses and neighbors we encountered along the way and how chilly were their replies to Mina's greetings. When I saw a woman up ahead deliberately cross to the opposite side of the street to avoid us, I drew Mina close and pointed out an interesting cat in a parlor window just to distract her.

Ten minutes later, with stinging cheeks and ringing ears, we at last arrived at Madame B.'s, a cozy little café two blocks off Rittenhouse Square, wedged between a cigar store and an electric shoe-repair shop. A nice enough place, in a shabby Left Bank sort of way, with blackboard menus and dull silverware and cats given free rein of the kitchen, as well as a great collapsing soufflé of a proprietress—the eponymous Madame B. Mina and I lucked into the last of the café's tables, and though it was a rickety affair covered with a stained linen cloth and decorated with a bud vase of roses going brown around the edges, it offered the best seats in the house, by the front windows, away from the other tables and clear of the floor traffic of harried garçons. Madame B greeted Mina with a theatrical kiss on each cheek and, after exchanging a few further pleasantries in French (accompanied by much fluttering of false eyelashes and suggestive glances my way), hurried off to dry our hats and gloves on the radiators.

When Madame B had gone, Mina leaned across the table to whisper, "She thinks you're my lover!" Her eyes shone with the wicked light of a naughty little girl, and she covered her smile with her hand to stifle a giggle.

"And she approves?"

"Of course—she's French! She said you are a very handsome *jeune homme.*"

I looked around at the other couples, noticing for the first time that the businessmen all seemed much older than their lunch companions. "Is that the sort of place this is?"

"I like to think so. Of course, I usually dine here alone, so I need something to entertain myself."

"Dr. Crawley never meets you for lunch?"

"Oh, on occasion. But never here. Arthur doesn't like the French." She leaned close again to confide, "He says they're immoral. That's why he won't take me to Paris—I think he's afraid I might fall in love with a handsome art student and contract tuberculosis!"

"That's funny," I said, recalling Pike's contradictory claim that it was her skittishness that prevented them from going abroad.

"What is?"

"Your husband doesn't strike me as the jealous type."

"He has no reason to be," Mina said, "but I'm afraid he can be frightfully jealous. Of younger men, younger couples—anything, really, that reminds him of the difference in our ages." A cloud seemed to pass across her sunny mood, and we both fell silent.

Fortunately, Madame B's daughter arrived then to take our order, and I was rescued from having to make some insincere comment about what nonsense it was for her husband to be jealous. Maybe Crawley had every reason to worry. After all, here was his wife with a younger man at a favorite assignation for afternoon lovers, and, however innocent it might have seemed at the time, last night Mina *had* asked me to kiss her. But if this were the case, why had Crawley asked me just this morning to keep his wife company? Was I such a palace eunuch that I fell outside the range of the man's jealousy?

"*Et deux cafés au lait, s'il vous plaît,*" Mina told Madame B's daughter.

"*Merci,*" she muttered grudgingly, and left us. I followed her with my eyes to the kitchen and, when I turned back, found Mina watching me with a sly smile.

"She's very pretty, isn't she?"

"It's the accent."

"Oh?"

"There have been studies done at Harvard. It's a scientific fact: A French accent makes a woman eleven percent prettier."

"As much as that!" Mina said, laughing. "Well then, I'll just have to work on my French."

"You don't need an accent," I heard myself blurt out. Mina's own cheeks colored at the compliment, coaxed so effortlessly from me. I had the distinct impression I was being tutored in this game of flirtation, like a novice on the tennis court playing against a more experienced partner. And like a novice, I was all knees and elbows, nearly knocking over the bud vase at one point with my nervous fidgeting and constantly bumping my long legs against Mina's beneath our table.

"Why are your ears so red, Martin?"

"Someone must be talking about me."

"Perhaps it's Madame B's daughter—"

"Or my colleagues. In which case I'm happy I can't hear them." Though I knew it was highly unprofessional, I found myself confiding, "I'm afraid they don't think very highly of me."

"Oh?" she said. "Well, if it's any consolation, Arthur doesn't think very highly of *them.*"

"Really?"

"Yes," she said, and then our *deux cafés* arrived in their mismatched saucers, and I was left in suspense while she fussed over hers: sipping, wrinkling her nose, adding sugar. "Mr. Fox is a buffoon, bless his heart," she said, stirring and sipping, "Mr. Flynn stared at my chest the entire evening"—adding more sugar— "and Mr. Richardson has the personality of a praying mantis." Finally satisfied with her coffee, she laid aside her spoon and raised the cup to her lips, peering at me over the rim. "Arthur says you are the only one on the investigating committee he respects."

I should have been immediately suspicious of this secondhand flattery, should have at the very least pressed Mina to elaborate on what precisely I had done to earn her husband's high regard. But this would have required a presence of mind, an emotional distance from the moment, I did not possess. Guilt weighed heavily on me, pulling my gaze again and again to the table.

When she covered my hand with her own, I flinched.

"And I hope you know I share my husband's opinion of you."

"Oh?"

"I'm very fond of you."

I forced myself to look up at her, saw her regarding me with such openhearted affection you would have thought I was her oldest friend in the world, and it was this that finally proved too much for my conscience to bear.

I retrieved my hand from under Mina's and, fixing my eyes on a small hole in the tablecloth, told her, "You shouldn't be."

"Your friend?"

"So trusting."

She smiled, thinking we were playing a game. "And why not?"

"Because," I said, steeling myself, "I spent this morning planning ways to better secure your hands and feet tonight."

I don't know what sort of reaction I was watching for: feigned surprise, perhaps, or a casually dismissive laugh. Or no reaction at all, which would have been nearly as revealing—and even more damning—than these others. But I never expected the look of hurt I saw now on Mina's face, I suppose because it would have been too terrible to consider.

"You . . . you don't believe me?" The color had drained from her face.

"It's not whether I believe you or not. It's just that—I don't have any *choice*—I have to consider every real-world explanation for what we witnessed last night before I can begin considering otherworldly ones."

"You don't believe me . . . ," she repeated, and this time it wasn't a question.

Madame B appeared then with our salade aux lardons and croque monsieur and immediately sensed the pall that had befallen the table.

"No, no!" she scolded us. "No quarreling!"

Mina looked up, running a knuckle beneath one eye in that careful way women have to keep from ruining their mascara. "We aren't quarreling," she said, composing herself. "Martin just asked me this very moment to run away with him!"

"Oh!"

"Unfortunately," Mina said, trapping my hand on the table and giving it a squeeze, "I had to break it to him that, no matter how adorable he may be, my heart will always belong to my husband."

The proprietress clucked sympathetically and, turning to me, said, "If you are too heartbroken, *mon petit chou,* let an old lady console you." She ran her fingernails across the scruff of my neck, wished us both *bon appétit,* and breezed off.

Mina took out a compact and began powdering her face to hide that she'd been crying. I watched, fighting a powerful urge to lean across the wobbly table and surprise her with a kiss.

But instead I asked, both as a distraction for my baser self and by way of a peace offering, "Did she just call me a little cabbage?"

Mina nodded, touching up her makeup. "It's a term of endearment." She snapped shut the compact and looked at me, and I felt my heart thump twice in my chest, like someone knocking on a door. Two knocks and no more—that was all and everything. I had hurt Mina, and she had forgiven me, and according to some ancient calculus neither of us had invented, we were wed. Or at least I was wedded to her. Whether the incident that afternoon in the little French café had worked a similar alchemy on her emotions, I do not know. She remained as always, inscrutable, beautiful.

After our lunch we strolled home through the snowy streets, Mina holding my arm tighter now to keep from falling—for the snow had surprised us both and begun to lay on the sidewalks, making the bricks slippery. I found myself fantasizing about what might happen if she were to lose her footing and fall, and I was debating whether I would rather catch her in my arms or be pulled down on top of her in a laughing heap when Mina suddenly asked, "So what did you decide?"

Was mind reading part of her repertoire, too?

"Decide?"

"About securing my hands and feet," she prompted. "You said you spent the morning planning better ways to do it. What did you decide?"

"Oh. Well, after some discussion we settled on luminous ropes around your wrists and ankles. Not too tight, of course."

She listened, nodding, as if I'd asked her opinion on the subject. "So you can see what my hands and feet are doing at all times, yes?"

I nodded. "Then you don't mind?"

"It's not whether *I* mind," Mina said as we arrived on her street, "it's whether *he* does. He can be terribly stubborn some nights."

"Dr. Crawley?"

"My spirit control."

We had arrived at the front steps of her house. As Mina began to climb them, I caught her sleeve. She turned to look at me, two stairs below her.

"Are you telling me if we bind your hands, we could experience a blank séance?"

Mina laughed, then pulled one of her hands free of its calfskin glove and laid it on my cheek.

"Poor dear Martin," she said with a tender expression. "Of course you don't believe me. You haven't any reason to! You haven't even met him yet." She bent forward to give me peck on the forehead, then, with a click of heels on salted stone, hurried up the stairs to her front door.

"Wait!" I called. "*Whom* haven't I met?"

Mina paused at the open door and looked back at me with a playful smile, as if I had just asked what she'd bought me for Christmas. She waggled a finger at me to show she wasn't about to spoil the surprise. Though she'd give me a clue:

"Walter."

. . .

Supper that evening was a less elaborate affair than the previous night. Before leaving with Pike, Mrs. Grice had left us several covered dishes: snapper soup (a local specialty whose star ingredient was an aggressive breed of tortoise) followed by watercress salad and roast squab a colleague of Crawley's had shot in Bucks County. The squab were small and stringy and a chore to eat, and conversation at the table was minimal as we all concentrated on digging out the birdshot and piling it in little cairns on the edges of our plates. I looked up in frustration at one point and caught Mina smiling at me across the candle centerpiece. She was radiant in her evening dress, a black crepe frock with a leaf pattern of tiny crystals and seed pearls.

Afterward, while Mina retired upstairs to change, we showed Crawley the bracelets and anklets I had made that morning from lengths of heavy butcher's twine coated with luminous paint.

While Crawley examined these, I studied his reaction closely but saw no indication that he was concerned by our request that his wife consent to wear them.

"Whose idea were these?" Crawley asked, holding up one of the luminous restraints.

"His!" Fox and Flynn all but tripped over each other in their eagerness to blame me.

"I suspected as much," Crawley said, caressing one of the ropes between his fingers as if it were a swatch of fine cloth. His eyes grew distant, and I thought I saw his nostrils flare ever so slightly. Then he seemed to snap out of his trance and turned an admiring smile in my direction.

"Very clever, Finch."

Mina called down that she was ready, and once more we all filed upstairs. I caught Crawley's arm and drew him aside on the landing.

"Excuse me, Doctor," I asked quietly, "but who is Walter?"

Crawley smiled. "Why don't you ask him yourself?" Then he gave my arm a companionable squeeze and continued upstairs.

The nursery looked smaller than I remembered, in that opposite-end-of-the-telescope way of childhood places: as if it were reality that was constantly receding from memory and not the other way around. Black muslin had once more been pinned over the windows to thoroughly screen out any stray light from the moon that might have leaked in. Mina was waiting at her place at the Crawford table, wearing a light summer dress that offered little more covering than a camisole. As we entered, she greeted us with a distant smile—as if she were watching us from the deck of a departing ship already some distance from shore.

Crawley administered her usual injection of Twilight Sleep and afterward bent stiffly at the waist and pressed his lips to her brow with tender formality, as one might kiss a child who had been brave at the doctor's office. Then he straightened and, turning to address the rest of us, asked, "Now, gentlemen, who will do the honors of tying up my wife?"

There was an embarrassed silence, until finally I could stand it no longer.

"I will."

I glared at the others and began securing Mina's slender wrists, careful not to knot the bindings so tightly that they would endanger her circulation. With her wrists immobilized, I knelt to repreat the process with her ankles. As I did, I found myself at eye level with her knees and glimpsed several dark bruises on the fleshy inside of her thighs. I glanced away, reddening. Mina wasn't wearing her slippers tonight, and as I looped one length of luminous rope around her ankle and the chair leg behind it, I felt her bare toes brush the inside of my wrist. Whether this was reflex or deliberate—a private sign that she forgave me for what I was doing, perhaps?—I couldn't say. To all outward appearances, Mina seemed to be in a deep trance now and completely unaware of the room around her.

Without being told to, we all took the same positions around the table we had occupied the night before. Crawley selected a different phonograph record as the score for this evening's séance, Drdla's mawkish "Souvenir." We joined hands, and Crawley extinguished the oil lamp, and once again the nursery plunged into a darkness that was absolute except for Mina's luminous cuffs and the few glowing trinkets in their hatbox.

As was the case the night before, I felt in those first lightless seconds a flurry of panic, as if the membrane of consciousness had just become porous and was no longer able to contain me. But a few seconds later, this passed, and I began to relax and even enjoy the sensation. This was how I thought death would be: an effortless dissolution of the chemical self into the alkaline black.

A fragment of Emily Dickinson floated up from the past and an undergraduate literature course: *"We grow accustomed to the Dark / When Light is put away—"*

The gramophone finished playing, and we were each left to our private silence for several moments, with the only sound Mina's deep and regular breathing. This went on for quite some time, until Fox's own quiet snores began to accompany Mina and I began wondering if the evening would be a blank.

But then, from two floors below, we heard the shudder of heavy furniture being moved across the hardwood.

"What in the name of God was *that?*" asked Fox, startled awake by the crash of china.

"Should we go see?" This from Richardson.

"Shhhh!" Crawley hissed at them. "He's coming. . . ."

We listened but heard only the usual sounds of an old house settling, like an octogenarian made to sit too long in an uncomfortable chair: the sigh of water pipes, the grumble of a constipated coal furnace. We heard no approaching footsteps, no confused chimes from the grandfather clock on the stair landing. I was listening so intently, antennae extended into the gloom, that I could hear my wristwatch, as well as Richardson's and Flynn's, and to my ears each had a distinct and separate tick. Crawley's pocketwatch was silent, but I could hear his quick, shallow breathing providing a counterpoint to his rapid pulse, which was so strong I felt it fluttering against my own palm. *He's afraid,* I thought, and it struck me that fear wasn't something a man could easily fake. Whatever Mina was doing, Crawley genuinely believed it.

Crawley's hand tightened on mine, and he uttered a choked whisper. "He's here."

From somewhere inside the locked room, we heard the familiar masculine chuckle. But this time it was followed by a silken voice speaking from the darkness.

"I see you've brought me company, Crawley."

A thrill ran through the circle of hands. The voice was that of an educated man in his late twenties or early thirties; and at the risk of sounding like one of those pretentious types who claim they can detect a dozen traits in a wine's "nose," I believed I could hear in that voice a hint of second-generation wealth and the boredom it breeds—as well as a fashionable cynicism of more recent vintage. It was the voice of the young men who frequented Harvard's snootier dining clubs and wrecked their roadsters on Massachusetts Avenue without suffering a scratch, and loitered around the outskirts of society weddings looking for cousins to seduce.

It was the voice of the mysterious "Walter," and the instant I heard it, he seemed to step fully formed out of a rotogravure photo and onto the proscenium of my imagination, wearing a bemused expression and a rumpled tuxedo.

Now Crawley called out to our spectral guest. "These are friends, Walter."

"Mina's—or yours?"

"Both."

Walter gave a skeptical harrumph. I tried to pinpoint where the sound came from in the nursery but couldn't get a fix on it. The owner of that disembodied voice seemed to be on the move, and when he spoke again, it was from over near the muslin-covered windows.

"I can believe they're your friends, Crawley, the way they dress."

Crawley cleared his throat, embarrassed. "Yes, well . . . in any event, these four gentlemen have traveled all the way from New York City just to meet you, Walter. You should feel honored."

"I'd feel more honored if they'd brought something to drink."

Flynn was the first of our group to find his voice. "Would you be able to drink it even if we had?"

"I believe I'd manage."

Crawley explained delicately, "Walter no longer possesses what we think of as a mouth—"

"What I have is more interesting," the voice interrupted, "and better suited for some things."

"Ouch!" Flynn let out a cry of pain. His chair overturned as he leaped to his feet.

"Don't break the circle!" Crawley shouted.

"But the son of a bitch just bit me!"

"For heaven's sake, sit *down*. You're hurting her!"

Beside me I could feel Mina convulsing. Hearing her moan, Flynn grudgingly returned to his place in the circle between Fox and Crawley. As Mina's convulsions subsided, we could hear Walter laughing from the corner of the nursery like a naughty schoolboy.

"I think my neck is bleeding," Flynn complained.

Now Fox cleared his throat, putting on his elder-statesman voice. "Walter, we represent an investigating committee formed by *Scientific American*—I assume you are familiar with the magazine?"

"I haven't been receiving my subscription."

"Ha, yes, that's very funny," Fox said stiffly, then attempted to return Walter's backhand serve. "And I imagine where you are the newsstands are a bit out of date, eh?"

"Where I am it's too dark to read," he growled.

"That's interesting," I called out, deciding it was time I joined the conversation. "Why don't you describe where you are so we can picture it?"

Silence. And then Walter spoke from a new location.

"At the moment I'm standing right behind you, old man."

I stiffened instinctively, straining my head as far as it would go to peer into the darkness behind me. My mouth had gone dry, and it took a moment to wet my lips sufficiently to speak. "Prove it."

"How?"

I took a breath. "Slap Fox."

At this, Walter began laughing, loudly enough to drown out Fox's indignant protests. But I hadn't meant it as a joke. I wanted to find out how this so-called spirit would respond to any deviations from the script.

"I like you, sport," Walter said. "But I'm afraid I'm not in the mood to jump through your hoops this evening."

"Oh? Then, what *are* you in the mood for?"

Walter purred in my ear, "Maybe I'll pay you a visit later tonight and show you. . . ."

Something cold and coarse like elephant hide brushed across my cheek. I bit down on my lip to keep from crying out and was grateful a heartbeat later when Walter turned his attention from me to the group.

"Frankly, gentlemen, I feel like redecorating . . ."

There was a loud crash of something heavy coming down on the Crawford table and smashing it to splinters (". . . fucking eyesore . . ." Walter growled). I winced as the broken tabletop barked against my shins. With the table gone, I could see Mina's two anklets glowing faintly, their luminescence growing faint; something seemed wrong, though I couldn't have said at the time exactly what it was about them that bothered me.

"Oh, and I hope you don't mind, Crawley," Walter continued, "but I took the liberty of moving the china cabinet downstairs—though I'm afraid a few pieces were destroyed in the process."

"That was my mother's good china!"

"Your mother was a silly bitch with atrocious taste."

There was a silence as Crawley struggled to control his temper. "I'm sure it was an accident, Walter," he said finally, swallowing his pride. "You know that Mina and I want you to think of our home as your home as well."

"My, my. Aren't we magnanimous when we have an audience," Walter said with contempt. "You do like an audience, don't you, Crawley? Gives you squirrel fever. It must drive you mad in the operating theater, one woman in stirrups and three others watching. Tell me, old boy, is it difficult to conceal an erection beneath your gown—"

"Enough!" Crawley bellowed.

"Watch you don't break the circle," Walter chided. "You don't want to hurt your precious Mina, now, do you? Or do you?"

Beside me, Mina let out a low moan, and it was clear she was rousing from her trance, like one of Crawley's patients waking from the ether.

"I believe I hear Mother calling," Walter said and then, to the rest of us, in the receding voice of a man walking down a long tunnel, "Gentlemen, much as I'd love to stay and chat, I have to go see a man about a dog. So I will bid you all adieu." And with these parting words the nursery fell silent, as Walter took his leave of this world and returned to whatever spectral plane in which he existed.

The oil lamp had been smashed when Walter destroyed the Crawford table, and so we had to fumble for a few minutes in darkness until Flynn finally struck a match. By its flickering light, we saw Mina slumped in her chair. I untied the luminous ropes that bound her ankles to the chair legs while Crawley chafed her wrists briskly to get the blood flowing again. A moment later she was fully conscious, though significantly drained by the experience. She looked up at me with the weak smile of a Vermeer.

"Did he come?" she asked.

"Yes, my love," Crawley said, pressing his lips to her knuckles, "Walter came."

"And how did he seem?" Mina asked. "Did he seem at peace?"

"He was in one of his moods," Crawley said. "But he made me promise to send you his love."

I listened to this exchange between husband and wife until my curiosity couldn't take it any longer.

"I'm sorry to interrupt—but just who is this Walter fellow?"

A smile played across Mina's wan face, and she exchanged a look with her husband.

"Why, I thought you knew! Walter is my brother."

PART TWO

WALTER AND MINA

· 7 ·

He was handsome, with deep, expressive eyes that looked as if they had been rimmed in kohl, and the sensuous mouth of a matinee idol. He wore an expression of amused nonchalance, and as I studied the face in the photograph, I thought he must have been quite a cake eater in his day. Something off to the right had caught the attention of those bedroom eyes, and though I knew this was only a staged pose in some portrait studio, I couldn't help reading into his look an eerie prescience, as if he had just caught sight of a stage door left open in the wings of this world. The doorway through which he would soon make his exit.

"You can see the family resemblance," Crawley said as I scrutinized the hand-tinted photograph of his brother-in-law, the only extant image of Walter Emerson Stenson. Mina's brother.

We were in Crawley's first-floor medical office, where the five of us had adjourned so the doctor could treat the "bite" Walter had inflicted on Flynn's neck: a nasty-looking welt with three shallow punctures, like the bite of a lamprey or an oversize leech.

"The resemblance *is* striking," I said. "He and Mina could almost pass for twins."

"They nearly were," Crawley said. "Their mother had them just thirteen months apart."

"Irish twins," Richardson muttered into his brandy. His face had gone as colorless as wet linen, and he wore the same shell-shocked look I saw echoed in all our expressions.

Flynn sucked in his breath as Crawley disinfected his wound with hydrogen peroxide.

"Will I need a tetanus shot, Doc?"

"I'm not sure," Crawley said. "This has never happened before. I'm afraid I don't know the protocol for treating the bite of a ghost."

Tetanus. An image flashed to mind from a medical text, a photo plate of a man with risus sardonicus, the "sardonic smile" of lockjaw.

Crawley must have been recalling something similar, because he told Flynn, "I believe I *will* give you five hundred units of anti-toxin after all—just to err on the side of the angels."

As Crawley turned to retrieve a hypodermic from the medical cabinet, I passed the photo of Walter on to Fox and saw that my hand was shaking. Fox saw it, too, and though he made no comment, I caught a glimpse of smug satisfaction on his face. It was clear he considered the night an unqualified victory—and me among the vanquished. And maybe he was right. I certainly felt defeated, my ears ringing as if something had exploded nearby and an unpleasant rumble low in my guts warning me to locate a bathroom in the near future. Even worse was the sensation that overcame me whenever I closed my eyes, akin to the "spins" that often follow a night of heavy drinking: the sensation of standing up to your ankles in an outrushing tide, as the sand streams away underfoot.

To distract himself from the impending tetanus shot, Flynn asked Crawley if the Red Cross had informed them of the circumstances in which Walter had been killed during the war.

"Drove his ambulance over a Boche land mine," Crawley said,

swabbing Flynn's shoulder and then stabbing the spot with the needle. "Blew the poor bugger to Kingdom Come."

"Is he buried overseas," Fox asked, "or in a family plot?"

"Wasn't anything to bury," Crawley said. "Mina was devastated, of course. She and her brother were very close."

"Then, you knew him well?" I said.

Crawley tugged the needle free. "As well as I cared to."

I watched him putting away the hypodermic and the bottle of peroxide, a question slowly forming in my mind. "Would you say the man we heard this evening was the same Walter you knew before the war?"

"I don't think I follow you."

"I suppose I'm asking if anything strikes you as different about Walter's personality. Do you sense that the experiences of the last five years have changed him in any significant way—I mean, besides the obvious?"

Crawley pondered this a moment. "I would like to say that he has matured, but I'm afraid I cannot." He looked at me, his face growing pinched with old resentments. "The Walter you heard is the same arrogant . . . selfish . . . *unprincipled* young man I knew before the war."

"Aren't you being a little unfair?" Fox said, rising to Walter's defense. "He was a Red Cross volunteer, after all."

"The only reason my wife's brother joined the ambulance corps," Crawley said, "was because he was a coward and because he enjoyed keeping company with incapacitated young soldiers."

Crawley's words had the desired effect. Fox's expression curdled, and he took an urgent sip of his brandy as if to rinse an unpleasant taste from his mouth. It would be the last we'd hear from him that night and seemed as good a note as any on which to end this unsettling evening. As Crawley fetched the other men's overcoats, I caught him in the hallway.

"Do you mind if I have another look around upstairs?" I asked. "You have my word I won't disturb anything."

Crawley showed a wry smile. "I should be very surprised if you found anything left in this house to disturb."

I thanked him and returned upstairs to the third-story nursery. To my surprise I found Pike gathering up the pieces of broken Crawford table like kindling.

"Oh, I'm sorry," I said. "I didn't hear you come home."

The Filipino butler looked at me, his expression stony.

"Dr. Crawley said I might have another look around up here."

Pike had a butler's keen sense of when he was being dismissed. He added a few last big splinters to his armful of scrap wood and exited, giving me a wide berth as he went.

He had lit a second kerosene lamp to replace the one that had been broken during the séance, and I turned up its wick now to chase the shadows back into their corners. Even with the flame turned high, the nursery felt cramped and low-ceilinged, with a queer sweet smell like the inside of a cigar box. The room was just as we had left it, our chairs still arranged in a circle, the gramophone in its corner like some night-blooming trumpet vine, four scraps of luminous rope still resting on the seat of Mina's chair where I had laid them after untying her. I picked up one of these scraps and carried it with me like a talisman as I made a slow circuit of the room. I looked for some change in the nursery, the way you do when you first enter a place after someone has died and the body has been removed and the bed neatly remade again. And just as I had felt years before, when I'd entered the bedroom where my mother had died, I was struck by the nursery's utter indifference to what had happened here.

I took a seat in Mina's chair and listened to the silence, a seething rush like the ocean inside a shell, or the hiss of the empty airwaves received on a crystal radio. I imagined Walter crouching behind that hiss, a Cheshire cat grinning at me while his tail twitched the chintz curtains. Though if Mina's brother *was* watching, it was with the patience of a bigger cat.

I looked down at my lap and saw that in my nervousness I had tied the short length of luminous rope into a circle. Now I leaned over and slipped my foot out of my shoe, rolling the rope anklet up over my stockinged foot and then—with a bit of force—past my heel and up to my ankle. On an impulse I dimmed the kerosene lamp. In the dark the anklet glowed dimly, just as I'd seen it glowing on Mina's ankle after Walter had smashed the Crawford table—

No. Not quite the same.

All of a sudden I understood what had bothered me about the luminous anklets during the séance: Both had been unbroken circles, not the half crescent that appeared before me now like a backward letter C. Which could mean only one thing. . . .

There hadn't been any ankles in them at the time. Mina's feet had been free.

I put on the second anklet and, through a bit of trial and error, discovered how it might be done. Tipping the chair back a few degrees lifted the front two legs off the floor; the bottom of these could then be used to "scrape" the rope anklets down over their biggest obstacle, the heels. It took some practice, but before long I was able to slip even my oversize feet in and out of their rope bounds with relative ease. Of course the rope anklets would have posed less of a challenge for Mina's feet.

But then what? Were those dainty white heels capable of smashing a sturdy wooden table in a single blow? Or of somehow "biting" a man sitting two yards away from her? Supposing for a moment that they were? That still left unexplained the more baffling question of Walter's identity.

I took this question with me as I retired to my room for the night. I stripped to my underclothes and crawled beneath the goosedown comforter that had once comforted Sir Arthur and Lady Doyle. I had exhausted myself beyond the point where sleep came easily, and so I tried the next-best thing to warm milk: a recent issue of *Zeitschrift für Psychologie*, my trusted German-English dictionary propped open against a pillow before me. But my insomnia proved resistant to even this usually surefire soporific. And so it was that I came to be still awake in the small hours of the morning, when through the wall behind me I heard the low sound of Mina and Arthur Crawley making love.

God only knows how long I had been listening without recognizing what it was I heard. They must have been going at it for a while, because by the time the noises rose to a volume and urgency sufficient to register in my awareness, Mina sounded close to her crisis. Immediately I forgot my reading, as well as any remnants of propriety, and knelt among the bedclothes in order to press my ear to the wall. My heartbeat threatened to drown out Mina's moans, until I plugged my other ear with a finger. But instead of bringing them into better relief, this only produced greater confusion, for now I could no longer tell with any certainty if what I was hearing was ecstasy or anguish. Surely the former: Hadn't Crawley mentioned just that morning how affectionate Mina became after a séance? Why, then, did she seem now to be sobbing? And soon I was beginning to wonder if it was Mina at all I was hearing. Could that be Crawley? Was it "oh!" I heard him groaning again and again, or a more protesting syllable that had lost its *n* somewhere in its trip through the walls? Didn't it concern them that I might hear their most intimate moments? Even if Mina assumed I was sleeping, Crawley must have noticed the light beneath my door as he'd crept down the hall to their rendezvous. Wouldn't this be enough to give most men pause, for their wife's sake if not for their own? Or at the very least to cover her mouth with his to prevent her from crying out? Perhaps he thought I'd fallen asleep with the light still burning, the way they'd found me my first night under their roof.

The protests—Crawley's, I decided—quickened, approaching some climax. I shut my eyes, tried to flatten my head further against the wall. And in doing so accidentally knocked a small framed oil painting off its hook. The painting slid down the wall with a scraping sound and crashed behind the headboard. I froze, afraid I might make some additional incriminating sound to tip them off to my shameless eavesdropping. From Mina's bedroom the sounds of urgent lovemaking abruptly ceased. Low voices exchanged unintelligible words. Bedsprings creaked as weight left them; footsteps thumped across the floor. I could imagine Crawley belting his dressing gown, stepping into his leather slippers as he prepared to investigate the crash. Then I heard more voices in hushed conversation, Mina stopping him at the door (I prayed), imploring Crawley to return to bed (please). After what seemed an eternity, he relented, and I could let out the breath I had been holding.

I sank back down beneath the bedcovers and made a solemn vow never again to eavesdrop on any amorous encounters. As the adrenaline subsided in me like a tide, I discovered my eyelids growing heavy, and not much longer after that, the sleep that had eluded me all night at long last pulled me down like an undertow into the dreamless deep, where a single question drifted like kelp among the shadows:

Who was Walter?

· · ·

"An impostor," McLaughlin said the next day when I put the question to him, reporting in from the apothecary's phone booth. "We don't even have to assume he is a particularly clever one either—since none of you on the committee has ever met the real Walter."

"I thought you might say that," I said, "so I asked Crawley if the Walter we heard last night sounded like the same man he knew before the war."

"And?"

"He said yes—without question."

McLaughlin grunted. "And that's it? You're prepared to take Crawley at his word?"

"I think he's telling the truth."

"What makes you say that?"

"Everything . . . ," I said, struggling to articulate what was essentially a hunch. "Crawley's behavior. His reactions to Walter. Just the way he looks at his wife . . ." Hearing myself flounder, I broke off my attempts to explain. "I'm sorry, it's difficult to put into words."

"Well, until you can," McLaughlin said, "I would advise you to regard Crawley as your prime suspect. He's the most likely accomplice."

Did my opinion really count for so little? "With all due respect, Professor," I said, "I genuinely don't believe he is."

"Don't argue, Finch. Now, when is the next sitting?"

"Tomorrow. Mina requested an evening off to recover."

There was a pause on the line. "So it's 'Mina' now, is it?"

"I meant to say 'Mrs. Crawley.' "

My face felt hot, a mix of embarrassment and anger at how little he seemed to trust me. Maybe Flynn was right. Maybe I *was* just his mouthpiece.

McLaughlin chose to let my slip go, circling back to more urgent matters. "Is the committee also taking the night off?"

"No. We're meeting for dinner to draft a list of questions for Walter."

McLaughlin made an exasperated noise. "Why not? And while you're at it, maybe you can find out his opinion on this spring's fashions." I didn't think sarcasm was his strong suit.

"Is there something else I should bring up?"

"Yes—controlling Mrs. Crawley."

"Any recommendations?"

"You can start by better securing her feet," McLaughlin said. "And requesting that her husband *not* join the circle."

I bit my tongue. Agreed to do as he instructed.

A few minutes later, we rang off. I sat in the phone booth quietly fuming, until the businessman standing outside grew impatient and rapped on the glass.

I exited the telephone booth and waited in line at the cash register while the old apothecary sold a bottle of Blondine to a neighborhood deb and a couple of two-cent stamps in a sanitary isinglass capsule to an irritable governess. I observed the governess's young charges—fraternal twin little girls—fight over a sock puppet with button eyes. The darker of the twins finally won possession of the sock and slipped it over her tiny fist, launching into an impromptu puppet show.

I watched the governess collect her girls and exit, and by the time it was my turn at the register, I had fallen so far down the rabbit hole of my own brooding that the apothecary had to greet me twice before I realized he was talking to me.

"I said g'morning, Professor." He had been calling me this ever since learning I was from Harvard—a fact I'd been forced to reveal when he confronted me with the suspicion I was running numbers out of his establishment.

"Just the phone call today?" he asked, and when I nodded absently, he used the back of an old receipt to calculate how much I owed. He was a funny little fellow, hairless and pink as a baby fresh out of the bathtub and toweled vigorously—a baby with liver spots, that is. Still in a daze, I paid him for the long-distance call, said good-bye, and was about to wander off when the murky thoughts triggered by the twins and their sock puppet suddenly became clear. I turned back.

"I wonder if you can help me, sir?"

The old man tensed, casting a quick glance around the shop to make sure we were alone.

He leaned closer and said in a low voice, "I might be able to. But I only sell half-pints, so if you're lookin' for gallon goods, you gotta go elsewhere." And from somewhere underneath the zinc counter, he produced an unlabeled bottle of soda-pop 'shine, a local concoction notorious for having a heavy content of isopropyl alcohol. "I don't wanna be responsible for any young fellas like yourself going blind."

"That's not the kind of help I'm after."

"No?" He blinked at me from behind rimless spectacles.

"I need to find a ventriloquist."

"Ohhhh," he said, nodding, as if this were no more unusual than any other of his customers' requests. I explained that I thought he probably knew the city better than just about anyone else. He must have been close to seventy, probably had memories stretching back to the War Between the States.

"Ventriloquists . . . ventriloquists . . ." He sucked on his few remaining teeth, as if the minerals they contained might fortify his memory. "Used to be one down the shore wasn't half bad, out on Steel Pier."

"Anything closer to home?"

"Closer . . ." He frowned, then snapped his fingers. "Come to think of it, there *was* a fella out on North Fifth, called himself 'Professor Vox.' "

I picked up the stub of pencil and scribbled this all down on the back of the scrip below his chicken-scratch calculations.

"Right there on the corner," the apothecary continued, pleased at his recall. "Right next to one of those Hebrew churches. You can't miss Vox's place—whole thing's plastered in playbills."

"I knew I'd come to the right man!" I said, folding the address and stuffing it into my breast pocket. I shook his hand, which was soft as an old ballet slipper, and thanked him.

This time I made it as far as the door before turning back.

"Actually," I said, "how much do you want for that bottle?"

· · ·

The neighborhood the old man had sent me in search of was only a dozen blocks or so across town as the seagull flew—but it might as well have been on the other side of the world from Rittenhouse Square. The two districts were as different as the rivers with which they were allied: to the west the Schuylkill, with its pretty boathouses and stone bridges and early-morning scullers, like a misplaced Thames; to the east the Delaware, dark and deep channeled, a river of industry whose banks were barnacled with wharves and shipyards and customs houses and whose environs were a warren of breweries and lace factories and railroad spurs and blind alleys. Gone were the shade trees, I noticed as I walked up Fifth Street and crossed Spring Garden Street; now the only flora to be seen were the occasional scrawny ailanthus or an empty lot of crabgrass. Gone as well were what seemed entire segments of the color spectrum, as if anything other than this dusty brick red weren't hearty enough to survive here—or perhaps were simply unwelcome. I was feeling a bit unwelcome myself, alone on these monochromatic streets of leaning tenements and unfriendly trinity town homes. I saw few people outdoors, and those I did encounter—an old woman dressed from head to toe in black, a gang of urchins tormenting a stray dog—fixed me with looks of open mistrust.

Luckily, the old chemist had been correct when he said I

couldn't miss the ventriloquist's place. There it stood in the 700 block of North Fifth, sharing a corner the "Hebrew Church"—in actuality a Greek Orthodox temple. The establishment I had come looking for was itself unexceptional: a three-story building of drab brick, with unshuttered windows and an awning in disrepair. But the manner in which the place was decorated made it remarkable, for every square inch of brick was plastered with playbills and hand-painted signs, the most histrionic of which shouted:

PROFESSOR SAMUEL L. VOX
THE CELEBRATED VENTRILOQUIST!

Beneath which smaller banners advertised VOCAL ILLUSIONS and SHOWS DAILY and VOX'S INTERNATIONAL SCHOOL FOR VENTRILO-QUY and ENROLL NOW! There were banners with cartoon ducks going QUACK! and pigs going OINK! and patrons looking amazed, as well as a weather-beaten mural of the good professor himself in bow tie and top hat beneath the legend CAN BE ENGAGED FOR ANY OCCASION. In fact the only information one couldn't find among these displays was the hours of operation and whether the place was indeed open.

After a few minutes of banging on the front door—where the buzzer should've been was what looked like an empty nostril sprouting wires—I began to wonder if I had missed a sign reading BY APPOINTMENT ONLY. I was about to give up and admit defeat when the door opened and an elderly Italian custodian peeked out, blinking in the wintry light. He looked distressed when I told him I had come to consult Samuel Vox on a professional matter, but after considering a moment, he decided finally to admit me.

Inside, I was met by the smell common to theatrical places, greasepaint and moldering talent. Visitors must have been an unusual occurrence in the afternoons, because the shy custodian fretted and fussed and generally looked uncomfortable to have been caught with a mop in hand. He was a squat, large-bellied man with short hands and a rolling gait that hinted at one leg jointed differently than the other. He took my coat and ushered me back through the musty darkness to what looked like the anteroom of a bordello, all Persian rugs and paper lanterns and brushed-velvet wallpaper. To one side of the room was a small glass case displaying various chapbooks and instructional pamphlets for sale, with titles like *The Vox Method in a Month* and *Principles of Theek Voice.* A metal cash-box atop the case suggested it doubled as ticket counter for the show that awaited patrons on the other side of the curtained doorway.

Now a man could be heard behind that curtain, calling from somewhere at the back of the house, "Who is it, Albert?"

"Is a young man, *Professore,*" the custodian called in reply.

"Well, tell him we discontinued matinees," Vox called back, then launched into what sounded like vocal exercises, do-re-me-fa-sol-la-ti-do. He had that flowery, formal manner of speech that so many theater people affect.

Albert turned to me, made an openhanded gesture. "You can hear what he say, yes?"

"If I could just . . . ," I began saying to the custodian, then decided to cut out the middle man and shouted back through the curtain to Vox, "If I could just trouble you for a few minutes, Professor. I'm here on rather important business."

Now from deep in the house came gargling noises. Albert touched my arm, said quietly to me, "Is no a good thing for him to speak now, yes? You hear how he make ready his throat for the performance. So you go away now, come back later, yes?"

"I only need a moment of the professor's time," I said. "I promise I'll do most of the talking."

Vox shouted, "Has he left yet, Albert?"

"Presto, presto!" the custodian called to his employer, then, seizing my arm, whispered urgently, "You see how you must, yes?"

The old custodian took my elbow and began to steer me toward the front door, but I surprised him and myself by pulling my arm free and dashing back through the curtains into the dark hallway.

"I only have one or two questions," I called toward the dirty yellow light I saw spilling out of another room at the far end of the hallway, to give Vox fair warning I was coming. The gargling abruptly ceased as I strode toward the end of the hall and rounded the corner to find—

An empty dressing room.

"Back here, my boy," a voice said from behind me.

I spun around and saw Albert the custodian in the curtained doorway, watching me with a sheepish expression. He shrugged, explaining in Vox's voice, "I fear I am a bit understaffed these days."

My mouth dropped open in surprise. When I could finally speak again, I said, "Well, I think you just answered my first question."

"And what was that?"

"Is it really possible to throw one's voice?"

Vox chuckled. "Strictly speaking, it is not—it's all just an illusion. A matter of fooling the ear." He squeezed past me in the narrow hall, gesturing that I should follow him. "Come. We can talk more comfortably in the kitchen."

Vox led me back through the house to a tiny galley kitchen that smelled of old linoleum and the ghosts of suppers past—and not lavish ones either, but the sort of starchy subsistence meals that were my own mainstay. He offered me a seat while he put a teakettle on the stove and went in search of matching cups and saucers. Small voices heckled him as he shuffled about the kitchen, calling "Over here!" and "Let us out!" from behind cupboard doors and inside the icebox. But I was onto Vox now, and though the movement was subtle, I caught his Adam's apple bobbing within its wattle of skin with each vocalization.

While we waited for the water to boil, Vox offered me an abbreviated history of what the public called "ventriloquism"— "Though I much prefer George Smith's term, 'alioloquism,' " Vox said, removing the teakettle once it began to whine, "or the less prosaic but more correct 'pectoraloquism.' " He filled two cups with boiling water, plopped in tea bags that had been used before but which he considered to have some life left in them, and added a shot of a licorice-flavored liqueur from an unmarked bottle. Then he resumed his survey. "The first practitioner of the modern art was Louis Brabant, in the court of King Francis I. At the time it was commonly held that the spirits of the dead resided in the stomachs of certain prophets and soothsayers—hence the word 'ventriloquist,' which in Latin means 'belly speaker.' Today we might call them—"

"Spirit mediums."

Vox nodded. "Rabelais has a delightful scene in *Gargantua and Pantagruel* with ventriloquists he called the Engastrimyths and Gastrolaters. . . ." He continued on in this vein, but I'd stopped paying attention, still hung up on this unexpected intersection between ventriloquy and spirit mediumship. Could Mina really be the voice behind her brother, Walter?

I put a variation on this question to Vox once he concluded his literary survey. "Do you think it's possible," I asked, "for someone to master the art of ventriloquism in a few months?" This was the length of time, in my best estimation, between Crawley's first interest in Spiritualism and the reappearance of Walter—the time Mina would have had to become adept at the vocal illusionist's art.

"Master?" he said. "Impossible! Why, it takes years just to learn how to produce the more rudimentary fricatives without moving the lips!"

"Good." It was what I had come hoping to hear, and I knew I shouldn't linger now but rather rise and thank Vox and make my exit before I had time to think about his answer. Because I knew there was a part of me that could not leave well enough alone—a seditious little voice in the back of my brain like Poe's Imp of the Perverse, goading me to leap from bridges and laugh at funerals, and pull the thread that unravels a perfectly fitting explanation. And so I started to rise. But it was too late; the question was already on my tongue.

"For the sake of argument," I heard myself begin, "let's say this individual didn't have to worry about moving her lips. She's performing in the dark—she can move her lips as much as she likes. All that's required is that she convincingly imitate the voice of a man and create the illusion he is speaking from various locations in the room." Vox listened with a grave face, as if I were describing a crime. "Given the scenario I have just laid out," I said, "do you still believe that it is impossible?"

Vox's brow knit in concern as he considered my question. After some deliberation he asked, "What would you say are the dimensions of the room?"

"About the same as this one. Perhaps a bit larger."

"A hundred and seventy square feet, then, give or take," Vox said. "Tell me what the walls are constructed of."

"Plaster, covered with paper."

"And the ceiling?"

I tipped my head back at the kitchen ceiling—dead flies in the frosted bowl of a light fixture, a water stain shaped like Japan—and struggled to conjure up a memory of the nursery's ceiling.

"Wood, I should think." It was only a guess, since, like the sky or the eye color of a stranger, ceilings weren't something I noticed unless they were extraordinary.

"Do you know what sort of wood?"

"I'm afraid I don't."

Vox grunted, factoring another unknown variable into his mental calculation of the nursery's acoustics. He let out a long sigh. "It would be difficult," he said, and my heart sank in anticipation of what was next. "But not impossible."

"How difficult?"

"First of all, performing in darkness is a great liability, not an asset, since so many of our effects depend on stagecraft, on suggestion and misdirection—for instance, inclining one's head as if listening to a 'distant' voice. In the dark, of course, you cannot do this, and therefore your success depends entirely on the sophistication of your vocal talents." I heard a note of professional jealousy enter Vox's own voice, the admiration of one high-wire artist for another who works without a net. "If, as you suggest, this is a case of a female imitating a man, then her achievement is all the more remarkable."

"Why?"

"Because masculine voices are among the most difficult to learn and among the last a student attempts," Vox said. "The young men who come to me begin their course of study by learning 'theek' or 'rush' voice—a reedy sound produced via the mouth and nose. With theek under their belts, they are able to create their first 'near' voices: A Small Boy, The Little Girl, The Crone. In the meantime they are developing discipline, learning the proper manner of breathing, perfecting their 'bee drone'—that cornerstone of the 'distant voices' which are the truest measures of a vocal illusionist's art."

"It sounds like quite an apprenticeship."

"It takes years, a lifetime," Vox said, then gave a shrug as he admitted, "but every art has its prodigies. It isn't fair, but that's the way God works. And what you describe would require a prodigious talent, a God-given talent." Vox looked at me with watery blue eyes, sad and extraordinary, and asked in a shy voice, "And you say you know someone like this?"

"No," I told him soberly, "I don't believe I do."

I finished the dregs of my tea, tepid now, and rose from the kitchen table. Vox gave me a quick tour of the rest of the house, a parlor converted into a Museum of the Voice, a sitting room turned into a twenty-seat auditorium, then accepted the few dollars I offered him as a contribution to his work, courtesy of the *Scientific American*. This seemed to cheer him considerably, to the point that for old times' sake he playfully resumed the character of Albert the Italian custodian as he escorted me to the front door. On the way there, we passed through the Museum of the Voice, where an old book in one of the dusty glass cases caught my eye. I peered down at the frontispiece of the first edition on display: *Wieland, or The Transformation*, by Charles Brockden Brown, published in 1798 by T. & J. Swords of New York.

I asked Vox about the book and learned it was an early gothic about an evil ventriloquist who uses his gifts to destroy a family in a small Pennsylvania town . . .

Something went cold inside me.

· · ·

When I returned to 2013 Spruce, I found the entire household—minus Crawley, who was no doubt buried up to his elbows in some poor woman's reproductive organs—convened in the front parlor with a fresh-cut Christmas tree.

"A little more to the right," instructed Mina from the settee where she reclined in a pale yellow tea dress. Mrs. Grice stood by with dustpan and brush, clucking in disapproval as Pike and Freddy shifted the shivering Douglas fir a few inches to the right, sending pine needles raining down on her nice clean floor. The mismatched men made a comedy duo worthy of a Buster Keaton production as they waltzed the tree around the room: the giant Freddy clutching it in a bear hug while the pint-size Filipino cursed in Tagalog and was engulfed by its branches.

I tossed aside my gloves and rushed forward to lend a hand.

"Careful, guv," Freddy cautioned through clenched teeth. "Don't get pitch on your coat."

"I won't."

I thrust my arms through the branches and found a handhold on the sticky trunk. Freddy's face grew a few shades lighter as I relieved him of some of the burden. With much grunting on our part and much indecision on Mina's ("Do you think we should turn the bald spot toward the wall . . . ?") we finally succeeding in positioning the tree to everyone's satisfaction.

"Bravo!" Mina applauded in girlish delight. She came forward to help me brush pine needles from my sweater. As she reached up to pick more needles out of my hair I chased her hands away.

"I can do it."

"All right, grumpy."

We stood clear as Mrs. Grice swept up pine needles and Pike began opening cartons of ornaments and Freddy climbed a wooden ladder to scrub at the streaks of green the treetop had made on the ceiling. The Siamese came slinking around the corner to investigate, with the Boston terrier scuttling close behind.

"Oh, isn't it just a lovely tree!" Mina said, her spirits lifted considerably, though her complexion remained pale and her voice was hoarse. She linked her arm through mine. "I was worried you wouldn't be home in time to help us trim it."

"Seems to me you have more help than you need," I said, and extricated my arm from hers. "Now, if you'll excuse me, there's some reading I really need to do." And with that I left.

Twenty minutes later Mina came searching for me upstairs in the library.

"Martin?" she called timidly from the doorway.

I shut the book in my hand with a loud clap. She flinched.

"Yes?"

"Is anything the matter?"

"Of course not," I said, irritated. "Why would there be?"

"I don't know . . . you seem upset by something." She came closer, perched on the arm of the Morris chair opposite me. "You would tell me if anything was bothering you, wouldn't you, Martin?"

"I very much doubt it."

"Why not?"

"I'd hate to impose on my host."

She reacted to this just as I had intended her to. "But we're friends."

"Are we?" I asked, as if the idea had never before occurred to me. I felt an almost sexual thrill at the look of hurt this caused Mina. And I'm ashamed to say I wasn't through with her. "Well, that changes everything, doesn't it? Friends . . ." I spoke the word as if it were foreign and I was tasting its shape for the first time on my American tongue. But all I tasted was ashes: I was strictly an amateur sadist, and the moment Mina's eyes began to glisten, the game lost any thrill it had once held.

"What's happened, Martin?" she asked, her lip quivering. "Please tell me what I've done to upset you so badly."

"Nothing," I said, sick of myself now, wanting only to be left alone. "I just woke up on the wrong side of the bed this morning. If you knew me better, you'd know I get into these moods sometimes, for no particular reason."

"Honestly?" Mina asked, wanting to believe it was true, and when I nodded, she gave a shuddering sob of relief that was halfway to a smile and threw her arms around my neck. I felt her tears against my collar, her breath hot as she spoke into my shirt. "Promise me that's all it is, darling . . . that you will tell me if it's ever anything more."

"Why does it matter so much to you what I think?"

"I . . . ," she began, then, pulling back slightly and turning her face to the fire, confessed in a small voice, "I'm lonely, Martin. I know that's a silly thing to say with a houseful of people—but I am."

"What about Dr. Crawley?"

This brought a smile to her lips, as if I had reminded her of an old friend. "Poor Arthur," she said with affection. Saying his name seemed to warm her from within, restoring color to her cheeks. "I think sometimes my husband must find me dreadfully boring."

"I don't see how anyone could."

If she had heard me, she did not acknowledge it. She stared at the fire, her thoughts still on her remarkable husband.

"Arthur always keeps a dozen books on his nightstand," she said, and I felt a pang of unwanted jealousy at this mention of his bedroom. "Books on every conceivable subject. Poetry, economics, history, politics—"

"Occultism?"

She gave me a cautioning look. "Metaphysics."

"Well," I said, "at least that's one interest you share."

Mina nodded. "Now you understand why my brother's return has been such a godsend. Walter has brought Arthur and me so much closer as husband and wife. Which I suppose is ironic."

"Why ironic?"

"Walter was very much opposed to our marrying."

"Because of the difference in your ages?"

"And because of how we met . . ." She trailed off, worried she might be revealing too much.

Before she could change her mind, I leaned forward, prompted, "How *did* you come to meet your husband?"

"I was Arthur's patient at Jefferson."

"Oh?"

She nodded. "I was hospitalized for many weeks, and we became friends. My brother seemed to consider it terribly unethical of Arthur to let the friendship become anything more." She smiled, as if at some private joke. "Which is also ironic, since Walter was the last person who should criticize another man's ethics." Despite her smile there was a tightness in her voice that spoke volumes. "I suppose Walter was just playing the overprotective brother."

"Still is, from the sound of it."

She frowned. "What do you mean?"

"Never mind."

But Mina wouldn't be deterred. "Did something happen last night between Walter and Arthur?" she asked. "Was there another row?"

"You mean to say you really don't remember?"

"No."

I studied her, watching for some clue that she was playacting. But she seemed entirely sincere in her amnesia. I could feel anger struggling to assert itself inside me, but Mina's utter lack of guile had rendered it helpless: a beetle on its back. And so in the end, I had no choice but to tell her about last evening's séance, sparing no detail—Walter's assault on Flynn, his suggestive remarks to me, the ugly things he'd had to say to his brother-in-law. Mina listened to all of it in silence, her hands folded in her lap and the last bit of color draining by degrees from her already pale face, and when I had finished, she thanked me for my candor.

"I'm sorry to upset you," I said, "but I thought you should hear it all."

"No, don't apologize," Mina said absently, reaching for my hand and give it a reassuring squeeze. "There are enough people already in this house trying to protect me." And she leaned over to give me a sisterly kiss, to seal this pact between us. I felt my pulse quicken and instinctively leaned forward to prolong the kiss.

Mina laughed as if I'd just amused her with a magic trick, then, rising to her feet, hurried downstairs to oversee the trimming of the Christmas tree.

· 8 ·

After dusk I hailed a cab to Sansom Street, a narrow alley of jewelers and oyster houses where Fox and Flynn and Richardson had agreed to meet me for supper. I jaywalked across Ninth Street, nearly getting myself flattened by a laundry wagon taking soiled linens from the back of the Continental Hotel. It took me ten minutes of back-and-forthing before I finally spotted the green awning of Carl's Oyster House, an old rathskeller that made up in sawdust what it lacked in charm. In its subterranean dining room, I found Flynn already camped out at a corner table and whispering something off-color in a waitress's ear.

"Kid!"

Flynn beckoned me to a chair as if I were his long-lost brother and said to our waitress, "And bring a dozen Lynnhavens on the half shell for my eggheaded friend here."

I caught her arm before she could leave with the order.

"Actually, I'd be just as happy with a bowl of the stew."

After she'd left, Flynn made a face. "Stew won't put lead in your pencil, kid."

"Who am I writing?"

"Our waitress seems your type," Flynn confided, bathtub gin on his breath. "I've been talking you up to her."

"I'm touched, Flynn. That's very selfless of you."

"Not really. Her sister is the real prize."

"There's a sister?"

"In the kitchen. Unfortunately, there's also a husband."

"And I suppose he's in the kitchen, too?"

"No, working the raw bar." Flynn gestured toward the front of the restaurant, where a red-faced brute with great tattooed forearms was shucking oysters.

"He looks like a reasonable man."

A short time later, Richardson arrived, overdressed as usual, tonight in a vicuña overcoat, dinner jacket with silk lapels, and expensive Balmoral boots. He took a seat, crossed his legs, and draped a napkin over his knee like someone doing a magic trick. Our waitress returned with our starters then, a tray of Lynnhavens for Flynn, and for me a steaming bowl of oyster stew flecked with bright yellow knobs of butter.

"What's the matter," Richardson asked me, "don't like them raw?"

"I don't like the idea of eating something still living."

"Hear that, Flynn? We have a conscientious objector in our midst."

"Lay off the kid," Flynn said, throwing an arm protectively around my shoulders. "He's saving himself for marriage."

I shrugged off Flynn's arm. It was going to be a long night.

Fox arrived ten minutes later, cheeks flushed from the cold. He stopped our waitress to place his order before he'd even removed his overcoat, and when she returned a few minutes later with a net bag of shrimp steamed in Old Bay, he fell on them as if they were his natural prey.

"Jesus, Fox—you want a bib?" Flynn asked.

"Or perhaps a baleen?" Richardson suggested.

Personally, I would have enjoyed seeing them all fitted with muzzles. But at least Fox's table manners had shifted the focus off me for the time being. The rest of our supper proceeded in a similar vein, as tray after tray was set down on our table, and Fox grew more and more flushed from the effort of dispatching each successive species—I couldn't help thinking of the Chinese brother from the children's fable, the one who swallowed the sea—and I kept my nose down to stay out of the sarcastic sniper fire between Richardson and Flynn. Never was the topic of Mina Crawley broached, and before I knew it, supper had concluded and my dining companions were lighting after-dinner cigars and calling for the check.

"Did anyone take a stab at writing questions for Walter?" I asked.

"Plenty of time for that later," Flynn said, then announced to the table, "Right now I propose a change of venue for this little soirée."

All the cigar smoke in such a confined space was making me feel a bit green around the gills, and so while Fox settled our bill, I went outside and waited on the sidewalk. The night was brisk and cold, and by the time the others emerged from the restaurant, I was feeling a little better.

Unfortunately, the chill night air also had an invigorating effect on Flynn—as had, apparently, the two dozen oysters he'd devoured at supper. With plenty of lead in his Eversharp and his mind set on finding a pen pal, Flynn strode into the middle of the street and flagged down a taxicab.

"Pile in, fellows," Flynn said, waving us over. Richardson ducked inside, followed by Fox on all fours. Flynn put a foot on Fox's well-padded rear and gave a shove, then waved me in.

"Shouldn't we go someplace quiet and discuss tomorrow's séance?" I asked.

"Later," Flynn said, holding the door for me.

"Where are we going?"

Flynn grinned, the stogie clenched in the corner of his teeth. He waggled his eyebrows and answered enigmatically, "A wake."

. . .

Ten minutes later the cab delivered us outside a funeral parlor on a back street in South Philadelphia—a neighborhood that, judging by all the stone lions and Virgin Marys on display, was predominantly working class and Italian. Struggling to keep my supper down after the nauseating cab ride, I fell into step behind the others as Flynn led us up the funeral parlor's slushy front walk. Flynn rang the bell, and we all waited, hugging ourselves against the cold.

A moment later the door was answered by a hulking pituitary case in a suit two sizes too small for him. Organ music floated out from somewhere inside.

"Yeah?"

"We've come to pay our respects," Flynn said.

The doorman checked the street behind us. "Youse any relation to the deceased?"

"On my mother's side."

These, we would later learn, were the passwords Flynn had purchased off a Western Union messenger that morning. It proved to be a sound two-dollar investment; hearing it now, the hired muscle working the door gave a grunt and admitted us.

Inside the faux funeral parlor—what we used to call a "blind pig" in those dry days—we followed the somber organ music back through darkness redolent of furniture polish and wilted gardenias. We passed a young man snoring quietly in an open coffin, pushed our way through a final set of heavy velvet drapes—and emerged in the middle of the most raucous memorial service any-one had ever seen. An electric nickel-slot piano provided music for a dozen couples dancing among the tables, while two bar-tenders in aprons served up gin and rye at fifty cents a shot.

"I must say, old man," Richardson said, clapping a hand on Flynn's shoulder, "your mother's family certainly knows how to throw a funeral!" He and Fox went off to commandeer a table while I trailed Flynn to the bar.

The bartender eyed me with suspicion.

"You old enough to be in here?"

"Are you serious?" With some indignation I said, "I'm twenty-four."

The bartender turned to Flynn. "He telling the truth?"

"Hard to say," Flynn replied. "Maybe we should cut him in half and count the rings."

"Flynn!"

The bartender scowled. "I'll let him go this time. Now, what can I get you fellows?"

"A bottle of your best coffin varnish."

"How many glasses?"

Flynn held up four fingers, and the bartender left.

Beside me, a girl was carrying on a conversation with her cock-tail olives. "That's a helluva thing to say to a girl you supposedly love, dontcha think?" I felt her arm on my elbow and turned. She looked like a bad mimeograph of a pretty girl, her mascara smudged by some earlier crying jag. She batted her eyes, less an effort to flirt than an attempt to bring me into better focus. "Dontcha think, mister?"

"Don't I think what?"

"That it's a pretty shitty—pardon my French—a pretty awful way to treat someone you're supposed to love? Calling her a phony and a liar . . ." The girl clutched my sleeve, tears clumping in her false eyelashes. "Honestly, mister, ain't that an awful mean way to treat a girl who's never done nothing but love you?"

"I'm the wrong person to ask," I mumbled to the girl, then grabbed the glasses off the bar and fled after Flynn.

Back at our table, Richardson lined up the four glasses and poured out shots of what the bottle's label claimed was Johnnie Walker, though it wasn't quite the right color and it smelled suspiciously of grain alcohol. The bartender had sworn it came directly from "Mr. Hoff's private reserve"—meaning Max "Boo Boo" Hoff, the notorious Philadelphia bootlegger.

"Fellows, I would like to say knowing you has been a pleasure," Flynn said, raising his glass, "but the past few days have been a pain in the neck—literally!" And he hooked a thumb toward the plaster on his throat where Walter had bitten him.

It dawned on me then that Fox and Flynn and Richardson had no intention of discussing tomorrow's séance. They were celebrating, enjoying a final lavish night on the town, compliments of the *Scientific American*'s expense account.

Richardson raised his glass. "To Flynn's neck!"

"Wait," Fox said, "shouldn't we propose a real toast?"

"I don't see why," Flynn said. "This isn't real scotch."

"For posterity," Fox said. "After all, this is a historic occasion."

"You're right," Richardson said, lowering his voice to a paranoid whisper. "And there might be biographers lurking."

"Isn't that one over by the piano?" Flynn asked.

"She strikes me as more of a linguist."

"Really?" Flynn said, craning to see. "Wonder how much she'd charge to strike me?"

"I'm serious!" Fox said.

"All right, don't cast a kitten," Flynn said. "What do you want us to drink to? But I'm warning you, Fox: If you say the *Scientific American*, I'm gonna sock you in the mouth."

Fox frowned, racking his brain for a toast suitable to the occasion. Just then inspiration hit him, and a smile spread across his face like a broken yolk. He raised his glass, said,

"To Mrs. Crawley!"

The others made appreciative noises at the correctness of Fox's toast. They raised their glasses to his.

"The beguiling Mina."

"And Walter!"

Expectant eyes turned my way, waiting for me to join their toast. Finally I raised my glass and clinked its rim to theirs. Drank. Shuddered as the denatured alcohol corroded its way through my GI tract, not stopping until it reached the basement, where my tailbone and testicles resided like an old croquet set. While Flynn began pouring the second round, I reached into the pocket of my overcoat and felt the small cloth-bound book I'd been carrying around with me all night in anticipation of the right moment. But although my moment had arrived, I felt a sudden compulsion to let it pass—to leave the book in its hiding place and later return it to the Crawley library where I had first discovered it. I have always been a companionable drunk, and as the bootleg liquor found its way to my brain and began dissolving the hard particles of resentment that had accreted there over the last seventy-two hours, I started to see Fox and Flynn and Richardson in a more charitable light and the book in my pocket as an eleventh-hour revelation of questionable significance, which would only spoil our evening. And so I took my hand out of my pocket and joined my colleagues in a second toast. But this time the liquor tasted metallic and wrong, and its glow was slower in coming; and when I closed my eyes to wait out the aftershocks, the memory of Mina's kiss that afternoon was there waiting for me.

I slipped out the book and set it on the table.

"What's with the King James, kid?" Flynn asked, refilling our glasses.

"It's not a Bible."

Fox contorted his head to read the spine. *"Wieland?"*

"It's about a con artist," I said. "A ventriloquist."

"Loan it to me, old man," Richardson said. "I could use a little light reading for the train ride home."

"I found this copy in Mina Crawley's personal library."

The hitch in Flynn's pour was almost imperceptible. But he finished filling our four glasses, then raised his and looked me in the eye as he proposed a new toast.

"To well-read women."

He tossed back the drink and set the glass down hard.

"Also," I said, sure that if I didn't get it out now, I never would, "I don't know if anyone else noticed during last night's séance, but Mina's feet were out of their ropes."

The room had fallen quiet. Even the nickel-slot piano had stopped playing, in one of those coincidental hushes people always blame on the angels.

Fox asked quietly, "What are you getting at, Finch?"

"Only that we shouldn't celebrate prematurely," I said, trying to sound reasonable. "The professor recommends we ask Crawley to recuse himself from any future sittings," I said. "I don't necessarily agree, but I don't see how it would hurt to ask. However, I do think we should request Mina to allow us to gag her."

Flynn looked daggers at me. "And just what in the hell is that supposed to prove?"

"That Mina isn't the voice of Walter."

I was surprised how quickly they were able to marshal their arguments.

"And what if she is?" Fox said. "All you will have proven is that this isn't a case of direct voice."

"After all," Richardson said, joining Fox's protest, "Walter wouldn't be the first shade to require a human intermediary to speak with the living."

"Maybe not," I said, "but he *is* the first shade to speak with the *Scientific American*. And the magazine's rules clearly state that 'purely auditory phenomena will not be eligible for the award.' "

The table fell silent. But not for long.

"If Walter's words can't count *for* Mina," Richardson said, proving himself a wily defense attorney, "then in all fairness they shouldn't be used *against* her. Which makes this *Wieland* inadmissible as evidence of any wrongdoing."

"I'm not trying to make a criminal case out of this."

"Oh, no," Flynn cut in, "you're just trying humiliate the poor woman."

"What is that supposed to mean?"

"First you tie her up, now you want to gag her," Flynn mumbled into his drink, his consonants becoming sloppy. "I'm no headshrinker, but I'm starting to think maybe you're gettin' off on this."

"You're tight."

Flynn's voice became a growl. "Not so tight I won't put my foot up your ass, you lousy son of a bitch—"

And he leaped to his feet so abruptly his chair overturned with a clatter. I rose from my chair defensively, so he wouldn't catch me sitting. Every eye in the place was suddenly on us, and I could feel myself perspiring beneath my shirt, and I had no idea and very little instinct whether I was about to be hit.

"Flynn, let it go."

Fox and Richardson attempted to defuse the situation. Flynn allowed himself to be walked away from the table. I was still trying to understand the precise instant at which the conflict had turned combustible when Flynn without warning broke free and lunged at me. His drunken punch caught me beside the left eye, and he followed it into me, head down like a charging bull. His skull plowed into my sternum and sent me reeling backward. I heard a tremendous crash, followed by the sound of breaking glass, and then I was falling ass over elbows, and then I was landing hard. I saw stars—actual stars, in vivid constellation—and when these finished their slow turn through the seasons and faded away, I found myself sprawled in a corner between a potted fern and a radiator, thinking, *So that's what it's like to be hit.* I wished I could have added to this insight what it felt like to hit Flynn back, but I was learning that second great truth about violence as it exists outside the movies: It's over as swiftly as it begins. Flynn by this time was gone, ejected by the hulking doorman, and Richardson was busy righting the overturned chairs, and as Fox helped me to my feet, I understood that any opportunity for retaliation had long since passed.

Fox hurried to the bar and returned with a handful of ice in his handkerchief.

"What's that for?" I asked.

"Your eye," he said.

No sooner were the words out of his mouth than the pain announced itself. I raised my hand to my left eye and winced as I felt the welt swelling my lid shut. Fox and Richardson caught me by the elbows as my knees buckled.

"Get him outta here!" the bartender called to them, stabbing a blunt finger in my direction. Fox and Richardson each took one of my arms and escorted me to the door.

Outside the speakeasy I stood swaying on unsteady legs while Richardson went in search of a cab and Fox spoke with the doorman to find out in which direction Flynn had wandered off. I looked up at the December stars. Whether confused or concussed, I couldn't make sense of them; they seemed to have rearranged themselves according to some strange cosmology, arrows and archers chasing a Cheshire moon across a crowded sky. *This is thy hour, O Soul,* I serenaded the stars, *thy free flight into the wordless.* It must have been the dram of Sicilian blood in my veins, stirred to verse by alcohol and injury. Though the poet I turned to in my sodden hour was American. *Away from book, away from art, the day erased,/the lesson done./Thee fully forth emerging, silent, gazing, / pondering the themes thou lovest best—* Damn it, how did the last part go? Suddenly my legs gave way, and I was flat on my back, gazing up at my answer:

Night, sleep, death, and the stars.

. . .

"Good Lord, what happened to you?" Crawley asked the next day, rising from the breakfast table at the sight of my black eye.

Though the swelling had subsided, the discoloration had intensified, so that the side of my face resembled an overripe peach. I was glad Mina wasn't there to see it. She was sleeping in, had left word for Mrs. Grice she would take breakfast in bed that morning in an effort to conserve her strength for tonight. And so I had only one worried host to reassure.

"It looks worse than it feels," I told Crawley.

"Who did this to you?"

"Johnnie Walker."

This came out more flippantly than I intended, so I added, "Afraid I had a little too much to drink last night and slipped on an icy sidewalk."

Ignoring my efforts to make light of the injury, Crawley asked, "At any point did you lose consciousness?"

"No."

"Have you experienced any nausea?"

I shook my head.

"Confusion?"

"No more than usual."

He steadied my head with both hands and had a look at my eyes, lifting first one eyelid and then the next as he checked for discrepancies in the pupils. I had already done as much the night before in my shaving mirror.

"Well," Crawley said when he was satisfied I hadn't suffered a concussion, "I'd like to see how the other fellow looks this morning!" He showed me a smile, then had a glance at his pocket-watch. "I'm due in surgery in thirty minutes. Otherwise I'd stay and look after you. I'll tell Pike to have a look at that eye."

"I'm sure he has better things to do."

"Nonsense. He's a *manghihilot*, you know."

"I beg your pardon?"

"A healer." Crawley tucked the morning paper under his arm and cast a final look over the half-eaten breakfast that had once again defeated him. "He was born in breech—that's the next best thing to a medical degree so far as the Filipinos are concerned." He gave me a wink and turned to go.

"Wait, Doctor." I hurried to catch him. "I won't keep you. I just wanted a few words with you about this evening."

"Yes?"

"I wonder if you'd mind terribly not joining the circle?"

"Why?"

I'd anticipated this and had spent a sleepless night preparing my arguments.

"To avoid antagonizing Walter. We'd like to question your brother-in-law at greater length but fear that your presence might be too much of a distraction. Also, we're concerned that agitating Walter takes a heavy toll on Mrs. Crawley."

"I'll thank you to let *me* to worry about my wife's health!" Crawley said.

"Of course."

I studied his face as he considered my request, just as I'd studied the face of the Reverend Betty Bell Harker months ago, watching for some "tell" that hinted at duplicity or a guilty conscience. But I saw none.

Crawley gave his head a firm shake. "I'm afraid it's out of the question."

"Do you mind if I ask why?"

"You said it yourself—Walter's visits take an enormous physical toll on my wife. I need to be there to monitor the sessions and end them if the strain becomes too much for her."

"This probably won't change your mind," I said, "but I've had a year of medical school. And I spent a summer assisting an internist in my hometown."

"Medical school?" Crawley said, surprised. I could see him reevaluating me in light of this revelation—and, more important, my request that he recuse himself from the circle.

"All right," he said. "I suppose if I can trust anyone to look out for my Mina, it's you, Finch."

I shook his hand. "Thank you, Doctor."

"Don't thank me yet," Crawley said, slipping into the fur-collared overcoat Pike was holding open for him. "There's no guarantee Walter will make an appearance if I'm not there. You could very well experience a blank sitting."

"Oh?"

Crawley pulled on his calfskin gloves, said on his way out the door, "It's an irritated oyster that makes pearls."

. . .

Yet these weren't the words that haunted me the rest of that morning, but rather what Crawley had said immediately before them.

If I can trust anyone to look out for my Mina, it's you.

By lunchtime I had begun to worry that in my desperation I might have oversold my medical training, and so I decided as a precautionary measure to have a Dictograph installed upstairs in order that Crawley could monitor the proceedings from the next room. God knows I couldn't bear any more responsibility for Mina's failing health than I already felt, as chief advocate for extending the investigation. I retained a stenographer to disguise my real motives for the Dictograph and then spent the remainder of the afternoon experimenting in the basement with more humane ways of controlling Mina's voice than a gag. If it weren't for the dark, there wouldn't have been any difficulty at all: I would simply have had her drink a glass of water whenever her brother spoke. But since this wasn't an option, I was forced to consider more baroque devices, such as tubes in which luminous Ping-Pong balls might be suspended so long as someone blew into the mouthpiece. After an hour of this, I gave up, realizing that my efforts—even if successful—would be deemed inadmissible in the court of committee opinion.

I was just dismantling the experimental contraptions I'd constructed when Mina called down the basement stairs.

"Martin? Are you down there?"

I hurried up from the basement and found her dressed in fur coat and gloves.

"What happened to your eye?"

I told her the same story I'd given Crawley. She looked skeptical. To deflect attention from myself, I gestured to her coat and asked, "You're feeling well enough to go out?"

"I'm too bored to stay in," Mina replied. "Will you come with me?"

"Where?"

"Christmas shopping. I want to buy some clothes for

Arthur—new silk pajamas, a golfing outfit for spring. I thought you might model them for me," Mina said. "You and Arthur have similar builds."

The request made me uneasy, yet I couldn't think of an excuse quickly enough. Mina took my hesitation as consent, and the next thing I knew, we had set off in a taxi for center city and Wanamaker's department store.

To describe Wanamaker's merely as a department store does the place an injustice. With twelve granite stories and almost 2 million square feet of marble floor offering the buying public everything from furniture to books to mourning attire, it was a veritable retail coliseum. More: a city unto itself, with its own power plant, post office, cable and telegraph center. As Mina and I entered the Grand Court, my eyes rose to take in the seven soaring galleries, and I had a sense of what it would be like to live inside a wedding cake. Mina caught my hand and led me to the great bronze eagle at the center of the marble court, set in a nest of red-and-white poinsettias, and from this vantage we caught an afternoon concert of Christmas music played on the largest pipe organ in the world, an instrument originally built in 1904 for the Louisiana Purchase Exposition and shipped from St. Louis in thirteen freight cars by Mr. Wanamaker, a man not given to modest gestures.

When the concert concluded, we rode an elevator up to the men's clothing store on the third floor, where I embarked on a second career as a mannequin. First came sports- and leisure wear. Hoping to encourage her husband to exercise (like most of the men in his family, Crawley suffered from hypertension), Mina had me outfitted for a day of bicycling, golfing, riding. This last getup left me feeling most foolish, standing there in fawn knee breeches and tall leather boots.

"What's wrong, darling?" asked Mina.

"I feel like a fop."

"Don't be silly."

"Maybe I should try on some powdered wigs?"

"Shall I ask if they have one in your size?" Mina teased.

"I'd like you to decide if you're going to buy this ridiculous outfit so I can take it off."

"I don't know why you're in such a hurry—you look very handsome in it."

I would have been happy for the compliment if I didn't think she was teasing. She was enjoying this little game of dress-up, and I suspected she was choosing outfits solely on the basis of my discomfort. I would be lying if I said I wasn't enjoying it, too, though the rules of the game required me to act aggrieved.

The salesclerk who had been helping us appeared at my elbow. "Would the gentleman care to try on a different color?"

"No thank you. Though perhaps you'd show me your selection of tricornered hats—"

"Martin."

The clerk peered down his nose at me. Mina informed him she would be purchasing the riding suit—in both the cotton cord and wool tweed—and I was sent packing to the dressing room to strip out of it. In my absence my own clothes had been folded neatly by some servile department-store elf. My shirt and trousers seemed to have become more threadbare and wrinkled, despite Mrs. Grice's valiant efforts to launder them into respectability. There's nothing like playing dress-up in expensive clothes to make one feel down at the heels. I tightened my belt and ducked out, avoiding my shabby reflection in the dressing-room mirror.

Outside, I found Mina at a nearby haberdashery counter debating the relative merits of a trilby versus a bowler. As I approached, she held both hats up for my inspection.

"Which of these do you like better?"

"The less expensive one."

"If money were no object?"

"I'd just wear my crown."

Mina rolled her eyes, exasperated. "You're impossible."

"I don't mean to be. I just don't have much experience making these kinds of decisions."

She handed the hats back to the salesman, said, "Will you box them both for me, please?"

"Perhaps madam's husband would like to try them on for size first?" the salesman asked, shifting his eyes toward me.

"Oh, I'm not her husband—"

"He's my fiancé!" chirped Mina.

"That's right," I said after an embarrassed beat, doing my best to play along. "We're eloping later this evening. I do hope you can keep a secret."

"Of course. My congratulations to the happy couple," the salesman said with something less than sincerity. "Now, if sir and madam will pardon me while I disappear in the back and find boxes *pour vos deux chapeaux.*"

"We'll come back for them later," Mina said, taking my arm.

As she steered me toward the elevators I inquired, "Where to now?"

"I thought we'd have afternoon tea."

"How very civilized."

"Yes, I'm hoping it will have that effect on you."

I looked over at her. "I'm sorry, am I being that awful?"

"Just grumpy," Mina said. "Arthur gets the same way when he hasn't eaten. It's funny sometimes how similar the two of you are. . . ." She trailed off, leaving me to wonder what other similarities she was thinking of.

We rode the elevator to the Crystal Tea Room, where I gorged

myself on petits fours and watched Mina nibble prettily on crust-
less finger sandwiches. My blood sugar must have been low, because almost immediately my mood became sunnier, allowing
me to view the hoity-toity scene—the chandeliers and Circassian
woodwork, the waiters carrying little silver trays of paper-thin
lemon slices, the overweight matrons stirring their tea with dainty
spoons, the pianist playing Debussy's "Golliwog's Cakewalk"—in
an appropriately ironic light. Much as I hated to admit it, I'd inherited my father's ambivalence toward the rich, though I liked to
think I was more aware of it and therefore less a victim of my own
prejudices. Certainly I'd had more experience than my father at
moving among the privileged classes and could comport myself
in a way that didn't draw attention to the fact that I belonged in
Wanamaker's subterranean "DownStairs" shop, among the more
budget conscious.

"You certainly have a sweet tooth," observed Mina as I started
on a second tier of petits fours.

"My mother's, unfortunately."

"Why unfortunately?"

"Because it killed her."

This came out more bluntly than I intended, so I tempered it
with an explanation. "She had diabetes mellitus. She couldn't me-
tabolize carbohydrates." I took a sip of my tea, found it tepid. "The
more sweets she ate, the more she wasted away, until in the end
they killed her."

"Hungry ghosts . . . ," Mina said to herself quietly.

"I beg your pardon?"

"Nothing," she said, looking up. "I was just thinking of
something I came across in one of Arthur's books of Oriental
mythology."

"Your husband keeps quite a library."

Suddenly she brightened. "Thank you for reminding me!"

Reaching into her purse, she produced a small gift-wrapped package tied with a silver ribbon. "I sent Freddy out scouring all the bookshops on Ludlow Street this morning." She set the package on the table before me and ordered, "Open it!"

I left the package sitting there between us.

"I can't."

"But you don't even know what it is yet."

"It doesn't matter. I can't accept it, Mina."

She frowned. "Why not?"

"Because it would compromise the investigation if I were to accept a gift from you." I felt disingenuous saying it, given the fact that I had already accepted the Crawleys' hospitality—not to mention Mina's friendship.

But she was ready for this argument.

"It was secondhand," she said, sliding the package toward me insistently. "I only wanted to do something nice for you, a little keepsake to remember me by." As if it were possible I could ever forget her.

I looked at her and knew immediately there would be no refusing her gift. I picked it up and slit the paper with my thumbnail; the gift wrap fell open, and I found myself holding a leather-bound copy of *Wieland* by Charles Brockden Brown. The book may have been secondhand, but it was still a first edition.

"I saw you admiring it yesterday!" Mina said, beaming at her own cleverness. Then she fluttered her hands excitedly at me. "Look inside! Look! I wrote something!"

I opened the front cover and saw the message she had inscribed in her delicate hand:

"For my adorable skeptic, on those evenings when he has difficulty sleeping. All my love, Mina."

· · ·

Dinner that evening was another informal affair, just Crawley and me hunkered over steaming bowls of pepperpot soup—another local delicacy—in the upstairs library. Mina was taking a medicinal soak to gather her strength before Fox and Flynn and Richardson arrived; the recipe for the restorative bath was purportedly invented by the late Sarah Bernhardt for use before strenuous performances and included two pounds of barley, a pound of rice, six pounds of bran, two pounds of oatmeal, and a half pound of lavender boiled in two quarts of water and mixed with an ounce each of borax and bicarbonate of soda. Now that her husband considered me a kind of junior medical colleague, the topics of our dinner conversation—or, more accurately, Crawley's disquisition—ranged from the largest fibroid he had ever removed (the size of a honeydew) to the ethicality of administering experimental truth serum on criminals (Crawley saw nothing wrong with it) to the recent awarding of the Nobel Prize for Medicine to Canada's Drs. Banting and Best, discoverers of "insulin" (in Crawley's opinion the award should have gone to Serge Voronoff, the Russian surgeon who believed he could reverse the signs of aging by transplantation of the interstitial cells of monkey gonads). While Crawley rambled on, I made the occasional attentive noises that were expected of me and kept myself entertained by dredging around in my soup in an attempt to determine exactly what a "pepperpot" might be.

After supper I asked Crawley to come with me so I could show him the Dictograph. On the way upstairs, I told him how I had done my best to find the least obtrusive location for the transmitter and chosen one of the nursery's windowsills.

Crawley froze midstep, one hand on the banister.

"What did you just say?"

"That I put the transmitter on the windowsill?"

"In the *nursery*," he said, with deadly emphasis.

"That's right."

His voice was low, dangerous. "Why did you call it that?"

"I . . . I'm not sure," I said, realizing I had strayed into an un-marked minefield. "I couldn't have just made it up on my own. I must've heard you or Mrs. Crawley refer to it at one time as 'the nursery'—"

"No," Crawley hissed, "you most certainly did not."

"I'm sorry," I said. "Then I honestly don't know where I might've picked it up. But I hope you will believe me when I say I didn't mean anything by it."

"Just so long as you never call it that again," Crawley said brusquely. "Especially around my wife."

"Of course."

"Good." Like a wind-up soldier that had been nudged, he re-sumed climbing the stairs, only to stop again on the landing and turn to me once more. "I'm sorry if I spoke sharply a moment ago."

"There's no need to apologize."

"It's just . . . ," he began, then confided quietly, "Mina miscar-ried last year, and she is only just beginning to come to grips with the fact that she may never be a mother."

I offered my condolences. Crawley flashed a brief smile and gave my arm a squeeze to indicate that my *faux pas* was forgiven. Then he continued on his way up the stairs to the third floor, leaving me to wonder at the coincidence of Mina's loss a year ago and her sudden discovery of her latent psychic gifts. I recalled something my mother used to say at news of family loss: "When God closes a door, he opens a window."

If that was the case in the Crawley house, then at that moment the open window was admitting a draft of uncomfortably chill air that sent me shivering up the stairs after Crawley.

. . .

Forty minutes later we sat in darkness listening to the gramophone scratch through its third playing of a popular show tune of a few seasons earlier, "I'm Just Wild About Harry."

Before receiving her usual pre-séance injection Mina had repeated her husband's warning that Walter might not appear this evening, in protest of our changes to the circle's "spiritual chemistry." It pained me to hear her offer excuses, and I felt myself sink into a funk as we joined hands. With each nasal refrain of the irritating show tune, my mood worsened, until I was certain the night would be a blank.

And so it was with great relief when, during the closing measures of the third reprise of the song, I heard someone whistling along.

The whistling grew louder by degrees, as if the whistler were approaching us down a long paved street. I imagined him strolling toward us via some lonely metaphysical thoroughfare, hands in his pockets and his collar undone.

"Walter?"

"Shhh," a voice hissed from somewhere inside the room. "This is the best part," he said, and began singing along in a surprisingly mellifluous voice:

Oh, I'm just wild about,
Cannot do without,
Can't you hear me shout?
Could you ever doubt?
He's just wild about me!

He made us wait until the phonograph finished playing, then gave a loud and exaggerated sigh. I had begun to sense a theme to these musical selections of Walter's, and when he spoke a moment later, my suspicions were confirmed.

"Aren't you just wild about that tune, Crawley?"

There was no reply.

"Crawley?"

"He isn't here," I said, electing myself spokesman for the group. Walter's surprise was genuine. "What?"

"We asked your brother-in-law not to join the circle tonight."

"Why?"

"An experiment."

"And Crawley agreed?" Walter said. "He should've known better. My brother-in-law knows I don't like surprises."

"In all fairness, Dr. Crawley *did* warn us."

"Then listen to him next time," Walter replied testily. "Now I will have to retune the apparatus. You have no idea how much trouble you've caused me."

"There is equipment involved?"

"Of a sort. It's teleplasmic . . ." He searched for words to describe his technology, then gave up in frustration. "It's too complicated to explain. All you need to know is that there are several large pieces of equipment in this room that are terribly sensitive and temperamental. Which is why I don't like anyone mucking about in here during the day, especially not that toothy little bastard with the peg leg. So henceforth I would appreciate it, gentlemen, if you'd save your 'experiments' for the lab!"

"I'm sorry," I said. "I had no idea."

Walter seemed to accept my apology grudgingly. Something caught his attention. "What's this on the windowsill?"

"A Dictograph transmitter," I explained. "It's allowing Dr. Crawley to hear everything that's being said in this room."

"Can he reply?"

"I'm afraid not."

This appeared to cheer Walter considerably, and I sensed that his chilly mood was beginning to thaw. "Who's the girl with him?"

"A stenographer."

"You're keeping a record of this?"

"Unless you have any objections."

"Not at all," he said, flattered. "I'll have to think of something clever to say."

"You're by no means under any obligation to," I said. "Though perhaps you wouldn't mind answering a few questions we prepared for—"

"She's a choice bit of calico, isn't she?"

"Who?"

"The stenographer."

"Oh," I said, caught off guard by the question and aware that the stenographer was at that moment waiting to hear how I might reply. "Yes," I concurred, "she's very pretty."

"Was my sister jealous?"

I thought back to Mina and the stenographer shaking hands as they were introduced. "Not that I could tell."

"Funny," Walter remarked, "she usually doesn't like to share the spotlight."

"She doesn't seem to mind letting you have the stage."

"That's different," Walter said. "She has no choice."

"Why is that?"

"For reasons I don't entirely understand, we seem incapable of being in the same place at the same time," Walter said. Then he added on a wistful note, "It's by far the cruelest irony of this little metaphysical arrangement. But thems apparently is the rules."

"Whose rules?"

"Wish I could tell you, sport—then I'd know where to send my letter of complaint."

This roused Fox enough for him to enter the conversation. "What do you mean, you don't know?"

"I mean," Walter said casually, "that on the subject of the Divine I'm just as much in the dark as you."

"But . . ." Fox struggled to understand what he was hearing. He shifted his line of inquiry, asked, "Is there no one else there with you?"

"There are others," Walter said. "I hear them sometimes off in the distance."

"What are they doing?"

"Oh, the usual. Moaning and weeping in the valley of tears. That sort of thing. Or calling out 'Hello? Hello?' *ad nauseam.* It's rather like an interminable game of Marco Polo."

"My God!" Fox gasped, then said in a whisper, "You're in *hell.* . . ."

"No, I've been there," Walter said, "and I distinctly recall the inhabitants speaking French. This is someplace else."

"Purgatory?"

"There's a thought," Walter said. "Although my first guess was Delaware."

"Perhaps you wouldn't mind describing your surroundings," I asked, "to help us imagine it."

"*Locum refrigerii, lucis et pacis.*"

I tensed. "Is there a reason you just answered in Latin?"

"That's what you're after, isn't it, sport?"

"After?"

"Proof—something Mina couldn't possibly know."

"The contest rules don't recognize auditory phenomena," I said, retreating from what I felt had been a personal attack. "That includes all forms of 'automatic speech.' I'm afraid you'll have to do better if you want to win the *Scientific American* prize."

"*Non do un cazzo del tuo premio!*" Walter snapped. As quickly as it appeared, his anger faded, and he asked in a silken voice, "*Cosa bisogna, carissimo, per convincerti che veramente esisto?*"

My chest tightened. I counted off the seconds until my own temper had subsided, refusing to rise to his bait.

"My father insisted I speak English growing up," I said. "I don't speak Italian."

"Neither does Mina," Walter said.

Somewhere nearby I imagined the stenographer scribbling frantically in an effort to transcribe Walter's words. But if she was frustrated by his Italian, she was about to be defeated by the torrent of gibberish that poured forth from the darkness:

"Gaanong kalayo ang iyong malilipad sa tu-too lang, ibon? Ang iyong bang pak-pak ay matibay at malakas okaya kailangan mo pang mas malakas?"

I concentrated, willing my ear to become a photographic plate on which these exotic-sounding phonemes might leave an impression. But it was like trying to photograph birds in flight—a study in blurs. I was about to ask if anyone in the circle recognized the dialect when there was a violent flapping commotion, as the pregnant dark was delivered of a feathered wet *something* that beat the air with furious wings.

"What the devil . . ."

"Where is it?"

I smelled the musky reek of bird shit and feathers, felt my face spattered with gelatinous droplets thrown from wet wings, prayed that whatever was flapping above our heads didn't have talons.

"Sounds like a parrot."

"Or a pigeon."

I knew there was one person who could tell us.

"What is it, Walter?" I called into the dark.

"Not much. Just a little keepsake," Walter said, in a weary voice that bespoke the great and exhausting effort it had taken to summon it. "A token of affection. For you, sport."

"Why me?"

In reply I heard only his famous chuckle, growing fainter now, receding into the fathoms. I repeated my question but heard no answer.

To my right Fox said, "I think he's gone, Finch."

To my right I heard Mina's breath catch in her throat.

"She's coming out of it."

"Someone get the lights."

As the kerosene lamp was ignited and the room warmed with its rosy light, we had our first glimpse of the "keepsake" Walter had given me: a drenched pigeon, perched on the sill beside the Dictograph transmitter. Its feathers were slick with what looked like well-beaten egg white, the same gelatinous stuff I felt clinging to my cheeks, saw speckling the surprised expressions of the others: "teleplasm." I scraped some of the jellied goo off my face, to send off to a lab for analysis.

Crawley appeared in the doorway, and I showed it to him.

"Shouldn't be too difficult to have it analyzed," he told me, studying the whitish slime. "I'll have a pathologist at Jefferson take a look at it."

We turned our attention to our living specimen. The pigeon pecked the window once and cooed a question at its reflection, as if inquiring of its twin how the two had managed to change places on opposite sides of the looking glass.

. . .

After the others had left (Flynn giving me a wide berth) and Mina was helped to bed and the pigeon toweled dry and given a home in an old bamboo birdcage from the attic, I retired to the upstairs library with a very large brandy and the transcript of the evening's séance.

I had been pleased to discover that our stenographer, Miss Binney, had a good ear for languages and thus had done a fair job of transcribing Walter's outbursts. I reviewed the transcript now in the library, the caged pigeon my only companion.

Q. Perhaps you wouldn't mind describing your surroundings, to help us imagine it.

A. Locum refrigerii, lucis et pacis.

A place of comfort, light, and peace. Another one of Walter's jokes. I sensed something else lurking behind the words, which had clearly been meant for me alone. Not because it was couched in Latin: I had no doubt Fox and Richardson, given their backgrounds, had a working knowledge of the dead language. But the quote itself would have been lost on anyone but a Roman Catholic. It was a quote I recognized from my days as an altar boy, a snippet of the *Commemoratio pro defunctis*—the Prayer for the Dead.

My eyes skipped ahead to another part of the transcript.

Q. Is there a reason you just answered in Latin?

A. That's what you're after, isn't it, sport?

Q. After?

A. Proof—something Mina couldn't possibly know.

Q. The contest rules don't recognize auditory phenomena. That includes all forms of automatic speech. I'm afraid you'll have to do better if you want to win the SCIENTIFIC AMERICAN prize.

A. Non do un cazzo del tuo premio! Cosa bisogna, carissimo, per convincerti che veramente esisto?

Q. My father insisted I speak English growing up. I don't speak Italian.

Strictly speaking, I had been truthful. My father *had* insisted I speak English exclusively, and as a result I was limited in my speech to only the most rudimentary Italian phrases. But like many a child who is curious what his parents are arguing about, I'd picked up quite a bit by listening and could understand the gist of conversational Italian.

As I looked at Walter's words now, my heart stilled and I felt the hairs along my arm stand up. Though the house was asleep and I was alone in the library, I couldn't shake the feeling that Walter was standing somewhere just behind me . . . speaking angrily, and then with an unsettling intimacy.

A. *I don't give a fuck about your prize! What will it take, darling, to convince you I truly exist?*

· 9 ·

"Does he seem melancholy to you?"

This was the question Mina greeted me with the next morning as I came downstairs to breakfast.

"Does who seem melancholy?"

She gestured for me to have a look at the guest of honor at the Crawley table—Walter's pigeon.

It was typical of Mina to worry about another creature's well-being when her own health was suffering, and I had to hide my distress at her appearance. Her face was sallow, and her eyes had lost much of their vibrancy and most of their color. When she spoke, it was clear her throat was raw and uncomfortable.

But then she hadn't asked my opinion of her own health, so I peered through the bamboo bars at the bird, blinking at me from its perch, and offered my inexpert opinion.

"It does look a bit, well . . . *underfed.*"

"Ha!" Mina said triumphantly. "Did you hear that, Arthur?"

From behind his open newspaper, Crawley muttered, "You're welcome to feed it the rest of my toast."

"He won't take it," Mina said, trying to tempt the pigeon with a crust from her own plate.

"Perhaps he doesn't like marmalade," I suggested.

176 · *Joseph Gangemi*

"Do you really think so?"

Crawley gave me a look over the top of his newspaper that said I shouldn't encourage her.

"I'm joking," I said. "Pigeons aren't exactly known as picky eaters."

"Filthy beggars," Crawley grumbled. "Rats with wings is all they are."

"Arthur."

"It's true," Crawley said, folding his newspaper and laying it beside his untouched breakfast. "I've seen the dreadful creatures fighting over a chicken wing. Can you imagine that? How would you like it, my dear, if you came downstairs one morning and found Finch and myself playing tug-of-war with Mrs. Grice's wishbone?"

"I believe," Mina replied, "I would be relieved to find you with an appetite for a change." And she leaned over to give her husband an affectionate peck on the cheek.

Crawley took a last sip of coffee and rose from the table. He left his wife with instructions to spend the day resting and me with orders to make sure she did. Before he could escape the breakfast room, Mina called to him.

"Don't forget to ask Freddy to stop at Woolworth's for birdseed."

"I will," Crawley promised. "Did I mention I seem to have lost another set of cuff links?"

"Which ones?" Mina said, with polite disinterest.

"The platinum-and-gold caducei, from the Twilight Sleep Association."

"Poor forgetful darling," Mina said, kissing him on the temple.

"Take my advice, Finch," Crawley said, "when you reach the age of forty-five—stop. Any older is a dreadful nuisance." And he wandered off.

No sooner had Crawley departed than the Siamese leaped up

onto his empty chair at the breakfast table to investigate the bird-cage. Mina shooed the cat away, then resumed worrying over her feathered patient.

"Do you think the cage is too small for him?"

I studied the lachrymose bird. "You really should consider setting it free."

"But what if he's unwell?"

Before I could respond to this, we looked up to see Crawley standing there in the doorway in his hat and gloves, his face ashen.

"Darling, what's wrong?" Mina asked.

"There are reporters outside."

"Reporters!" I rose from my chair. "What do they want?"

"They wish to speak to 'Margery.' "

"Who is she?" Mina asked.

"Apparently *you* are, my dear. According to this morning's *New York Times*."

"I don't understand. . . ."

But I did. My stomach seized like a fist. "Flynn."

Crawley nodded. "He's given us all pseudonyms," he said, sinking into a chair without removing his overcoat. "I'm called 'Archibald Crumley.' "

"And Walter?" Mina asked.

" 'Chester.' " Crawley raised his confused eyes to mine. "I didn't know what to say, Finch, so I just . . . came back inside."

I threw down my napkin, was surprised to hear myself reassuring the Crawleys, "I'll deal with them." I left them huddled in each other's arms, looking shell-shocked.

Outside, I found the three reporters loitering on the sidewalk, trying to bribe information out of Crawley's driver with cigarettes and thermoses of coffee. Freddy shot me a look that asked something on the order of, *Shall I put the boot to these tossers, guv?* I gestured for him to hold his ground and, in doing so, drew the attention of the reporters, who left Freddy and converged on me like horseflies.

The first to reach me was a bright-eyed kid of about twenty, eager as a spaniel, in a suit that he'd obviously purchased off the rack for his first city job.

"Good morning, can you spare a few minutes to comment on the Margery case for the *Inquirer*—"

But before the spaniel could get any further, he was elbowed aside by one of his older colleagues, a weather-beaten veteran in a shapeless fedora and rumpled suit.

"Name's Livoy," he said. "I'm with the *Public Ledger*."

"How do you do, Mr. Livoy."

"Call me Frank," he said, stuffing his hand into my own, then offering me a cigarette. "What can I call you, champ?"

I nearly slipped and told him my name but caught myself. " 'Champ' will do."

I heard Freddy snort. Livoy's expression took on the long-suffering look of a statue that had just sighted an approaching flock of pigeons. I might have felt sorry for the man, except for the fact that he had camped out here on the Crawley doorstep with the intention of ambushing Mina.

Livoy took out a hand-rolled cigarette and gestured with it toward the house behind me. "Is Margery in there?"

"I think you're mistaken."

"Doubt it," he said, opening a copy of the early edition of the *Times* and scanning its columns until he found Flynn's, which I saw bore the headline THE WITCH OF RITTENHOUSE SQUARE. The son of a bitch must have filed the story immediately after leaving last night's séance.

Livoy read aloud, " 'The home where Margery lives and which Chester haunts is on the corner of a quiet, tree-named street in one of the Quaker City's nicer neighborhoods. It might not look like your typical haunted house, but then the chatty spook who shows up nightly isn't your typical ghost, and neither is the pretty witch he calls 'sister.' Typical or not, the brother-and-sister act performed nightly in a séance room on the third floor is certainly the most convincing *Scientific American* has yet encountered, which is why it seems increasingly likely Margery will clinch the esteemed magazine's five-thousand-dollar prize—' "

Livoy looked up. "Should I keep reading?"

"No."

"Good. I hate reading copy out loud," he said, wrinkling his nose in distaste. "Feels like wearing another guy's damp swim-suit." He tucked the newspaper under his armpit like a man headed for the toilet and got back down to business.

"So, champ. Maybe now you'd care to comment on Margery?"

He stared me in the eye, knowing he had me on the ropes. When I grudgingly gave my statement, it was through clenched teeth. "The *Scientific American* investigation is still ongoing."

"Have you spoken with Chester?"

"I'm not going to answer that."

"Why? It's a harmless question."

"There's no such thing as a harmless question," I replied, then told Livoy and his loitering colleagues, "Now I'm going to have to ask you gentlemen to leave." I was hoping to purchase their coop-eration with a little courtesy, but Livoy wasn't buying it.

"Sorry," he said. "My editor told me not to come back without a statement from Margery."

"Then you'd better start looking for another job."

Livoy's eyes went dead. "You're a real wise guy, aren't you?" He picked tobacco off his tongue, scrutinized the fleck on his pinkie finger a moment before flicking it away. "Let me tell you some-thing, champ—I know how to wait. I've outwaited a kaiser"—he lit his cigarette—"three wives, and more kidney stones than I can count. So I sure as shit can outwait some Joe Zilsh from Harvard."

"I think you've given that speech before," I said, trying to maintain a hard-boiled exterior, though inside I was reeling at the speed with which these jackals had sniffed out a story.

Livoy blew a smoke ring at me. "I've given 'em *all* before, champ." I waited for the smoke ring to dissipate in the morning chill, but it only hung there whirling between us, obstinate as the man who'd made it.

. . .

The Crawleys remained indoors the rest of the morning, prisoners in their own home.

Crawley phoned the hospital to cancel all of his surgeries scheduled for the day and learned from the ward sister that a reporter from the *Bulletin* had been there earlier inquiring about him. Mina passed several hours on the low divan in Crawley's waiting room, peeking through the curtains from time to time at the reporters lurking outside. By silent consensus Crawley and I had agreed to keep the details of Flynn's *Times* article from her, as if it were a diagnosis of some terminal illness. I could only imagine what it would do to her already delicate health to learn she had been branded "The Witch of Rittenhouse Square."

I stayed with the Crawleys for the duration of the morning, providing distracting conversation and what little moral support I could muster. But I was eager to confront Flynn, and so after lunch, when the Javelle-water man came with his monthly delivery of bleach, I asked if he would allow me to sneak away in the back of his wagon. He agreed and dropped me off a few blocks away. I wasted no time, making a beeline for the Bellevue-Stratford.

There I found Fox and Richardson enjoying a leisurely lunch in the Oak Room, the Bellevue's enclosed roof-garden restaurant.

To my surprise, neither seemed particularly upset by Flynn's article in the *Times*.

"It was bound to happen," Fox said, buttering a roll. "You might be accustomed to receiving extensions on your term papers, Finch, but the rest of us have editors to answer to."

I was aghast. "And it doesn't bother you that he scooped the *Scientific American*?"

"He didn't 'scoop' anyone," Fox said. "Oh, he might have tipped our hand a bit more than I'd have liked. But he didn't give away the game."

"What's to stop him from giving it away next time?"

"A gentleman's agreement."

"Flynn isn't a gentleman!"

Richardson rolled his eyes. "For goodness' sake, sit down, Finch, you're making a scene."

A waiter brought their lunch, while the maître d' inquired at my elbow, "Shall I bring another place setting, sir?"

"No thank you, I'm not eating."

"You should," Fox said around a mouthful of roast duckling. "You need to learn to relax, Finch—before you worry yourself into an early grave."

"Take time to smell the roses," Richardson said, gesturing with his fork through the windows. "They're right out there."

I thought this was his way of telling me to take a flying leap, until I looked and saw a rooftop rose garden just beyond the restaurant's French doors. Although there were no roses in bloom at this time of year, a few of the hardier hotel guests were braving the gusty cold to take in the panoramic views of center city.

I turned back to the table. "I can't relax—not when we gave the Crawleys our word we would protect their privacy."

"I don't recall giving anyone my word," Fox said.

My mouth dropped open in surprise, and I noticed that my

hand had gone white-knuckled where it gripped the back of a cane chair. Suddenly it became clear to me, and I understood why they were taking Flynn's column with such equanimity.

"You're glad Flynn jumped the gun, aren't you?" I said, then continued, without waiting for his denial, "You think by dragging this investigation before the court of public opinion, you're going to force my hand, force me to vote your way."

"Careful Malcolm," Richardson said over the rim of his wineglass. "He must be angry—he's mixing his metaphors."

"I *am* angry," I said, then added the threat that the imp I kept on retainer had just whispered in my ear: "Angry enough to go to the press myself."

Fox laid down his fork. "What are you saying?"

"I'm saying that I'm giving serious consideration to going to the papers with the *real* story behind this investigation," I said. "How the *Scientific American* is more concerned with its circulation than with conducting a serious inquiry. How its investigators spend more time in speakeasies than séances. And how the only things anyone really seems interested in testing are the upper limits of an expense account!"

For once Fox seemed to have forgotten about his food. His voice went cold and flat as he asked, "What do you want?"

I opened my mouth to speak, but nothing came out. I hadn't planned this far ahead.

"If you're going to play the blackmailer," Richardson said, fastidiously removing the bones from his fish with a knife, "you really should come prepared with a list of demands." And then, to Fox's astonishment, not to mention my own, the mathematician offered a suggestion to get my list started. "For instance, you might demand that Malcolm here issue a statement to the press—"

"What are you *doing?*" Fox hissed.

"—reiterating that, regardless of what people may read in the newspapers, this committee has yet to reach any conclusions regarding the authenticity of the 'Margery' mediumship."

"Do you think he'll go for that?" I asked.

Richardson rinsed his palate with a sip of wine, mulled this question a moment, concluded, "I believe so. After all, so far as I can see, you have him by the short hairs."

I turned to Fox, indicated that this indeed was my first demand. In that moment Fox resembled one of those sideshow performers who are able to swallow various small items—a silver dollar, a lightbulb, a watch—and regurgitate them in whatever order the audience requests. The item he was currently struggling to bring forth from his throat was a single word: "Done."

It had taxed Fox enormously to croak this simple response. But this particular audience member wasn't satisfied yet. And anyway, Richardson had inspired me.

"I have another demand."

"You little—"

"Did I mention the reporter I met outside the Crawley house this morning?" I said innocently. "From the *Inquirer*? Young fellow, my age or thereabouts. No doubt struggling to make a name for himself. I'm sure he would love nothing more than an opportunity to break a *Scientific American* scandal."

I cut my eyes to Richardson to see how I was doing. "Don't press your luck," he warned.

Fox hissed, "What else do you want?

"That you make a gentleman's agreement with *me*."

"What are the conditions?"

"One more week of séances," I said, "with no interference from you, employing whatever experimental controls I deem necessary."

Fox made a strangled noise and stood up from his chair. He glared at Richardson, at me, at the other diners witness to his public humiliation. Then threw down his napkin and stormed off to the elevators. It took a moment for an express elevator to arrive, so Fox was forced to stand there a dozen yards off, pretending he was invisible and quietly fuming.

I turned back to Richardson. "Thank you."

"It wasn't a favor," Richardson said, pushing his lunch away and signaling a waiter for coffee. He looked at me with eyes clear as gin. "Don't mistake me for an ally, Finch. I find this little witch-hunt you are on just as distasteful as Fox does."

"Then what was that all about a few moments ago?"

Richardson took out an Egyptian cigarette and tamped it against the white ibis on the tin. He lit the cigarette and inhaled deeply, as if my question required a more rapid infusion of nicotine than his pipe could offer. "That was about leveling the playing field."

I looked at the mathematician, with his tailored suit and affected manners, and narrowed my eyes. "So this is just a game to you, is that it?"

"Game?" Richardson's brows lifted in surprise. "No, it certainly isn't a game—otherwise I never would have risked making an enemy of Malcolm just now." His expression took on the gravity of a military officer's estimating casualties on the eve of an important campaign.

"I don't understand."

He filled his lungs with smoke. "I don't expect you to. You're young; this is just an intellectual challenge for you. A little puzzle en route to your Ph.D. But there is considerably more at stake for the rest of us." He fingered the unlit end of his cigarette with his thumb, his eyes unfocusing. A waiter brought coffee, inquired if I would like him to bring a second cup and saucer.

"No," Richardson answered for me. "My young friend here was just leaving. He has very important business to attend to," he said, meeting my eyes across the linen tablecloth, "not to mention a great many people counting on him to see it through to its finish. Isn't that right, Finch?"

"Yes."

"Very good, sir," the uncomfortable waiter said, and left us. I was about to follow him when Richardson stopped me.

"One question before you go, Finch."

"Yes?"

"How do you explain the pigeon?"

"It's a fairly routine illusion," I said with an offhand shrug. "The bird is concealed in a hidden compartment, under the floorboards, say. Or in a chair with a false bottom."

"A hidden compartment, of course," Richardson said, nodding. "And the teleplasm?"

"A nice touch," I conceded, "but it doesn't prove anything. At least not until the pathologist's report comes back."

"Indeed."

Richardson flashed a wan smile, indicating he had anticipated as much. But as he reached for another cigarette, he forgot his composure, and I glimpsed disappointment. I said good-bye and left him there in his sunny aerie overlooking the city, surrounded by animated diners and bustling waiters, looking for all the world like the loneliest man alive.

. . .

Richardson was wrong on one point: This investigation meant far more to me than just an "intellectual challenge." And I had the black eye to prove it.

Just what it did mean remained a tangled question in my mind—and, at present, my conscience. How was I going to make good now on McLaughlin's promise to safeguard the Crawleys' privacy? *No,* I thought, revising the question, *not McLaughlin's promise*—your *promise.* I might have come here to Philadelphia as McLaughlin's representative, but at some point over the last few days, I had taken upon myself Mina and Arthur Crawley's fate. Which was why the three reporters on their doorstep that morning felt like a personal failure. I didn't hold out much hope that the statement I'd just blackmailed out of Fox would deter these newshounds. I would have to come up with something more clever if I wanted to throw them off the scent.

I knew I should return to 2013 Spruce, but I wasn't yet ready to face the besieged house. So I found an Automat and bought a birch beer and a liverwurst sandwich, then walked to Cugley & Mullen's (which advertised itself as "The Largest Pet Shop in the World") for a ten-pound sack of birdseed for the pigeon. Finally, unable to procrastinate any longer in good conscience, I slung the birdseed over my shoulder and trudged back to Rittenhouse Square with all the enthusiasm of a soldier on a forced march.

As I approached the corner of Twentieth and Spruce Streets, I was surprised to find the sidewalk outside the Crawley residence empty and all the reporters gone. What was this? Had they really lost interest in "Margery" so soon? But then I saw a reporter arrive and scurry up the front steps of the house; a moment later the front door opened to admit him. I felt my heart sink. With a feeling of dread, I followed, and soon discovered Crawley's new strategy for dealing with the press.

There were a dozen reporters convened in the downstairs parlor, the three men I had seen that morning—Livoy gave me a wink—along with several more from outlying papers and radio stations. Mrs. Grice was serving coffee in Mina's best china, while Pike made rounds with a bottle of his employer's good brandy.

Crawley looked up as I appeared in the parlor doorway.

"Ah! Here he is." Before I had a chance to draw him aside and question the wisdom of this impromptu press conference, Crawley announced to the room, "Gentlemen, allow me to introduce Mr. Martin Finch, chairman of the *Scientific American* investigating committee."

"I'm not the chairman—"

"Is that 'Finch' like the bird?" someone asked, and before I knew what was happening, I was spelling my name and detailing my affiliation with Harvard University. I felt the heady sensation of being on a runaway train and knew I had better put on the brakes before we jumped the tracks and wound up in a public-relations disaster.

"Gentlemen—please," I called, motioning for silence. "I cannot comment on any details of this investigation until it has concluded and our findings are announced in *Scientific American*. In the meantime I'm going to have to insist you refrain from printing any of our names in your newspapers. Also I'd ask that you please respect the privacy of Dr. Crawley and his wife—"

"It's all right, Finch," Crawley said, sidling up beside me and sounding very like a politician on the stump as he addressed his audience, "We have nothing to be ashamed of! My wife has a very rare and special talent—and I don't care who knows it!"

"Your patients might care," I warned in a low voice.

"Let them hang, then!"

The reporters laughed, raised their coffee cups to Crawley in salute. Now my old friend Livoy called out, "C'mon, champ, you gotta give us something we can run. Can't you give us a little hint which way your committee is leaning?"

I could feel Crawley looking at me, just as interested as the reporters in my reply.

"It is this committee's opinion," I said carefully, "that *Margery* is a remarkable woman."

Around the parlor heads bowed and Eversharp pencils began scribbling furiously in notepads. All except for Livoy's. While his colleagues took down my nonstatement, he only stared at me with the crafty eyes of an old crocodile.

"You enjoying your visit to the Quaker City, champ?"

"It's been very pleasant."

"You're staying at the Bellevue?"

"Most of the committee is, yes."

Livoy pretended to be surprised. "But not you?"

"No," I replied, wondering where the newshound was headed with all this. By now a few of the other reporters had looked up from their scribbling, and so, for their benefit, I explained, "The Bellevue was booked up when I arrived, and Dr. Crawley and his wife were kind enough to invite me to stay here as their guest."

"Isn't that a conflict of interest?"

"What?"

"Accepting their hospitality."

"Maybe you should tell me—you're drinking his brandy."

Livoy showed me a smile that was all teeth, raised his cup. *This man is dangerous,* I thought.

Luckily, I was saved from further cross-examination when one of the radio reporters called out, "Can we speak to Margery?"

"Well, now," Crawley said, "she's a bit bashful, but I can see if she might not be willing to come downstairs for a few—"

I stepped in. "I'm afraid that's out of the question, gentlemen." Gripping Crawley's arm, I whispered sternly, "If you don't mind, I'd like a word with you in *private,* Doctor."

I steered him out of the room to the front hall, where we could confer out of the reporters' earshot.

"I understand that you feel you have nothing to hide," I began, "but I don't think this was a very good idea."

"You're overreacting," Crawley said, eager to return to the parlor. *You do like an audience, don't you, Crawley?* Walter's words of a few nights earlier came floating back. *Gives you squirrel fever.*

"I don't want to see you and Mrs. Crawley made laughing-stocks," I said, "just so those men in there can sell a few newspapers."

At last I seemed to have gotten through to Crawley. After musing a moment on my warning, he nodded, said, "You're right, Finch. We mustn't make it too easy for them. What is it show people always say? *Gotta leave 'em wanting more!*"

He gripped my shoulder and gave it a squeeze.

"That's not quite what I meant—"

But Crawley was already on his way back to the parlor— and his adoring public. I caught up with him in time to hear him announce to the reporters in the voice of a veteran impresario that Margery was resting in anticipation of her next session before the *Scientific American* committee and thus could not be disturbed. He thanked the reporters for coming, invited them to stay and enjoy Mrs. Grice's refreshments, and with a short bow made his exit.

I might have been heartened by this performance if I hadn't found him on the kitchen phone a few minutes later with Gimbel's department store, arranging for the rush delivery of a cabinet radio so that he and Mina might hear themselves—or at least their pseudonyms—mentioned on the evening news. I leaned in the kitchen doorway and watched Crawley barking orders into the phone, transformed before my worried eyes into that harried and vainglorious species of *Homo sapiens*—the Celebrity.

. . .

Within the hour two men in caps and overalls delivered a new Florentine cabinet radio to 2013 Spruce.

The commotion had woken Mina, who sat on the bottom stair in a robe of tangerine silk and watched with amusement as the deliverymen installed the radio in the parlor by the lone electrical outlet. She had long been campaigning for a radio—everyone was buying them that Christmas, now that all the department stores had started radio stations—but until now Crawley had refused to allow one into the house. Crawley, a Luddite through and through, distrusted anything that had to be plugged in; his disdain was not limited to radios but also included the latest laborsaving devices—vacuum sweepers and the like—touted in the Sears catalog, which Pike and Mrs. Grice were always pining over.

But now, in the space of a single afternoon, Crawley's mistrust seemed to evaporate in the radiant glow of the cabinet radio's warming vacuum tubes. He ran his hand over the fine woodwork, admiring the exquisite cherry inlays and smooth satin finish; he tuned the dial tenderly, as he might palpate a patient's ovary, and clucked in wonderment as this miracle of Marconi's plucked from the ether heavenly music—which at this hour and frequency just happened be "Yes! We Have No Bananas" reinterpreted as a rumba by the Ray Lamere Orchestra and broadcast live from the studio of Lit Brothers department store. So tickled was Crawley by this technological marvel that he didn't even seem to mind the song and listened with a silly grin on his face, as if he had taken a snort of nitrous.

I watched Crawley delight in each new station he came upon. WLIT, "The Quaker City Siren." WCAU, "Where Cheer Awaits U." The irony was not lost on me that he seemed more amazed by the radio's ability to pick up Gimbel's and Wanamaker's stations than by the fact that his wife could communicate with her dead brother. But then Crawley and I were the products of different centuries; and for me, who had built my first radio out of a cat whisker and a Quaker Oats container nearly a decade before, electromagnetism was as second nature as supernaturalism must have seemed to him. I could only assume I wore the same amazed look in the séance room hearing Walter's disembodied voice as Crawley did listening now to the evening stock-market report.

As the broadcast segued to other topics, Crawley called his wife over to join him before the radio. Mina knelt at his feet, hugging his calves protectively, as if they were on some high precipice and he was threatening to leap. Crawley sat on the edge of his seat and absently stroked her hair as we listened to the international news of the day: revolt in Mexico, squabbling in the Ruhr. The United States was entering the war-reparations debate, while the Greater Tokyo Reconstruction Board was picking up the pieces from September's devastating earthquake. The biggest local news was Mayor-elect Kendrick's successful bid to bring Brigadier General Smedley Butler to Philadelphia in an attempt to clean up its crime-ridden streets—a move the outgoing administration had tried vigorously to block. Crawley attempted to give me the short course in Philadelphia politics—something about City Hall's being a cog in the greater Republican machine controlled by the Vare brothers, which was subsidized at the ward level by graft and vice—but I wasn't really interested, and I sensed Crawley wasn't either. He was only trying to distract himself from the agony of waiting.

When the local news concluded soon after without mention of their story, Crawley sat for several moments in confused silence. He looked winded, like a man who'd just tripped on a false step and gone sprawling. But then I suppose it *had* been a fall for him: from the heights of raised expectations. He looked at the radio as if he'd been betrayed by science itself. It taunted him with a Christmas program for children, broadcast live from the Adelphia Hotel.

"Well," he said at last, clapping his hands on his knees and rising to his feet stiffly. "I wonder what's for dinner?" he asked, and wandered off to the kitchen to find out.

"Poor darling," Mina whispered, staring after her husband. "He puts on a brave face, but he's suffered so terribly for his beliefs. People don't understand how sensitive he is. I wish those awful reporters hadn't gotten his hopes up."

But I was only half listening. Mina's silk robe had fallen open partially, revealing the top of one pale breast. There I saw a small raised discoloration, too perfect to be a birthmark or a blemish or anything so innocent as a freckle. It resembled a drip of candle wax and could only have been a scar. For reasons I couldn't explain, an image flashed to mind: a martyr's breast pierced by a flaming arrow. But now I was mixing up my saints, since it had been St. Sebastian who had been shot full of arrows, and so far as I remembered, none of them had been flaming—

I realized then that Mina had stopped talking, and by the time I looked up, I knew it was too late, that she had caught me red-handed. Given the scar's location, I couldn't very well ask her how she'd gotten it without admitting I'd been staring at her chest. I dropped my eyes, blushing furiously. But when I stole a glance back up at her to see if she was angry with me, I found something in her face I hadn't expected and didn't understand: permission.

She caught my eyes with her gaze and held it, then, without uttering a word, took my hand. She guided it inside her robe, pressed my fingers against her breast so they were forced to feel its soft weight. The scar felt like a wax seal on a letter as I caressed it with the pad of my thumb. Mina shut her eyes, seemed to lose herself in that secret inner place where she retreated in séances. She raised my hand higher, forcing it to cup one breast. I could feel her heart beating against my hand. Her expression was inscrutable, at first urgent, then listening, then lost. What did she want me to understand? My fingers instinctively strayed to her nipple, and her expression changed, becoming troubled, as if she'd just received unpleasant news. She came out of her momentary trance, blinked at me like a waking amnesic, seemed surprised to find my hand inside her robe. I pulled it away, and she reached up to pinch closed the neck of her robe.

With a fierce look full of confusion and hurt, she rose to her feet and fled upstairs, leaving me alone in the dim parlor before the quietly hissing radio.

· · ·

"Gising ka na!"

A hand shook my shoulder roughly, rousing me from a dream in which my mother had returned from the dead but refused to eat any of her favorite dishes at her welcome-home supper.

I opened one sleep-sticky eye and discovered Pike and Crawley standing over my bed, both men wearing hats and overcoats. The butler switched on the bedside lamp, filling the guest room with rose-tinted light.

"Get dressed," Crawley whispered.

"What time is it?"

"Half past four. There's a cab waiting for us at the other end of the alley."

"Cab?" I sat up against among the tangle of blankets, yawning and disoriented. "Where are we going?"

"Lying-In Hospital."

"In the middle of the night?"

"Lower your voice, old man—you'll wake Mina."

Before I knew what was happening, Pike had thrown back the covers and swung my bare legs around so he could help me into my trousers. He was surprisingly strong for such a little fellow.

"Would somebody mind telling me what's going on?"

Crawley checked his pocketwatch, explained, "Pike and I are needed in surgery. I thought you might find it amusing to come along."

"Surgery? But I—"

"Just put your shoes on," Crawley called on his way out the door, promising to fill me in further once we had successfully slipped down the alley and past the few insomniac reporters out front.

I did as instructed—not that I had much choice, given how the Filipino valet was manhandling me—and within moments found myself sandwiched between Pike and Crawley in the backseat of a taxi speeding away from the alley behind 2013 Spruce.

As promised, Crawley briefed me en route to the hospital. It seemed that shortly after midnight, the daughter of a city alderman had been admitted in advanced labor, her os dilated to three and one-quarter inches. Despite the mother's minor pelvic deformity, the physician on duty had decided to proceed with a natural delivery; but when attempts to manipulate the infant's head into the brim failed, it was determined Crawley should be summoned to deliver the child via cesarean section.

"Barring complications, we'll be home before Mina realizes we ever left," Crawley told me as the cab stopped outside Jefferson Lying-In.

As Pike paid the driver, I caught Crawley's arm and drew him aside to ask the question that had been nagging me throughout the ride.

"What's Pike doing here?"

"Oh, he assists me from time to time," Crawley replied airily. "In addition to being a *manghihilot,* he is also a damned capable anesthetist"—lowering his voice—"certainly better than the old battle-ax on duty tonight." He brightened as the cab drove off and Pike joined us on the sidewalk. "We make quite a team, don't we, old friend?" Crawley said sentimentally.

The Filipino gave a monosyllabic grunt that was the extent of his effusiveness, then strode on ahead of us through the hospital's entrance.

"He certainly seems in a hurry."

"Has to be," Crawley said, then explained that induction by ether required half an hour and thus necessitated a significant head start for the anesthetist.

We went indoors. Crawley ushered me upstairs and turned me over to an exhausted-looking intern. I was shown to a dressing room, told where to hang my belongings, and given a pair of sterile linen overalls. As I began stripping out of my clothes, I became aware of a tremor in my hands; until that moment I'd been too preoccupied to give much thought to what was waiting for me in the next room, but now that I was here and donning a surgical gown, the reality of what I was about to witness hit me full force. A chill that had nothing to do with the temperature crept up my legs from the floor tiles and settled in my intestines.

"Well, don't you look the part!"

I startled, nerves taut as mandolin strings. Crawley retrieved a pair of overalls from the metal drum in the corner of the dressing room and began changing. What had taken me fifteen minutes to accomplish, he managed in three. I wasn't usually in the habit of studying how a man dresses, but I couldn't help noting how ritualized Crawley's movements were as he donned his surgical garb, like a priest or a fencing instructor. Whistling some chipper tune I didn't recognize, he pulled on a pair of black gum boots, then helped me tie my mask before securing his own. These were elaborate affairs with hoods that covered nearly the entire face and head, leaving only the eyes exposed. Crawley then led me into an adjoining room, where I saw a long porcelain trough with rose jets and foot taps delivering hot, cold, and tepid water. I mimicked Crawley's ablutions, lathering my arms to the elbows and giving my cuticles a thorough scrubbing with a nail brush. Next came a quick plunge into an enameled basin of biniodide of mercury before thrusting our hands into India-rubber gloves.

Throughout this ritual I wondered if any of it was really necessary—surely I didn't need to observe aseptic technique if I was only observing—but when I mentioned as much to Crawley, he seemed surprised.

"Observe?" he said. "Why, I wouldn't have bothered bringing you if all I meant was for you to *observe,* old man."

Above his mask Crawley's eyes shone with droll amusement, and he gestured that I should follow him.

The operating theater was a hive of activity as we made our entrance—the theater sister at her instrument table threading needles with No. 2 bichromate catgut, the ward sister painting the expectant mother from navel to pubes with iodine solution, the first assistant making incremental adjustments to the degree of the table's tilt—and there, at the still center of it all, Pike, perched at the patient's head like some Oriental version of the sandman. His eyes met mine briefly across the top of the anesthetist's screen before returning to his delicate task—administering sleep drop by drop to his patient's gauze mask.

Crawley greeted each member of his staff in descending order of station ("Parker . . . Agnes . . . Sister") before addressing them as a group. "If I may have your attention for a moment, we are fortunate to have with us this morning a visitor from Harvard University."

Three masked faces turned my way, eyes revealing no opinion whatsoever with regard to my presence.

"Hello." My voice came out flat and metallic. With all its ceramic tile and enamel surfaces, the operating theater had the acoustics of a men's room.

Crawley continued to his staff, "I trust you will make young Finch here feel welcome to our little operating theater, as well as answer any questions he may have about the procedure we are about to perform."

With these introductory remarks out of the way, Crawley took up his position at the operating table, where he fell into quiet consultation with Pike. The nurses resumed their work, the first assistant began preparing a hypodermic, and for the next few minutes I was relieved to be entirely forgotten. I wasted no time falling back to a corner where I might continue to be overlooked and where I might have the worst possible view of the incision.

But just when my racing pulse was slowing to a more reasonable rhythm, Crawley turned and, with a gloved hand, beckoned me over beside him.

Reluctantly I joined Crawley at the operating table. He administered 1 cc of pituitary extract via a hypodermic in order to "ensure good retractility of the uterus." If this phrase struck an ominous note in my imagination, what Crawley said next to his assistant produced an entire chord.

"Lower her head a little more, Parker—we don't want the poor woman's intestines prolapsing through the wound."

"Yes, Doctor."

The assistant adjusted the table. Then the two surgeons began draping their patient with a sterile linen sheet, taking care that no corners accidentally brushed the tiles underfoot. With drape in place and fastened to the table by towel clips, nothing remained in view of the woman's anatomy (at least on this side of the anesthetist's screen) beyond a swell of iodine-stained belly rising through the sheet's oval cutout. I had read once that draping patients served a psychological—in addition to an antiseptic—function, that it was a crucial piece of ceremony that permitted surgeons to forget for the time being that the violence they were doing with scalpel and bone saw was being committed on another human being.

Another one of the thousand little self-deceptions life demanded of us, I realized, and recalled my own misadventures in gross anatomy, where my lab partner and I had kept our cadaver's face covered with a handkerchief for weeks while we disassembled the thoracic cavity. The human face—that was the memento mori every first-year medical student dreaded dissecting. (Hands, it would turn out, were just as unnerving.) But while I hadn't been alone in my fear of what waited beneath that handkerchief, in the end I had been among the minority in every class who proved constitutionally incapable of overcoming it. *Nothing to be ashamed of,* my faculty adviser had consoled in a highly condescending way. *Some simply aren't cut out for medicine.* But of course I *had* been ashamed; and I carried the shame with me still, like shrapnel.

"Shall we begin?" Crawley asked the room, and requested a Bard Parker No. 15 scalpel.

He took the blade in his right hand like a cellist's bow and, with his left steadying the abdominal wall, made the first cut.

I averted my eyes and, when I braved a glance back, was surprised to see Crawley already clamping the few bleeding points at the periphery of the incision he'd opened from umbilicus to symphysis pubis. It was difficult to say which detail most unsettled me, given how many were in the running. Was it the band of vivid yellow fat, perhaps? Or the way the incised skin lost its elasticity and puckered at the edges? Surprisingly enough, the blood was running a distant third; beneath the operating lights it shone so brightly as to almost look pretty.

"Now," Crawley said, "we incise the linea alba and begin separating the recti." This entailed inserting his index fingers to the second knuckle into the wound and roughly separating the tough muscle fibers that girdle the abdomen. It was close work, and the lips of the incision shook and seeped fresh blood with Crawley's exertions.

Once more I turned away, taking several deep, slow breaths. But instead of steadying me, the influx of oxygen—smelling powerfully of sulfuric ether—only multiplied the swarm of colored gnats swimming in the air before my eyes. My face felt hot, so that I wondered if I were coming down with a fever. I cast about for something other than the wound to focus on and spied one of the patient's hands peeking out from the edge of the drapes; the sight of manicured fingernails and a gold wedding band only served as a reminder of the woman being butchered before my eyes.

"Have a look, Finch!" Crawley exclaimed with the excitement of a man laying eyes on a new ocean. "The peritoneum!"

I forced myself to look. There, indeed, was the peritoneum— that shiny membraneous sac that encases the abdominal cavity and cradles its organs. I glimpsed a white cord running through the membrane and was surprised when its Latin name came springing forth from some dusty cupboard in my memory. The urachus.

I was still marveling at my powers of recall when Crawley offered me a pair of forceps.

"What am I supposed to do with those?"

"Assist me."

Was this a test Crawley was presenting me, or an honor? With his mask obscuring two-thirds of his expression, I couldn't tell. Crawley's assistant seemed to think the latter, judging by the jealous looks he gave me. Opening the peritoneum *did* carry a certain symbolic gravity, the moment when the body's own hermetic seal was broken and the abdominal cavity exposed to the microbe-laden air.

"For heaven's sake, hurry, man—we've a baby to deliver!"

I took the forceps in my hand. Crawley selected an identical pair and demonstrated how to gingerly pinch and lift the membrane. I imitated him, and together we stretched the peritoneum taut. Crawley then expertly nicked the membrane with the tip of his scalpel, explaining how this would allow air to enter the cavity and displace any intestines or omentum that might be adhering to the peritoneum's underside. Working rapidly, Crawley now widened the nick enough for him to slip first his fingers, then his entire hand, inside.

"Now," Crawley explained, "some of my colleagues prefer to deliver the uterus through the abdominal wound before opening it"—he manipulated the pale pink organ so that its anterior side came into view—"but I see no reason for that unless the uterine contents are septic and pose an infection risk. . . ."

But I had stopped listening. I felt woozy, as if my own contents were turning septic. A bead of perspiration itched its way down my back between my shoulder blades.

"Give me your hand, Finch."

I wondered at my disloyal arm rising up at Crawley's command. Taking my hand, Crawley guided it inside the wound, so that before I knew what was happening, I found myself buried to the wrist in another living person, my fingers enveloped in slippery warmth and my only thought at the moment, *Oh.*

"Hold it steady while I open the uterus."

Crawley made another swift incision, and the muscular organ split, spilling liquor amnii. The rush of warm fluid had the effect of temporarily flushing away any blood, leaving the uterus glistening and clean, and revealing through the gap in the uterine wall a miniature blue-mottled foot.

But before I could marvel any further at this perfectly formed miracle, the darkness that had been stealthily encroaching suddenly irised shut—and I fainted dead away on the hospital tiles.

· · ·

An uncertain while later, a vial of ammonia salts was waved beneath my nose, and for the second time that night, I was forcibly awoken.

I coughed, cracked my eyes, found myself stretched out on a leather couch in a dimly lit physicians' lounge. Crawley stoppered the smelling salts and gave me my glasses. I slipped them on, noticed that my hand still smelled of French chalk from inside my rubber gloves.

I started to prop myself up onto my elbows when Crawley put a hand on my chest.

"Lie still."

"What happened?"

"Your appendix burst, I was forced to remove it." And he set a specimen jar on my chest in which a diseased appendix sloshed. To his credit, Crawley maintained his deadpan expression for a full five seconds before breaking into convulsive laughter. Relief washed over me, diluting my anger.

"Very funny."

"Cheer up, old man—you just fainted."

I felt the smallish lump hiding in my hair at the back of my head like an Easter egg. I winced. "How masculine of me."

"The orderlies had a devil of a time carrying you out." He felt my wrist for my pulse and, after ten seconds of silence, inquired in a concerned voice, "How do you feel?"

"Embarrassed."

"No reason to be, old man," he said. "If I had to guess, I'd say your fainting spell was most likely the result of hypoglycemia. You barely touched Mrs. Grice's cassoulet at supper."

I very much doubted that Crawley believed this theory about low blood sugar, but I accepted his kindness nonetheless. He smiled, gave my knee a pat, and stood.

"Do you feel strong enough to stand?" he asked.

"I think so."

"Come along, then—our patient should be coming out of the anesthesia right about now."

As I followed Crawley to the recovery room, he recounted the rest of the cesarean section: the delivery of the child via traction to its leg, the clamping off and cutting of the umbilical cord, the removal of the placenta and membranes, and finally the suturing shut of the uterus. It was this last bit of surgical prowess Crawley seemed most proud of and most disappointed that I had missed.

"I put in three stout mattress sutures of number-four silk and then a single continuous thirty-day catgut to approximate the edges of the uterine wound. . . ."

He trailed off as we arrived at the recovery room and found his patient—a church mouse of a woman aged about twenty—awake and resting against her pillows while her nervous-looking young husband held an emesis basin beneath her chin for her to retch into.

"Hello, my dear," Crawley said, congratulating the mother on the birth of a robust baby boy and reassuring the father that the newborn's off-putting smell of ether was only temporary. They conversed quietly for a few minutes more while I stood by feeling like an extra wheel, until Crawley lifted the woman's dressing to show off the four-inch line of suture he'd used to close the skin incision.

"Some don't bother suturing the subcutaneous fat," he said as I studied his handiwork, "but I believe that the aesthetic advantage outweighs the risks of additional time beneath the ether."

"Oh?"

"Prevents the skin from adhering to the fascia; you don't see any of that dreadful 'guttering' that makes abdominal scars so unsightly." Crawley smoothed the dressing back into place and cast a tender look over his patient, who had drifted off to sleep. "Very important, aesthetics. Especially with the young ones. Just look at her, Finch. Have you ever seen such a sweet face? All of motherhood ahead of her—not to mention a lifetime of marital relations. . . ." This thought seemed to carry him off for a moment, before he snapped back to the present and gave me an arch look. "Far be it from me to interfere with the sacred covenant between a husband and wife, eh, old man! Otherwise I might very soon find myself out of a job!"

· · ·

In the morning we awoke to find a dozen reporters waiting on the sidewalk in front of 2013 Spruce, some of whom had even managed to befriend Freddy. Pike dropped an armload of morning papers on the breakfast table—the Philadelphia *Inquirer*, *Tribune*, *Record*, *Dispatch*, *Bulletin*, and *Public Ledger*—and, leafing through them, we found that each carried at least some mention of "Margery," her "wisecracking spirit control, Chester," and her husband, "celebrated surgeon Archibald Crumley." Even I received mention, under the fairly transparent pseudonym "Morton Bird." The *Bulletin* went so far as to describe me as "a bookish Valentino." Seeing myself compared to a film star gave me a taste of the narcotic allure of the press's affections. Not to mention a better understanding of Crawley's new addiction.

He scrutinized every column inch as if it contained the coded answer to the Sphinx's riddle, chuckled over the choicer bits of journalistic hyperbole, huffed whenever he came across anything in a skeptical key.

"Rubbish," he muttered as he finished Frank Livoy's column in the *Public Ledger*. "He'll be eating crow by week's end."

I picked up the *Ledger* Crawley had tossed aside and skimmed the offending article to see what Livoy had written.

PHILADELPHIA. She is beautiful. He is rich. And together they are charming the wool over the bespectacled eyes of the SCIENTIFIC AMERICAN. Perhaps next time that magazine's editors should consider sending someone more experienced to chair its investigating committee. The young man who currently holds that position hails from the ivy-covered halls of Harvard University and looks as if he was still in short pants when Pershing crossed the Rhine. . . .

My throat constricted. What was Livoy up to? It wasn't his personal attacks that surprised me, nor the fact that he was condemning the Crawleys solely on the grounds of privilege. But just what did the reporter hope to achieve by misrepresenting me as committee chairman? It didn't seem a big enough hook to hang an article on—Stop the presses! Look how inexperienced the committee chairman is!—and so I assumed that Livoy must've had a different reason for intentionally publishing an inaccuracy. It was almost as if he wanted to drive a wedge into the committee, had devised an angle guaranteed to foment unrest within our ranks.

Thus was I introduced to that least distinguished member of the press, the muckraker.

"Are you all right?" Mina asked.

"Fine," I said, returning Livoy's article deep in the folds of the *Public Ledger*, where I hoped it would stay buried. "It's amazing the sort of garbage newspapers get away with printing."

"That's not what I meant," Mina said, feeling my hand and then, finding it warm, my forehead. She pulled her hand away sharply, as if stung. "You're burning up, darling!"

"I'm just angry."

Crawley peered over the top of the paper he was reading and took notice of my color. "You do look a bit peaked, Finch. Let me ring Mrs. Grice for some aspirin—she keeps a bottle in the kitchen."

He reached for the little service bell on the breakfast table, but I stopped him.

"I'll go ask her myself."

Normally Crawley would have insisted I stay put and allow the help to wait on me, but today he was too engrossed in his reading to argue. I got up from the breakfast table and left.

In the kitchen Mrs. Grice looked up from her own newspaper (I noticed she was reading the latest installment in a serial novel called *The Man Tamers* by Mildred Barbour) and blanched at the sight of me standing in her doorway. I don't think she would have been so discomfited had I entered her bedroom and caught her in her peignoir.

"Is something the matter, sir?"

"Headache," I said, nodding hello to Pike, who was trying to coax the pigeon to eat its breakfast seed. "Dr. Crawley said you might help me out with a couple of Bayer tablets."

"He knows I won't have those in the house!" Mrs. Grice said, aghast, as if I had just requested opium. Funny how the tiniest things can touch you: watching Mrs. Grice take down a bottle of American-made aspirin from a cupboard, I was suddenly reminded of my mother and her conviction that the flu epidemic of '18 had been cultured in the Bayer laboratories by the kaiser and his germ warriors. And though five years had passed since those paranoid days, Mrs. Grice's reaction reminded me it would be some time before "Liberty cabbage" could go back to being sauerkraut and "Alsatians" to German shepherds.

I took the aspirins Mrs. Grice offered and swallowed them with a gulp of water from the tap. The tablets seemed to go down sideways and lodge somewhere short of their destination. I thanked Mrs. Grice and was about to exit when I stopped abruptly and turned at something Pike had just said in Tagalog to the caged pigeon. Though I couldn't understand what he was saying, one word he kept repeating seemed to float free from the rest and find its way across the kitchen to me—where it clicked with another in my memory.

"What does that mean, Pike?"

Pike's shoulders tensed. "Eh?"

"That word you keep saying—it sounds like 'ee-bohn.' "

"*Ibon,*" he said, correcting my pronunciation subtly. "It mean 'bird.' " He nodded toward the sullen pigeon in its bamboo cage. "I tell him to eat, that he too skinny he cannot fly."

Ibon: a word I had heard before. Spoken by Walter during his final outburst of glossolalia. An outburst my Western ears had mistaken for gibberish, but which I now understood had been in Tagalog.

"Pike," I said, gripping his arm, "I need your help."

He looked at me with suspicion. I made him promise to wait there in the kitchen for me, then hurried upstairs to my room to fetch the transcript from the séance wherein Walter had spoken in tongues.

Our stenographer had made a valiant effort at capturing the shade's last outburst, transcribing as best she could the long chain of exotic phonemes. Now Pike slipped on a pair of old reading glasses and examined her efforts. I had hoped Walter's message would be immediately clear to the Filipino butler, but one look at Pike's face told me otherwise. I shouldn't have been surprised; it wouldn't have been any easier for me to decode a passage in English if it was broken up phonetically and filtered through the ear of someone other than a native speaker.

I was starting to give up hope when Pike began sounding out the syllables and, in so doing finally managed to crack the code. Our stenographer had heard pauses where there were none, had

been forced to approximate sounds that didn't have a clear ana-
logue in English. Speaking them aloud helped them return to
their proper place. Pike's face lit up with sudden comprehension
as he began to translate.

"He asking, 'How far are you willing to fly for the truth, little
ibon?' "

Little bird—Finch.

"What else does he say?"

The butler ran a finger along the words in the transcript. "He
ask are your wings strong enough," Pike translated, "or do you
need him to give you stronger ones?"

Stronger wings than a finch's . . . My eyes went immediately to
the pigeon, watching me now with that quizzical look of caged
birds. These were the stronger wings Mina's brother wanted me
to have, the stronger wings he'd "given" me. But what was it he
wanted me to do with them?

And then I knew.

. . .

It took the better part of the morning to convince Mina we
should set the pigeon free, that captivity was the real cause of the
bird's melancholy. Mina worried that the pigeon might have sustained internal injuries in its journey through the membrane separating Walter's realm from our own. Or what if it had a broken
wing? she fretted, saying she'd never be able to forgive herself if
we freed the bird only to have it immediately fall victim to one of
the neighborhood's many cats.

I seized on this last argument of Mina's and used it to my
advantage.

"I'll take him to the square," I said, surprised how easily the lie
came to me, "and set him loose among the other pigeons."

In spite of her husband's warning that pigeons carried disease,

Mina extended a finger through the bars of the cage and stroked its feathers.

"Do you think the others will accept him?"

I assured Mina I fully expected the pigeon to be welcomed back into feathered society, where he would no doubt enjoy all the rights and privileges due him.

"Must you always be so flippant?" Mina said irritably.

I wondered what other times she was thinking of. I apologized, then watched in silence as she bade her temporary pet farewell.

Twenty minutes later I was striding across Rittenhouse Square with the Malaysian birdcage in one hand and a borrowed pair of binoculars in the other. I'd requested the latter as part of my second lie: that I wanted to observe our bird from a safe distance once I had released him, to make certain the other pigeons didn't mistreat him. Of course, I had no intention of releasing the bird in the park. I had other plans for him.

And so I continued across the square and out its northeast corner, turning up Walnut on my way to the Bellevue-Stratford.

You might think it would be difficult to smuggle a pigeon into a first-class hotel, but that would be to underestimate the bizarre foot traffic even the best hotels see on a daily basis. No one raised an eyebrow as I crossed the lobby, and the only question directed my way on my ascent to the roof garden came from the elevator boy, who wanted to know my bird's name.

"Don't know," I admitted, thinking, *I just hope it doesn't turn out to be Icarus.*

Outside on the rooftop garden, it felt like a different day: blustery and blue, a Sunday-colored sky—as if the hotel had imported better weather for its wealthy clientele. The gusts had kept most sightseers indoors, so I had the garden to myself. I carried the birdcage over to a remote corner of the rooftop, doing my best to ignore the fact that I was twenty stories above the side-walks of center city. But it was hard to avoid the dizzying view. It kept turning cartwheels in the corners of my vision—sunlight flashing off a bend of river, a hundred blackbirds startled at once from a church steeple—so that in the end I had no choice but to chance a look at it.

Acrophobia is a curious thing. The thinnest pane of glass can defeat it, transform a scrotum-tightening panorama into a paint-ing of foreshortened angles and forced perspective. But with no window to give lie to the illusion, the height felt wide and fero-cious, a raw, raging thing that pushed my phobia to the brink of panic. Intermediate distances were the worst, so that when I tried to look at the statue of William Penn atop City Hall, my stomach lurched and I had to grip the balustrade for fear my knees might buckle under me. I steadied my nerves on distant objects: the par-tially constructed Delaware River Bridge, the tawny dry banks of southern New Jersey. I took slow breaths until my panic sub-sided, then crouched beside the birdcage. I reached inside and caught the bird in cupped hands, cradled it like a Christmas or-nament as I brought it out of the cage. Then I stood, said a silent prayer the poor bird wasn't concealing a broken wing, and pitched it underhand into the sky.

The moment the bird left my hands, a gust tried to blow it back at me, like a balled-up racing form; but then the pigeon opened its wings and beat them against the blue, and, for a few graceless seconds, held itself clumsily aloft. Then it seemed to re-member the trick to flight, ceased flapping and fell—and in a blink became a perfect paper airplane sailing across the clear, wide canyon of air.

I fumbled the binoculars out of their leather case, found the pigeon in the eyepieces—already some distance away—and followed its thrilling glide past the bronze buckle on William

Penn's shoe. Watching its effortless flight, I knew I had guessed correctly. This was no garbage-eating pigeon, no disease-ridden rat with wings.

This was a carrier pigeon. And it was flying home.

Watching the damned thing go was exhilarating. Though disappointing, too, since I had secretly been hoping the pigeon would return to a neighborhood roost. A long shot, I knew—which was why I had tried to hedge my bets by releasing the bird from the highest ground in center city (with the exception of William Penn's tricornered hat). But all the panoramic view afforded me now was a clear vantage of the stupid bird flying hell-for-leather toward Connecticut or, for all I knew, Canada.

And then a curious thing happened. The bird, now no more than a speck of confetti in the twin disks of shimmering blue I held to my eyes, began to bank and circle back around. For a moment I lost the bird in sun glare. I let the binoculars drop around my neck and shaded my eyes with my hand. There—soaring above Kensington's factories and tenements. Was it possible the bird was returning to me? Had I somehow become confused in the bird's pea-size brain with its keeper?

No sooner had these questions occurred to me than the bird suddenly went into a shallow dive and dropped out of sight a few blocks north of Market Street. I raised the binoculars to scan the rooftops where it had disappeared, saw no evidence of coops among the chimney stacks and cold-water cisterns.

But I was far from discouraged. For now I knew—within a few blocks—where in the city the pigeon's keeper lived.

· 10 ·

Being neither a Philadelphia native nor a Pinkerton detective, I needed quite some time to narrow this four-block area of the city's tenderloin to an address.

Eighth and Race Streets. The Liberty Hotel.

Finding the place was a comedy of investigative trial and error, though in my defense probably no more so than the average police rookie's learning to "canvass" a neighborhood. I quickly learned that saloon keepers, cigar-store proprietors, and pool-hall attendants were useless as informants, their reactions to my inquiries ("Do you know anyone in the neighborhood who keeps pigeons?") falling within a narrow spectrum of indifference and irritation.

Outside on the street, I tried hitting up a local bluecoat for information, but all he had for me was a warning to stay clear of Chinatown after dark, so I wouldn't become another white victim of the territorial tong war then raging between the Hip Sings and the Five Brothers. On Arch Street I approached the bored-looking fellow at the Trocadero's box office (today's matinee: Vivian Lawrence, Edith Hart, and a chorus of thirty-five "Vampire Girls"), only to discover that he didn't speak English. I quizzed a grizzled rummy panhandling outside a five-and-dime, who advised me to forgo my quest for pigeons and seek instead the Dove of Peace. I tried bribing newsboys and striking up conversations with slack-faced men loitering outside the Galilee Mission. I peddled my questions in barber schools and pawnshops, in dingy restaurants where hot lunches could still be had for a dime, and in drugstores offering live leeches four for a quarter. As the day wore on with no results, I became so desperate I began considering having my teeth cleaned by one of the area's ubiquitous unlicensed dentists (BE SURE You get in the Right Office, a sign above the sidewalk warned. There are lots of FAKERS Practicing Dentistry in this Neighborhood) just to talk to someone who couldn't immediately dodge my questions.

When at last I caught a break in the case—as a Pinkerton dick might say in his memoirs—it came in the uniform of a Western Union messenger. I was sitting on a curb, giving my blistered feet a rest, when the kid sauntered over with his little gold hat canted at a cocky angle and a cigarette dangling from his bottom lip.

"Got a light?"

"Don't smoke."

The kid huffed, continued patting down his many uniform pockets. Unable to find a match, he tucked the cigarette over his ear for safekeeping. He looked down at me on the curbside.

"Everything okay, buddy?"

"I'm fine."

"You tight?"

"No."

"You sure? Looks like you might be about to pull a Daniel Boone."

My stomach gave a feeble flop like a mackerel lying on a hot pier. I wondered if I should have eaten breakfast.

"You want," the kid offered, "I know a place not far from here where you can get a little hair of the dog that bit you."

"You're a regular entrepreneur, aren't you, kid?"

"Fella's gotta keep himself in kale," he said, shrugging his skinny shoulders inside his oversize uniform jacket. He couldn't have been older than sixteen. Now he took a different tack. "Say, you look sandbagged. You want me to recommend a hotel?"

"No thanks."

"I know a swell dump around the corner," he said. "You go check in, I'll send over a nice coal-scuttle blonde to keep you company."

I kneaded my temples. "You're giving me a migraine."

"Rather play with China dolls?"

"Beat it, kid."

"C'mon," he cajoled, "tell old Cholly what sorta bird you like. I run messages for them all—I can fix you up straightaway."

Bird. If I weren't so exhausted, I might've laughed.

"What sort of bird?" I repeated, then told him, "Pigeons."

"Come again?"

I stood up, shifted my feet in their shoes. Winced at my sore blisters. I should never have sat down in the first place.

"I'm not interested in finding a girl, kid," I said, "but maybe there *is* someone you can help me find."

His face turned all business as he stuck out his hand. "Gonna cost you."

"Don't you want to hear what I want first?"

He shook his head. "If it was anything regular, you woulda asked for it right away. So you gotta pay up front."

I plucked a damp dollar bill from my wallet, stuffed it into his breast pocket with enough force to let him know I could easily take it back, and asked my question.

"You know anyone who keeps pigeons in this neighborhood?"

He pulled a wise-guy face. "Yeah, about two thousand Chinese."

"I mean the carrier kind," I said. "Type you keep in a pigeon coop on the roof, exchange messages with other folks with the same hobby."

His face screwed up as he pondered my question. He was a calculating little bugger, I'd give him that; fortunately, he was only equipped with an abacus. He stewed for so long I began to suspect he didn't have any answers, was only stalling to concoct a lie that would let him keep my money. But then, to my surprise, the kid produced a name, with enough corroborating details to convince me he was telling the truth.

"Was this fella named Ernie," the kid began, "lived over at the Liberty Hotel. Management let him keep a coop on the roof. Don't ask me why—the goddamn things shit all over the place."

"You know this Ernie's last name?"

He shook his head. "Haven't seen him in a while."

"How did you know him?"

"Used to take him deliveries."

"What sort of deliveries?"

He gave me sly look that said I'd asked a question out of my price range. With eyebrow arched, he answered, "Birdseed."

I knew I wouldn't get much more out of him, so I tipped him another two bits, and set off on sore feet toward Eighth and Race.

The Liberty was a four-story fleabag, with spindly fire escapes and grimy windows stenciled with the word HOTEL.

A social reformer might say its lobby reeked of despair, which was polite society's euphemism for urine. I approached the front desk and leafed through a water-warped guest register, where I saw visits by frequent guests "Mr. & Mrs. John Smith" (I counted eleven), alongside entries for President & Mrs. Calvin Coolidge, Charles Chaplin & Pola Negri, and Pope Pius XI—no doubt in this part of town searching for Mary Magdalene.

"The hell d'you want?" a voice croaked at me from behind the desk. I started. The manager came shuffling out from a back room, like the troll emerging from under the bridge in "The Three Billy Goats Gruff." Short and shapeless, held together in the middle by a stained truss, the old man brought with him a whiff of the toilet he'd just vacated.

"I'm looking for a guest named Ernie."

"Ernie?" His eyes narrowed, as if to conceal the light of recognition before I noticed it. "Never heard of him."

"You sure? Funny fellow, keeps pigeons on the roof?"

"Who wants to know?"

"His cousin." Lying was still novelty enough to send a thrill racing along my spine. Which isn't to say I was any better at it.

"Like hell you are," he said. "Go chase yourself, sonny."

"Your guests aren't allowed visitors?"

"Not the unannounced kind."

My patience was wearing thin. "So call upstairs and announce me."

"What d'you think this is, the Waldorf-Astoria?" He began searching his handkerchief for a clean spot to blow his nose, informing me between phlegmy honks, "Anyway, Ernie ain't in."

"Too bad," I said, "because I brought him a present."

I reached into the pocket of my overcoat, brought out the half-pint of soda-pop moonshine I'd been hoarding for days. It gave a melodic gurgle as I stood it on the desktop in front of the manager. Music to the old man's ears.

"I might be willing to let you keep it if you'll do me this favor."

"Room 128," he said, making a grab for the moonshine. I held the bottle out of reach until he agreed to my conditions:

"I want to wait for him upstairs—in his room."

The old man's eyes were fixed on the bottle. His mouth hung slack, a lone tooth on display. He gave a sigh, any vestiges of resistance hissing out of him like a bled radiator. "He's two weeks late with the rent anyway," I heard him grumble under his breath as he searched for the passkey. He found it, shuffled out from behind the desk, and waved for me to follow him.

The old cage elevator had long since given up the ghost, so we were forced to take the stairs—less of an issue for me than for the old man. He led me upstairs through progressively dank and fly-blown corridors. The wallpaper seemed to have contracted a venereal rash, and I buried my hands in my pockets to prevent catching anything. The place smelled of unwashed dishes, cigarette smoke, cats; somewhere an emphysemic coughed himself to death behind a closed door. At some point in the stygian journey, I learned from the manager that the man I'd come to find was named Ernst Stanlowe.

Stanlowe's room was on the fourth floor, at the end of a long hall whose only source of illumination—a dishwatery sort of light—came courtesy of the dirty window that looked out on a fire escape and an inspiring view of brick wall. The numbers on Stanlowe's door had long ago disappeared, though the impression of the number was still visible in the painted grain.

The manager kicked the door four times and, when there was no answer, unlocked it and ushered me in. He seemed in a hurry to get back to his bottle and left me with these parting words: "Don't make trouble—I got a good memory for faces."

I assured him I had no intention of causing trouble. The old man grunted, hitched his pants around his middle, and shuffled off, leaving me alone in a stranger's hotel room.

I raised one of the roll shades to let a little light into the room and onto its spartan furnishings: a bare mattress, a hot plate, a washstand with a chipped porcelain bowl and a strop hanging nearby. The top of the dusty bureau held the scattered contents of what could have been any man's pockets: forty cents in loose change, a mangy rabbit's foot, a pack of Chesterfields. The walls were stained yellow from decades of cigarette smoke, and I chided myself for forgetting to ask the manager how long Stanlowe had been a resident of the Liberty. Looking around his hotel room, I found it hard to imagine anyone living there more than a few days, the place was so drab and unwelcoming. Yet Stanlowe had been long enough in residence to befriend the management, winning permission to coop his pigeons on the Liberty's roof. Where were his books on practical pigeon keeping, then? Where were his journals recording correspondence with other far-flung bird lovers? The room's austerity was more than strange, it was suspicious, and when twenty minutes passed and I had completed my cursory search with no more insight into Stanlowe's character than when I arrived, I began to wonder if the man existed at all—or if I was merely supposed to think so.

I flopped down onto his bed, the springs bouncing beneath me with a metallic screech. I waited another quarter of an hour. The room filled with a late-afternoon light that stirred dust from the mutt-colored rug. I was reminded of the ghoulish Scot I'd had for gross anatomy back in medical school, how he'd reveled in details such as the composition of common house dust: *Skin and hair, lads,* he'd said, cheeks rosy above his rubber apron. *Skin and hair.* Now I watched the slow motes turning through the sunbeams and had the drowsy thought, *Maybe this is what's left of Stanlowe. . . .*

Why did it take an hour of this sort of daydreaming before it occurred to me—as sharply as if someone had rung a gong—to look under Stanlowe's bed?

Because I was a novice. Because this was another man's room. Because it no more occurred to me to poke around in Stanlowe's bureau or look under his bed than it occurs to a small child to look for a toy that's been removed from his sight.

Now that I'd made this cognitive leap—or ethical stumble, as my father might call it—I embraced it with the zeal of the same child a few years later searching for Christmas presents. Stanlowe's bureau held the most promise, but just to be thorough, I dropped to my knees on the rug for a quick peek beneath the bed.

Where I discovered what Stanlowe didn't want found.

Among the dust balls, beside a pair of old work boots, was a small case of cracked leather. I slid it out, felt several metallic somethings clink as they shifted inside. I didn't jump to the more likely (though just as inaccurate) conclusion: that what I'd found was a shaving kit. For reasons known only to my baroque imagination, the first thing that occurred to me was that Stanlowe collected Civil War memorabilia, that what I held in my hands was a field medic's surgical kit. I opened the case, and a length of rubber tubing sprang out like a novelty snake. But I wasn't startled, only confused. Weren't the tourniquets used by military surgeons made of leather?

Of course, at some level I registered the hypodermics, the empty ampoules of morphia hydrochloride, the blood-spotted gauze. But now that the leather case was open, something else caught my eye that immediately took supremacy over the other contents.

A photograph of Mina. Younger than I knew her. She wore a peasant blouse that left her upper half daringly exposed. Her hair, longer than I'd seen before, fell in thrilling ringlets to her bare shoulders. Except for a glimpse of decorative fern, the picture could have been taken in heaven, with its backdrop of altocumulous, its beatific light. Like the portrait on a holy card. One of the mystic saints, Our Lady of the Incorporeal . . .

I held Mina's picture gingerly by its one uncurled corner,

understood that what I held in my hands as I knelt there on the floor in the dying light was a desperate man's last article of faith.

Which is how Ernst Stanlowe would find me a moment later as he came listing suddenly and drunkenly through the doorway.

"Who the hell are you?" he growled at me.

I recognized him. It was the man I'd seen lurking in the alley outside 2013 Spruce earlier in the week when I'd been out walking the Crawleys' terrier. The man I'd taken for a hobo.

Two things saved me from a beating at the hands of the enraged man: first, the ravages of Stanlowe's addiction, which had stripped him of any spare flesh and left him a scarecrow in oversize clothes; and second, that I immediately leaped to my feet and stopped his shambling advance by shouting, "Walter sent me!"

Why these were the first words that came to mind, I cannot say. Wasn't it more plausible that Stanlowe himself had sent for me? Under different circumstances I might have argued so, but at present I was interested only in forestalling his attack.

It worked. Stanlowe cocked his head like a thrush as he repeated the name. "Walter . . . ?"

I caught a trace of an accent, a Slavic way with consonants, that agreed with his features—or what was left of them since the morphine had begun cannibalizing him. His hair, formerly coarse and dark, had gone brittle and prematurely gray, so that it was a struggle to estimate his age. Thirty-five, I guessed—though he could easily have passed for fifty. He had arrived at that advanced stage of emaciation when a man becomes an effigy: a skull stuck on the end of a ragged broomstick, puppet for a public burning. Though if Stanlowe had been made for protest, it was clear the fight had long since left him.

"Who are you?" he asked with effort, sagging against the doorframe.

"My name is Finch," I said. "I'm from *Scientific American* magazine. We're investigating the mediumship of Mina Crawley."

"Mina?" he repeated. On his lips it became a plea.

"That's right." I held up the photo. "You know her?"

He made a sound that was his laugh.

"Yes, I know her," he said wryly. "She was my wife."

. . .

They had met a dozen years earlier, when Mina was eighteen and Stanlowe twenty. She had been a student at Bryn Mawr, where he worked as an assistant groundskeeper. Their courtship, such as it was, had been brief and was conducted largely at the labor rallies and protest marches that substituted for mixers among the more social-minded coeds of that Quaker college. Their marriage had been equally brief, and in the end had gone the way of so many other failed social experiments.

I learned all this in fits and starts from Stanlowe as he withdrew into a corner of his bed and hunkered down for another long night of hallucinations and tremors that accompanied narcotic withdrawal. He had injected the last of his morphine two nights earlier, had been out all day scouring the neighborhood for his usual supplier—a West Indian called "Sweets" Beauregard, who it turned out had stopped paying for the protection of the local ward boss and earned himself a one-way trip to Moko, otherwise known as Moyamensing Prison.

And so Stanlowe had tramped wearily home to the Liberty and an addict's last recourse—"needle freaking." I thought he might ask me to leave, or at least turn away, but he didn't. His need must have been too great. Or perhaps at some level he wanted a witness for what he'd become. He lit a cigarette, left it dangling in the corner of his mouth. Then he pushed up his shirt-sleeve and with an empty hypodermic began pricking the skin on the inside of his wasted forearm. It was morbidly fascinating, watching him search for a patch of open skin among the dried specks of yesterday's efforts, then pricking himself with the pointillist precision of a tattoo artist. Finished, he closed his eyes, and his face took on a look of rapt anticipation. It was the same look I had seen on Mina's face as she entered her hypnotic trance. Which is why it occurred to me that the morphine addict's was no different from the ceremony we enacted around the séance table: tricking our senses with ritual, until the dark yielded up its dragon.

Now Stanlowe tensed, as if he had heard something far away. Scales? He listened. Suddenly the deep lines in his face seemed to melt and his jaw went slack. I looked at the forgotten hypodermic in his hand, raised my eyes to his smooth face. Was his rapture any less real because the needle had been empty?

He wasn't asleep, despite the fact that his cigarette had dropped from his lips and lay smoldering on his chest. When I reached across him to remove it, he thanked me without opening his eyes. I knew that if I had any remaining questions, I should ask them now. So I leaned forward and asked him quietly how his marriage to Mina had ended.

"*Crawley.*"

"She left you for him?"

"He took her," Stanlowe said, then made a gargling noise low in his throat, emotion pooling in his chest. "Took her from me . . . and the boy . . ."

I sat a little straighter in my chair.

"Boy?"

". . . was a boy . . ."

"What was a boy?" No answer. "Stanlowe?"

He was drifting, the tide towing him out to sea. I tried dragging him back to the shallows. "Stanlowe!" Slapping him.

Our conversation, if you could call it that, continued in this fashion over the next half hour, during which I was able to piece together what had happened, at least in Stanlowe's mind: The Pregnancy. The Complications. The Hospitalization. . . .

Now Crawley made his entrance in the grim story, all but twirling his waxed mustache. Stanlowe's voice filled with venom as he told me about his wife's purported "turn for the worse," the sudden "hemorrhaging," Crawley's claim that he had done everything in his power to save the child that would have become Stanlowe's son.

The anger went out of his voice, was replaced by remorse. He recounted Mina's convalescence with as little enthusiasm as a schoolboy giving a book report: How she'd fallen into a deep depression. How grief had made her vulnerable to Crawley's obscene affections. How in the end she had confused gratitude for love, attributing what had been her spontaneous recovery to Crawley's near-mystical powers of healing.

Stanlowe's eyes were open now, black slits like twin lines of sutures. The dragon had tossed him out of the waves, and he lay tangled in bedsheets like something discarded by the sea.

"Mina," he said, as if he saw her standing there before him.

I asked when he had seen her last. His reply surprised me.

"Last week." He frowned, doubting his answer, mustered the strength for a boneless shrug. "I suppose it might have been last month. . . ."

"What did she want?"

"Nothing."

"I don't understand—didn't she say?"

"She never comes up."

"You mean she's come before?"

He nodded feebly. "She leaves packages at the front desk. Food. Sometimes clothing . . ." He plucked at the shirt he was wearing, rank with his sour perspiration. Despite its wrinkles, it was unmistakably a garment of superior cut and quality, finer than anything in my own wardrobe. That was when I noticed his cuff links: twin caducei, winged staves entwined with serpents.

"Your cuff links," I said. "Are they Crawley's?"

He grunted, seemed to take a grim satisfaction in this.

"Why haven't you pawned them?"

"They come in handy."

"Handy?"

Stanlowe indulged my naïve question. "For those times when it is useful to impersonate a doctor."

His scam was simple: Costumed in Crawley's expensively tailored clothes, sporting his gold cuff links, Stanlowe would ride a commuter train out to the unsuspecting suburbs, where he would convince local chemists he was a visiting Lithuanian lung specialist so they would sell him prescription cough syrups and patent medicines. The amounts of morphine, cocaine, and heroin in these medicines were minimal—never more than a quarter of a grain per avoirdupois ounce, as legislated by the Harrison Act—which was why this was Stanlowe's scam of last resort. Of late, however, his gaunt appearance made it impossible to put one over on even the most gullible chemists. Which brought us back to my original question: If the cuff links were no longer any use to him, why hadn't Stanlowe pawned them?

But Stanlowe had already demonstrated he wasn't interested in answering this question, and so I asked another.

"Does Mina know your condition?"

"No."

"You've made no effort to contact her?"

"What purpose would it serve? She is in love. . . ." He gestured listlessly at the window, hand flopping on the hinge of his wrist. "Once when I was on the roof with the birds, I looked down and saw her getting back in a taxi. I shouted down to her, and she looked up. She was so"—the word he wanted caught in his throat—"beautiful. She had put on weight. I thought she must be very happy."

"I don't think so." Even though I believed it was true, it was a cruel thing to say. But I was too young, too unschooled in the diplomacy of estrangement to know better. Stanlowe's eyes cut to mine, urgent, then angry: at me, for bringing this hope in his eleventh hour, at himself, for wanting so badly to believe me.

He turned his face away. "Why are you here?"

He had asked the question earlier, when he'd first found me in his room, and I had told him about Mina's séances, his former brother-in-law's coded messages, the pigeon. Now, hearing him repeat the question, I knew that Stanlowe wanted something more: the truth.

And so I told him, "I'm looking for Mina's accomplice."

He turned his face toward mine. "And do you think you've found him?"

I looked at Stanlowe, his skull grimacing at me behind taut skin the color of tallow. I shook my head. "No."

"Keep looking," Stanlowe said. "You will find him."

"You don't believe she speaks with the dead?"

"If I did, I would have cut my throat long ago," he said, nodding toward the straight razor on the washstand. "No, she must have someone assisting her—an 'accomplice,' as you say. Perhaps a lover. Perhaps not." He flashed a ghoulish grin, "Perhaps *you*."

He was becoming incoherent, the light draining from his eyes as rapidly as it was from the hotel room. I glanced at my wristwatch, saw it was quarter past five: I had a hundred other questions for Stanlowe—what his relationship had been like with his brother-in-law, Walter; why he had granted his wife a divorce in the first place—but I knew if I wanted to see his pigeon coops on the roof, these would have to wait.

So I stood up from my chair, turned on the room's one lamp to offer some resistance against the encroaching gloom, tucked the old horsehair blanket around his shoulders. His teeth were chattering.

"Do you mind if I go up on the roof?"

Stanlowe rocked his head feebly from side to side. "Suit yourself. The birds are all dead. I tried setting them free, but they kept coming back."

I crossed to the window and forced up its lower pane with much protest from the old counterweights, then climbed out onto the fire escape. I ascended the rusted ladder, doing my damnedest to avert my eyes from the precipitous view, and scrambled onto the roof. There I was greeted by the sight of a tar-paper moonscape, and, set down squarely in the middle of it like one of Verne's squat rocket ships, an old cold-water cistern. In the lee of the cistern, I found the pigeon coop, a blighted tangle of wood and chicken wire. Now I lifted away the broken door and looked inside, saw the remains of Stanlowe's flock: miniature rib cages upturned, tufted with fluttering gray feathers. And lying on its side in the midst of it all a fresh corpse—Mina's pet.

How it had worked its way inside the ruined coop, I do not know. It was hard enough for me to crawl through the tangle of chicken wire. I knelt beside the pigeon. Ignoring Crawley's cautions about disease vectors and the general unsavoriness of the species, I extended a hand to touch the pigeon, Walter's messenger. It was cold and hard as a stone covered in felt, as if it had been dead already for days.

I extricated myself from the collapsed pigeon coop, walked to the low wall that ran around the perimeter of the roof, watched

226 · *Joseph Gangemi*

the shadows reach across the neighboring rooftops, pooling in the alleys of Chinatown. I thought of Mina, summoned her smile to my mind's eye. Was Stanlowe right? Did she have an accomplice? A lover? I felt my chest tighten at the thought of Mina in the arms of a paramour. Why was I willing to entertain the notion of her being a fraud but not an adulteress? And why was I resisting these in favor of the wilder supposition that she was telling the truth: That Walter was real. That Mina was in danger.

I took my glasses off, pressed the heels of my hands into my eyes. The darkness brought my mental image of her into sharper contrast, cool and inscrutable, a girl glimpsed in the midst of a wicked thought. Who was she? And what was she thinking?

I put my glasses back on. I dreaded returning inside to Stanlowe, dreaded it more than anything I could have encountered in a dark séance room. But I had no choice. There was no way down other than through his window. And so I steeled myself and took hold of the fire-escape ladder.

The light had changed in Stanlowe's room since I had left, the walls now a hellish shade of orange, like the inside of a decaying pumpkin. Mina's former husband lay where I had last seen him, sprawled across the bed with arms outflung. His mouth was agape, lips forming an inverted triangle. And while I knew it could only be an olfactory illusion, I thought I caught a whiff of formalin coming off him.

"Stanlowe?"

I put my ear to his mouth to listen if he was breathing.

"Finch."

I nearly leaped out of my skin. "Jesus—!"

Stanlowe lunged forward, clutching my shirt. Launched into a gibbering rant that phased in and out of coherence like a ten-watt radio station: something about Crawley being a monster, a mesmerist, Svengali in a surgeon's mask, with Mina cast as his helpless patient and me his unwitting assistant. It was Grand Guignol performed in an operating theater, and I recoiled from its lunatic vision of infanticide and sexual enslavement.

I seized Stanlowe's wrists and, with a violent jerk, broke their grip on my collar, dragging him and half the blankets off the bed. He landed in a heap on the dirty floor—but I didn't linger to help him up. In that moment of blind panic, he ceased being Stanlowe and became instead the cadaver I'd been given to dissect in medical school, pallid as poached veal. It clutched at my pant cuff, and I kicked it free, kicked it again, might not have stopped if it hadn't cried out and become Stanlowe again.

I left him like that, mewling, bleeding. And fled.

. . .

"This is ridiculous," I said, then called out to the dark for what seemed the thousandth time, *"Walter!"*

The darkness seethed but gave no reply. We'd been waiting for him for three-quarters of an hour and a dozen playings of "Somebody Else Took You Out of My Arms" by Barney Rapp and His Orchestra. Now, as the gramophone began its thirteenth reprise, I extended my foot and kicked the plug from the socket. The foxtrot groaned to a halt.

"Have you lost your mind, Finch?" asked Fox.

"Just my patience," I said, and called out once more to the obstinate shade, "Talk to us, Walter—I know you're there!"

"It won't do any good to provoke him," Fox said. "The discarnate rarely manifest if they sense tension in a circle."

Bullshit, I thought. *This one thrives on it.*

Richardson asked, "How long do we wait before declaring the session a blank?"

"All night if we have to."

"Like hell," Flynn said. "I propose we vote."

"Flynn's right," Fox said. "All in favor of adjourning, say aye—"

"No!" I shouted. "He's here. I can feel it."

Flynn complained, "All I can feel is the right half of my ass going to sleep."

"May I remind you there's a lady present," Fox said.

"She can't hear us," Flynn said. I suspected he was right. Beside me, Mina's somnolent breathing was deep and regular, her hand several degrees cooler than mine.

"I was referring to the young lady taking dictation."

"Oh, right," Flynn said. He apologized to the Dictograph on the windowsill. "Sorry, sister."

"Now, we were about to vote on—"

"I finished your scavenger hunt!" I blurted out to the darkness, a last-ditch effort to bait Mina's brother. "I found the Liberty Hotel."

From the darkness near the windows came a familiar voice, more subdued than usual. "Congratulations, sport."

Was it my imagination, or was that his silhouette I saw lounging in the corner of the nursery?

"So," Walter said, "did you like the place?"

"Not especially."

"Really? I would have thought an inquisitive fellow like yourself would be fascinated to learn how the other half lives."

"Don't you mean 'better half'?"

"Careful, sport—the walls have ears."

Crawley. As if I needed a reminder Walter's brother-in-law was listening from the next room. I'd spent the last few hours pacing the library, agonizing over how to mention Stanlowe in tonight's séance without betraying Mina, then berating myself for protecting a woman who in all likelihood was playing me and the *Scientific American* for suckers. Though I was no clearer on which

Mina was—victim or vamp—I erred on the side of caution now as I broached the subject of her former husband.

"I ran into an old friend of yours at the Liberty."

"I had a feeling you might," Walter said. "How is he?"

"Dying."

He grunted, unimpressed. "Has he gotten any better at it?"

"Another week or so and I think he'll have it licked."

"I doubt it," Walter said. "Dope fiends have a way of hanging on."

("Who are they talking about?" Fox whispered, before being silenced by Richardson. "Hush, Malcolm, let them speak.")

"You don't seem terribly sympathetic," I remarked.

Walter was on the move now, speaking from a position near the silent gramophone. "I have a strict policy against pitying the self-destructive, sport. I've seen too many beautiful young men with their jaws blown off." The gramophone wheezed its way through another melancholy half measure, like music from a far-off garden party to which none of us had been invited. I imagined him standing there in his sad tuxedo, using one finger to give the gramophone record a contemplative turn.

Stop it, I thought, *there's no one there!* And yet he was; I could hear him speaking.

"Sad as our friend at the Liberty may seem," Walter said, "never forget that he is there by choice."

"He doesn't seem to think so," I said. "To hear him tell it, he's been the victim of a terrible crime."

"I don't doubt it."

I asked, "Should I?"

He considered my question. "No, you can believe him. He isn't blameless, of course, but then I trust you have lived long enough to know there are two sides to every story, between which lies the truth. I do wonder, though, if you have learned enough to know what to do once you've found it."

I bristled. "And what might that be?"

"Let it lie."

He spoke it in a whisper, inches from my ear. Gooseflesh crept up from my collar and across my scalp, a prickling beneath my hair. I took a breath to help my heart return to a reasonable time signature, fought to still the tremolo in my next question.

"If that's the case, why did you want me to find the Liberty in the first place?"

"You left me no choice," he said, all amiability gone from his voice. "You would have dragged on this little Inquisition of yours until there was nothing left of my sister but a puddle of milk!"

"It's not an Inquisition—it's an investigation."

"Please." He made no effort now to hide his contempt. "It's a witch-hunt. Only instead of a public hanging, you're going to pillory her in the press. You've already started. Do you honestly think in a city this small, people won't figure out the identity of 'The Witch of Rittenhouse Square'?"

"I thought you said you didn't get the papers?"

"You son of a bitch."

There was a terrific crash at the center of the circle, as if someone had dropped an anvil. Our chairs leaped in place, and I braced for some assault, but all that came was a threat.

"I should string you up myself," Walter snarled.

"Do it!"

I heard a collective gasp from my colleagues.

"I'm getting tired of all your talk," I continued. "You boast a good game. And you're always ready with an insult. But when it comes to showing us any proof—anything substantial, anything we can *use*—the best you can come up with are a few tired old parlor tricks."

We heard a rumble, like distant thunder or the growl of a big cat, and then Walter warned, "You had better watch yourself, sport. You're getting me sore."

"Do you know what I think?" I asked, pressing on before I lost my nerve. "I think you only pretend you want this investigation to end. I think you love the attention and the toll it's taking on your sister—" Hearing myself, I stopped abruptly, as if encountering the word for the first time. *"Sister,"* I said to the imposter, whoever he was. "Mina's no more your sister than she is mine!"

"Is that your expert opinion, sport?"

"No," I said defiantly. "It's Stanlowe's."

The nursery seemed to experience a sudden drop in air pressure. Silence, and then Fox asking, "Who's Stanlowe?"

"Fools!"

Two voices, male and female, croaked in guttural unison from a single larynx. Then Mina let out a sudden piercing cry and convulsed. The chair she sat in began bucking under her like a mare startled by a starter pistol.

The next few moments were chaos, voices calling:

"We need light!"

"Don't break the circle!"

Then a sudden flood of electric light as Crawley threw open the nursery door.

"Quickly! She's having a seizure!"

By the time Richardson lit the kerosene lamp, Mina was in full grand mal, eyes rolled back in her sockets and mouth white with foam. Her heels drummed the floor in chaotic rhythm as we struggled to hold her down and force Flynn's belt between her teeth. I shut my eyes and held her shoulders, praying for the clonic spasms to pass. A full minute passed before the tremors diminished, the electrical storm drifting off the coast of her startled cerebellum. I opened my eyes and saw her curled in a fetal ball, whimpering.

I backed into a corner, though it felt as if I observed the next few minutes from an even greater distance. Pike telephoned for an ambulance, and while we waited for it, Crawley ministered to his wife, checking her pulse, stroking her hair, whispering soothing words of which she seemed only dimly aware. The cat slipped in and sniffed its fallen mistress, tail atwitch, and I was surprised when Flynn picked it up in his rough hands and began stroking it. Richardson kept watch at the windows.

"The ambulance is here," he said with relief.

A few moments later, two attendants shuffled into the overcrowded room and collected Mina on their litter, while the rest of us stood helplessly by.

Crawley was about to follow the ambulance attendants out of the nursery when he stopped on the threshold, looked back at me for the first time. I braced myself for what he might have to say to me, but when he spoke, it was to the others.

"Have Pike put on coffee and make you something to eat," he muttered distractedly, then cast a bitter look my way. "And I would very much prefer it if he isn't here when I return."

Crawley left. I received variations on the theme of his accusing glance from each of my colleagues as they filed out of the nursery and retired downstairs; only Richardson's bore any spark of sympathy.

After they had gone, I went directly to my room—the *guest* room, I thought, relinquishing possession of it—and packed my few things. Why is it that our clothing so resists being returned to the luggage it came in? As if the inanimate had some interest in reinforcing our domesticity. Struggling to close the lid of my bulging suitcase, I looked up and saw the Siamese perched on the needlepoint cushion of the room's lone chair, watching me. It licked its paw and seemed to comb its hair, its velvet ear springing straight with each swipe. A Filipino would have read in this feline gesture an omen of imminent arrival; Mina had told me Pike saw the cat grooming itself many times the afternoon before our committee had turned up on their doorstep.

At this memory of my arrival—could it have been only a week ago?—I felt a stab of longing behind my sternum, as if a dial had caught in the clockworks of my heart. I sighed, said good-bye to the saturnine cat, and set out upon my exile.

· · ·

Of course, I had nowhere to go. Even if the Bellevue had found lodging for me, I had no way to pay for it and could no longer claim—as Fox had informed me on my way out the door of 2013 Spruce—to be in the employ of the *Scientific American*. And so I wandered. The night was raw and full of sirens. I drank a pot of coffee at an all-night diner near Broad and South, in the company of tipsy couples who staggered inside to seek refuge from the tilting sidewalks. A girl in a dress missing many of its sequins struck up a conversation with me at the counter and offered me a furnished room in her Aunt Ethel's place for $1.50. I might have taken her up on it, too, if another girl hadn't cut in to warn me off this notorious "pocket joint." This incited an argument that quickly escalated into a catfight, and when I heard someone yell that the police were on their way, I decided it was time I made my exit. Out on the streets of center city, I walked and walked and walked, with no real sense of where I was going, though in retrospect I was approaching my destination as inexorably as if I had a map. A fire engine went by with a clanging bell, and I walked on, past the dark windows of Strawbridge & Clothier, Lit Brothers, Snellenberg's, with their unlit scenes of Christmas. A tanker truck rode by, spraying down the street ahead of it and in the process soaking my ankles. I continued north, beneath the ornamental gate at the entrance to Chinatown and, only after emerging unmolested from its few exotic blocks, remembered I had been warned once never to venture there. I continued walking, past McShea's Lucky Dollar Saloon and Shim Loo's Shanghai Tea Gardens, conscious now of where I was heading: the only place I knew where a bed could be had for next to nothing.

I rounded the corner of Eighth and Race, and found where all the sirens had been going.

The Liberty. All four stories were ablaze, fire streaming from its windows and throwing sparks at the sky. A half dozen fire companies had converged on the scene, and the street was black with water. I stepped carefully among the hoses and took my place among the bystanders, many of whom had the bewildered look of residents, and watched as the bricks blackened and the fire escape collapsed and the windows popped in unison—all while the beleaguered firemen pumped municipal water up from the sidewalk and trained it on the blaze. The heat was so intense that the trucks could not be positioned close enough, and thus the streams never quite reached the flames but only came apart in a lacy spray full of monochromatic rainbows from the streetlamps.

"You!"

It was the hotel's manager, the little homunculus I had bribed to let me into Stanlowe's room. He thrust an accusing finger at me, which wouldn't have alarmed me if not for what he said next to the bluecoat with him.

"He tried to kill one of the residents!"

And that was how I came to be taken into custody for the first and only time in my life, hauled off in handcuffs to a Sixth Precinct holding cell on suspicion of arson and attempted murder.

PART THREE

SCIENTIFIC AMERICANS

· 11 ·

"I'm through with the goddamn police!" my cellmate announced to no one in particular. "There hasn't been a ticket they were selling, hasn't been a carnival or an appeal for their pension fund that I haven't helped them out, and done a bunch of the men personal favors, too, not to mention the hundred bucks a month I already pay (you know exactly what I mean)—and they can't leave me alone with what little business I have left? They gotta come on a Saturday night and load my customers in the wagon and drag the women off to morals court to be sentenced to six months in the workhouse? I tell you, my heart breaks for some of them girls. It's damn near impossible for 'em to make a dollar anymore since *His Honor* and that crooked bunch at City Hall started in with all this reform bullshit (and Kendrick won't be no better—you're only kidding yourself if you think he will). All these so-called reformers are doing is making graft bigger. People are always gonna drink liquor just as they will always sport. I tell you, this country's been on the bum ever since Prohibition—"

"Shut your bung, Coyle," the desk sergeant shouted in the saloonkeeper's face, giving the man's fingers a sharp crack with his nightstick. Coyle let out a yelp and retreated from the cell doors, pouting over his bruised knuckles. The desk sergeant strolled a few paces farther, to where I stood staring out through the bars.

"Anything you'd like to get off *your* chest, professor?"

"No."

"Good."

And he jabbed the nightstick through the bars into my groin. I staggered back to one of the wooden benches bolted to the walls and curled up on my side. A few inches from my glasses, some jailhouse wag had scratched EVERY DAY IN EVERY WAY I AM GETTING BETTER AND BETTER! I shut my eyes and appealed to my aching testicles for clemency.

I was in my fourth hour of incarceration and my twentieth without sleep. Herewith I offer a summary of how I had spent those early hours of Sunday the sixteenth of December, in the Year of Our Lord Nineteen Hundred and Twenty-three:

12:10 A.M. I am denied bail and ordered held by Sixth District Magistrate Carson, pending an investigation into the cause of the blaze by the fire commissioner.

12:33 A.M. I am granted one call and use it to ring Jefferson Hospital to inquire after Mina's condition. The dragon on night duty refuses to give out any patient information over the telephone but invites me to pay my regards during regular visiting hours.

1:47 A.M. My attempts to sleep are thwarted by a noisy disquisition in the next cell by a besotted streetwalker on how "damned tight" this town was, as well as the general untrustworthiness of the Wassermann test.

2:40 A.M. While thumbing through the Bible that has recently failed me as a pillow, I find that there is no Book of Stanlowe with a 128th verse (his room number); however, there *is* a

1 Samuel 28 (close enough), which relates the tale of the Witch of En-dor, who spake to the skeptic Saul in the voices of the dead.

3:12 A.M. The desk sergeant informs me I am no longer a murder suspect, since through some miracle none of the Liberty's residents perished in the fire. However, the sergeant can give me no information on the whereabouts of my cousin Ernst.

4:48 A.M. I discover that the letters in the name "Ernst Stan-lowe" can be rearranged to spell the words "noEl ratS newts" as well as the names "tannEr slotSew" and "waltEr stenSon"—

"Wake up, Coyle," the desk sergeant barked at my cellmate. "Your lawyer's here."

I peeked open one eye—I was on my back now, with an arm thrown across my face—and saw outside the bars a tall, bemused man in his late forties wearing a raccoon coat, accompanied by a much younger woman in a mink wrap.

"Gee, thanks for coming, Mr. Patterson," Coyle said, shaking hands with his defense attorney through the bars. "I hated like hell having to phone you so late."

"Don't give it a second thought, Jimmy," the attorney said. "We hadn't turned in for the night yet—had we, Ginny?"

"Heavens no," the brunette replied, studying her manicure. "Chiff and I don't reach that station of the cross until at least six."

"Virginia."

"Yes, darling?"

The brunette batted her eyelashes at him innocently. I noticed that neither of them was wearing a wedding ring.

Patterson offered his client a cigarette, took out a gold-plated lighter.

"Have they been treating you decently, Jimmy?"

Coyle leaned closer to accept the light, whispered through the bars, "The desk sergeant's been a real strap."

"I'll have a word with him." Patterson snapped the lighter shut, returned it to his vest pocket. "I've spoken with Judge Phelan about your case."

"And?"

"He seemed amenable to the idea of reducing your bail. Of course, I had to give him my word you wouldn't hop on the first train to Atlantic City. Can I trust you not to prove me a liar, Jimmy?"

"I swear, Mr. Patterson—on my mother's grave."

"Good. How is she, by the way?"

"Better."

"Do send her our regards."

"I will—and god bless you, Mr. Patterson, Miss Virginia."

Coyle's benediction brought a faint smile to Patterson's face and for a few moments seemed to chase away the storm clouds that darkened his sky-blue eyes. But the effect was fleeting, and, as they clouded again, his eyes became restless, famished for further absolution. He looked past Coyle, took notice of me at the back of the cell.

"What's your friend in for, Jimmy?"

"Rape."

I sat up on the bench. "I didn't rape anyone!"

"Of course you didn't," the defense attorney said. "She was a conniving little seductress, wasn't she?"

"No! I mean—I'm charged with arson, not rape—I don't know why he said rape."

"Oh, don't mind him, he always says rape," Patterson said. "You look more like a firebug anyway. So tell me—what are they claiming you tried to burn down?"

"The Liberty Hotel."

"Ha!" the brunette exclaimed, poking Patterson in the ribs, then explaining to me that they had passed the scene on the way over.

"That's right," Patterson said, taking out a billfold from an inner pocket and removing a crisp new dollar. "And Virginia, who can always be relied upon to take the more cynical view of humanity, bet that someone set the blaze deliberately."

"Someone may very well have," I said, "but it wasn't me."

Patterson shot a look at the front of the brunette's dress, where she had tucked her winnings, then returned his attention to me.

"Why do the police suspect you of arson?"

"I don't know," I said. "I mean, I *do* know—I was there in the afternoon inquiring after one of the residents—but I don't see how that makes someone a pyromaniac."

Patterson chuckled. "Don't try to understand Philadelphia jurisprudence, son; you'll only do yourself an injury. Speaking of which—" He indicated my black eye, asked, "Did one of Philly's finest give you that shiner?"

"No."

"Didn't think that looked like their handiwork," he said. "On the whole they prefer the kidneys. Leaves a fellow a little something to remember them by whenever nature calls."

"Charming," I said.

"Welcome to the City of Brotherly Love," Patterson said. "Cheer up, son. Let me speak to a few people I know in the front office, see what we can do about getting you released on your own recognizance."

"Wait!" I called as he started to go. "I can't afford a lawyer."

Patterson approached the cell bars. Looked me in the eye.

"Did you set fire to the Liberty Hotel?"

"No."

He nodded gravely. Turned to the brunette. Plucked the dollar bill from between her lovely breasts so quickly she let out a startled hiccup. He held up the dollar, folded lengthwise along his index finger.

"We'll consider this my retainer."

. . .

He was a remarkable man, this C. Stuart Patterson, Esquire. In the hour before the attorney got him released on bail, my cellmate regaled me with stories about the legendary "Chiffy," as his friends on both sides of the law called him: How he had been born to privilege but from an early age had exhibited a preference for greasy spoons over silver ones, and the company of rapists, racketeers, dope peddlers, bootleggers, kidnappers, abortionists, gunmen, and gamblers over the more backstabbing rogues' gallery who comprised Philly's social register. How he was one of the few Occidentals who could walk through Chinatown after dark without having his skull split by a hatchet-wielding tong foot soldier (I didn't tell my cellmate that only last night I had managed this same feat), and the sole attorney who could cross the exercise yard at Moko or Eastern without being gutted like a mackerel with a homemade shiv. How he'd once sold a judge on his Indian client's squatting rights outside the Ritz-Carlton on the principle that the hotel was situated on an Indian reservation. How he had turned his back on the family practice—his father was legal counsel to the Pennsylvania Rail Road—and chosen to represent clients who paid him in bathtub gin he wouldn't touch, pearl-handled pistols he'd never fire, checks that couldn't be cashed because they'd been written on overdrawn accounts, and greenbacks that couldn't be deposited because they were counterfeit. And yet Chiffy never complained, because the goodwill he accumulated from bad people gave him a satisfaction that couldn't be bought, leased, or inherited.

But remarkable as C. Stuart Patterson might have been, he was no miracle worker, and so I would remain behind bars for the rest of the morning.

A curious lucidity is available to the sleep-deprived mind, if you are willing to put up with a few hallucinations—garter snakes, chimney swifts—darting in and out between the bars of your cell. With the critical part of my brain temporarily mute, my thoughts buzzed through the events of the last week like a honeybee visiting the most vivid blooms: the séances, the look in Stanlowe's eyes as he teased himself with an empty needle, the same dreamy look repeated in Mina's that first night as she whispered, "Kiss me." Now I made a connection I might not have had I been better rested: to the look on the face of Wick Halliday's girl when I hypnotized her months and months ago. Were the séances we had conducted on the third floor of the Crawleys' house just more elaborate versions of that old parlor trick? And if they were, who was hypnotizing whom?

"On your feet, Finch!"

I startled. Saw the latest in a line of interchangeable jailers unlocking my cage. Patterson was with him, dressed for a day of motoring in a tweed jacket, baggy plus-fours that ended just below the knee, and a soft English cap.

"Rise, Lazarus, and come forth!" Patterson boomed, opening his arms to me as I shuffled from the holding cell.

"You posted my bail?"

"There is no bail, my boy," Patterson said, clapping me heartily on both shoulders. "Judge Phelan threw out your case."

"I . . ." Emotion washed over me. "I don't know how to thank you, Mr. Patterson."

"Don't thank me," he said. "All I did—if you'll pardon a bad pun—was light a fire under the magistrate. The police would have gotten around to releasing you in a few more hours."

"But what about the Liberty?"

"An accident," Patterson said as he escorted me to freedom. "I could have told the fire commissioner as much. With all the rummies flopping there, it's a wonder the Liberty didn't go up in flames ages ago. Place was a tinderbox."

We emerged from the dark police precinct into dazzling sun. I stood there on the sidewalk blinking and disoriented among the people out strolling on a Saturday afternoon. Something smelled rank, and only after looking around in vain for the wino I assumed it was coming from did I realize that the ripeness was my own.

Patterson saw me sniffing my armpits and laughed. "Come on, my office isn't far. You can wash up there."

He started off toward Broad but stopped when he saw I had no intention of following. He came back alongside me, touched my arm gently. "You feeling okay, son?"

I pointed in the opposite direction down Chestnut. "I'm going that way."

At least this was the plan, once marching orders finished trickling down to my feet.

Patterson looked the way I had indicated, guessed where I intended to go. "The Liberty?"

I nodded.

"Isn't much left of it to see. You do realize that, right?"

I nodded again, more slowly this time, guilt turning all my movements leaden. I looked up, met Patterson's patient gaze. Confessed quietly, "I didn't set fire to the Liberty. But I'm the reason someone did."

The defense attorney received this without expression or, so far as I could tell, judgment. Though I did catch a glimmer of curiosity in his eyes, which in the midday sun were calm and colorless. He showed me the smile of a kindly uncle you turn to when your own father is being unreasonable, the man who secretly takes your side in family disagreements, who sneaks you your first drink and provides a sofa for you to sleep off your first hangover.

"Come on," Patterson said now, throwing an arm around my shoulders. "You can tell me all about it on the way there."

And so I did. It was a relief to unburden myself at last of Mina's secrets, though I knew I was taking considerable risk in doing so to a man I had known less than twelve hours—and a "Philadelphia lawyer," no less. I started with my arrival and ended with my arrest, sketching all the station stops along the way: Crawley, Mina, Munson, Walter, Vox, *Wieland*, Stanlowe . . . Stalemate. I omitted nothing, not the kiss I had shared with Mina, not the burn I had seen on Mina's breast nor my eagerness to examine it. I flushed, hearing myself recount my role in the whole sordid affair, for, in my own retiring way, I seemed as culpable as Crawley in Mina's exploitation.

Unless of course it was she who was exploiting us.

Patterson listened without comment, his expression growing graver by the minute; and when I reached the end, just as we arrived at Eighth and Race, he told me to go on ahead, that he'd wait for me here on the opposite corner. I left him looking pensive, then crossed against traffic to inspect what remained of the Liberty.

The fire commissioner had erected wooden barricades and posted warnings to prevent curiosity seekers from entering the burned-out building, but I ignored these and ventured as deep into the lobby as debris permitted. The place stank of scorched bricks and charred bedding and was still smoldering in spots. I saw a dozen mattresses heaped at the foot of the broken stairs, saw an abstract sculpture made of ruined iceboxes and a blackened chest of drawers, saw a mountain of carpet scraps and plaster atop which rested a child's tricycle.

I retreated from the ruin and approached a gathering of tooth-less old rummies—former residents—seated on milk crates out-side the condemned property. I asked if anyone knew what had happened to their neighbor, Ernst Stanlowe. The old men sucked on their corncob pipes and bandied the name back and forth be-tween themselves with no sign of recognition. Once again Stan-lowe had proven even more of a phantom than his brother-in-law Walter.

I returned to the street corner where I had left Patterson, found the defense attorney passing the time in conversation with a former client who had happened by: a pockmarked celestial known around Chinatown as "Whispering Willie." ("He was nearly decapitated by a tong hatchet boy," Patterson would tell me later, explaining how Willie—a stool pigeon—had come by his speech impediment.) The two men shook hands and parted ways.

Patterson fell into step beside me on the sidewalk. "Learn any-thing about Stanlowe's whereabouts?"

I shook my head. "I'm beginning to think I imagined him."

"Oh, he's real enough," Patterson said. "I've met him." I must have looked stunned. He explained, "There aren't many people in this town I haven't met—or represented, for that matter. Though in this case the circumstances were social, as it so happens, a wed-ding. The reception was held at the Germantown Cricket Club. This must have been—what?—a decade ago. I brought a lady client I was representing at the time, the proprietress of one of the more fashionable and discreet parlor houses on Poplar Street. The sort of place that catered to a very well heeled clientele. As you might imagine, we were quite the *cause de scandale* that day, since there were a number of Miss Mary's well-to-do customers in at-tendance with their wives. We were shunned like lepers, but that was all right; we managed to make our own fun. . . ." Patterson drifted off momentarily, lost in the pleasant memory of his date with the society madam, then resumed his story. "And then all of a sudden Mary and I found ourselves upstaged by an even bigger scandal—the first public appearance of Mrs. Ernst Stanlowe, formerly Mina Stenson, with the socialist gardener she'd run off with that spring. Well, we wasted no time in going up to offer our congratulations. I remember being struck by how all grown up little Mina Stenson seemed—"

"Wait," I interrupted. "You already knew her?"

"Knew *of* her," he specified. "She's from Chestnut Hill, where I was raised. Of course, I was long gone by the time she and her brother arrived on the scene—I was off at law school when they were still attending ice-cream parties. But my mother had written me that Judge Stenson had remarried, and when I came home on holidays, I would see his new family at church. I remember there was a great deal of loose talk at the time about a man of his years starting a second family so late in life . . . which is funny looking back on it, since the judge was younger than I am now."

"What were Walter and Mina like as children?"

"Peculiar," Patterson replied with a ruminative frown. "Secretive. Inseparable." He glanced over at me. "And from everything you've told me today, they still are."

"Assuming she hasn't been playing me this whole time like a cheap accordion."

"Yes, I've been wondering about that," Patterson said.

I waited, hoping he might offer some insight that would clarify the enigma of Mina Crawley. Unfortunately, what he had come up with only further complicated matters.

"I think you may be overlooking a third possibility, Finch."

"Which is?"

"That your Mina *is* deceiving you—but isn't aware of it."

I looked at him sharply. "You mean that she's crazy?"

"I'm sure there must be a more scientific term."

If there was, I wasn't in a position to know it. I had no clinical experience to speak of, had only my limited reading of the works of Freud and Charcot to draw on when it came to the complicated topic of neurosis. Of course, this didn't prevent me from forming an opinion, one of the bad habits of my school days that I recall with greatest embarrassment and am least inclined to forgive.

"I suppose a psycho-analyst would say Mina's behavior is consistent with that of a hysteric," I said.

As guesses went, this was fairly conservative, since hysteria—an ancient affliction first diagnosed by the Greeks and believed to have some connection with a wandering uterus—was a kind of catchall neurotic condition, with a poorly understood etiology and a laundry list of symptoms that included everything from nervous cough to cataleptic seizure. I was basing my guess entirely on Mina's grand mal of the evening before, the first of its kind I'd ever witnessed, though it had followed the classic phases—epileptoid seizure, arched back, vocalization, contracture—as the hysterogenic fits described by the great neurologist Jean-Martin Charcot in his legendary *Leçons sur les maladies du système nerveux faites à la Salpêtrière*.

While I was struggling to reconcile myself with the idea of Mina-as-hysteric, Patterson tossed out a second possibility.

"What about dementia praecox?"

"Schizophrenia?"

Patterson raised an eyebrow. "Is that what they're calling it these days? Well, that just goes to show you how long it's been since I mounted an insanity defense."

"Did it succeed?"

"What?"

"The insanity defense."

Patterson shook his head, still smarting over the old defeat. "I put the superintendent of Pennsylvania Hospital for the Insane on the witness stand—a funny old duck by the name of Newcastle, has the most unsettling stare. . . . Anyway. He swore up and down under oath that my client heard voices—and we aren't talking two or three, but an entire Boy Scout camp. . . ." Patterson trailed off, gazing down at his foreshortened shadow. "But the jury wasn't buying it. Sent the poor devil to the electric chair singing campfire tunes."

We walked on for another block, each sequestered with his own thoughts. As we crossed Broad just north of City Hall, I emerged from my brooding to declare, "Mina's no schizophrenic."

"You don't think so?"

"No," I said. "For one thing, we've all heard Walter speak, so he isn't just a voice in Mina's head. Second, schizophrenics are highly disturbed individuals. Their thinking is disorganized, they lose touch with reality, they are either highly agitated or emotionless— none of which even remotely describes Mina." I could hear the protesting note in my voice, and yet I couldn't stop. "Schizophrenics can't carry on a *conversation*," I said, "let alone host elaborate dinner parties or entertain famous *authors*."

Patterson shot me a questioning look. "Authors?"

I explained that it had been Arthur Conan Doyle who first brought Mina to the *Scientific American*'s attention.

"You don't say?" Patterson looked impressed. "I wasted many a night at Penn reading Doyle's detective stories when I was supposed to be studying tort law." He raised an eyebrow. "What is it Holmes is always telling Watson? 'Never make the mistake of theorizing before you have all the facts.' Splendid!" Patterson showed the smile we reserve for memories of childhood, when life was

250 · *Joseph Gangemi*

lived by a gentler light. "Of course, that has very little to do with the way real police work gets done," he said, stopping on the street corner and checking to see if it was safe to cross.

"No?"

He shook his head. "Life rarely affords us the luxury of waiting for all the facts, Finch." And, tired of waiting for a break in traffic, he darted across Chestnut Street before the belligerent horns and shaken fists of a dozen angry motorists.

. . .

The law practice of C. Stuart Patterson & Associates occupied a shabby suite of offices on the fourth floor of 1523 Walnut Street, upstairs from the Goodman Barber Supply Company and across the hall from the assistant city solicitor. So far as I could tell, Patterson had no "associates" in the traditional sense, though he did employ a small staff of misfits overseen by a former Western Union boy–turned–majordomo named Ben Zion, whose principal duties, I would learn, included fending off creditors and fielding calls from the dozen or so lady friends Patterson was avoiding at any given time.

Arriving upstairs that Saturday, we found Ben—a tough little pug with the crooked nose and cauliflower ears of a reformed street brawler—in heated argument with the phone company.

"Pleased to meetcha," Ben said to me, then covered the phone's mouthpiece so he could inform his employer, "They're threatening to cut off service."

"Again?" Patterson asked, hanging his tweed jacket on a coat stand from which dangled an old Boche gas mask. "Who do you have on the line—a manager?"

"Some dame," Ben said. "A Miss Glasser."

Patterson factored this into his mental calculation of the bullshit-to-believability ratio. "In that case kindly inform Miss Glasser she's infringing on our First Amendment rights and exposing the Bell Telephone Company to immediate legal action."

"Gotcha, boss."

Patterson winked at me. "That should win us a stay of execution." He turned again to Ben. "I'm famished. What's the status of our petty cash?"

Ben fished around in a desk drawer and pulled out a fat envelope. The defense attorney's eyebrows shot up in surprise.

"Don't tell me one of our clients actually paid his legal tab?"

Ben shook his head. "Beefsteak habeas corpus."

"Ah."

Patterson gestured for me to follow him into his cramped corner office. The tall windows were unwashed, which lent the sunlight flooding the room a Sunday-after-a-hangover feel.

"What's a 'beefsteak habeas corpus'?" I asked as I took a seat in the space he cleared for me among the avalanche of dusty books and petitions and blue-backed legal briefs.

"Oh, that," Patterson said, rummaging in his rolltop desk. "It's just a little contingency plan we cooked up for those times when the practice hits low tide. Ben chats up the fellows awaiting trial down at Moko, finds out if any of them are getting tired of prison food and might like a twenty-four-hour release for a steak and a snuggle with their girlfriends. We charge fifty bucks to file the writ of habeas corpus—I tell the judge the defendant wants to develop fresh evidence on his behalf—and make them promise not to get into any trouble. Next day they surrender voluntarily with a full stomach and a smile on their face— Aha!" He emerged from the rolltop with a menu from a Chinese restaurant. "You in the mood for some chop suey?"

At the mention of food, my stomach rumbled, and I realized it had been nearly a full day since I had last eaten.

"I'm afraid at the moment I'm at low tide myself."

Patterson waved this off. "My treat. We'll send Ben out as soon as he's done fighting with the phone company. Speaking of which"—Patterson looked up from the menu—"isn't there anyone you want to call to let them know you're okay?"

A feeling of terrible lethargy settled over me, Patterson's question weighing on me like a lead vest. I sighed, knowing I couldn't put off calling McLaughlin forever.

"I suppose I should telephone the professor."

When Ben was through with the line, I accepted his boss's offer and made the dreaded call from the reception area. My mouth was dry. I waited for the operator to connect me to Klondike 5-6565. I heard a click and then the voice of the McLaughlins' housekeeper. I told her my name and asked to speak with the professor.

"I'm sorry," she said, "but he was called out of town on urgent business."

"Out of town?" I repeated, surprised. When last I'd seen McLaughlin, he had been barely capable of moving from study to bathroom. "Do you mind if I ask where the professor went?"

"He left very early this morning for Philadelphia."

. . .

Of course I felt awful about this. But beneath the guilt, which clamored in my ears like one of Schoenberg's discordant operas, there stirred a more gratifying submelody. I was touched that McLaughlin was willing to travel four hundred miles to come to my rescue—something my own father would never have done. I held out hope that McLaughlin's concern for my well-being would outweigh any disappointment he might harbor about my botching of the Crawley investigation. Oh, I didn't doubt for a minute that he would be angry, but I consoled myself with the knowledge that any harsh words he might have for me when he

arrived later that afternoon would be an expression of parental relief. And thus, as I headed off to Broad Street Station to await
McLaughlin's train, I did so in good spirits, confident that I was
embarking on an excursion that would end in forgiveness.

I couldn't have been more mistaken. No sooner had his wheelchair been lowered from the Pullman by two colored porters than
our eyes met across the crowded train shed, and I knew in a
glance that the scene McLaughlin and I were about to play would
not be a reconciliation. I crossed the platform on shaky legs.

"Professor."

"Finch."

I had spent the last hour rehearsing my act of contrition, but
now that the time for it had arrived, it flew out of my head.

"Here, let me help you, " I said, and was about to take up position behind his wheelchair when he raised a hand to stop me.

"You needn't bother," he said, "Tom will be along in a
moment."

Before I could ask who Tom was, a young stranger with ginger
hair and mustaches and an outdoorsman's winter tan climbed
down off the train and approached McLaughlin's wheelchair.

The professor made introductions. "Finch, this is Tom
Darling—another doctoral fellow."

"At Harvard?" I asked, shaking Darling's hand. "I don't understand how it is we haven't run into one another before."

"Darling's been abroad," McLaughlin explained, "conducting
research for his dissertation."

"I see."

I suppose it was rude of me not to inquire about his research or
his impressions of life on the Continent, but the truth of the matter was, I didn't give a good goddamn about Tom Darling and
didn't care if he knew it. For his part, Darling seemed entirely
oblivious of my efforts to slight him, only glanced at the watch on

254 · *Joseph Gangemi*

his freckled wrist and asked McLaughlin in a New Englander's accent, "Should I call us a cab, Doc?"

Doc?

"Thank you, Tom, yes."

"Wait," I said, stopping Darling with a hand on his chest. "The Bellevue-Stratford is just a block or two away. Tom here looks like a strapping fellow—I'm sure he can wheel you that far."

Darling narrowed his eyes at me and seemed on the cusp of some cutting remark when McLaughlin signaled him to leave us.

"We aren't going to the Bellevue," McLaughlin explained once Darling had left on his original mission. "We are going straight to the Crawley house, to attempt to repair the damage you've done."

He fixed me with a stare of such withering disapproval that I wanted to slink away and escape on the first outgoing freight. But in the end I stood my ground and resigned myself to the full force of his disappointment.

"What are you going to say to the Crawleys?" I asked.

"First I intend to apologize on your behalf," he began. "After that I will ask Mrs. Crawley to consent to a final séance—to be conducted under my own test conditions."

"Crawley will never allow it," I said. "I think he's had his fill of publicity."

McLaughlin smirked. "You underestimate the allure of the limelight, Finch. Only yesterday the good doctor contacted the *Scientific American* to inquire if his wife's participation in its contest in any way forfeits their publishing rights. I suspect Mrs. Crawley's collapse last night was due to her husband's inability to secure a satisfactory reply from the magazine's legal department before the weekend."

I frowned, admitted I wasn't following him.

"A stall tactic," McLaughlin explained, "meant to buy time until an answer can be had on Monday. If the lawyers come back with an answer in the Crawleys' favor, then you will no doubt see Mrs. Crawley make a full and miraculous recovery in time for Monday night's performance."

"And if they learn they *are* forfeiting their rights?"

"Then I expect Crawley will declare his wife too fragile to continue, forcing the magazine to abort its investigation before a verdict can be reached. So that when the public next sees the Crawley name, it will be on a book jacket—with lecture tour to follow." He looked up, saw my anxious expression. "What's the matter, Finch? I should think it would come as a relief to know you weren't responsible for this Crawley woman's collapse."

"It doesn't."

"No?"

"Of course not. She's a friend. It doesn't make me feel better to hear you accuse her of being a fraud."

"Oh, she's a friend now, is she?" McLaughlin said. "I wonder— is she anything else?"

"What are you getting at?"

"I think you know," he said mildly. "From where I'm sitting, you look for all the world like a man in love." And taking hold of the wheels on either side of his chair, he propelled himself toward the station exit, leaving me there on the platform, quietly reeling.

He was wrong. What I felt for Mina wasn't love: affection, certainly, perhaps even infatuation. But love was a more symphonic feeling, wasn't it? Not this anxious chamber piece playing in my inner ear at all hours of the day and night. I searched my feelings and decided what I felt must be something other than love— sympathy, perhaps, as well as a deep concern for her welfare. Mina was in grave danger; that was the ache I felt now in my bones.

Turning, I broke into a run and caught up with McLaughlin's wheelchair near the station's exit.

"What if you're wrong?" I asked breathlessly, striding beside him. "About . . . ?"

"What if Crawley calls an end to the investigation because Mina really *is* too sick to continue?"

"He won't," McLaughlin said with sly confidence, revealing the ace up his sleeve. "Because I have brought the good doctor the answer he's been wanting."

"And what is that?"

"He retains all publishing rights to his wife's story."

I didn't see how this guaranteed Crawley's acquiescence to McLaughlin's request for a final séance—and said so. "Then he doesn't need the *Scientific American* anymore. What's to keep him from showing you the door as soon as you tell him?"

"The chance to double his money."

"But he's already said he doesn't want the five thousand."

"I was speaking metaphorically. Fame has become the coin of Crawley's realm. The publicity he and his wife have tasted thus far is only a drop in the ocean compared with what awaits them if she wins the *Scientific American* prize."

I remembered the gleam in the surgeon's eye as he entertained a parlorful of reporters, and I knew that what McLaughlin had predicted would come true: that Crawley, having tasted fame, would risk everything for a permanent seat at the banquet table. Yet as cunningly as McLaughlin had anticipated his opponent, exploiting Crawley's egotism to maneuver him another step closer to checkmate, he had overlooked one thing:

"What if Mina no longer wants to compete for the prize?"

A muscle in McLaughlin's cheek flickered, and the doubt that had landed there briefly was brushed away like a horsefly. "I'm sure she will go along with her husband's decision."

"Yes, even if it kills her!"

McLaughlin looked at me as if I had started speaking in

tongues. I began pushing his wheelchair toward the station doors, emboldened by the fact that I couldn't see his face to press my argument.

"You're assuming that Mina is in conspiracy with Crawley to dupe the *Scientific American*. That her declining health is just part of the charade. But what if it isn't? Forget for a moment whether or not Walter is real—what if her seizures are? What if Mina is just a pawn in this little chess match you're playing with Crawley? Are you willing to sacrifice her? Don't we have a responsibility to look out for her welfare?"

"Our only responsibility," McLaughlin said, smoothing the tartan blanket across his lap as we arrived outside in the cold, "is to the readership of the *Scientific American*. You seem to have lost sight of that, Finch. But then I suppose that is to be expected when you break the cardinal rule of psychic investigation."

"What's that?"

"Never fall in love with the medium." For a fleeting moment, McLaughlin regarded me with pity, as if he knew all too well the temptation that had brought about my downfall. Then his expression hardened like setting plaster, and he wheeled himself away toward the taxi Darling had hailed.

· · ·

With McLaughlin's words still echoing in my head, I trudged back to Patterson's office on Walnut Street.

The sun was going down, and a few orphan snowflakes swirled cheerfully among the pedestrians hurrying home from evening Advent services. If there was any Christmas spirit in the air, it was lost on me; I felt only the intermittent gusts of wind off the Schuylkill cutting through my overcoat and gnawing at my rib cage. In addition to the toll it had taken on my psyche, McLaughlin's rebuke seemed to have cost me something of my physical substance, so

that pedestrians kept bumping shoulders with me on the sidewalk as if they didn't see me. At one point I passed the pretty
young mother I had encountered on my first night in Philadelphia, but just as I was about to reprise our pleasant exchange in
front of a Christmas display, I saw her eyes slide past mine and
continue on their way. I stopped, listened to the retreating click of
her Louis heels on the pavement, smelled the whisper of orange-
blossom water that was her signature on the air, and wondered if
perhaps McLaughlin's words had done more than wound me.

I needed sleep. Thankfully, Patterson had offered me the ciga-
rette-scarred couch in his office for as long as I wanted to make a
bed of it. He couldn't guarantee any warm water in the wash-
rooms, but with him away on a fishing retreat to Corson's Inlet
with a few corrupt city officials and the office closed, I would at
least enjoy a little peace and quiet for the next twenty-four hours.
My intention was to sleep for twelve of them and spend the remaining twelve mixing self-pity with liberal quantities of whatever local embalming fluid I could lay my hands on. There would
be plenty of time to sober up on the train ride home to Cambridge. Not that it mattered: Lab rats don't care one way or another if you are tight when you feed and water them, and it
actually helps when it comes time to lug them up to the roof in a
trash bin and dump chloral over their heads. It might not be the
most glamorous of careers, but it offered a measure of job security, of which my father was sure to approve.

The world doesn't need another psychologist, I could imagine him
saying, *but the city park service always can always use a good rat
killer.*

I found the key under the doormat, right where Patterson had
promised to leave it, and let myself into the dark suite of offices.
Speaking of rodents, it smelled as if one had died in the walls

while I was out. I collapsed on the cracked-leather couch, which had the texture and smell of a stuffed hippopotamus in a second-rate taxidermist's. I had arrived at that point of exhaustion where you forget the trick of sleep and finding its elusive groove becomes as difficult as locating a favorite bar of music on a gramophone record.

I stared up at the ceiling, thoughts circling back to an earlier conversation in the day, when Patterson had posited his "third explanation" for what was going on in the Crawley household—that Mina was neither a genuine spirit medium nor a calculating fake, but something else altogether: an *unconscious* fraud. As the light waned in the law offices, my initial resistance to Patterson's theory faded with it, so that by the time I lay in total darkness, I was willing at least to entertain the possibility that Mina was suffering from . . . what? Some species of nervous disorder, most likely. One that didn't impinge upon the normal psychical processes or in any way diminish higher mental functioning. A condition that allowed Mina to carry on her public life: overseeing the thousand little domestic details of a busy household, managing all the social engagements and charity functions that attended marriage to a prominent man—the invitations to the Union League's Christmas Ball, fund-raising galas at the Obstetrical Society of Philadelphia, the American début of Wanda Landowska at the Academy of Music—all the while suffering a private anguish that expressed itself only in the séance room. Did such a condition exist? Or was Walter unprecedented in the annals of neurosis? God knows I wasn't in any position to say. Nor was I prepared to believe—at least not until I had heard a diagnosis from someone more qualified.

"The tricks the brain can play without calling in Spiritualistic aids are simply astounding. . . ." So had written the superintendent

of Edinburgh Asylum, in the annual report McLaughlin had given me to read long ago, during my indoctrination in the art of psychic investigation. *"Only those who have made a study of morbid as well as normal psychology realize the full truth of this."*

I sat up on the leather couch in the dark, trying to recall the name of Patterson's expert witness from Pennsylvania Hospital for the Insane. Funny old duck . . . unsettling stare . . .

Newcastle.

It took me a full sixty seconds to find a light switch and an hour more to locate the secret hiding place where Ben Zion stashed the office address book. I rang the number listed in its pages for L. W. Newcastle, M.D., and within a matter of minutes had learned two things from the hospital's helpful receptionist: that the good doctor would indeed be in attendance tomorrow, as he was every Sunday and most holidays, and that the Pennsylvania Hospital for the Insane had changed its name to the less excitable sounding "Institute of the Pennsylvania Hospital Department for Mental and Nervous Diseases," in 1918.

Five years ago: Patterson hadn't been exaggerating when he said it had been a while since he'd last tried selling a jury on an insanity plea. I returned the phone to its hook and slumped down into Ben Zion's chair, recalling the grim outcome of that trial and wondering if the jury Mina was about to face on Monday would show her any more leniency.

. . .

"Excuse me, but I'm a little lost. I was wondering if you know where I might find the Pennsylvania Hospital for Mental and Nervous Diseases?"

The face inside the old Gypsy's shawl puckered into a toothless scowl. "Never heard of it."

"The Home for the Insane?" I prompted, glancing around the

gray neighborhood of stone row houses and streetcar junctions: not exactly the sort of landscape where one could easily hide an asylum. "The trolley conductor told me it wasn't far from Haverford Avenue—"

"Oh, you want Kirkbride's!"

"Do I?"

Evidently I did, though when I asked how the hospital had gotten this third name, the old woman only shrugged. I might as well have asked who had named the days of the week. Eager to be on her way to mass, the old Gypsy pointed with an arthritic finger, crooked as a chicken bone, indicating the direction I'd just come. I thanked her and, with overcoat flapping around my ankles, set off once more on my walking tour of West Philadelphia.

It was an unseasonably mild December morning, quiet even for a Sunday: cemetery weather. A dry wind swept leaf grit along the gutters, shivered the tall weeds that had sprouted up around telephone poles. I wandered another ten minutes, glancing back every so often to reassure myself that center city was still there to return to. It was, massed darkly on the other side of the Schuylkill like a gathering storm. I was about to give up and catch the first streetcar home when I rounded a corner and stumbled on the place—or, more accurately, stumbled on the fieldstone wall that encircled Kirkbride's twenty-seven acres. As I walked alongside the wall, I caught glimpses of the buildings beyond: a large administrative building of brick and stone with a central dome and pedimented portico along its western façade and, radiating off the main structure to the north and south, two patient wings with gabled roofs and ventilation cupolas and rows of cheerless windows. In time the stone wall brought me to an open iron gate with a gravel drive leading onto the grounds, and it was here that I hesitated, where countless visitors had hesitated before me, struck down by a sudden acute case of second thoughts.

Why had I come to Kirkbride's? For answers, of course—sober medical explanations to help me make sense of Mina, her odd marriage to Crawley and even odder relationship with Walter, and most of all her way of looking at me with hazel eyes that were flirtatious one instant and full of fear the next. Who was behind those eyes? The question seemed larger than one woman's sanity.

Just then the sun appeared through a break in the overcast, returning my shadow and temporarily brightening the gloomy surroundings. I filled my lungs with fresh air and held it—as if the human suffering I was about to encounter might be catching—then made my way through the hospital gates.

Inside, I was informed that Dr. Newcastle was on morning rounds and would be unavailable for another twenty minutes. I passed the time in conversation with the rather plain but friendly receptionist, who shed light on the lingering mystery of just who this fellow Kirkbride was and how he'd come into possession of a mental institution. Turned out Thomas Story Kirkbride had been the institute's first superintendent, hired for the post in 1841, when Pennsylvania Hospital had transferred its insane from center city to what were then the bucolic climes of West Philadelphia—over the river and through the woods, so to speak. A Quaker by faith and a surgeon by training, the thirty-year-old Kirkbride had discovered his true calling among Philadelphia's mentally degenerate, those unfortunates who had been driven mad by tobacco use, religious excitement, excessive masturbation, or prolonged lactation; unfortunates Kirkbride rescued from public ridicule (apparently a favorite pastime in that entertainment-starved age) and dedicated the next five decades of his life to treating with dignity and compassion.

All of which helped me understand why Kirkbride was spoken of in the reverential tone usually reserved for secular saints. "Can't you just *feel* the kindness in his eyes?" the receptionist asked as we stood before Kirkbride's dour portrait in the visitors' lounge, and I nodded gravely and said, "Mmm, yes. . . ." Though secretly I thought Kirkbride looked about as kindly as Captain Ahab, with those walruslike dundrearies and that scowl of Victorian disapproval.

Must be difficult living in that long shadow, I thought, wondering about the man I'd come to see today. Though from everything the receptionist told me, Newcastle was cut from the same humanitarian cloth.

"Dr. Newcastle is *always* here," she said, leaning close to confide. "One morning when I came in, I found him sleeping on that sofa right over there. I don't think he'd been home to Narberth for three days."

"His wife mustn't have been very happy about that."

"Oh, Dr. Newcastle's a bachelor," she informed me solemnly, fussing with the lace collar of her dress in an attempt to conceal the blush blooming at her throat.

When the object of her affection made his appearance a short while later, he turned out to be an elfin man of about forty-five, wearing an oversize hospital coat that gave him the appearance of a boy playing dress-up. A very sober, unsmiling boy with a preference for broken toys.

"Sorry to have kept you waiting, Mr. . . . ?"

"Finch," I said, shaking his hand. "And it's no trouble at all. I'm grateful you agreed to see me on such short notice."

Patterson had been right in singling out Newcastle's stare as his most disquieting characteristic. By the time we'd gotten these introductions out of the way, I was already squirming under the scrutiny of the physician's unblinking eyes, which were an unusual shade of mineral gray and shone with an intelligence as dispassionate as a rock formation.

"You are a colleague of Mr. Patterson's?" he asked.

"Yes."

"This is about a trial?"

"In a manner of speaking . . ." I let out a stillborn sound somewhere between a laugh and a cough. Best to come straight to the point: "Is there someplace we can speak in private, Doctor?"

"My office," Newcastle said, "though I'm afraid if we go there, I can only spare you a few minutes. Of course, if you don't mind accompanying me on rounds, we could speak at greater length."

"Didn't you just finish rounds?"

He showed a polite smile at my question. "We have sixteen wards at Kirkbride, so it's something of a never-ending process. It's a bit like bridge painting, really—when you have finished one end than it's time to start all over again at the beginning."

"I see." Adopting the nonchalance of a braver man, I said, "In that case, lead the way!" And felt a cold sweat break out beneath my shirt as he proceeded to do just that.

The first few wards were innocuous enough, not altogether different from those of any big-city hospital. I saw no overt signs of insanity in the female patients, most of whom were melancholy grandmothers with wet eyes and uncombed hair. The wards themselves, built according to Thomas Story Kirkbride's exacting and oft-imitated specifications, were bright, high ceilinged, and well ventilated, and while it would be a stretch to describe the atmosphere on the wards as homey, I *can* say at least they didn't suffer overly from the reek of disinfectant and unwashed bodies one expects of such places.

Between patients I laid out my own baffling case to Newcastle, sketching "Margery's" personal history in as much detail as I'd been able to gather. When I finished, Newcastle fell silent, his other patients temporarily forgotten, so that at least I had the satisfaction of knowing I'd intrigued him.

"Of course, without examining her myself, I'd only be speculating," Newcastle cautioned, by way of qualifying his thumbnail diagnosis: that the woman I described did indeed sound as if she was suffering from a rare nervous disorder, one that allowed the outward appearance of normalcy while manifesting under hypnosis (for Newcastle confirmed my suspicion that the séances were just elaborate hypnotic sessions) the bizarre collection of symptoms we had come to know as Walter.

"Then you've encountered patients like this before?"

"Once, very early in my career," Newcastle said, "though my patient suffered a less highly developed form than the one you describe—her abortive personalities were really just artificially dissociated groups of memories from various periods in her life; none ever developed into anything so sophisticated that it might pass for an entirely new ego."

Dissociated memories? Abortive personalities? I was having difficulty keeping up with Newcastle—literally and figuratively, as he moved briskly from one patient bed to the next—and am pleased to say that for once I admitted I was floundering. Despite his brusque exterior, Newcastle proved to be a patient teacher.

"Sometimes you will hear them referred to as 'multiple' or 'split' personalities," he said while skimming the medical chart of a listless woman with bandaged wrists, "though I share Morton Prince's opinion that a more correct term is 'disintegrated'—since the secondary personalities never achieve full independence." He looked up from his reading and warned, "Convincing as your 'Chester' may seem, Finch, you must understand that he is not a separate and sentient creature like you or me."

"What is he, then?"

"A fragment," Newcastle said, closing the chart, "a splinter of this woman 'Margery.' Inhabiting her subconscious. Sharing her memories. Leading what he believes to be a separate existence, in order that he may defend her against what he considers an imminent danger. But he is like a character in a play—just the illusion of a real man. Oh, he may linger in the dark after the curtain has gone down, but he can no more vacate the stage than Hamlet can. Nor does he especially want to—since it's in front of an audience that he truly comes *alive,* becomes for a brief time a creature of three dimensions. I don't know if you attend the theater much, Finch, but when you've gone as often as I have, you come to understand that a successful Hamlet owes as much to an audience's willingness to believe as it does to acting talent."

"Then you think Chester was invented for our benefit?"

"No," Newcastle said, "but I *do* think your committee's interest may be giving this secondary personality greater authority, as well as autonomy. May, in fact, be feeding into an existing disintegration and, without intending to, exacerbating it. I warn my interns against this danger all the time, that they should never underestimate the power of the therapeutic relationship. One of the first lessons these wards teach you is that patients feel a great desire to win their physician's approval, will often go to extraordinary lengths to please us—sometimes so far as to generate new symptoms that confirm our diagnoses. Little tokens of affection, if you will. You see how easily it becomes a vicious circle? Though I should add, in the right hands it can also be a powerful ally in treatment."

I glanced up at this hint of a silver lining. "Then the condition isn't permanent? There's a possibility she might be cured?"

Newcastle's expression grew even more dour, which is why I was so surprised when he spoke encouragingly. "Dr. Prince *has* succeeded in reversing disintegration—most notably in the case of his patient Miss Beauchamp. In effect he assisted her in reintegrating her secondary personalities back into the original one.

But not without great difficulty." He led me out of earshot of the nurses delivering the noonday meal to the convalescing patients. "If this Margery woman is indeed suffering from a similar condition, it is urgent her husband have her committed immediately."

"That could be difficult."

"Why?"

"He'd say there's nothing wrong with her."

"You will have to convince him otherwise."

"And if I can't?"

Newcastle grew pensive. "Does she have other family?"

"None that I'm aware of."

"And I don't suppose you can reason with her to have herself committed?"

"I've been forbidden to speak with her ever again."

Newcastle shook his head in resignation. "Then I'm afraid my hands are tied. If she hasn't broken any laws, I can't have her forcibly committed. I suppose I could try reasoning with the husband myself. Tell me again what he does for a living?"

"He's an obstetric surgeon."

Newcastle cursed softly under his breath. "In that case he won't give a damn what I think." He buried his hands in his pockets, seemed to deflate inside his hospital coat. "It never fails to amaze me how stubborn and difficult they can be."

"Surgeons?"

"Spouses," Newcastle said, leading me off the ward. "I shouldn't be surprised. In a great many instances, they are a large part of the problem in the first place."

As we descended the stairs, I followed up on this last comment of Newcastle's with a question that had been nagging at me for the last half hour.

"What causes this splintering of the personality?"

Newcastle paused on the landing and shrugged. "What causes

any nervous disorder? Disease. Duress. Chronic alcoholism. Up-bringing. Even—much as we in the medical profession hate to admit it—iatrogenesis: the treatment itself. Take for example my own dissociative patient. In hindsight there is no question in my mind that I inadvertently caused the spontaneous 'birth' of several new personalities. All a direct result of my inexperience."

"I'm sure you can be forgiven for making a few mistakes so early in your career."

Newcastle's face clouded. "Regrettably, there is only one person who can forgive me," he said, gazing out the wavy window glass at the hospital grounds, "and she slashed both of her carotid arteries with the sharp end of a bedspring twenty years ago."

· · ·

"The patient is a 48-year-old female who suddenly took ill after the funeral of her eldest daughter; she was admitted on the 10th of April, 1904, with symptoms suggestive of neurasthenia or nervous exhaustion (sleeplessness, depression, lassitude, pains in the limbs, &c). Since that time her condition has worsened to include paralysis of the lower extremities and right arm with complete loss of sensation. She is irritable and abusive toward myself and the staff, and suffers bouts of hysterical vomiting as well as hallucinations that she is being tormented by unseen persecutors. It was for the purpose of alleviating these more severe symptoms that hypnosis was first attempted this morning, the 18th of April. In a deep trance her anesthesia was tested and as expected found to be functional (hysterical), i.e., she was capable of counting the number of pinpricks to her lower extremities. During this session she exhibited a sudden inability to orient to season, year, or surroundings (something she has had no difficulty doing prior to now). Further questioning revealed that she believes herself to be a young woman of twenty years, residing in Boston and planning her wedding. She is unaware of her deceased daughter, her five re-

*maining children, or the man who fathered them and later deserted
her. Future hypnotic sessions are recommended to fully explore this
patient's curious conviction that she is herself at a younger age. . . ."*

I looked up, surprised to see by the humming electric clock on
the law-office wall that it was nearly eight-thirty. At some point
during the last four hours, evening had stolen over the offices.
Not that it had required much stealth, so immersed was I in
Newcastle's case notes. Three times now I'd crawled through the
loose collection of handwritten impressions, transcripts, medical
charts—and had the headache to prove it, a tight band stretching
from temple to temple.

Now I set the file aside and swung my legs off Ben Zion's desk,
jiggling them up and down on the floor to get the circulation going again. I ran a hand over my face, rubbing the place where my
glasses pinched the bridge of my nose. When the pins and needles
subsided, I stood, stretched, wandered on heavy legs to the windows, wishing I had more to show for my effort than aches and
eyestrain. But the fact of the matter was that each successive reading of the file only eroded the certainty I'd felt that afternoon—
until what had started as a compelling explanation for Mina now
felt merely plausible. True, Mina shared some things in common
with Newcastle's patient: an unsavory husband, a dead child, a
double who appeared under hypnosis and then vanished like
smoke into the amnesic aftermath. Her health might be deterio-
rating, but Mina suffered no hysterical paralysis, no vomiting or
violent hallucinations. She was troubled, no question about it—
but she wasn't mad.

(Or was I simply unwilling to admit she could be?)

Goddamn it! I brought both palms down on the windowsill
hard, my heart rising in my chest on a swell of frustration that felt
like the onset of flu. My eyes burned as I glared out at the warm
drizzle falling on Walnut Street, sick of this goddamn gray city

and everything deceitful in it, its speakeasies masquerading as funeral parlors and its winters pretending to be spring. I had done what I'd been sent to do, damn it, had asked the difficult questions and then followed them through to their logical ends: Mina was real. Mina was fake. Mina was neither. Was it my fault the evidence refused to corroborate any one of these conclusions? Or, more perplexingly, corroborated them all?

It's no longer your problem.

From now on, this would be my mantra whenever my thoughts turned to Mina. Or so I solemnly swore. And to hell with the ordeal she would face tomorrow, when McLaughlin cross-examined her. She had only brought it on herself by competing for the *Scientific American*'s five-thousand-dollar prize.

Except in my heart I knew this wasn't true. Mina never wanted the money, had only consented to sit for our committee under pressure from her husband. What else could she have done? To refuse would have been to call into question the one thing keeping Crawley's appetites in check. *Walter.* Real or imaginary, he was the only thing that kept Crawley cowering at the foot of Mina's bed like a chained wolf, naked and sobbing, his erection clutched in his cutting hand. Unless this, too, was just part of their elaborate ruse. A midnight performance I'd been meant to overhear. To lure me into their scheme, and fool me into working for them.

She isn't your problem!

Turning from the windows, I flung myself down on the leather sofa, heartsick and miserable and certain of nothing anymore, least of all what was going on in the Crawley household. I lay that way for a long time and must have drifted off at some point, because when I startled awake a while later, it was with a full bladder and a single thought.

I need to know.

Not for the *Scientific American*'s sake. Not for McLaughlin's; not even, when it came right down to it, for Mina's. I needed to know for myself. Because now I was ready to admit to myself what I'd been unable to that afternoon. McLaughlin had been right. I had made the psychic investigator's cardinal mistake.

I had fallen in love with the medium.

Which was why I had to see her again, even if it meant for the last time. To leave Philadelphia without meeting with Mina would be to condemn myself to a life of uncertainty and doubt. I had to look one last time into the eyes of this woman with whom I'd made the terrible mistake of falling in love and know if she was what she claimed—in every way other than words—to be: a woman who loved me in return.

We had to meet. Soon, in secret. Somehow.

· 12 ·

I debated whether to approach Pike the next morning with a message for Mina when he took the Boston terrier on its walk, and even staked out the house waiting for him emerge.

But when Pike finally did, it was without the dog. I watched, puzzled, as the Filipino butler scattered handfuls of what looked like table salt around the foundation of the house. (This, I would later learn, was a Filipino custom for ridding a house of unwanted guests.) However, at the last moment I aborted my plan, deciding I couldn't trust the butler's feelings for his mistress to outweigh his long-standing allegiance to her husband. Mrs. Grice seemed an even less trustworthy courier for the message I had in mind *(Meet me at the Waltham Hotel—come alone)*. I even considered enlisting the aid of Frank Livoy, my old friend from the *Public Ledger*, who I was certain would jump at the chance for an exclusive interview with a former member of the *Scientific American*'s investigating committee. But after seeing the Saturday papers' coverage of Mina's collapse (MARGERY CRACKING UNDER THIRD DEGREE), I decided now wasn't the time to take the news media into my confidence.

In the end I settled on a solution that didn't require the involvement of any third parties. Though it came with its own risks: chiefly that Mina would break with tradition and skip her afternoon-before-the-séance visit to St. Patrick's Catholic Church.

As I sat waiting in a rear pew in the candle-scented quiet, I thought of a dozen reasons why Mina wouldn't come. Hadn't she only just been released the day before from Jefferson Hospital? And why would anyone risk leaving the house, when to do so meant running a gauntlet of newspaper reporters? Mina would have to sneak out the back—disguised as Mrs. Grice, perhaps. And even then odds were she'd only run into more reporters lying in wait for her in the alley.

With each passing minute, I grew more glum, convinced that Mina wasn't coming. I watched the caretaker enter by a side door and freshen the holy water in the cisterns, dust the altar, replace used votive candles with fresh ones. Old women arrived singly and in pairs throughout the morning to pray as long as their arthritic knees would let them. Later, lone penitents wandered in from the cold on their lunch hour to light a penny candle and offer up silent appeals for promotions, proposals, pregnancy. I yawned and was about to give up on my pointless vigil when one of these young women turned from the row of votives and revealed herself as Mina.

She had not come incognito after all, though her fur collar and knit cloche had disguised her well enough to slip inside the church and right under my nose. As she came up the center aisle, her eyes were downcast and troubled, and she might have exited without noticing me at all if I hadn't reached out to touch her sleeve.

"Martin!"

I would like to say I studied her reaction with the cool detachment of a detective, or at least a defense attorney, but the truth was, I watched with a lover's fervent hope she would be happy to see me. And she was, once the initial surprise passed.

"Oh, Martin," she said, embracing me. "I was so worried."

"*You* were worried?" I said. "The last time I saw you, they were carrying you out of the house on a stretcher."

"Ugh, that." She rolled her eyes.

"How are you feeling?"

"Angry with myself," she said. "I wasn't raised to be the sort of hothouse flower who faints at the drop of a hat."

"Is that what you think happened—a fainting spell?"

Her eyes cut to mine, uncertain, afraid. "I don't know. Arthur won't tell me. I just assumed I suffered some sort of . . . fit. All I know for certain is that I woke up in the hospital, with Arthur angrier than I have ever seen him." She caught my hand, implored, "Please tell me what happened, Martin. Why did Arthur send you away?"

"Not here," I said, glancing at the few noonday worshippers scattered throughout the pews, any of whom might recognize their notorious neighbor if we lingered here. "How long can you be away before Dr. Crawley becomes suspicious?"

"A few hours," she whispered. "Arthur knows how tired I am of being cooped up in that gloomy old house. He won't expect me to come home straightaway."

"Good." I took her gloved hand, was about to lead her out, when she stopped.

"Where are we going?"

"The Waltham." Despite my protests, Chiff Patterson had insisted on loaning me enough for a room at the hotel around the corner from the Bellevue-Stratford, and now I was glad he wouldn't take no for an answer. "We can talk there."

"All right." She let go of my hand, said, "But it probably isn't such a good idea to be seen arriving together, don't you think?"

"Oh, yes, of course," I stammered, feeling like an amateur.

She nodded. "I'll tell Freddy I need to do some shopping in

the square," she said, then promised to meet me at the Waltham within the half hour.

· · ·

Twenty minutes later she entered Room 76, cast her eyes over the cramped quarters and the narrow bed, and declared my temporary home "cozy."

"It's a little dark," I said, shutting the door behind her, "but at least it's private. No one will bother us."

Immediately Mina took possession of the room, crossing to the windows and throwing open the drapes. She pouted at the view, or lack thereof, then said brightly, "Well! We'll just have to pretend we're at sea."

"Sorry?"

"On the *Aquitania*," she said, letting me slip her coat from her shoulders. "In our adorable little cabin belowdecks. You were dreadfully ill the first night, but now you've gotten your sea legs."

"Where are we going?"

"We don't care," she said. "All that matters is that we're together." She fussed with a loose button on my shirt and, looking up at me, asked, "Where would you like to go, my darling?"

"After Reno, I should think someplace cool."

"Reno?"

"Where we've been living the last six weeks," I explained nonchalantly. "Waiting for your divorce from Crawley to be finalized."

Mina frowned at my unwillingness to play her game.

"You don't have to go to Reno in make-believe."

Now that I had invoked Crawley, there would be no evicting him from our little party. I watched as Mina tugged off her gloves one finger at a time and paired them atop her coat on the bed. She opened her beaded clasp purse and took out a cigarette.

"You smoke?"

"Only when I'm upset," she explained, searching the room for a box of matches and finding one on the bed stand. "Promise you won't tell my husband. He can be a tyrant about these things."

"He and I aren't exactly on speaking terms these days."

As I lit her cigarette, she asked, "Will you tell me why?"

She had taken a seat on the edge of the bed and sat now with legs crossed and one arm wrapped protectively around her middle, as if guarding herself against whatever I might have to say. Seeing her like that, I began to reconsider my policy of truthfulness, which had never been as high-minded as I liked to pretend. The fact of the matter was, I brought Mina the truth the way other hapless suitors might bring bouquets or expensive gifts: because it was all I had to offer her. Now that I had used the truth to lure her here to a hotel room, it seemed cruel to have a change of heart. And so I told her.

"If you ask Crawley, he'll say its because of what happened Friday night," I began, "but the truth is, it's because of what I did earlier that day that he's become so angry with me."

"What did you do?"

I met her eyes, said, "I spoke with your former husband."

For a few heartbeats, she seemed confused, as if unsure she'd heard me correctly. "How . . . ?" Then understanding flooded her face, and she was able to answer her own question: "Walter."

I nodded. "He seemed to think it was important that I hear Stanlowe's side of things."

"Did he," Mina said without inflection, examining the nails of the hand holding the cigarette. "My brother has always been overprotective, ever since we were children. He worshipped our mother, and when she died, I inherited his devotion. Which has been suffocating at times. . . ." She looked at me. "Do you have any siblings?"

When I shook my head, she frowned, deprived of common ground that might make this easier to explain. She resumed her story.

"He used to get into beastly scraps with young men who showed me any attention. He wasn't much of a fighter, but that didn't stop Walter. He would come home bloody as an old tomcat and sit there purring while I cleaned him up. Once he tried to run over the neighbor's boy in our old Auburn. Father had to beg the family not to press charges. Later he stopped trying to run young men over and would simply attempt to seduce them." Her eyes shifted to mine. "I'm sorry, have I shocked you?"

"No."

"Good. Because there was nothing especially shocking about my brother. He was terribly old-fashioned, really. My annulment positively scandalized him." She held the stem of the cigarette holder to her lips, tipped her head back to exhale the smoke in a thin stream. I looked at the ivory sweep of her throat, heard her ask the light fixture on the ceiling, "What was my point in all of this? Oh, yes—that you shouldn't believe everything my brother tells you."

"I'm still trying to decide whether I believe *any* of it."

If the look of surprise and hurt that came over Mina was just an act, then she possessed a talent rivaling that of Eleonora Duse. But although her eyes grew liquid and her chin trembled, no tears ever came. Instead she stood abruptly, crushing her cigarette in the ashtray on the bed stand and gathering her coat and gloves.

"I'm a fool," she said, flustered. "Forgive me. I just assumed once you met Walter— It never even occurred to me that you still might not believe—"

"Mina, wait," I said, catching her shoulders and forcing her to look up at me.

Before I could say more, she interrupted. "You must think I'm a horrible person."

"I could never think such a thing."

"What then?"

"I . . ." My mouth had turned to cotton. "I don't know."

At this her face crumbled and she lost her battle with her tears. Amid her sobs she begged, "Please, *please* . . . tell me what I can do to convince you I'm not lying. I'll do whatever you ask—"

I opened my arms to her, and she buried her face against my chest. I said into the crown of her hair, "You don't need to convince me. I'm not the one investigating you anymore."

"But you're the only one I care about," Mina said. "You're the only one who matters. There must be something I can do to convince you to believe me."

"There may be a way."

"How?"

"Let me hypnotize you."

Mina's expression became guarded. "Why?"

"So I can question you about your brother."

"But I'll tell you whatever you want to know."

I shook my head firmly. "People speak more freely under hypnosis. They're less inhibited, less inclined to censor themselves—"

"You mean they can't lie." Mina shifted her mascara-streaked eyes away from mine. I studied her face in profile. Was it anger and hurt that were causing her jaw to clench? Or something cooler—a mind calculating the moves that would keep her out of checkmate?

I had almost convinced myself of the latter when she turned her eyes back to mine and asked timidly, "What does it feel like to be hypnotized?"

"No different from one of your trances during a séance."

This seemed to reassure her. "And you've done it before?"

"Many times," I said, exaggerating only a little. "It was popular at campus parties for a while. People did it for a laugh."

"A laugh."

She tasted the word, like an exotic sweet. I took her hand to show her that this was something we'd be doing together, not something I would be doing *to* her. At last she relented, squeezing my hand. Her smile was like the sun after a spring shower.

"If it will make you happy, darling."

I sat her back down on the edge of the bed and gave her a glass of water to settle her nerves while I went in search of a candle. As I walked to the front lobby, I felt my confidence in what we were about to do beginning to waver. What had worked on extroverted Radcliffe girls in the context of a party wouldn't necessarily work on a sober woman of thirty; though Mina had already demonstrated a gymnastic nimbleness of mind, slipping in and out of autohypnotic trance with no difficulty at all. I only prayed that this nimbleness would survive the change of venue.

When I returned from the Waltham's reception desk with a candle in hand, I found Mina lying back on the bed with her shoes off, preparing herself mentally for what was to come. At first I thought she might be sleeping, but as I shut the door quietly behind me, her eyes opened partway. She watched through slitted lids as I shut the drapes to darken the room, then lit the candle and dripped wax into the ashtray to make a base. When everything was ready, I indicated that she should sit with her legs over the edge and took my position on the floor at her feet like a shoe salesman.

"What do I do?" she asked tremulously.

"Relax. Take deep breaths. This won't be difficult."

She did as she was told, her chest rising and falling beneath her silk dress. I was acutely aware that we were reaching the point of no return and that I had lied to get Mina there. I had no intention of questioning her about Walter; I wanted to hypnotize her for one reason and one reason only: to hunt him. To find where the Cheshire cat was crouching in Mina's unconscious and flush him into the open. It was for selfish reasons that I was putting Mina into a trance, but not, I must believe, entirely heartless ones.

"All right, Mina," I began, "I want you to look closely at this flame. See how it is actually made up of several colors? Orange . . . yellow . . . even a little blue if you look hard enough. Can you see the blue, Mina?"

She gave a tiny nod, never taking her eyes off the flame. Her pupils had dilated, so that there was only the thinnest ring of iris left in each eye.

"Now," I continued, "I want you to look even closer, Mina. Notice how there is a tiny space around the wick? Almost like the eye of needle or a keyhole. . . . Can you see the keyhole?"

Another nod, though her reaction time had slowed considerably.

"There's a room on the other side, Mina. You are very curious about what is in there. It's all right to be curious. Why don't you try to peek through the keyhole? . . . Can you make out what's in the next room?"

This time she gave a sleepy shake of her head. Her eyelids were at half-mast, and her breathing had settled into the placid give-and-take of surf at midnight. My heart was racing. I had never induced a trance state so quickly. I fought to keep the quaver of excitement out of my voice as I guided her deeper.

"Now I want you to imagine yourself becoming smaller, Mina. Shrink yourself down until you can fit through that keyhole. It shouldn't be difficult. Are you small enough yet? Good. Then I want you to pass through the keyhole into the next room. You needn't be afraid. You can always follow my voice back here. But you don't want to just yet, because the room you have found is so comfortable and safe and quiet, far away from any worries. You could rest here for hours, it's so peaceful. Let yourself rest in this quiet place, Mina, you've earned a long rest. . . ."

"Mmmm." A low moan escaped her throat. She was gone.

Now, Mina, I thought, *let's see who's in there with you.*

"Walter?"

Silence. Just the sound of Mina's slow respirations.

"Will you speak with me, Walter?"

Nothing. Only the sound of my wristwatch ticking off the seconds. I waited, watched the twin flames reflected in Mina's heavy-lidded eyes. Her breathing hitched and held, the way it does when you have heard a noise in the distance. Mina was listening. Or was it someone else?

"Tell me how to help her, Walter," I said softly. "I'll do anything for Mina. Do you understand? *Anything.*" With a voice wrecked by emotion, I confessed what I had been unable to before that moment: "I'm in love with your sister."

It had taken every ounce of courage in me to say the words, and now that I'd said them, I was rewarded with . . . nothing. Just a woman staring into space in a claustrophobic hotel room. Defeated, I closed my eyes and rested my forehead against one of Mina's knees, taking a moment to collect myself before bringing her out of the trance.

I heard a hiss of silk, felt her knee shift. Startled, I opened my eyes, saw Mina still staring blankly into the candle flame with her legs open. I could see where the thick silk stockings ended in a dusky pink roll high on her white thighs and, further up between them, that she wasn't wearing any underclothes.

"Mina?"

The candle sputtered out in my hand, a filament of smoke

unspooling from its wick. She continued staring at the place where the flame had been, though now the absence in her hazel eyes was replaced by an unsettling *something else . . .* as if an intelligence other than Mina's was looking out of them.

I asked quietly, in a cracked voice, "Walter?"

In the poor light, I could just make out a wicked smile as it played across her features. Then she was coming forward and gripping my shirt, pulling me up to her mouth. Her lips were cold and dry, but her tongue when I found it, when she offered it to me, was soft and warm. Kissing her, I could taste the good burgundy she'd had with lunch, resinous and sweet, as well as the waxy taste of lipstick and the Chesterfield she'd just smoked. She pulled me down after her as she fell back against the pillows among our coats and gloves, her hands clutching at my ears, my shoulders, the scruff of curls at the nape of my neck. I felt the strength in her hands, the strength of a sleepwalker. We tangled like contortionists on the bed, shedding clothes, liberating her from her ridiculous bust flattener and me from my trousers—all the little domestic preparations that give lie to the illusion, popular in French novels and the more purple descriptions of sex, that passion is a breathless headlong rush that cannot be interrupted once set in motion. Much as I would like to claim that passion made me incapable of stopping our adulterous slide into each other's arms, I cannot in good conscience, not when I maintained a clear enough head to see my glasses safely set aside on the bed stand, where they wouldn't get broken.

Without them Mina was vague as she sat astride me, so that I couldn't be certain during our lovemaking if what I saw across her breasts were scars or birthmarks. Her face was vague as well, an upturned mask, either unaware of or indifferent to the reality of me beneath her. Though it occurs to me now, with the advantage of hindsight and greater experience in such matters, that her expression could simply have been that inward-looking one a woman gets when she is close to climax.

Afterward we collapsed among the bedclothes and slept, lulled by the muted city sounds outside the window that might as well have been the sound of the sea.

I woke a short while later and, reaching carefully so as not to disturb Mina, retrieved my glasses from the bed stand. Her face had returned in sleep to the one I knew, uncomplicated and kind. I laid my head back down beside hers on the pillow and drew her closer to me, knowing full well we would have to rouse ourselves in time and take stock of the damage we had done. I lay there listening to the gentle sound of her breathing, the untroubled rise and fall of it, watched the flicker of her pulse in her throat.

"I'm sorry," she said in the dark, surprising me.

"You're awake?"

"I was never asleep," she said, yawning, stretching her legs beneath the covers. "I'm sorry it didn't work."

"Work?"

"The hypnosis," she said. "I was never in a trance. I heard you talking the whole time."

"What did you hear?"

Sadly: "That you've fallen in love with me."

It took a moment to find my voice. "I can't believe it."

She turned to face me, said, "I wanted so very badly for it to work, darling. So that you'd believe me. . . . Now I don't suppose anything has changed." A tear spilled down her cheek and soaked into the pillowcase. With a corner of the bedsheet she dabbed at her eyes, and raising her arms exposed the marks on her breasts I had wondered at before. This time there was no question in my mind what they were.

"Where did you get these scars?" I asked, tracing with a fingertip a crescent-shaped dimple below her right breast.

"Don't." A shiver ran across her flank. "That tickles."

"Tell me."

"I don't remember."

She rolled away from me, dragging the bedclothes with her. She sat on the edge of the bed with her back to me and retrieved her stockings. "Walter probably threw a bottle at me. He could be a frightful bully sometimes. You know how little brothers are."

"I don't, actually."

"You'll just have to take my word for it."

"I'd rather not. I'd rather you tell me the truth."

She heaved a great sigh of exasperation, shoulders sagging. "Honestly, darling, you can't expect a person to remember the story behind every little bump and scrape she suffered a million years ago."

"I'll settle for one."

She bunched one stocking into a doughnut and slipped it over her toes, unrolling it along the length of her leg. Her movements as she plucked and adjusted the seam were quick, irritated.

"You don't believe anything I say. Maybe you should just go ahead and make up one for me."

"All right," I said. "I think Crawley is responsible for them."

The muscles in her back tensed as she froze in the act of rolling on her second stocking. I crawled across the bed on my knees until I was behind her, reached around to touch the four-inch scar below her navel, the smaller round burn on her breast. I spoke quietly, my face beside her ear.

"He made this one with a cigarette, didn't he?"

Mina closed her eyes, seemed to fight a wave of revulsion. I pressed my lips to the spot on her neck where her hair became fine as down feathers, and whispered, "McLaughlin is going to try to take your brother away from you, Mina. Tonight. What happens once Crawley reads in the *Scientific American* that Walter isn't real? What happens when he knows no one is watching? Goddamn it, I won't let him!" I said, though I had little more than a vague idea of what we might do—run away together, I suppose, as we had envisioned in our daydream. But details of how and where were secondary to the more immediate concern: convincing Mina to accept me as her rescuer.

"Please, Mina. Let me help you."

"Don't you see you already have?"

She laid her hand on my cheek. Then she rose from the bed and slid her dress over her head. She gave a little shimmy to help it settle over her breasts, her hips, then stepped into her shoes and whisked up her coat and gloves from where they had ended up on the floor. Before I could stop her, she was across the room.

She looked back at me from the door. "Walter is real. . . ."

She said it with less conviction than I might have expected. She heard the hitch of uncertainty in her own voice, and her eyes clouded, as if she had just overheard a bit of cruel gossip spoken in the next room. She glanced at me once more in the bed, blew me a kiss. And slipped away into the afternoon.

• • •

That night Walter never came.

After two hours and more playings of "Swanee River Blues" from the Ziegfeld Follies than anyone could count, the séance was reluctantly declared a blank. The transcript of the evening is rather dry-eyed about the whole thing, but I had it on the good authority of my undercover agent Miss Vivienne Binney, the stenographer, that Mina was visibly upset by Walter's failure to come through. In a personal aside, the stenographer confided to me that the professor's new graduate assistant, Tom Darling, had offered a sarcastic running commentary on the proceedings as he listened with her via the Dictograph. Also that he smelled. This so tickled me that I treated Miss Binney to coffee and a slice of pie at the Horn & Hardart along with the other Quaker City insomniacs. We agreed to meet again at the same time and place the following night and as many nights thereafter that McLaughlin's Inquisition continued.

But we never expected our standing engagement at the H&H to stretch into a week. For four consecutive evenings, Miss Binney dutifully reported to the Automat with news of another unsuccessful séance, as well as her impressions of the effect these failures were having on the personalities sitting around the newly rebuilt séance table. Crawley, embarrassed, made excuses for his wife's faltering powers: Mina was tired, Mina was menstrual, Mina was distracted by the fact that she hadn't yet finished her Christmas shopping. Crawley's equivocations found a sympathetic audience in Fox, Flynn, and Richardson (though the stenographer suspected that their solidarity might be weakening), but McLaughlin remained unmoved. And Mina? The medium seemed oblivious to the men around her, caught up as she was in a crisis of diminishing self-confidence. That Friday, Mina herself asked for a night off to rest and meditate—an unprecedented request that suggested just how serious the situation had become.

On that day, while Mina was resting in her four-poster bed a few blocks away, I was tossing and turning in my narrow bunk at the Waltham Hotel with my face buried in a pillow that still bore her scent. This was no accident. Each morning I stripped the pillowcases and hid them under the mattress so the chambermaid couldn't remove them.

At last I managed to fall into a restless sleep and, in the small hours that Saturday morning, dreamed I had completed medical school and was a resident on a hospital ward. Many of the details were cloudy and contradictory, so that it remained unclear in my mind whether the ward was part of a lying-in hospital or an asylum. Crawley was the attending physician, and I was his chief resident. As he led me on rounds, I saw that all the patients were wild-haired females of child-bearing age. *Hysterical pregnancies, every one,* Crawley told me with a conspiratorial wink, as if we were something more than colleagues. And yet his diagnosis hadn't jibed with what I saw on the dream ward, or for that matter knew about hysterical pregnancy, since many of the women were nursing newborns: pale, groping creatures, slick with the same teleplasmic slime we had scraped off Walter's pigeon. At last, and at the far end of the ward, we came upon Mina in a hospital gown. *Now, Finch, here's an interesting case,* Crawley said by way of an introduction. Mina turned her face from the wire-cage window and asked, *Which one of you is going to give me my baby?* I was dumbfounded, but Crawley had an answer ready for his patient. *It saddens me to inform you, my dear, the child was born without gills. I had no choice but to send it to the incinerator.* Mina accepted this news without expression or surprise. She replied calmly, *Well then, I will just have to make another one myself.*

And, hiking up her grubby hospital gown, she lay back against her pillows and began to masturbate feverishly.

· · ·

On the evening of Saturday the twenty-second, the séances at 2013 Spruce Street were resumed—and resulted in a fifth blank.

"Things are getting pretty tense," Miss Binney reported that night over eggnog and sticky buns at the H&H. (We had exhausted the Automat's selection of homemade pies and sworn off its "bottomless" coffee.)

"I can imagine," I said. "How does Mina seem?"

"Sad."

"How so?"

"Mostly little things," Miss Binney said, accustomed by now

to my obsessive interest in Mina's every nuance of mood. No doubt her female intuition had long ago tipped the stenographer off to my feelings for Mina, but to her credit she never commented on my infatuation—only did her best to bring me the details I so desperately craved.

"Usually Mrs. Crawley makes a point of saying hello," she said now. "She'll linger a while afterward, when the rest have gone downstairs and I'm reading over my notes. She always goes out of her way to say something nice about my dress or compliment me on how I'm wearing my hair. She isn't at all snooty or stuck up, like you would expect a doctor's wife to be. Then, for instance, just this Monday I had a little difficulty of a female nature, and Mrs. Crawley took me to the powder room and fussed over me like a mother hen. She was very sweet, asking me all sorts of questions about how I like living alone and don't I get scared riding streetcars by myself. I get the feeling she doesn't have any close girlfriends." The stenographer made a sympathetic face, then came to her point. "Anyway. So the last few nights after the blank séances, Mrs. Crawley has looked right through me—like she never laid eyes on me before in her life. I tried saying hello to her, but I might as well be talking Swahili."

"She doesn't respond?"

She shook her head. "The poor thing just gets up from her chair and sort of *floats* out of the room. Without saying a word."

I looked down at my earthenware mug of eggnog, cloying as uncooked cake batter. Soft Christmas music was coming from a radio somewhere back behind the Automat's bank of little glass windows, a sound as sad as a foghorn or a distant train whistle. I glanced at my watch and saw that while we were talking, the hour had slipped over quietly into Sunday.

"I've kept you too long," I told Miss Binney. "I had better see about getting you home."

"All right."

She rose, gathering her purse and spiral-bound steno books.

Her apartment building was only a few blocks away, and as I walked her there, she prattled on about the people left on her Christmas list (a baby brother off at college, a spinster aunt) and how she had been fending off the crude advances of Tom Darling, McLaughlin's boorish apprentice. I knew she was only making an effort to distract me, but she was fighting a losing battle, and when I failed to offer any of the polite noises people make to show they're listening, she gave up trying. We walked the last two blocks without speaking. And yet when we arrived outside her building, it was I who broke the silence—with a question it had never occurred to me before to ask this young woman who all along had been a kind of unofficial fifth juror.

"Do you believe she's genuine, Miss Binney?"

"Vivienne," she corrected, then answered solemnly. "And yes, I do." I thought she might leave it at that, but she continued. "I believe it's her blessing and her curse."

"Why curse?"

The pretty stenographer met my eyes. "Because now that it seems to be fading, she is losing her brother all over again."

. . .

December 23. Two days before Christmas. A Sunday.

The bitter cold had winnowed the number of reporters outside the Crawley home to one. Frank Livoy was in the midst of a drink from his hip flask when I stepped out of the shadows.

"Shit!" Livoy startled, squinted at me in the dim light from the single streetlamp. "Well, well, well, if it isn't the Ghost of Christmas Past."

"I thought you didn't believe in ghosts, Livoy."

"I don't," he said, offering me the flask. "Drink?"

"Thanks."

I took a swig, wiped my mouth on the back of my hand. "Looks like you're the last man standing, Livoy."

"In my line of work, that's who usually gets the story."

"Did you get yours yet?"

"Bits and pieces," Livoy said. "Had a coupla new faces show up a little while ago. Fellow about your age, with an older gent in a wheelchair. Didn't catch their names, though."

"McLaughlin and Darling," I said. "McLaughlin is chair of Harvard's psychology department. Also president of the American Society for Psychical Research. Darling is the new assistant he found to replace me."

"You feel like telling me your side of the story?"

"Someday," I said, "once I figure out what it is."

I took a second swig from the flask, handed it back to its mystified owner, and hurried up the steps of 2013 Spruce Street. I rang the doorbell and waited. On the windowsill to my right, I saw the imperious Siamese watching me, and I was struck by a sudden overwhelming sense of déjà vu. I rapped on the glass to scare the cat away.

The looks on the faces of my former colleagues when Pike escorted me into the parlor a moment later were priceless. The cigarette nearly dropped from Flynn's lips, and in the stunned hush you could almost hear Fox's blood pressure whistling like a teakettle. I was relieved that Mina and Crawley weren't downstairs yet, since I was a few drinks away from being ready to confront them.

McLaughlin wheeled himself toward me with a scowl on his face that could have curdled milk. Fortunately, I was drinking sherry—or would be as soon as I finished pouring a glass for myself.

"What are you doing here, Finch?"

"Helping lure your shade back to the table."

McLaughlin's eyes narrowed. "I wasn't aware that this was a negotiation."

"No?" I tossed back the sherry, refilled my glass. "Then I suppose that explains why you've had so many blanks."

Fox came forward, incensed. "That's your fault, Finch, not ours! Frankly, I'm shocked you can even show your face here after what you've done. Do you realize your meddling may have driven off the only family this poor woman has left in the world?"

"Walter hasn't gone anywhere," I said, feeling the alcohol working its magic on my confidence. "You just haven't offered him any reason to talk to you."

"Don't be idiotic—" Fox began, before McLaughlin cut in.

"All right, Finch. What do you suggest we offer him?"

"For starters," I said, "his brother-in-law. I see now it was a mistake to have asked Dr. Crawley to leave the circle."

"Anything else?" McLaughlin asked.

"Yes." Sufficiently fortified with liquid courage, I added, "Me."

"What makes you think this will make any difference?"

"Because, gentlemen," I said to the gallery of grim faces surrounding me, with special emphasis to Tom Darling, "it's the irritated oyster that makes pearls."

A disgruntled murmur ran through the other committeemen, but I ignored them, knowing that in the end it was McLaughlin's decision that mattered. I could see him weighing his distaste for my suggestion against the very real possibility of another blank séance. At last McLaughlin spoke, and the room fell quiet around him.

"All right, Finch. But I believe you have your work cut out for you convincing Dr. Crawley."

"Convincing me of what?" Crawley stood in the entranceway dressed in his usual formal dinner attire. The climate in the parlor became wintry as he saw me under his roof, sipping his sherry. "What is *he* doing here?"

"I've come to ask your permission to rejoin the circle."

"Absolutely not."

"Please hear me out." I drew him aside so we could continue our conversation in private. Crawley cast a chilly look at Pike, presumably for having admitted me in the first place, and then followed me reluctantly into the foyer. Out of earshot of the others, I made my case. "I'm only doing this for Mina. Each day this drags on, another little piece of her dies."

"So now you're an expert on the state of my wife's soul?"

I ignored his question and said, "Think how suspicious this all looks to Professor McLaughlin. He shows up and overnight the most talkative shade this side of the Holy Ghost goes mum. Trust me, Dr. Crawley, I know McLaughlin, and he is *this* close to pulling up his tent poles and going home."

Crawley's jaw tightened, and he looked over my shoulder in the direction of the parlor, where the others were waiting. He pursed his lips. "What makes you think you will be any more successful than your colleagues?"

I was ready for this. "Because Walter relishes having the last word—something I denied him last Saturday. Put me in that séance room tonight and your brother-in-law won't be able to resist giving me a piece of his mind."

"You had better hope that's all he gives you," Crawley said with a nasty smile, "since I'm all out of tetanus antitoxin."

And with that he turned on his heel and made his way back to his guests.

I may have been reinstated to my former position on the *Scientific American* committee, but I knew I wouldn't be welcome at cocktail hour in the parlor. So I retreated to the kitchen, empty now that Pike and Mrs. Grice had gone out for the night, and passed the hour before the séance with a piece of mail that had been delivered to the house for me earlier that week: the pathologist's analysis of the sample of teleplasm I'd scraped off Walter's pigeon. Much of the report was highly technical, and I found it depressing how much organic chemistry I had managed to forget over the last few years. *"The sample is an albuminous exudate made up of at least 50 percent water,"* the pathologist had written, *"with traces of sulfur, phosphates, and fats, as well as cellular matter consistent with that typically found in the human mouth and esophagus."* The report came to an inconclusive finish, with the pathologist unwilling to make even an educated guess at the formula for the mystery substance.

At half past seven, Darling poked his head into the kitchen. "You wanna give me a hand carrying the professor upstairs?"

I followed him out, and together we lifted McLaughlin from his wheelchair and transported him up three flights of stairs to the nursery. I was surprised by how little he weighed; it seemed his wife's excellent cooking hadn't been enough to stay the considerable wasting in the aftermath of his accident.

As we entered the tiny third-story séance room, I saw Mina for the first time in a week and was shocked by her transformation. She had cut her hair since last I'd seen her and wore it now in the short Eton bob of a woman ten years younger. It was obvious she had spent a great deal of time before the vanity mirror in anticipation of tonight's performance, powdering her face and painting her eyes to give her features an exotic, almost Oriental cast. She had replaced her usual loose-fitting tunic with a shimmering silk kimono of midnight blue—another souvenir of Crawley's years overseas, I could only assume—on which was embroidered a dragon with golden scales that turned and twined and climbed the length of her before perching finally on her shoulder like a celestial pet.

What Mina meant to accomplish by this getup, I couldn't guess—nor could I ask, since she had already embarked on her journey into the kerosene flame and gave no indication that she was aware of our entrance. Her hazel eyes were as blank and un-blinking as a waxwork dummy's, and only by peering closely at her was I able to detect the subtle rise and fall of her breath.

We installed McLaughlin in the chair immediately to Mina's left, and once he was settled, I wasted no time staking my claim to the place on her right. I could see McLaughlin making note of my eagerness to claim this second position of honor in the circle. We engaged in a brief staring contest as Fox, Flynn, Richardson, and Crawley filed in and took their customary places around the séance table.

Crawley fussed with the gramophone's electric repeater, then glanced at his pocketwatch and announced to the room, "Half past seven. I suppose we should begin."

As Crawley extinguished the kerosene lamp, we all joined hands with our neighbor. In the corner of the nursery, the gramo-phone crackled, and then we heard the opening bars of "Sou-venir," one of Walter's favorite tunes.

I gave Mina's frigid fingers a squeeze, expecting her to squeeze my hand back or indicate in some other way that she was aware of my presence, but she remained unresponsive. I recalled then what the stenographer had told me about Mina's failure to recognize her. Had the anxiety of the last two weeks finally become too much for her already fragile mental state? I felt a wild impulse then to throw Mina over my shoulder and bolt from the house under cover of darkness. How far would we manage to get before the police caught up with us?

You can see that my instinct was still to regard myself in the role of romantic hero, instead of the lesser part for which I had been cast in the Crawleys' strange little domestic drama. But self-delusion is key to playing the foil—not to mention the fool.

We waited as the gramophone record played through to its finish and started over again, with no sign that its intended audience was listening. I could feel tension running through the human circuit we made, a current of apprehension and dread. When a second and then a third playing of "Yes! We Have No Bananas" failed to lure the Cheshire cat out of his tree, we broke the circle for a moment and waited while Crawley dashed downstairs to retrieve his secret weapons: a dozen more Victor Red Seal records purchased the day before at Wanamaker's music counter. Dance records, light vocal selections, sacred songs for the Christmas season. I wondered what the girl at the music counter had made of this middle-aged gentleman buying copies of "Shake Your Feet" and "Walk, Jennie, Walk!" and "Ev'ry Night I Cry Myself to Sleep Over You."

Now we listened to them all—once, twice, three times, until we knew every sentimental lyric by heart. We played them until the grandfather clock on the landing chimed midnight and Crawley announced that we had worn through the last of the steel needles.

"Well," Fox asked in the dark, "what do we do now?"

The room fell silent, as each man in the circle waited for one of his neighbors to be the one to propose adjourning. And it was in this odd moment of communal indecision that I began to sing the most ridiculous song I knew.

Jimmy was a soldier brave and bold,
Katy was a maid with hair of gold,
Like an act of fate, Kate was standing at the gate,
Watching all the boys on dress parade.

I ignored the discouraging comments of my colleagues ("Who's that singing?" "It's Finch—he's finally lost his mind!") and continued singing.

> *Jimmy with the girls was just a gawk,*
> *Stuttered ev'ry time he tried to talk,*
> *Still that night at eight*
> *He was there at Katy's gate,*
> *Stuttering to her this love sick cry—*

What I lacked in talent, I made up for with enthusiasm, and by the time I arrived at the chorus, my voice had lost its nervous warble. I found I was actually enjoying myself.

> *K-K-K-Katy, beautiful Katy,*
> *You're the only g-g-g-girl that I adore*
> *When the m-m-m-moon shines,*
> *Over the cowshed,*
> *I'll be waiting at the k-k-k-kitchen door!*

As I brought the chorus home with all the lumbering grace of Babe Ruth rounding bases, I was surprised to hear another voice join mine: Flynn. The newspaperman was an even worse singer than I, and together we did a bang-up job of massacring the second verse, as the lovestruck stutterer proposes on the eve of being shipped off to France.

Soon Richardson joined us. With volume now on our side, we had become an unstoppable force, and as we came down the home stretch, Fox made us a quartet.

> *Jimmy thought he'd like to take a chance,*
> *See if he could make the Kaiser dance,*
> *Stepping to a tune,*

All about the silv'ry moon,
This is what they hear in far off France.

To this day I don't know what made me break into song that night or moved Fox and Flynn and Richardson to set aside their animosities and join me. Fatigue, I suppose, coupled with a desire to salvage what little dignity was left to us by mocking the whole ridiculous situation. We were, after all, a group of grown men holding hands in the dark. What else could we do but go out singing?

K-K-K-Katy, beautiful Katy,
You're the only g-g-g-girl that I adore;
When the m-m-m-moon shines,
Over the cowshed,
I'll be waiting at the k-k-k-kitchen door.

Crawley applauded as we reached our rousing finale and collapsed in laughter. We laughed for a full fifteen seconds, forgetting the fact that we disliked one another, until it occurred to me that we were still holding hands and therefore it couldn't be Crawley who was clapping.

"Bravo," a familiar voice said from the darkness.

"Walter!"

A thrill ran through the circle.

"We thought you weren't coming!" Crawley said.

"And miss the debut of the *Scientific American* Follies?"

"Were we really awful?" Richardson asked.

"To the contrary! You'll be the toast of Broadway—assuming, of course, you can find some sequined tuxedos."

"We're so glad you're here!" Crawley enthused. "We thought we had heard the last of you."

"No, you're hearing that now."

"What?"

"I've only come to say good-bye."

A stunned beat; then Crawley asked the question on all our minds. "But where are you going?"

"West."

"There's something there you want to see?"

"Mountains," Walter replied, "though it's what is on the other side of them that most interests me."

In a timid voice Fox asked, "Do you think it is the City of God?"

"I hope not!" Walter said. "I would hate to go all that way just to find another dry town. No, I'll be quite content to find a few others like myself. I know I sometimes come across as hard-boiled, but I don't mind admitting to you gentlemen that it can get lonely here in the evenings with no one to talk to."

"But you have us to talk to!" Crawley said.

"It's not the same."

"Why not?"

"Because what goes on in this room isn't conversation."

"How is it any different?"

"For starters, there's a woman writing it down."

"You have my word she'll never do it again."

"Yes, because there won't be anything to write."

A note of desperation entered Crawley's voice. "Are you leaving because you're bored?"

"That's part of it."

"Because I could invite other people. . . ."

"What other people?"

"More interesting ones. Writers, artists."

"You don't know any artists."

"I'll find some," Crawley said. "We'll start a salon."

"I daresay the décor is better suited to a mortuary."

"We'll redecorate."

"You're wasting your breath, Crawley."

"There must be someone you want me to invite?"

"I'm drawing a blank."

"Homosexuals?"

"Good-bye, Crawley."

"Wait!" his brother-in-law cried, gripping my left hand with such force that I winced in the dark. "You can't leave. Don't you see, Walter? You've captured the public's interest. There are thousands waiting to hear your message . . . millions."

Walter responded in a subdued voice, "I'm only concerned with one."

I broke my silence. "Mina?"

"Would you mind taking a message to her for me, sport?"

"She's going to be upset."

"What I have to say will help take the sting out of it."

I agreed, and after a thoughtful pause, he began to speak.

"Start by telling my sister that I love her," Walter said, "and that I'm going to miss her terribly. She won't understand why I've chosen to go, so you might want to leave that part out and just tell her I was called away—or better yet, *summoned*. Yes, that has a more metaphysical-sounding ring to it."

"I'm not going to lie to her for you."

"No?" He sounded disappointed. "I suppose you're right, sport. She'd only see through a lie anyway, and it wouldn't do any good having her sore at the both of us. You might try consoling my sister with this, though, because it's the truth: I wouldn't be leaving if Mina hadn't proven she doesn't need me looking out for her anymore—" He broke off, then asked, "Do you have any younger siblings, sport?"

"I'm an only child."

"Too bad," he said, before waxing nostalgic. "When I look

at Mina sitting there, I can still see the little pigtailed terror who wanted to marry all of my classmates from Germantown Academy. Strange to think she has gone and done it—married someone, that is. Stranger still to think that that little girl is going to be somebody's mother."

To my left, Crawley suddenly came awake. "What did you just say?"

Walter ignored Crawley. "Will you give my sister the good news for me, sport? Afraid it's all I can offer in the way of a farewell present."

Beside me I heard Crawley muttering under his breath:

"Impossible . . . nothing short of a miracle . . ."

But I had gone numb and stopped listening.

"What's wrong, sport? You look as if you'd seen a ghost."

"I'm just wondering what I'm going to say to Mina."

"Don't worry," Walter reassured. "It won't come as all that much of a surprise. Women have an intuition when it comes to these things, you know." And I heard his famous chuckle. "In any case, I'm confident you'll think of something, sport. You haven't disappointed me yet."

Mina made a small sound and began to stir.

"She's coming 'round," her brother observed, his voice full of emotion. "I'd better be on my way. I say, fellows, would anyone mind loaning me a last cigarette for the road?"

"I've got a pack in my pocket," Flynn said. "But I don't know how to offer you one without breaking the circle."

"If you don't mind, I'll just help myself."

We heard Flynn gasp and then the soft sound of a dozen cigarettes spilling onto the floor, followed by a match flaring somewhere out of sight. *(Beneath the table?)* An ember danced into view like a wayward firefly.

"Ahhh, I do miss these," Walter said, luxuriating in the

smoke. "Here you go, Crawley. A little something to remember me by."

Crawley yelped in pain, his hand tightening on mine as the cigarette was pressed to his cheek. The sizzle of burning flesh seemed to go on forever.

"Careful you don't break the circle, Doctor," Walter hissed at his brother-in-law. "You wouldn't want to hurt our precious Mina, would you, now?"

Crawley's hand suddenly went limp in mine as his whimpers changed to a glottal, choking noise that went on and on. Terribly, interminably . . .

"Crawley?" I gave his hand a squeeze. No reply. Just the horrible croaking noises of a man choking on his own tongue. Or being strangled.

"Get the lights!"

"Don't break the circle—"

"The hell with the circle! Do as I say!"

I leaped from my chair, breaking the circle and striking out in the dark at Crawley's assailant. But there was no one standing over the surgeon, who had stopped making those dreadful strangling noises and now slumped in his chair with his head hanging forward. As the others fumbled in the dark to light the lamp, I brought my face down close to Crawley's and was relieved to feel a faint stir of his breath.

"He's still alive!"

But only just barely—as we discovered once Flynn succeeded in lighting the kerosene lamp.

Whether Crawley was awake and aware of us was impossible to say, despite the fact that his eyes were open. His face was expressionless. Worse, it had lost its symmetry, the left side sagging like waterlogged crepe. At the center of the slack cheek was a perfect round cigarette burn the size of a bullet hole.

His right cheek, the one nearest to Mina . . .

For a few stunned moments, no one spoke, until McLaughlin broke the silence. "For heaven's sake, someone call an ambulance!" he barked at us. "The man's suffered a stroke."

"Stroke?" Fox repeated in disbelief. "He was *assaulted.*"

Before McLaughlin could reply, Mina gave a sleepy groan and opened her eyes. She stared into space and then gradually focused on the faces around the table. When her eyes found her husband's, they went wide with a surprise and concern that seemed, so far as I could tell, entirely sincere.

"Arthur!"

She rushed to his side, hands fluttering about his sagging face. Bending at the waist, she tore a strip of material from the hem of her kimono and used it to wipe the drool from Crawley's lip.

"Mina?" I touched her elbow gently. She seemed unsurprised to find me beside her.

"Is my brother responsible for this?"

I answered truthfully. "I don't know."

Mina's expression tightened. "Help me get him onto the floor," she said, taking her husband by the lapels. He fell forward against her, a dead weight.

"Let us do it, my dear," Fox interceded. "You mustn't strain yourself in your condition—"

"Fox!"

Mina shot me a look. "What is he talking about?"

"Don't you know, Mrs. Crawley?" McLaughlin asked.

"This isn't the time!" I barked at him, helping Mina ease Crawley out of his chair and onto the floor. I half expected to see bruises or other ligature marks on him, but when we removed his jacket and opened his collar, his throat was unblemished except for an old shaving nick. As we waited for the ambulance to arrive, I ran scenarios through my mind by which someone might artificially induce cerebral apoplexy, and I decided it could be accomplished quite simply with a hypodermic full of air injected into a major artery. Of course, there was another even less complicated explanation for Crawley's stroke, one Ockham would have favored above any other: heredity.

It was in the midst of all this speculation that my eyes fell on something near Crawley's shoulder. A box of matches, embossed with the name of the Waltham Hotel. Had they fallen out of Crawley's pocket? Or fallen from where they'd been stashed beneath the lip of the Crawford table? Without calling attention to myself, I palmed the matchbox and was about to slip it out of sight when I heard McLaughlin ask, "What did you find, Finch?"

Reluctantly I showed them to him. "Matches."

"Well, well," McLaughlin said, reading the name embossed on the matchbox. "It appears our ghost frequents local hotels. Maybe the mattresses aren't firm enough in the afterlife."

I turned away from his accusing look and watched for some reaction from Mina, but she was too busy worrying over her husband.

"Here you are, Finch," McLaughlin said as he returned them to me. "You might as well keep them for a souvenir."

Without uttering a word, I took the matches and slipped them into my breast pocket, near my thudding heart.

Fifteen minutes later the ambulance arrived, and we all stood aside as the attendants carried Crawley out of the house. Mina was too distraught to speak, and though I wanted to comfort her, I checked the impulse and kept my distance, aware that McLaughlin was watching. And so it was that we passed our final fifteen minutes together outside on the sidewalk in silence, neither of us realizing it would be the last time we would ever see one another.

After the ambulance drove off with Mina and Freddy following in the Peerless, I turned back and wearily climbed the steps to 2013 Spruce.

Upstairs in the séance room, I found the others in heated debate over what we had just experienced. It was to be the final meeting of the *Scientific American* investigating committee.

". . . but how do you explain the cigarettes?" Fox was in the middle of asking when I arrived.

McLaughlin was about to respond when he saw me in the doorway.

"Perhaps Mr. Finch will answer your question, Malcolm."

Three sets of eyes turned toward me expectantly. How I would have liked to have shrugged then and joined Fox and Flynn and Richardson in their unwavering belief. Certainly nothing would have given me greater pleasure than to deny McLaughlin his victory over Mina. But the truth was, I knew he had already won, and he knew it too. Though he seemed to take little pleasure in the being right.

"Well, Finch?" McLaughlin repeated the question: "How do you explain the cigarette?"

"She could have taken the cigarette out of Flynn's pocket with her feet," I said in a flat, inflectionless voice. "Then lit it below the table using the matches we found." I looked around the circle of shocked faces. "Or she could have had an accomplice."

"But how would an accomplice enter?" challenged Richardson. "You locked the door."

"The door yes, but not the window. There's a small ledge outside where he could wait. It's too high to reach without a ladder, but if you climbed down from the roof, you could get to it without much difficulty. And escape that way, too."

A ghost of a smile had appeared on McLaughlin's lips as he listened. I hated him then.

Fox and Flynn and Richardson were following our exchange like a tennis match. Now they pounced on me with questions.

"Well, which is it, Finch?" Flynn asked irritably. "Did she use her feet or an accomplice?"

"And why would she do such a thing if she doesn't need the money?" Fox asked.

"It doesn't matter," I told them, though I was looking at McLaughlin as I spoke. "Our job was never to ask *why* she might be doing it. Or even to catch her doing it. All we need to do is show how she *might* be doing it and it's all over for her—isn't that right, Professor?"

McLaughlin nodded. "A real-world explanation trumps a metaphysical one every time. So says the great scholastic William of Ockham—as does, I might add, the contest rules set forth by the *Scientific American*." And with this, McLaughlin sat back in his chair, having rested his case.

But Fox wasn't going down without a fight.

"The contest rules also say a simple majority determines the winner," Fox said, glancing at Flynn and Richardson to make sure they were with him. "Three of us can still outvote you."

"Yes, I suspected you might say that," McLaughlin said, unconcerned. "But before you call a vote, there's someone I believe you should meet first." Turning to the Dictograph on the windowsill, he called out in a loud voice, "Would you mind coming in here, Captain Darling."

Captain?

"I hope you will forgive me, gentlemen," McLaughlin began once Darling had joined us in the séance room, "but I'm afraid I wasn't telling the truth when I introduced Darling to you earlier tonight as my graduate assistant. The truth is, Tom runs a successful Ford dealership with his father outside Providence. He is also a decorated war hero—a fact I hope you will keep in mind as you listen to what he has to say."

He turned the floor over to Darling. The car salesman scowled at each of us individually before making his statement.

"I knew Walter Stenson," he began. "We were stationed together at Base Hospital Number 38 outside Nantes, France. We were part of the same ambulance unit. We used to eat together, bunk together, crumb together—"

"Excuse me," Fox interrupted, "but did you say 'crumb'?"

"It means delousing your uniform," Darling explained. "You take a candle and go over all the seams inside and out, where the sons of bitches like to hide. Trick is to boil their blood without burning a hole in your uniform."

"Oh, dear, I see. Please continue."

Darling grunted. "My point is, Walt and I spent a lot of time together, just talking and so forth, and it got so that we became pretty good pals. Hell, we even ran around with a pair of French sisters. I'm not gonna pretend I was his best friend in the world or that I knew him better than his own mother or anything. But after what I heard tonight, I can say I knew Walt Stenson better than that sister of his downstairs. And I sure as shit knew him better than any of you."

"What are you trying to say, Darling?" Richardson asked, impatient.

Darling squared his shoulders and said, "That son of a bitch I heard tonight wasn't him!"

. . .

McLaughlin's gambit succeeded. Suspect as Darling's own motives might have seemed (at least to me), his eleventh-hour testimony—along with the matchbox I'd found on the floor and Flynn's grudging admission that the hand he'd felt searching his pockets for cigarettes could have been a foot—raised sufficient doubt in the minds of the other committeemen that they could not in good conscience award Mina the *Scientific American* prize, much as they might have liked to. And so in that tiny séance room, it was agreed that the investigation into the mediumship of Mina Crawley was concluded—albeit on a note of inconclusiveness. For his part, McLaughlin agreed that the announcement in the *Scientific American* would be worded in such a way as to reflect the difficulty of the committee's decision and that, unlike the Valentine and Harker statements, it would not insinuate—explicitly or otherwise—that Mina was a fraud.

With that, everyone shook hands, and the evening adjourned.

While the others carried McLaughlin downstairs and said their solemn good-byes, I lingered behind in the séance room, which, if Walter was to be believed, would in nine months finally become the nursery I'd always mistaken it for. What part I'd played in that transformation I wasn't yet ready to consider, still reeling as I was from the news. Pike entered, moving the chairs back into place around the Crawford table and sweeping the floor. When he was finished, the Filipino gave me a strange sidelong glance, as if reappraising me, then limped off on his dead leg.

The room felt small, the ceiling lower than when we'd first entered a few hours before. Colder, too, thanks to the window we'd opened to bring in some fresh air for Crawley. I walked over to it now and leaned out briefly into the alley. The small ledge below looked no wider than the spine of a book. *Wieland*, perhaps. I brought down the sash, and the curtains collapsed like a spinnaker in dead calm. Then I collected my coat and gloves, bade a silent good-bye to the Crawley residence, and made my way downstairs.

Outside, it had started snowing in earnest. McLaughlin and Darling were waiting for a taxi, the younger man smoking a Chesterfield. McLaughlin and I didn't shake hands but only nodded the way opposing attorneys do when they encounter one another outside a courtroom. I turned up my coat collar and was about to leave when I saw their cab's headlamps approaching through the curtain of snow. I lingered until it had come to a stop at the curb and offered to help Darling transfer the professor from wheelchair to passenger seat.

McLaughlin clenched his teeth, in obvious pain, as we installed him in the front of the taxi. While Darling and the driver were wrestling the wheelchair into the trunk, I arranged the tartan blanket across McLaughlin's lap. I said a second good-bye, then shut the taxi's door. McLaughlin sat in the cab's dark interior staring straight ahead, watching snow fall through the headlamp beams. I tapped on the window and motioned for him to crank it down.

"May I ask you something, Professor?"

He gave me a curt nod.

"Why go to all this trouble," I asked, "with the committees and the transcripts and the experimental controls, when you don't really believe in any afterlife in the first place?"

For once I didn't expect an answer. It was an insult wrapped in a question, a parting shot from a bruised ego: an effort to let him know I considered him a hypocrite. And yet though I never expected an answer, McLaughlin provided one.

"Because," he said, as if it should be obvious, "I dearly want to be proven wrong."

I must have looked stunned. "You mean to say you actually *wanted* Mina to win?"

"Of course," McLaughlin said with impatience, as if I were being hopelessly dim. "Why else would I send my most promising student to try to disprove her?" Snow swirled in through the open window, and he shivered and said, "Now, if you don't mind, I need to roll up this window before I catch my death."

Looking back now on our final exchange, I suspect that McLaughlin must already have known about the bone cancer hollowing him out like a diseased sycamore.

The trunk slammed, and a moment later the taxi drove off into the night. I watched until its taillights were swallowed by the storm, and then I turned back for a final look at 2013 Spruce. Pike had emerged silently from indoors and was scattering salt around the base of the house.

"You can stop now," I told the Filipino, nodding toward the bag of salt in his hand. "It worked—all the unwanted guests are gone."

The butler cocked his head at me as if I were an idiot.

He held up a fistful of rock salt. "This for the snow." Then, having finished salting the slippery walk outside the Crawley house, he limped back inside and closed the door.

EPILOGUE: CHESTER

In the spring of 1924, *Scientific American* released the following statement on the status of its ongoing psychic investigation:

> We the undersigned members of the committee appointed to investigate the mediumship of "Margery" (as she has come to be known in the papers) report as follows: Though startling phenomena were observed which in many cases resist easy explanation, nothing this committee witnessed during the weeks of December 8–23, 1923, can be conclusively proven "supernormal." Therefore, it is our judgment that Margery's powers, while worthy of further study, do not entitle her to the $5,000 currently on offer by the SCIENTIFIC AMERICAN.

The statement was signed by Malcolm Fox, H. H. Richardson, and W. M. Flynn. Notably absent was McLaughlin, who had passed away quietly in his sleep two weeks earlier.

The memorial service was held in the Quaker tradition, an informal affair that couldn't have been more different from the operatic Catholic send-offs I was used to. The few hundred mourners crowded into the meetinghouse were invited to rise as the spirit moved them and say whatever came to mind about the deceased. Or not. McLaughlin had been well respected, which is different from being beloved, and so the afternoon consisted mostly of long silences punctuated by the occasional dry eulogy. A subdued Houdini had come up from New York with his wife, Bess, and afterward I saw them talking quietly with the Conan Doyles: a meeting of titans on the eve of their final estrangement. By the end of the year, their public feud over the existence of the supernormal would come to an ugly head, and thereafter the two old friends would cease to be on speaking terms. (Of the efforts to apply scientific rigor to the supernormal, Houdini would write, *"I have read with keen curiosity the articles by leading scientists on the subject of psychic phenomena. . . . The fact that they are scientists does not endow them with an especial gift for detecting the particular sort of fraud used by mediums, nor does it bar them from being deceived."*)

The end of 1924 was momentous for other reasons as well. In September the newspapers reported that "Margery," the society psychic whose reputation had managed to survive the skepticism of the *Scientific American*, had given birth at Jefferson Lying-In Hospital to a healthy baby boy. I received a birth announcement, along with a few hundred other people, and learned the name Mina had chosen for her son—"Chester." What Crawley thought of this choice was anyone's guess, since the surgeon had been unable to speak ever since that fateful night in 1923.

Three months later, nearly a year to the day since Mina's final séance in Philadelphia, I submitted my dissertation topic to Harvard's Department of Psychology for review. I had toyed with the idea of further exploring parapsychology (as the field was coming to be known), but in the end—perhaps in tribute to the Crawleys' one-legged butler, Pike—I decided to conduct research into that strange persistence of sensation called "phantom limb." On December 15 the department approved my topic. Oddly enough, it was my father who was most heartened by this news. I suppose all he really wanted was a son with "Dr." in front of his name.

On December 31, the *Scientific American*'s offer of five thousand dollars for tangible evidence of psychic phenomena expired, unclaimed. Readers were reassured that this did not represent any wavering in the magazine's commitment to psychic research. In fact, the contest rules stipulated that any applications still on hand at the expiration date would be investigated later. A number of such applications were on hand, the editors wrote in a special message to longtime readers, and would be investigated in due course, with the results published "from time to time."

· · ·

My dissertation became all-consuming—first the research, then the laborious writing and endless revisions—so that I had very little spare time for outside reading. Yet I always found time for the occasional posthumous works of McLaughlin's when they were eventually published.

I pored obsessively over these scraps of final writings, hoping to glean some insight into his character and answer the lingering questions I carried about our last conversation. If McLaughlin had secretly wanted to believe in Mina, why was he so hell-bent on disproving her? I could understand why a dying man might be interested in news of the afterlife, but I couldn't reconcile this with the bitter disbeliever who had turned up on Mina's doorstep. Which raised a further question: Why had McLaughlin agreed to send me to Philadelphia in the first place, when he'd managed the trip himself only a week later? Originally I assumed that McLaughlin had decided to risk the journey only after learning he was riddled with cancer and that mismanagement of the investigation had merely provided him an excuse. But as the years went by and

I replayed our final conversation outside the Crawley house (*Why else would I send my most promising student to try to disprove her?*) I began to wonder if there wasn't more to it. What that might be continued to elude me, though I found clues scattered throughout his posthumous writings. Such as this one, from the September 1925 issue of the *International Psychic Gazette*:

> Psychic investigation is a young man's game, . . . for after the age of forty or so, the outcome attains an importance that precludes all objectivity. This is why undergraduates make the best investigators, second only to atheists.

I thought I heard echoes of Richardson's words in this and wondered—as I had that afternoon on the roof of the Bellevue-Stratford Hotel—if I had been a pawn in a greater game than I realized. A game of strategy, and of tests. If so, I felt certain I had failed.

That is until, in March 1926, McLaughlin's memoirs were published, where I read the following:

> The unspoken goal of all psychic investigations is to fail; that is to say, for the Unexplained to defy our best efforts to explain them. Which begs the question: How do we know we have brought our best to bear on a problem, if all the while we've been hoping in our hearts to be defeated?

It occurred to me then that perhaps I had been McLaughlin's last, best hope. But in the end I had failed him in a way McLaughlin hadn't anticipated. Dispatched to be what he could not—incredulous, dispassionate, resolute—I had broken the psychic investigator's cardinal sin and fallen in love with the medium. I'd often wondered how McLaughlin had been so quick to diagnose my heartsickness, before I was even fully aware of it myself; it never occurred to me that he might have firsthand experience with the affliction.

As McLaughlin's posthumous publications slowed to a trickle and stopped altogether, I came to the conclusion that perhaps our failing had been the same. We had both wanted to believe—with a devotion bordering on desperation—that Mina Crawley was real.

McLaughlin had died disappointed. I, on the other hand, lingered on in limbo. Of course, I had no good reason to hold on to my suspicions. Tom Darling's testimony should have put an end to any question in my mind of Walter's authenticity, as it had for the rest of the *Scientific American* investigating committee. The case was closed. Yet Darling's words continued—if you will pardon the expression—to haunt me throughout my medical-school years.

I knew Walt Stenson . . . better than any of you. That son of a bitch I heard tonight wasn't him!

Age and experience may not grant much insight into the behavior of others, but at least—and if you are lucky—it gives you an understanding of your own character, and I knew that mine wouldn't rest until I had some resolution.

And so one hot late-August afternoon between my third and fourth years of graduate school, I took a train down to Providence and paid a visit to the Ford dealership Darling ran with his father. I waited on the lot among the new Model A's, admiring the phaetons and the roadsters in racy shades of Niagara Blue and Arabian Sand. Darling emerged in shirtsleeves and a huckster's grin that cooled several degrees once I introduced myself. Yeah, he remembered me—what had happened in Philly wasn't exactly the sort of thing a fella forgot. Darling was disappointed I wasn't in the market for a Ford, and when new customers arrived on the car lot, I knew I wouldn't have his attention for much longer. So I came straight to my question.

"That final night in Philadelphia," I asked, "you said there was no doubt in your mind the voice you heard didn't belong to your war buddy Walter Stenson."

"That's right."

"Do you still believe that?"

He narrowed his eyes at me, surly and suspicious. "Why wouldn't I?"

"I've just always been curious," I said quickly.

"Curious?"

"About what makes you so certain?"

He straightened his tie, eyes shifting over my shoulder to the prospective customers. In that unguarded moment, I caught a glimpse of the soldier Walter had befriended in the war, a man very different from this automobile salesman—this decorated war hero who was also a husband, a father, a man without secrets—and in that moment I suddenly understood why he had been so adamant then and why he remained so obstinate now. Darling glanced back at me, pupils sharp as pencil points in the strong daylight. And repeated what, once upon a time, he had told McLaughlin.

"Because I never would've been best pals with no queer."

· · ·

Nineteen twenty-eight was the year I finally received my doctorate from Harvard. It was also the year "Margery" announced she was coming out of her self-imposed retirement and would begin conducting séances once more in her New Jersey home. Since the departure of her brother, Mina claimed to have been contacted by a retinue of new spirit controls, including a prankish little girl named Lily, and Tedyuscung, a fierce Indian brave of the Leni-Lenape tribe.

When this news first reached me—via the newspapers, as it did everyone else—I was overcome with a disappointment that dogged me for the better part of a week. It seemed so out of character from the Mina I had known. By now it was an open secret that the celebrated medium was actually Mrs. Arthur Crawley. Her decision to go public with her real identity coincided with a flattering profile in the pages of *Collier's.* (*"What amazing things people are willing to believe,"* she was quoted as saying, *"in order to avoid believing the things they don't want to believe!"*) And yet, ironically enough, just as the public was learning the name of the woman behind the pseudonym, in my mind Mina was finishing her metamorphosis into a stranger I had never met—Margery.

I followed this stranger's career as it was reported in the newspapers over the course of my remaining time at Harvard and afterward, when I took a teaching position at Boston University. When the public lost its appetite for all things supernormal, as it eventually did, I continued to follow Margery's exploits in stalwart Spiritualist journals like *Light* and the *International Psychic Gazette.* It would be in the pages of those periodicals that I would first catch a glimpse of six-year-old Chester, in a photograph accompanying an essay on how to recognize latent psychic ability in children. The photograph—taken in the rose gardens of one of Mina's wealthy new admirers—was of poor quality, and it added few details to my mental image of the boy. It did, however, show a strange figure who had strayed within the frame, a gardener looking up from his clippers to glower darkly at the photographer. Stanlowe? As many hours as I have spent scrutinizing that photograph under a magnifying glass, I have never been able to tell.

One afternoon nearly a decade after the *Scientific American* investigations had come to an end, I received a letter from Mina. I had learned on a recent trip to Philadelphia—where I had attended the funeral of my old friend C. Stuart Patterson, Esquire—that Mina had put their longtime residence at 2013 Spruce Street up for sale and relocated the family "down the shore," as Philadelphians are fond of saying. With her husband confined to a wheelchair and unable to communicate, Mina had chosen the sleepy seaside town of Cape May, on the sandy southern tip of New Jersey. But although I had received this bit of gossip from a credible source, it remained unconvincing to my imagination, which could in no way picture the three of them there among the seagulls and the sand dunes.

Now I held in my hand physical proof the place existed: an envelope of heavy stock, postmarked "Cape May, New Jersey." (To my sparse mental canvas, I added gingerbread homes in Victorian hues, the smell of frying funnel cake and saltwater taffy.)

Inside was a brief letter on cream vellum, written in Mina's unmistakable hand. She made no attempt to bring me up to date on all the doings of her life or work but rather seemed content to send along a fragment of a poem she had recently discovered (on the recommendation of new admirer W. B. Yeats) that reminded her of me.

"It is a poem by Emily Dickinson. Perhaps you are familiar with it?" Mina wrote, and went on to quote me these four lines of verse: *"The Pleading of the Summer— / That other Prank—of Snow— / That Cushions Mystery with Tulle, / For fear the Squirrels—know."* Though it was a poem about death, Mina wrote that it had cheered her *(why did she need cheering?)* because it had reminded her of a breakfast-table conversation we'd had once about squirrels, on that long-ago morning when she and I had first met.

Mina concluded her letter by sending me the warm regards of the latest spirit to join her coterie. *"He requests that I pass along the following message to you,"* Mina wrote, *"which he says you will understand."* The message in its entirety read:

Forget the Arrow—I have met the Archer!

The sender of this message, or so she claimed, was William McLaughlin, D.Sc.

That night I dreamed of Mina and her little boy, Chester, strolling by the edge of the sea. Crawley was nowhere to be seen—my unconscious must have left him buried up to his neck in the sand somewhere offstage, attended by Pike—but there were plenty of squirrels scampering about on the dunes. Mina's son was attempting to catch them, with great delight but little success. A sense of urgency hung over the dream, as if the squirrels needed to be collected before the tide came in and drowned them. As the sun sank below the horizon, Mina called to Chester to run along, son, it's time we were going indoors to feed Papa his supper. Hearing his name, Chester turned to look at his mother over his small shoulder, and I glimpsed in that backward glance just how much the boy took after his father. . . .

The resemblance was more than striking. It was uncanny.

Acknowledgments

My thanks to: Theresa Park for her expert advocacy; Kathryn Court and Sarah Manges for editorial acumen; Terra Chalberg, David Colden, Charlie Ferraro, Chris Foust, Richard Green, Steven Katz, Keya Khayatian, David Mandelbaum, Mark Ross, Greg Schauer, and Deezha Winn for early encouragement; and Charles Gangemi, Eva and Armin Hartman, Pacifico Labajo, John Passarella, John Ramspacher, Vickie Tamboer, and David Ufberg, M.D., for answering my technical questions. Of the many authors who provided insight into the 1920s, I am especially indebted to Lewis Allen, Christopher Morley, Massimo Polidoro, and Thomas Tietze.

Acknowledgments

My thanks to: Theresa Park for her expert advocacy; Kathryn Court and Sarah Manges for editorial acumen; Terra Chalberg, David Colden, Charlie Ferraro, Chris Foust, Richard Green, Steven Katz, Keya Khayatian, David Mandelbaum, Mark Ross, Greg Schauer, and Deezha Winn for early encouragement; and Charles Gangemi, Eva and Armin Hartman, Pacifico Labajo, John Passarella, John Ramspacher, Vickie Tamboer, and David Ufberg, M.D., for answering my technical questions. Of the many authors who provided insight into the 1920s, I am especially indebted to Lewis Allen, Christopher Morley, Massimo Polidoro, and Thomas Tietze.